The Boy ... Th

A Strange Beginning

A Biographical Novel

Gretta Curran Browne

SPI
Seanelle Publications Inc.

ISBN: 978-1-912598-16-8

Typeset in Georgia 10/18

Cover Design: The Cover Collection
Cover image by permission of Mr Alain Delon
Painting of Newstead Abbey: British Government Art Collection.

www.grettacurranbrowne.com

ACKNOWLEDGEMENTS

To my husband, Paul, for all his tremendous help; and for being so valuable in my research.

To the staff at Newstead Abbey for their assistance; and to the Nottingham Trust for their preservation of Lord Byron's home and beautiful estate in Nottinghamshire.

To

GABRIEL

'aurora filii'

"a son of the bright morning"

PROLOGUE

The Boy

George Gordon

"He was undoubtedly the greatest poetic genius of our century."

GOETHE

Prologue

Aberdeen,
Scotland,
1798

"Am I to call this woman *Mother?*"

Whenever he could escape from the unpleasant chaos of his home, he walked, and walked far, amidst the peace and majesty of nature.

The mountainous beauty of the landscape of Aberdeenshire inspired in him his first great love, a love that was to stay with him for all of his life – a love of solitude.

Although a boy of only ten years old, here amongst the empty green hills and high mountains could his boy's mind rise above the petty bickering and bawling shouts of his mother. Here he could think, and wonder, and dream, and allow his passionate mind the peace and freedom it craved.

The long walks exhausted him, although the exhaustion never deterred him, despite the box-like shoe on his right foot which allowed him to do no more than limp along.

He had been born with a damaged foot, bent sideways and useless, and since then he had suffered his foot to be stretched and pulled and yanked and finally bound up in tight bonds by ignorant doctors who knew no remedy, yet never tired of *experimenting* their new ideas on him, regardless of his infant screams or his boyhood tears.

Sitting on the bank below the Brig o' Balgounie, a small stone bridge over the River Don, he looked down at the deep water, calm and smooth under the evening sun. Water had always been his friend, welcoming him with affection, and with no dislike of his damaged foot, always cool and soothing, slowly easing away the strain in his right leg.

He turned his head and looked searchingly around him, although he knew he was alone here, completely alone.

It took him some minutes to remove his right shoe, and then his left, and one by one all his clothes until he was free of all restrictions and he slipped into the river until the deep water surged around his neck, breathing out his joy in cool gasps, his hands disturbing the sun's streaky reflections on the water.

He struck out from the bank and began to swim as swiftly and easily as if he had born underwater. *Here* was his kingdom; *here* he could be a master and a prince. Not one of his schoolfellows could out-swim him or get near to him in a race, because *here* in the buoyancy and depth of the water, the problem of his foot was no longer an impediment. His arms and his body sped along as gracefully and as lightly as if he had wings, and the cool silky water caressed him with love.

~~~

Returning home, limping along Broad Street, he silently passed a group of local urchins who immediately stood alert to stare at him.

Always jealous at the sight of him in his fine clothes of velvet jackets and breeches, his head of shining black hair, and his face, which – unlike their faces – was always so free of dirt and *clean,* leaving them with only one insult left to hilariously jeer and shout after him:

"Come an' see the laddie wi' the club foot! Come an' see the wee cripple hobbling along!"

As usual, he did not pause nor respond, ignoring them as if they did not exist, his aloof and remote manner incensing them even more, forcing them to shout louder.

An approaching woman, appalled at the jeering, stopped to console him, telling him to "Pay no heed to those ruffians," and offering him kind words of sorrowful sympathy about his "poor lame leg."

He paused to glare at her with eyes of tormented blue fire. "Don't speak of it," he snapped, and limped on past her.

She stood to stare after him. "Well!" she muttered, deciding that the son must be as bad as his mother, a woman whom all knew to be "as haughty as Lucifer."

Although *why* Mrs Gordon should be so haughty in her manner – that was something she and her neighbours often wondered amongst themselves? Although it was said Mrs Gordon had once been a woman of some wealth – but not any more. Nay, not any more. And aye, although it was true that the Gordons lived in a spacious apartment and had the services of a maid, that apartment was still nothing more than a few rented rooms above a perfumery shop.

Nevertheless, as indignant as she felt about the Gordon boy's response to her, she still felt sorry for him having to suffer as he did. And although his mother was an ugly frump of a woman, the boy was as bonnie as they came, so his looks must have come from his father, whoever he was.

The urchins were still engrossed in their jeering when the woman reached them. She gave one of them a hard clout on the side of his head and admonished them all severely: "Ye young ruffians, away with ye and yer bawling! Tis no' a Christian thing ye be doing. Away now and leave the crippled laddie be!"

~~~

Broad Street was a long street, and today it felt even longer, so slow was his progress, so throbbing the pain in his right leg now from all the walking, and yet his anger was quickening with every slow step he made. He felt like an outcast, an ugly deformed being that no one could ever love, not even his own mother.

His mother!

If the first two people on this earth were Adam and Eve, and the first two *sons* were Cain and Able, then his own mother was certain that *he* must be a descendant of *Cain*, the cursed one. The mark was there — the deformed foot!

Even at ten years old, and already an avid and retentive reader of books, as well as having the Bible and the Calvinistic religion cudgelled into him every day at school and on Sundays at church, he was intelligent enough to be disgusted at his mother's stupidity and ignorance. But if she truly believed that he was a descendant of *Cain*, then so be it.

Tears were now filming his blue eyes while his intense imagination wandered off and away, back to the Garden of Eden and poor cursed Cain ...

> ADAM — *"Son Cain, my first-born, why art thou silent? Why do you not pray with us?"*
>
> CAIN — *"I have naught to ask. Nor aught to thank God for."*
>
> ADAM — *"Dost thou not live?"*
>
> CAIN — *"Could I not die?"*

His foot caught on one of the rugged cobblestones

5

and he lost his balance, feeling himself falling forward and going down towards the hard ground as if in a trance of slow motion ... yet still his mind could not stop writing his own version of the Garden of Eden.

EVE — "Alas! The fruit of our forbidden tree begins to fall.

PART ONE

"When he reflected, his mind always returned to the child."

GOETHE

Chapter One

~ ~ ~

It was a hot April afternoon and Catherine Gordon could not cope with another minute of it. At least, not without a rest in the comfort of her bed and a wee dram of whisky before dinner — but first, she decided, she would console herself with a few luscious sweet biscuits topped with almond-flavoured icing sugar.

Bending down to the bottom of her wardrobe, she pulled out box after box of shoes before she reached one of the secret boxes of biscuits that she kept hidden from her maid.

Lord save us, if May Gray knew about these lovely treasures she would have them all devoured inside her own mouth before nightfall.

The maid was a contrary girl, always rudely contradicting her mistress. Such impertinence! Earlier, when she had complained to the maid that the heat was making her feel faint, May Gray had the audacity to insist that the day was no more than "only a slight mild, and not hot at all."

A wench like May Gray did not deserve such a good mistress, such a kind mistress. Did she not allow the girl one night off a week? And did she not buy the girl a new frock or two whenever she needed them to replace the old ones and look respectable — and not a word of gratitude given back to her mistress who had to try and manage with such a limited amount of money these days, such a *limited* amount!

Pulling herself onto her bed and flopping back against the mound of pillows, she looked up at the ceiling and gave a deep sigh ... only the good God in His Heaven appreciated her kindness to everyone, and only the good God knew how much she was forced to suffer on a daily basis.

She pushed a sweet biscuit into her mouth and began to munch it quickly and miserably, feeling weak and exhausted and so very much older than her twenty-nine years ... the fact that she was actually thirty-four years old was a truth she now denied, even to herself.

In the kitchen, May Gray was also feeling peeved. The nerve of Mrs Gordon to insist that she must not cook dinner until she had awoken from her nap. And how long would that be? Some days she stayed in her bed for five or six hours.

May banged her fist on the table in frustration. Tonight was her evening off and now she would probably miss half of it. Oh, how she *hated* that woman and her selfish ways. And how young Geordie coped with his mother made him a true saint in May's eyes.

Mrs Gordon might be highly proud in her manner and although she always seemed unaware of her own faults, May Gray was a daily witness to her terrible mood swings and episodes of melancholy, as well as her regular explosions of rage against everyone, especially against her son — sometimes physically beating young Geordie so hard in her rage that May had been forced to turn away and hide in the kitchen, too terrified to intervene and protect the boy. Only the Devil himself would dare to obstruct Mrs Gordon in one of her furies.

No wonder the boy complained that his constant headaches were caused by his mother.

May Gray detested Mrs Gordon, but young Geordie ... such a beautiful boy ... May Gray could not stop herself from loving that sweet boy.

~~~

Half of the box of biscuits had been eaten, two glasses of whisky had been guzzled down, and now Catherine

Gordon lay back in readiness to sleep, her eyes glazed with carelessness and her mind calm. What could beat it? Whisky and sweet biscuits! The best medicine for a troubled heart and mind.

A rapping knock came on the door. Her eyes opened and glared.

"May Gray — I'm sleeping! Go away!"

The rapping knock came again.

Furious, she edged up the pillows a fraction and yelled, "May Gray, I have told you – I AM SLEEPING!"

The door opened ... surprised and disconcerted Mrs Gordon sat up in her bed, her eyes staring as her son entered, quickly shoving the box of biscuits under the eiderdown. "George ... I told you *never* to come in here."

George stood looking at his mother, at her heavy corpulent body and her sweating face, red and puffed with fat. Her gown was opened to the waist and the top laces of her corset undone. She looked repulsive, and he could smell the whisky.

He had known for some time that she drank in the afternoons, (and probably late at night) but he cared no more for that than he cared for anything else about his mother.

Her face reddened deeper, knowing he had caught her out in her secret sin of drink and gluttony — her, who regularly preached to him about the pure and simple life of the Calvinistic religion.

Her eyes lowered with mingled shame and wretchedness, and then just as suddenly her manner abruptly changed and she sat further up the bed, holding out her arms to him.

"Come to me, Georgeee, come to your poor dear mama. Oh, George ... you do not *know* how your poor mama suffers!"

Tears began to spill from her big glazed eyes. "Come and comfort me, George, come now!"

Too young and too frightened to disobey her, he forced himself to move towards her and then found himself grabbed and clasped hard against her chest.

"Release me," he mumbled, trying to pull away. "My head is sore."

"It's that school!" she declared, immediately angry again. "It's that school that gives you those fierce headaches all the time, making you study too hard with all that Latin, Latin, Latin! Surely they know we are *not* Catholics!"

Her lack of intelligence repulsed him even more than the smell of her sweat, yanking himself back out of her suffocating grasp. "My study of Latin is *scholastic*, not religious," he said impatiently, and then moved quickly towards the door.

"George," she called as he opened it, "you have not told me why you came in here. So *why*, pray, did you want to see your poor dear Mama, even though you knew she was resting?"

He stood looking back at her, noticing her hand already moving under the eiderdown to reach the box of biscuits.

"I wanted to know why you *eat* so much. All the time eating, eating, eating and making yourself as fat as a sow."

The shock of his angry words left her stunned, but only for a moment. A second later her upper body propelled forward, her eyes and mouth wide with fury as she screamed back at him.

"Why do I eat? I'll tell you why I eat! Because I have a lame brat of a son who thinks he's better than his mother! Now you listen here, m'laddie — you may think you are a Gordon but you are *not* a Gordon. There were no lame brats in the Gight clan of Gordons! All were good strong men!"

"Then I must have inherited my weaknesses from my

father," he replied, slamming the door behind him.

The blood was still trickling down the side of his face from his head, due to his fall in the street, but his mother had not noticed it, even though her bedroom was still bright with daylight; seeing only her own misery and seeking solace only for herself.

He went to his room and his dresser, lifted the jug, poured water into the bowl, soaked a flannel and held it to his head to halt the bleeding ... she had called him a *lame* brat ... his own mother adding her jeers to those of the ruffians on the street. For that he would never forgive her.

~ ~ ~

Catherine Gordon sat in her bed, fuming. Her son had called her fat! As fat as a sow!

How could he? How could any son be so *cruel* to his own mama? It was not her fault she was fat, it was *his* fault — people just did not know what she had to suffer with such a difficult boy to contend with. Any woman would have to be a saint to cope with his silent moods and quick temper. And now he had been so cruel to her — the mother who had cared for him so lovingly from the moment of his birth.

She threw back the eiderdown and hurriedly got out of bed. Well, now she would show him how *unloving* she could be! The back of her hand across his face might put him in a less insulting mood. Oh yes, she would quickly show that limping brat not to insult Catherine Gordon of Gight.

In such a heat to administer punishment she almost forgot to tie her corset and button up her bodice before leaving the room.

She looked down to pull the laces of her corset together and button herself up — letting out a sudden, terrified shriek — yanking open the door and screaming for her maid.

"May Gray! May Gray! Come quickly! I'm bleeding! Oh Lord save us, I'm dying!"

May Gray came running, a wet flannel in her hand. "Aye, Madam, what be it now?"

Mrs Gordon flopped back against the doorframe in a half faint, pointing a fluttering hand to her bloodstained bodice.

"Can't you see, I'm bleeding! He has made my heart burst open with his insult and now the blood is pouring out."

May Gray showed no sympathy. "'Tis not you that's bleeding, Madam, 'tis young Geordie. A fair crack on the head he's got too."

Confused, Mrs Gordon stared at her, and then lowered her eyes to her bloodstained bodice, to the place where she had clasped him to her.

"What? A crack on the head? Someone hit my George?"

She stood upright, no longer feeling faint, only murderous.

"Did he tell you who struck him? So now you tell *me* who it was and I'll go and strangle the mangy cur who dared to hit my George!"

"No one hit him," May said impatiently. "He tripped and fell on the street and banged his head."

A minute later when his mother rushed into his room, followed by May Gray, George jumped up from his chair and moved backwards to the farthest corner of the room, holding his palms up. "Stay back!" he shouted. "Don't come near me — either of you. Leave me alone."

"Now, George," his mother said cajolingly, "your mama just wants to take a look at the wound on your dear head."

"There's nothing to look at. The bleeding has stopped.

So go away!"

His mother began to weep, wiping at her eyes. "Oh, George, George, why do you treat your poor mama in this cruel way?"

"You called me lame."

She stared at him, puzzled. "But you are lame, George."

"No, I'm not. And even if I am – *you* did this to me. You made my foot all bent and useless."

"Me?"

"Yes, you! If you had not been so vain and kept wearing your tight corsets all the time I was in your womb, my foot would not have been squashed up and damaged. Is that not what the doctor said last year? I heard him say it – about your tight corsets. I heard him say that was the probable cause. So *you* did this to me!"

"That doctor was a fool and a quack, that's why I dismissed him." His mother was weeping real tears now. "Oh, George, why do you insist on hurting me so much. Do you not know how much your poor mama loves you?"

The blue fire was back in his eyes. "You have never loved me."

"I'm devoted to you!"

He stood looking at her, at this woman who called herself his 'Mother', remembering as a small child how much he had loved her, and the many times he had attempted to hug her and cling to her warm body for comfort, and she had always in a cold manner shoved him away, or – as she had just done in her bedroom – laughingly trifled with his affections by making fun of his infant caresses, pretending to love him, and then shoving him away with dismissive taunts about his foot, until pain and humiliation were the only emotions he knew.

"If you ever call me *lame* again, I will never call you

by the name of 'mother' again."

In the silence that followed, even May Gray was shocked, both women staring at this sweet-faced young boy who sounded so much older than his ten years.

May looked at him with deep condemnation in her eyes.

He looked back at her, at May Gray, a plain and flabby girl in her twenties who had her own secret way of persecuting him. He disliked her even more than he disliked his mother.

"Geordie," said May Gray in a fake rebuke, "you are a wicked, wicked boy to say such a thing to your dear mother."

The frustration and pain in his head exploded. "No, *you* are the wicked one, May Gray, a demon from hell you are! Both of you — wicked selfish women and I detest you both. Now go away, both of you, and leave me alone!"

Mrs Gordon was still feeling shocked, but now a confused frown was moving on her face. She had never seen George so enraged before, so erratically frustrated. His quick temper, yes, but there was something more going on here to disturb him in this terrible way, something more than her little slip of the tongue ... For the first time in her life she lost sight of her own problems and became aware that there was something terribly wrong with her son, but what?

Her dull brain could not conceive any kind of answer, so she dismissed it as nothing more than her own melancholy imagination, her own natural kindness in seeking to make excuses for his disgraceful rudeness to her. Being too soft was always one of her major faults.

Seeing his back turned to her and his brow and clenched fists pressed against the wall, she decided he was being over-dramatic and turned to leave the room with one of her favourite retorts.

"Stop whining about your crippled foot, my lad, and thank God you are perfect in every other way — unlike your poor mother who almost died giving birth to you!"

~ ~ ~

Later that night, in the dark stillness, May Gray crept into his room and slid into bed beside him, waking him immediately, making him jump with fright and then struggling to get out of her grasp, crying "No! No! No!" while at the same time hobbling distractedly around the bed towards the door — but being nearer to the door she caught him, grabbing his nightshirt, and then pulling him inside her strong arms.

"Oh, now, my bonnie sweet boy," she whispered. "You don't want to offend me again do you? You know I can be very wicked when you offend me."

His strength was pitiful against hers, a big rough and raw girl with the strength of a man, and seconds later he found himself pressed into May Gray's flabby body, her big breasts under her thin shift pressing into each side of his face, making him almost vomit with shame.

As soon as she moved to pull him back over to the bed, he twisted his hand free and slammed his fist up into her face — shocked and wide-eyed at his own strength when she stumbled backwards.

"Ye little bastard!" she hissed, but he was out the door, careening into a limping run to his mother's room and sanctuary.

As soon as the door was shut, he stood for a moment calming his gasping breath, before turning round to look at his mother in the bed.

The bedside lamp was still burning, the empty whisky glass still laying inside her limp hand on the eiderdown, a dishevelled big lump in her blue nightgown. Her head was back on the pillows, her mouth half open, fast asleep.

He gently took the glass from her hand and placed it on the bedside table, then quietly moved over to the ottoman chest containing her spare bed linen, and took out a blanket.

He turned down the oil lamp until the flame was extinguished, and then lay down on the thick rug near the fireplace and pulled the blanket around him in the darkness, his breath still trembling.

Chapter Two

~ ~ ~

The following morning was a Sunday morning. He had awoken while his mother still slept and had crept back to his own room.

When May Gray entered with his washing water, her face and manner showed no sign of that other person she could be late at night, urging him to get ready quickly because today was the day of prayer.

He delayed as long as he could, until finally she returned to tell him that his mother was already seated at the breakfast table and waiting for him.

His mother was reading a newspaper when he reached the table, her eyes squinting with concentration.

"Ah, George," she said, looking up. "Sit down and read this part of the newspaper to me while I eat. It seems there has been a big uprising over in Ireland, Protestants and Catholics together. Can you believe that, May?"

May Gray was also eager to hear the news, both women listening attentively as he read from the newspaper:

"In a contemptible insult to His Britannic Majesty, Lord Edward Fitzgerald, the son of the Duchess of Leinster and the first house of the Irish aristocracy, has attempted to lead a rebellion to separate Ireland from the Crown of England."

His mother sighed admiringly. "Lord save him, but I doubt the Irish will fare any better than our own Bonnie Prince Charlie did fifty-three years ago. So many of the Gordons of Gight died in that battle at Culloden. The

English can be brutal people, *brutal.*"

George looked up from the paper. "Was my father not English?"

"Aye, but he was not like the most of them. He was a liar to be sure, but he did not have an ounce of English hypocrisy in him."

Hypocrisy was something George saw in all its sickening falseness at church later that morning.

In church, May Gray was ostentatious in her display of religious fervour, beating her chest and praying louder than any other person there, condemning all sinners, and agreeing loudly with the Minister that every Christian should spend at least one hour of every day studying the Bible.

His mother was no better, nodding her head continuously when the Minister warned against the evil of strong drink and the regular imbibing of liquor.

"Amen!" his mother cried.

"Amen!" May Gray cried fervently — a woman who could not see a drop of liquor on the table without instantly lapping it up like a thirsty cat.

For some strange reason he found it all very funny and could no stop himself from smiling, and then quietly laughing, forcing him to bend his head and bite his lip in an effort to hide his mirth. For the first time in his life a new awareness of the *absurd* had been ignited within him, providing him with a release from the heavy tension of it all, and it felt good — no longer viewing people with painful anger but only high amusement.

Hypocrisy and false piety were playing out before his eyes and the more he watched it, the more uncontrollable his shaking shoulders and his attempts to stifle his laughter.

He was ordered out of the church, all declaring him to be a "wicked" boy, and his red-faced furious mother giving him a wallop across the head as soon as she got him outside, but still he could not stop himself from laughing at the absurdity of it all.

When they arrived home his mother's rage exploded in a torrent of abuse, and when that did not satisfy, the poker was lifted from the fireplace and thrown at him, followed by the fire tongs and anything else she could get her hands on while he escaped to his hiding place under the table, knowing her corsets would prevent her from bending that low.

"Ah, you little dog, you are a Byron all over, as bad as your father! I will *kill* you one of these days!"

May Gray brought her a cup of tea and she eventually calmed down, but only to announce his punishment – without any food or drink, he was to spend the rest of this Sabbath Day sitting at the table studying the Bible and, hopefully, finding his own path back to God's forgiveness, if not her own.

"And you can start with the Garden of Eden," his mother directed. "For in that you will learn the difference between a good son and a *bad* son."

May Gray solemnly placed the Bible on the table before him, but as she lifted the newspaper to take it away, the article about the rebellion in Ireland caught her attention again.

"Nay mind the Irish," she said. "When you've read enough of that Bible, Geordie, and you feel you have at last obtained God's forgiveness, then say a fervent prayer to Him on High that one day Scotland will gain her freedom from the hateful rule of England."

Giving no response, he opened the Bible at the first page of Genesis, certain that if he said any prayer at all today, it would be a fervent prayer for himself, that one day – dear God – he would gain his own freedom from the hateful rule of dominating females.

Chapter Three

~ ~ ~

Newstead Abbey
England.
1798

William, the 5th Baron Byron of Rochdale, had lived for all of his seventy-six years in Newstead Abbey, on the edges of Sherwood Forest in Nottinghamshire, the ancestral home of the Byrons.

The Baron had become decrepit with old age, a misfortune, because now all he could do was ruminate on his many regrets.

"Joe," he called from his bed to his valet and servant, Joe Murray, who was still in the room. "Joe, come and help me into the chair. I want to take a last look at the grounds of the estate"

"A last look? Oh, nonsense, my lord, you have a good few years left you in you yet."

"The doctor tells me otherwise, and he knows better than you. Bring the chair and take me over to the window."

Joe helped his master into the chair and wheeled him over to the bedroom window, watching him as he sat staring out sombrely at the large lake in front of the house ... a fine sheet of water measuring thirty-six acres on which the old Baron had often sailed in his small yacht.

Joe Murray had served him too long to not know what his lordship was thinking now, and the depth of his regrets.

So long ago it seemed now, that his lordship, being at

bitter enmity with his son who had married a girl not of his father's choice, had in his rage and hatred against his son, resolved that the estate of Newstead should descend to him in as miserable a state as he could possibly reduce it; and for this reason he had taken no care of the mansion, letting it fall into decay in parts, and furiously lopping down as many trees as he could lay his hands and axe on, reducing immense tracts of woodland country, although much still remained ... And then his son had died before him, and even his infant grandson was dead, and now all his rage was thrown away.

"I have spent years trying to destroy this place," the Baron said quietly. "Doing everything I could to ruin its grandeur and beauty. What a folly of mine that was, Joe, what a damnable folly."

"You were not to know how things would turn out," Joe replied soothingly. "You were not to know that your son would die in such a way, and your grandson too."

"My son went against me all the way. I was determined he would inherit nothing — nothing of much value anyway. I even sold off all the collier rights to the coal mines in Rochdale so not a penny of the income would go into his pockets."

Joe pursed his lips disapprovingly. "That is not all you sold, my lord. The house is not the same without all the good paintings hanging on the walls."

The Baron looked sidelong at him. "What paintings? There are hundreds of paintings still hanging on the walls."

"But not the ones by Rubens and Titian and Canaletto."

The Baron was in no mood to be reminded of even more of his own follies. "Gambling debts, Joe. They had to be paid."

When Joe gave no answer, the Baron sighed, shaking

his head slightly at the stupidity of it all.

"The problem with the aristocracy, Joe, is that we all gamble in the first place merely to relieve our own boredom; but then, alas, we are forced to gamble seriously in an attempt to recoup our great losses, and if we fail, then our treasures must come down off the walls."

He looked sidelong at his valet from under hooded lids. "Good God, man, those paintings were sold years ago. Don't tell me you are *still* fretting?"

Joe sniffed. "I was always very proud to live in the same house as them ... Rubens, Titian, Canaletto. And regrettably, the paintings of your ancestors do not instil in me the same pride."

"Nor in me, nor in me," the Baron laughed, and then erupted into a fit of coughing. "These damn lungs ... slap my back, Joe!"

Joe slapped his master's back until the coughing subsided, then both lapsed into another silence, gazing out to the lake.

The Baron suddenly sat alert. "Do you hear the murmurings of the monks, Joe?"

"No, my lord, it's your imagination. The monks left Newstead Abbey centuries ago."

"Yes, but the *dead* ones, the ones buried here in the grounds ... lately I believe I have heard their spirits, praying for me."

"Then I should take you back to your bed, my lord, and allow your imagination to rest." Joe turned the wheelchair around and began wheeling it back towards the bed.

"And you do remember, my lord, that Mr Hanson will be arriving from London this afternoon, so you will need a clear mind when he gives you his report."

"Mr Hanson? Who is he?"

"Your solicitor, my lord. He has been your attorney

for many years."

Back in his bed and propped up against the pillows, the Baron's eyes moved quickly around the room.

"Rot me but I am sure I can hear the murmurings of those monks again, praying for me ... always praying for me, God damn them!"

~ ~ ~

The Baron's mind was clear and lucid again when John Hanson, a solicitor in his forties, was shown into the bedroom later that afternoon.

"Well, Hanson?' he asked eagerly. 'Did you find him? The boy in Scotland?"

"It has been difficult, my lord, because —"

"Nonsense!' the Baron snapped irritably. "The boy is a Byron, not a common name, so it should have been very easy to locate him."

"It has been difficult, my lord," John Hanson continued, "because the boy has been brought up under the name of *Gordon,* not Byron."

"Eh, what? What poppycock is this? Is he Jack's son or is he not?"

"Oh, most definitely he is John Byron's son, but it seems that your nephew changed his name to Gordon at the time of his marriage."

"Eh?" The Baron turned his disbelieving eyes to his valet. 'You see now, Joe? You see now why I am not the least bit unhappy to be leaving this world — everyone in it has gone mad!"

He looked at John Hanson. "Now why would Jack do a mad thing like that — change his noble name of Byron to ... what was it?"

"*Gordon*, my lord. At the time of his marriage there were four relatives in front of John Byron to inherit the title as your heir," Hanson explained, "and the last of those, your grandson, being an infant boy at that time, I can only deduce that your nephew saw no hope of ever inheriting your estate and title, and so changed his name to Gordon in order to inherit his wife's estate and title instead. It was a condition of his marriage contract."

The Baron pulled a face. "Then it will be a condition of *my* will, and *his* inheritance, that the boy has his own noble name of Byron restored to him. You will legally see to that, Hanson?"

"Yes, my lord."

The Baron grunted. "Jack was my brother's son, and the boy in Scotland is Jack's son and therefore *my* great nephew. So he is a legitimate Byron in blood and flesh, I will have no other."

Chapter Four

~ ~ ~

There was a time, some years ago, when Mr Bowers, the headmaster of the Aberdeen Grammar School, felt sorry for Mrs Gordon, a widow struggling through life on her own, trying to make ends meet, with an afflicted young boy to care for; but now he considered her to be a hard woman to tolerate, and hard to feel sorry for.

In previous years, when she had protested to him that she could not afford to pay the school for this or that, especially not the outings the school occasionally arranged for the boys, she had always received his full sympathy — until he had learned that she was living on an annuity of £150 a year — which gave her an income of three pounds a week: a full two pounds *more* each week than he himself earned.

Also, on occasions, there were signs of real damage done to the boy, and not only physical damage, but also mental damage that caused the boy to start weeping, suddenly and silently, and for no apparent reason, and for which he would give no explanation.

The headmaster had, in the past, attempted to raise the subject with Mrs Gordon, but he had failed. She was truly a terrifying and overbearing woman who had dismissed his concerns with a wave of her hand, saying, "My George's emotions have always been near to the top. Whether it be his tears or his quick temper, *out* they come. A tempestuous boy is what I would call him."

"His temper?" The headmaster was very surprised. "Mrs Gordon, your son has one of the mildest temperaments of any boy in the entire school."

"Has he indeed? So that shows all you know about him, but I could tell you things about my George's temper that would make your hair stand on end. For example, when he was five years old he deliberately ripped his frock from top to bottom in a rage, and then stood there in sullen silence waiting for his punishment."

"And did you punish him?"

"Of course I did. He had to learn that wanting to wear breeches was no excuse for ripping up his new frock. No boy is unfrocked before the age of seven. Oh, he has not been an easy boy for me to rear, not easy at all."

And with that she had dabbed a handkerchief to her eyes in self-pity; and minutes later she was complaining heatedly about the enormous cost of his schoolbooks.

And now here she was in his office, yet again, sitting in the chair on the other side of his desk, a belligerent woman in a lavender outfit with a huge hat sitting on the top of her mop of black hair, and a hint of real grievance in her eyes.

The headmaster sighed, stirred some papers on his desk. "So, Mrs Gordon, how can I assist you today?"

"I've come about my son."

"Of course you have. Is there something wrong with George?"

"Yes, this school is wrong with him. It's causing him to suffer bad headaches all the time. I believe it's due to all the Latin you teach."

The headmaster's eyes blinked rapidly. "Did George tell you that?"

"No, that boy tells me nothing!" she retorted. "He is sullen and silent with his headaches all the time, and I am certain now — " she abruptly leaned forward and banged her fist on the desk — "that *this* school is to blame!"

The headmaster stirred his papers again.

"Mrs Gordon, I can assure you, any sullenness that George may be displaying to you is certainly not due to his life here at school. In fact, when he is here, he always appears to be a very happy young boy."

"Happy?"

"Yes. And very popular with the other boys."

"Popular?"

"Very."

She sat back in her chair, frowning, and then shot him a sarcastic look.

"Give me at least one example of all this jolly happiness and popularity that sends my boy home looking so sulky and miserable?"

"I can give you many examples, Mrs Gordon. Your son's foot may be afflicted, but his intellect is quite superior to the other boys. He is always reading books, devouring them would be a better description, especially the Bible, and he appears to have easily absorbed everything he has been taught so far."

"The Bible?"

"Yes, he has read it from front to back, many times, but only the *Old* Testament, I must add. He once told me it was the colourful history and battles and different stories in the Old Testament that he enjoyed so much; but alas, he says he finds the New Testament very dull in comparison."

She moved about on her seat, surprised and speechless.

"As for George's popularity with the other boys," he continued, "well, the best example I can give you of that is the day out in the hills which his class had in February, do you remember that, Mrs Gordon?"

She blinked a few times, and then remembered. "I remember that he was supposed to be back home by the end of the day, but the school did not return him until the following morning. Out of my wits I was with worry, out of my wits! But not one word of sympathy did I get from his teacher the next morning, nor indeed from you, Mr Bowers."

The headmaster's patience was quickly ebbing, but after a deep inhalation of breath, he cleared his throat and carried on.

"And the reason for that was explained to you, Mrs Gordon, on more than one occasion too, as I recall. The delay was due to the class being caught in a sudden snowstorm. Some kind of shelter had to be sought for the boys overnight, which, thankfully, they finally found in the back kitchen of a village shop. All the boys came back saying they had great fun."

Mrs Gordon's round eyes glittered with suspicion. "Why, what did they do to have such fun? Stand in the snow throwing snowballs at my George and knocking him down?"

The headmaster smiled rather scathingly. "No, Mrs Gordon. All the boys here at Aberdeen's Grammar School come from very good families, and all are very well behaved."

He paused briefly. "Although, it seems that all the fun of that snowstorm *was* provided by your George. The teacher feared the boys would become very mettlesome trying to sleep in a huddled group on a hard kitchen floor overnight, but it seems that George kept them all quiet and entertained by telling them story after story from the *Arabian Nights.*"

"He did that? My George?" A glow came into Mrs Gordon's eyes, but only for an instant, then dimmed again.

"So why then," she asked with confusion, "if he is not unhappy when he is here at school, why does George come home every day looking so miserable then?"

The headmaster pushed back his chair, gathering up his papers. "That's a question you must ask yourself, Mrs Gordon."

~~~

After leaving the headmaster and returning home, Mrs Gordon did ask herself that question, but finding no answer, she vented her spleen on the headmaster. Stupid man! If she had known the answer she would not have asked him the question. And the way he kept fiddling with his papers? Such disrespect shown to a respectable woman who was clearly grieved with concern about her son.

She flopped down into an armchair by her drawing-room window, gazing down on Broad Street, her mouth turned down, her mind dejected, wondering why her life was so hard.

She had been a very unhappy woman for a very long time, and she believed she had every reason to be so. Her life had not turned out as she had expected.

Fate had been cruel to her, very cruel. Although there were those who would say it was John Byron who had been cruel to her — relatives who had insisted on poking their noses and opinions in, but she would not listen to a word said against her dear Johnny. And as for her relatives, well she had long ago ostracised the lot of them.

Although now, sitting here in this rented room, it galled her to think that those same relatives were still living so close in their grand ancestral houses, still thriving members of the Scottish aristocracy, while she was reduced to a few rooms and penury.

If things had not gone so wrong, her son would now be a member of that same Scottish aristocracy. George would now be the Laird of Gight Castle and all of its surrounding lands ... but love and passion had destroyed his inheritance. Love and foolishness ...

At sixteen, Catherine Gordon had been a good-humoured girl full of romping energy and unbounded optimism. Not even the complaints of her elderly grandmother, Lady Gight, that she was "*too plain in her looks and too inclined to corpulence to attract a husband*" dimmed Catherine's hopes of finding the man of her dreams.

At the age of eighteen, she inherited her dead parents' estate and became the Laird of Gight Castle in her own right, also inheriting a small fortune as well as a £25,000 yearly income from the Gight farmlands, salmon fishing and other investments in shares; but still no proposals of marriage came.

"Because there are too few young men in the Scottish aristocracy," Lady Gight told her.

At the age of twenty-one, her grandmother took her off to the fashionable Spa town of Bath, a town much favoured by the English aristocracy who regularly hustled their daughters down there in the summer season of Balls and Dinner Parties in an attempt to get them married off to a suitable husband.

"Bath, in the summer season, is nothing more than a marriage market, and everyone knows it," Lady Gight had declared. *"But in this circumstance, why cannot we do what everyone else is doing, eh?"*

Catherine agreed, and began excitedly buying new clothes.

After two weeks attending Balls in Bath, Lady Gight and Catherine were beginning to give up all hope, until the night a handsome young man appeared before Catherine and asked her to dance — the man of her dreams — a young army officer who introduced himself as Captain John Byron.

She stumbled up from her chair, and even her grandmother looked surprised, and yet within minutes Catherine had forgotten her grandmother and everyone else in the entire room, swirling around in a dream of delight and, for the first time in her life, falling madly in love.

John Byron was not only handsome, he was charming and funny and in the following days he joined Catherine and Lady Gight for lunch, for dinner, and later escorting the two women to yet another Ball.

Finally it came, the night and the moment that Catherine had been praying for. After walking her out of the ballroom and through the moonlit garden, John Byron proposed to her — although he quickly warned her *not* to accept his proposal until he had told her the truth about himself, because in all fairness he wanted to be honest with her.

He then told her that he did indeed come from an aristocratic family, but being fifth in line to the Byron title, he was unlikely to ever inherit his uncle's estate in Nottingham. He was also a widower with a baby daughter and a mountain of debts.

His wife had died in childbirth and the baby was now in the care of her maternal grandmother. He had come to Bath for the sole purpose of finding an heiress to marry, hopefully one that possessed her own fortune and would be able to pay off all his debts.

Enthralled by his honesty, and already restless with love for him, she had eagerly accepted his proposal on those terms, joyously throwing her arms around him and laughing, "Ah, Johnny, I have enough money to last us for a lifetime!"

Lady Gight had been delighted. John Byron was, after all, a son of Admiral Byron of His Majesty's Royal Navy, and his family had very high connections within the English aristocracy — or so he said.

Even so, Lady Gight informed him that in accordance with the Last Will and Testament of Catherine's parents, no inheritance of hers could be attached to any marriage contract unless her prospective husband changed his name to Gordon. Only a Gordon could be the Laird of Gight and its estate.

A month later, in London, having changed his name to John Byron Gordon, he married her. Two years later their son George Byron Gordon was born in London, but by then his father had run through his mother's total fortune on gambling debts, yet she had forgiven him for doing so — still loving him so dearly.

Nothing could shake her love for her husband, not even when she returned from a visit of a few weeks down in London and discovered he had sold the roof over their heads and she had a mere four weeks to get out and find somewhere else to live. It was hard to take in, hard to believe - he had *sold* Gight Castle and all its lands for a mere £18,600 — a sum *less* than the £25,000 income the estate provided every year.

She was hurt, very hurt, and she had cried a lot, especially when she had looked down at the whimpering two-year-old boy clinging to her knee.

"My son was *born* to be a Laird!" she had cried ferociously. "A son of the mighty Gordons, born to be a Laird and hold a high station in life! But what now, Johnny? What lays before our son now?"

And her poor beloved Johnny was full of apologies, worn down as he was with his lack of sensibility with money and his addiction to gambling. He promised he would make it up to her and the boy. He would go to his rich relatives and try to get the money to buy back Gight Castle and restore to their son his rightful inheritance.

"*What* rich relatives," she had demanded, no longer believing a word he said. "Not one of your relatives came to our wedding, and not one came to our son's Christening."

"Now that's not true," he had argued. "Lord Carlisle agreed to become my son's Godfather."

"*In absentia*, Johnny, he agreed to become his

33

Godfather in absentia! What kind of a Godfather is that! Does Lord Carlisle even exist? And if he does, do you even know him?"

He had left her then, promising to return with enough money to restore her and their boy to their rightful position in life. These rented rooms were merely temporary. He would come back, he assured her, and he would come back rich!

She did not hear from him again until a year later, in a letter from France, telling her, "*I have now neither a sou nor shirt to call my own.*"

And then, a few weeks later, her beloved Johnny, still in France, had committed suicide by drinking poison, leaving to his son nothing more than his debts to pay off on his behalf. And those debts were still in George's name, still accruing interest. She could not pay them. All she had left to live on now was a small annuity from her late grandmother.

Of course, she had informed all her other relatives that her dear husband had died from tuberculosis, which was such "*a devastating loss*" for her, because she had "*ever so sincerely loved him.*"

Although nothing could have been as devastating for her as the letter she later found when rummaging through her husband's papers, which had been sent to her after his death — a letter only half-written with many words scratched out, a letter he had obviously started again on a new sheet of vellum and had probably posted. It was a letter to his sister — a sister she had never yet met — telling her all about his present wife.

Even now, she could still remember how her hands, holding the unfinished letter, had shaken with joy and excitement as she had sat down and began to read it, eager to find out if her husband's love had been as deep as hers, or even more so?

And even now, she could still remember the shock

and the pain cutting through her heart as she read, *"She is nothing more than my golden dolly..."* a crude way people often described a penniless man who had married a rich woman for her money, his 'golden dolly.'

But worse was still to come: *"She is very amiable at a distance, but I defy you and all the twelve Apostles to live with her two months, for if anybody could live with her that long, it would be—"*

The shock, the pain, the days and nights of drinking bottle after bottle of so much whisky until she could barely see through her glazed eyes and her legs would not allow her to stand. To know that their marriage had been such a sham, and his affection for her so fake!

But then, somehow, in the weeks that followed, she had found her strength again, pulling herself together and regaining her natural Scottish pride and her usual haughtiness in the face of the world, informing her relatives and everyone else – "My husband was always most devoted to me. We were all the world to each other. Our life together was pure bliss."

Oh yes, Fate had been cruel to her. And John Byron had been the cruellest of all, lying to her, robbing her, and giving her that lame brat of a son and then leaving her to bring him up on her own with little money.

Another of her regular black melancholy moods was beginning to descend upon her now, darkening her mind and her soul, making her truly hate every single person who lived in this world.

Finally, she turned her gaze away from the hateful Broad Street and the hateful world outside, and slowly rose from her chair, padding towards her bedroom.

The doctor frequently prescribed her with medicine to lessen her black moods; but really, there were only two kinds of medicine that helped and consoled her in her miserable life — whisky and sweet biscuits.

~ ~ ~

"One thing I want to know," she said grumpily to May Gray later that evening, "is why the cost of your grocery bills are getting so high? Every week you bring me less and less change from the money I give you, and yet you appear to be buying the same things and nothing more."

May Gray shrugged as she placed a tureen of soup on the table. "It's not my fault if prices keep going up and up, Madam, not my fault at all."

"Take the soup away, it's too watery. Either make a decent soup or none at all. You know George and I dislike watery soup."

With an air of grievance May Gray silently removed the soup to the kitchen and returned with a dish of lamb chops, followed by a tureen of vegetables.

"So, where is he?" Mrs Gordon asked, finally noticing her son was not at the table. "Am I to sit here waiting for him?"

"He says he wants no food tonight."

"No food?" Mrs Gordon had never heard anything so ridiculous.

"He's surling," May Gray informed her, "surly and silent. On his way home today he got a bad mocking from some of those ragamuffins and now he's shut him himself away and wants no food."

"Lamenting about his lameness again, no doubt," Mrs Gordon said sniffily. "And probably in there this minute blaming it all on *me*. Go in and get him, May."

When May Gray slipped into his bedroom he was standing at the window, gazing up at the sky. Her manner was soft and tender. "Still upset, Geordie?"

His glance was one of denial. "No."

"It's hard, I know," she said sympathetically, "but God is not so cruel as you think, so look on the bright side."

May Gray smiled at his frown of perplexity.

"There is always a bright side, Geordie, always. God may have left you a bit deficient in your foot and leg, but he made up for it *here.*" She grabbed his crotch and laughed, "Made very nicely down there you are!"

The horror, hatred and revulsion — he roughly pushed her away before limping at a run into the dining room where he confronted his mother.

"You have to stop her, Mother! Her trickery is evil!"

His mother put down her knife and fork and wearily looked at him. "What now?"

"She..." he said, pointing accusingly at May Gray who had followed him into the room, "she keeps trying to play tricks with me."

His mother looked at May Gray who flashed her eyes up to the ceiling for a second and then imitated her mistress's weary expression. "It was just a little jest, Madam, a bit of fun to brighten his mood."

"And your mood certainly does *need* brightening, George," his mother remonstrated. "You can't go off into a surl at every little offence. Those ragamuffins down on Broad Street are just jealous of you, aye, jealous, because they can see you are many stations above them and you wear fine clothes."

"But she..." he pointed to May Gray again, "she keeps trying to play tricks on my person!"

"Och, where's your sense of humour?" his mother replied irritably. "It might do you good to have some fun here at home instead of always gazing out of windows."

She looked at May Gray. "Those lamb chops are very greasy, May. I'll eat no more, George can have the rest."

He stood staring at her, his mother, so dismissive of what he had just told her ... although in those moments he realised that she was completely unaware of what he *had* just told her.

She moved heavily to her feet. "Come into the

bedroom and help me to get out of this corset, May. I fell asleep without loosening it earlier and now it feels so tight it's bursting the breath out of me."

"Aye, Madam, a tight corset is a curse at the best of times."

He was still staring at his mother. That there could be something immoral in May Gray's tricks had not entered her mind ... but then she had not stayed around long enough to find out.

May had undone the first hook when they both heard the loud crash – and another –crash – crash – crash ...

"Lord save us!" cried Mrs Gordon, wide-eyed with fright.

Hurrying down the hall, both women stopped at the open door of the dining room, staring in disbelief while George violently smashed plates and anything else he could get his hands on against the wall.

It was not until Mrs Gordon saw her most precious China vase smashing through a pane of glass in the window that she came out of her stunned trance.

"*George!* — George Gordon you stop that right now!"

"Why?" He flashed a violent look of hate at her. "You're not so swift at telling anyone else to stop when *I* ask you to!"

He violently flung another plate at the wall.

"George Gordon you stop that! Stop breaking my good china!"

He stopped, letting the plate in his hand fall onto the floor – looking directly at the repulsive May Gray. "I want you both to leave me alone!"

May Gray was silent, but his mother was simply aghast as she stared around at the debris over the floor. "I know what I'll leave you ... I'll leave you with my hard hand across your face for doing this!"

Yet a moment later she was staring at him in a befuddled way. "What made you do this, George, what?"

"You did, because you don't *know*, and you don't care!"

His mother was shaking her head in bewilderment. "What don't I know George, what?"

And then, suddenly, he felt too ashamed to tell her. "I want Agnes back. Agnes was my friend – and a better servant than *her*."

"Don't be stupid," his mother replied. "Agnes has her own child to take care of now, and damned lucky we are that May came in her place to help us out. I cannot do it all on my own, not with my list of ailments."

Which left nothing more to say. He turned and left the room, left the house, and left Broad Street, walking as far as he could until the pain in his right leg made it impossible for him to walk any farther.

He was far outside the town now, standing by a low stone wall at the edge of a field. The night had grown dark and there was no sound, no sound at all from anywhere.

He sat down on the wall and gazed up at the bright stars in the clear dark sky ... he had always been a stargazer, from as far back as he could remember.

After a time, he realised it was time to move, to go back or to stay ... he decided to stay, swinging his body around until he was over the low wall, his feet on the grass, finding a soft place to lie down and sleep, although he had no wish to sleep.

He lay down inside the wall and put his hands behind his head, his eyes still gazing up at the stars, enjoying the peace and the silence ... his storm of rage all gone.

A sound made him turn his head and look ... a dog was strolling over the dark grass towards him, a black dog. He reached out his hand and the dog came to sniff him, sniffing his face and his hair.

"Hello, boy ... hello..."

The dog licked the side of his face and he smiled,

pretending to lick him back. Then the dog sat down beside him, peaceful and quiet, as if he too had nowhere else to go.

His eyes turned back to the stars, gazing.

"*This* is what I love," he whispered to the dog. "The freedom of the night ... away from humans and voices and walls and ceilings..."

After a long silence, the dog planted his head on his chest and he put his arm around the dog, enjoying his warmth, two lost young animals together in the night.

His eyes were still on the stars, but his mind was drifting far beyond their lights –

I had a dream, which was not all a dream.

The bright sun was extinguished, and the stars

Did wander darkling in the eternal space ...

Chapter Five

~ ~ ~

Newstead Abbey
England.
1798

The month of May brought not only sunshine and spring blossom to the county of Nottinghamshire, but also some long-awaited good news for the Baron at Newstead Abbey.

The boy in Scotland had been found and verified.

The Baron's bony hands groped at the bedclothes, his eyes anxious as he looked at his attorney. "Have you spoken to Jack's widow yet? The mother?"

"I have, my lord, during the past two weeks, but in correspondence only. She is agreeable, very much so, and considers it fair and correct that the boy should be allowed to inherit his father's rightful title and estate, before her own. Although she insists that the boy will be very sad to leave Scotland."

"Do you have his full name?"

"Yes..." John Hanson wiped a hand over his brow, "but even in that there is some confusion ... the boy has two birth certificates."

"Two? Was he born twice? How can he have *two* birth certificates, or are they just duplicates of the same one?"

"No, my lord, not duplicates. It appears that the mother registered her son's birth in the name of George Byron *Gordon*, but a few days later his father went back to the Registry Office in London and registered the birth of his son under the name of George Gordon *Byron*.

Both certificates still exist."

The Baron gave a laughing "*Arrrrffff*" and looked at his valet. "That's Jack for you! He was always a charmer and a deceiver! But we liked him well, didn't we, Joe?"

Joe Murray nodded diplomatically, and then informed John Hanson. "His lordship always liked Jack because he was a gambler like himself."

"And he made me laugh," the Baron added. "Always such a cheerful and charming young rake. When did you last hear from his widow?"

"I received another letter from his widow yesterday."

Hanson glanced down at the wedge of papers in his hand. The eager widow was now sending him three long letters every day, eager to know as soon as possible of the Baron's demise, and also filling her long letters with her own demands and stipulations.

"She insists that her son's name will not be changed until the day of his inheritance. Until then he will remain a Gordon."

The Baron again struggled further up his pillows, the effort causing him to gasp on his breath. "But can you assure me, Hanson, that when he inherits, you will make sure his surname is changed back to Byron. I want you to assure me of that?"

John Hanson had no doubts. He was legally in charge of the Baron's estate, and if the boy's rightful name was not restored, then there would be no inheritance for him, and he could not see the eager widow allowing that to happen.

"I can assure you, my lord, that on the day your great nephew inherits your estate and title, his name *will* be Byron."

Chapter Six

~ ~ ~

Aberdeen,
Scotland,
1798.

It was the last week of the school term before the summer break, the week of tests and exams. He had no anxiety about the exams, fairly confident that he would pass them all, but he was now feeling even more confused about life.

The main cause of his confusion was his mother. That melancholy snarling woman who had often beaten him black and blue for no good reason, was now killing him with her love, smothering him with her sloppy kisses and affection.

And even May Gray had changed in her behaviour towards him over the past few weeks, keeping herself more distant, more respectful in her manner, and no longer creeping into his bed at night to try and play naughty tricks on him.

And all because some unknown relative of his father was going to give him a big house in England one day. Other than that, his mother would tell him nothing, saying he would be told all when the old relative died.

Since then, he had often heard her praying loud and long for the old man's death, kneeling in her bedroom beseeching God Almighty to "*please hasten his demise*" and while she waited for an answer to her prayers, she had been busying herself in selling off most of her furniture.

This morning she was busying herself again,

whipping the clothes brush out of his hand and pushing aside May Gray to brusquely brush down his navy velvet suit with her own hard hand.

"I have already brushed it,' he insisted, pushing her hand away. "I'm ten, not five! I can brush my own clothes."

He looked at the two women suspiciously, wondering why they were both fawning all over him. He looked more intently at his mother. "Are you worried I will do badly in the exams?"

"Och, Geordie, ye could pass those exams in your sleep!" May Gray answered with a laugh, and his mother nodded her agreement.

"I'm not worried about your exams, George, but when you get to school today, the headmaster will be giving you a nice surprise."

His interest quickened. "What kind of surprise?'

"No, my lips are sealed. If I had wanted to tell you myself about it I would have done so. But no, I thought, no, let the headmaster tell you in front of all those snooty schoolfellows of yours."

"My schoolfellows are not snooty. They are my friends!"

"Innocent children," May Gray said with a sly smile. "I just can't help loving them."

"Well, maybe the boys themselves are not snooty," his mother allowed, "but their *mothers* are! The snootiest bunch of bonnets I have ever come across. Not so much as a nod do they give to me these days, not even a nod. Now you go in there to school today, George — and shock the shite out of them!"

He recoiled at his mother's sudden vulgarity, but he had become used to it. Over the years, the more she drank, the more vulgar her speech, and he hated it. Given the chance, he would exchange her in less time than a flash of lightning for one of the mothers of his school friends, the sweet-faced ladies in their bonnets with their soft voices and kind smiles.

"I will be late for assembly if I delay any longer," he said, limping quickly towards the stairs. "If it is another Latin book the headmaster gives me, I will bring it home and *you* can read it."

He could hear his mother laughing as he reached the ground floor, and May Gray's voice had also broken into a rough laugh. He was glad to get away from them, out into the fresh air and into the company of his school friends again.

He was almost late for assembly, just managing to hurriedly slip into his place before the headmaster joined the other teachers at the top of the room to start the roll call.

All the boys remained standing while Mr Bowers called out their names in Latin.

Five names had been called when the headmaster paused, and then called out a name that left every boy silent.

"Georgius Dominus de Byron."

As the silence continued, the headmaster, now looking directly at him, called the name again.

"Georgius Dominus de Byron."

And in that dawning moment of realisation, and seeing the sympathetic expression now coming onto the headmaster's face as he, too, was also beginning to realise that the boy had not been told, had not been prepared.

Unable to give utterance to his usual answer of "*adsum*", he stood silent amid the stares of his schoolfellows, finally lowering his head as his eyes began to spill anxious tears.

It was his first crisis of identity and it frightened him. He had always been very nervous of change, and now, here, his very name had been changed.

All of his schoolfellows began to surround him, noisily, until the headmaster cut through the group and touched his arm.

"Lord Byron..."

He blinked through his tears at the headmaster, still in confusion. How could he be a lord? He was only ten.

Yet, later, in his office, the headmaster confirmed the change in his status, informing him that his great-uncle, the 5th Lord Byron, had died in his bed at Newstead Abbey in England, and he, George Gordon Byron, had been named the heir to the title.

"Your mother showed me all the legal documents yesterday."

The headmaster's hand moved to the open school register on the desk, turning it around to allow him to see that his old name had been scratched out — ~~George Byron Gordon~~, and replaced with the new name of *George Gordon Byron*.

As their time together went on, it was not the headmaster's words that added to his nervousness, but the complete change in his manner and the *way* he was speaking to him. Always a kind man, but now he was being more than just kind, displaying extreme deference in his attendance upon him, giving him cake and wine and treating him like a person of great importance.

It was then he got his first suspicion that the biggest change of all, due to his sudden rise into the aristocracy, would not be found in him, but in the change in manner and attitude of other people towards him.

"I hope," said the headmaster, "that when you leave us for England and continue your education there, you will not forget Aberdeen or your early years here in Scotland."

"No, sir."

"Of course, I know you were born in London and are English by birth, so I hope—"

"I am half a Scot by birth, sir, and a whole Scot bred, so my heart will always warm to the tartan, wherever I go."

The headmaster smiled and raised his glass to him. "And I doubt we will ever forget you, Lord Byron. The only boy in our school who could easily read and translate the Latin poems of Horace at the age of ten."

The wine was warming his mind, calming his nerves, and it was much more enjoyable to talk about Horace than a place in far away England.

"Every sentence written by Horace is like a string of jewels, sir."

"Jewels?" The headmaster smiled again. "Do you truly think so?"

"I do, sir. I worship the Horatian style."

"Then let me give you some words of advice to take with you to England. I want you to always remember these words as you grow older, and I am sure you will, because they were written by Horace ... *carpe diem, quam minimum credulo postero.*"

Smiling at the headmaster, he translated the words into English. "*Seize the day, trusting tomorrow as little as possible.*"

Later that night, in the darkness, sitting by his bedroom window and looking up at the ever-present and unconquerable stars, he wished he had possessed the courage to tell the headmaster that he had stopped trusting tomorrow, and every person in that tomorrow, a long time ago.

PART TWO

Newstead Abbey
1798-1801
~~~

"Newstead and I will stand or fall together."

BYRON

Chapter Seven

~ ~ ~

Newstead Abbey
Nottinghamshire.

John Hanson was making his inventory of the house, writing down every item for his records on behalf of the new owner, a task that would take him some weeks to complete, for the Abbey was vast in size, and full of antiquities that had been here for centuries, as well as numerous rooms that had provided accommodation to members of past royalty on the occasions of their visits to the Abbey.

As yet he had not gone anywhere near King Charles the Second's Bedroom, nor King Edward the Third's Bedroom, all hung with splendid pieces of tapestry and beautiful inlaid cabinets that even the old Baron had not dared to destroy.

Of the small number of servants now running the house, the only one he knew, and trusted, was Joe Murray, and Joe himself was another of the very real treasures within the Abbey.

Joe came to him now; standing at the door of the library, telling him a lunch had been prepared for him in the parlour.

"Oh, thank you. Will you join me? Keep me company while I dine?"

A moment of surprise, startled by this breach of etiquette, Joe shook his head. "Thank you, sir, but as you must know, I always take my meals in the Servants' Hall."

"Yes, of course I know that, Joe, but the servants are also part of the inventory. I thought you could help to save me some time and advise me on the valuable ones, and those who appear to be no longer of good service. The new master of the house is very young, as you know, and I need to ensure that all the servants will treat him with respect, and good care."

Joe paused a moment to reflect. "The old Baron could be very difficult, sir, aged and ill as he was these last years, so it's been a matter of relief and excitement in the Servants' Hall that the new master is one so young. As for respect, I cannot promise that the servants will give him that, not to a mere child, but I can promise that they will certainly give him plenty of good *care*."

Hanson nodded. "Thank you, Joe. Although..." he quickly added, "the new master will be accompanied by his mother. She will, of course, take on the role of mistress of the house and will wish to run it in her own way."

Joe Murray remained unperturbed. "I'm sure the lady will be made to feel most welcome by the staff, sir. Her feminine presence is already being happily anticipated by one and all."

The lunch of smoked salmon and fried mushrooms in a herb sauce was delicious and very welcome after a long stuffy morning in the library recording the inventory of books. John Hanson relished every bite, his eyes moving appreciatively to the golden apple pie and jug of cream that Joe carried in and placed on the sideboard.

"Is all agreeable, sir?"

"Delicious, Joe. My compliments to the cook."

"Thank you, sir."

As soon as Joe had left the room, Hanson had just pushed another forkful of salmon into his mouth when Joe reappeared, astonishment on his face.

"Mr Hanson ... I think they have arrived! I've just seen a coach coming up the drive. The roof of it is loaded down with leather trunks ... it must be them, the new young master and his lady mother."

Paralysed with dismay, Hanson stared at him. "But... they are not due for another three days."

Joe Murray moved to the window and looked out, watching as the horses and coach came to a halt outside the main door. "'Aye, it is them, sir ... the coach door is opening and a lady ... a large lady, is stepping down."

Hanson wiped his mouth with his napkin and threw it down. "Collect the servants to come outside and welcome them, Joe."

"But, sir, most of them would want to be dressed in their best clothes and aprons — "

"Too late for that now. Make them come as they are, and quickly."

The eager widow! John Hanson fumed: she could easily have sent a letter on from one of the staging posts on the route down from Scotland and given the house some warning of their early arrival.

He stepped outside into the August heat and saw a woman standing stock-still as she stared up at the first floor windows of the house, almost twenty feet long in size, her face entranced with joy, the fan in her hand motionless in mid air.

John Hanson also looked up: even though the old Baron had deliberately allowed the house to fall into some decay, it was still an impressive building of great width and length, surrounded by three hundred acres of green land and numerous lakes, as well as four thousand acres beyond that.

"Mrs Byron?"

She looked at him, the fan in her hand beginning to flutter again. "Are you the solicitor — Hanson?"

"Yes, Madam."

"You should have warned us that the drive is five miles from the gate up here to the house! Five miles up a lane of high trees. I was sure the coachman had taken a wrong turning."

"It's no more than one mile from the gate, Madam, I assure you."

"Well it *felt* like five. Still, I suppose it's a good thing – no more crabby neighbours knocking on the ceiling wanting me to lower my voice and talk only in whispers."

Hanson agreed. "As you can see, there is no other residence near here for at least two miles. Apart, of course, from the small farms here and there of some of the tenants."

"Oh this heat! Is it cooler inside? I pray to God it is! Now let's get inside," she said with heated excitement, "so I can at last get a look at my new home."

As soon as she stepped into the hall she was met by Joe Murray and a bustle of eight servants rushing behind him.

"Oh, Madam, our apologies for not being outside to greet you." A wave of his hand ordered the servants to get into line. "May I introduce — "

"Pleased to meet you," she swiftly replied, ignoring the other servants as she lumbered up the main staircase and then went into one room and then another with exclamations of delight:

"Oh, *look* at the size of *this* room, and the *height* of that ceiling! Oh ... Lord save us ... this room is even bigger! And all that lovely oak-panelling on the walls...!"

John Hanson was still standing outside in some confusion. Where was the boy? The coach driver and his assistant were now hefting the trunks down from the roof of the coach.

He called up to them. "Did a young boy not travel with the woman?"

The driver nodded down at him. "Aye, there was a boy with her. Is he not gone into the house?"

Hanson walked over to the open door of the coach and stood for a moment staring at the boy curled up fast asleep on one of the two padded benches. His hair was a mop of black curls and he looked fragile and innocent, reminding Hanson of his own children who often curled up and slept in the same position on long journeys.

"Lord Byron..."

The boy slept on.

Hanson gently touched his leg to awaken him, startled when the boy immediately sprang upright with a terrified "*No!*"

"I'm sorry ... did I awaken you from a bad dream?"

The boy sat staring at him with the lightest of blue eyes, a beautiful blue, and then he looked around him, blinking rapidly as if trying to grasp where he was.

"Lord Byron, you have arrived at Newstead Abbey. Your mother has already gone inside."

"Who are you?"

"John Hanson, the estate's attorney. I shall be staying here at Newstead for a few weeks to take care of the inventory and other legal matters." He smiled genially at the boy. "And to help you settle in."

After a short pause while studying his face with suspicious eyes, the boy suddenly smiled back at him, and it was the sweetest smile John Hanson had ever seen, a smile of sweet relief.

"Shall we go inside?" He stepped back, giving room for the boy to jump down, surprised when the boy stirred so slowly in his movements, as if his legs had become painfully stiff due to sleeping in the cramped smallness of the coach's interior.

As he put one foot on the step, Hanson immediately reached out to take his arm and help him down, as he would to any of his own children after a cramped long journey, and it was then he saw the boy's strange shoe, and realised he was afflicted.

"Oh, I'm sorry..." His hand moved into a tighter grip on the boy's arm, but the boy shrugged it away impatiently.

"I'm a slight slow, but I am not *lame*."

"My apologies, Lord Byron, I was just trying—"

"Yes, I know, I know," the boy replied in the same impatient tone, stepping down and pausing to stand and look up at the house, his eyes moving over the array of windows as he said, "Could you not just call me George?"

John Hanson made no answer, not knowing how to answer such a request, and unwilling to offend; but the boy clearly did not understand the formality of these things, or the firm standards of the aristocracy which had to be upheld at all times.

The boy moved towards the house and it was then that Hanson saw his limp. His feelings of sympathy were quickly followed by a strong flash of annoyance against the mother. Why had she just run into the house and left her afflicted son behind to find his own way?

But then, remembering the boy's earlier indignation and the way his own helping hand been impatiently pushed aside, she probably knew from experience that it was wiser to leave him to his own efforts.

Even so — not even to awaken the boy to tell him they had arrived!

Hanson thought it strange behaviour for a woman who had written in every letter that she was "a most devoted mother."

Once inside, and after walking up the staircase to the great hall, the boy took his time looking into each room, seeing not the stupendous mansion of a building that his mother had seen, but a dark and gloomy hall with family portraits, creaking doors, and so many rooms left empty and neglected.

> *'An old, old monastery once, and now*
> *a still older mansion of a rich and rare*
> *mixed Gothic.'*

He had inherited a ghostly and gothic palace, but he was not displeased, only fascinated by the strange and eerie images it evoked in his mind.

John Hanson remained standing in the great hall while the boy turned and limped back down the stairs to stand at the open oak front doors, staring at the scene before him.

> *Before the mansion lay a lucid lake,*
> *Broad as transparent, deep, and freshly fed*
> *by a river.*

John Hanson felt a wave of sympathy as he intently watched the silent figure, already suspecting that the boy was rather a *lonely* boy, due to his affliction if nothing else. And now here he was, so young, in a new country and in this strange place filled with strange rooms and peopled with strangers ... but time was moving on, and the boy's mother now appeared to be creating some kind of a rumpus with Joe Murray upstairs.

"Lord Byron."

The boy turned and looked at him, a slow smile moving on his face as he made his way back towards him.

"You really *can* call me George, y'know."

"Yes, my lord."

"Or even Georgius, if you prefer to be more formal."

"Yes, my lord."

The boy sighed. "So which name is it *yes* to? George or Georgius?"

"It is no to both, my lord."

Chapter Eight

~ ~ ~

There was no wind to cool the day's lingering heat, and it was still too bright an evening for sleep, but it had been an exhausting day.

In her bedroom, Mrs Byron was pouring herself a dram of whisky, excited by thoughts of her son's inheritance, which was a lot more than she had expected.

As well as the Newstead mansion, and the three hundred acres of gardens and parklands and woodlands surrounding it, her son now owned all the land and buildings in sight, in addition to even more land and buildings that were *out* of sight.

Mr Hanson has explained it all ... the Byron family estates were wide and complex, and included not only the adjacent forest and mill, but also the far-off manor at Hucknall, and a number of small villages and hamlets spread over three thousand acres. Rents were being paid by fifteen different tenants of the farms and mill, and even the local clergyman was paying rent for his house and paddock.

And yet ... and yet ... she took another gulp of her whisky. Mr Hanson had said the accounts of the estate were found to be in a state of great disorder and confusion, due to the 5th Baron's neglect. It all had to be sorted out, and that would take some time to do.

In the meantime, with this big mansion to live in and no rent to pay — an immediate income of one thousand pounds a year would be like a fortune to her in comparison to the measly £150 she had been living on. And what's more, it would now allow her to go to the expense of taking George to London to get him fitted for a special shoe.

She thought of the cost, and deliberated ... those English doctors in Harley Street charged the earth and a few of its oceans for a consultation, but if the foot could be put right and fitted into a proper shoe, then her George would look more like a Lord and less like a cripple.

In all other ways he was such a fine looking boy. To be truthful, his beauty was beyond compare in her eyes, and she was certain he got his good looks from *her* side of the family, the Gordons, and his sulky sullenness from the Byrons.

Of course, his father had been a handsome man in his own way, but then handsome is as handsome does, and her dear Johnny had not done very well at all. But all that was forgiven now. All his promises to repay her son's lost inheritance and make her rich again, had come to pass.

She sucked back the last dregs of her whisky, put down the glass and decided to go in search of her young lord.

She found him in the bedroom next door. She was now installed in the old Baron's bedroom and George in the adjacent room previously occupied by Joe Murray.

"Georgeee ..." He was sitting in a languid way on the window seat, looking up at the dusky sky.

"Mr Hanson told me something very important today George. Aye, he explained it all very carefully to me, and now I want to explain it to you."

He looked at her curiously as she sank down near to him on the window bench.

"You've become a young man of very special importance, George. You've been made a ward of the Court of Chancery until you come of age. And Lord Carlisle has officially been appointed as your legal guardian."

"A ward of the Court — what does that mean?"

She waved a dismissive hand and chuckled. "It means that they do all the worrying about you, but I am still your darling mother*!"*

More change! He sat up, feeling nervous. "Why must I have a guardian? Who is Lord Carlisle?"

"God knows! I was convinced he was dead or did not even exist, but it seems that all the lies that I thought your father had told me have turned out to be true. When you were christened, Lord Carlisle was named as your Godfather, but only *in absentia,* and he's been in absentia ever since. Still, now that he knows you are one of the nobility, just like himself, he might make an appearance and give us his acquaintance at last."

"Why must I have a guardian?" he asked again.

"Och! it's all to do with this estate and it's protection and you being a minor and not having a father to make decisions for you. The fact that you have a very good *mother* is of no importance at all. Your guardian *must* be a male."

"Then why cannot Mr Hanson be my guardian? I like him well."

"You have three legal guardians now, George, and Mr Hanson is one of them, along with Lord Carlisle and the Court and myself. Oh, that makes four in all, but Mr Hanson is really just a solicitor, a legal go-between who draws up all the papers and sends reports to the court. But now you sit back while I tell you about all the other places that Mr Hanson tells me that *you* now own."

He dropped back into his languid position, his eyes on her face as she told him all about the villages and hamlets and rents and farms and the list seemed endless. One of the female servants had told her that the old Baron had been a very wicked man.

"And as for the coal mines in Rochdale!" She pressed her palms together and looked up at the ceiling as if begging Heaven for patience.

"The old bugger sold all the lucrative collier rights of the coal mines purely out of spite against his son for some reason, but Mr Hanson said the sale was illegal and so a civil court action will now be started on your behalf to get the coal mines back, and when they are got back, the income will come back to Newstead — to us! We will be rich, George, rich enough to afford you a proper shoe. So what do you think of that?"

When he gave no answer, she turned round more fully to look at him and saw his head drooped and his eyes closed in sleep.

She gazed at him dumbly, wondering why he was always so unkind to her? After all the information she had found out for him, the ungrateful brat had lazily fallen asleep and not listened to a word of it.

Chapter Nine

~ ~ ~

He was standing alone, enjoying the solitude, an ascetic look on his face as he gazed around him, lost in thought.

The day was again hot, but grey and cloudy with strong warm winds rustling the trees. Yet all else was quiet and the grounds empty, due to it being the dinner hour of the new gardeners hired by Mr Hanson.

His eyes moved over the scale and eerie grandeur of the building that had belonged to his ancestors and was now his home, still trying to absorb it, to understand it, his eyes fixing on the spire of the ancient and neglected church, it's roof long gone.

> *Thro' thy battlements, Newstead,*
> *The hollow winds whistle;*
> *Thou, the hall of my fathers,*
> *Art gone to decay.*

And yet he loved it.

The Abbey was three storeys high and square: built in a complete quadrangle with a beautiful water-fountain in the centre courtyard.

Of all the rooms and corridors inside the huge house, he had felt little interest, preferring to spend day after day exploring the parklands and woods surrounding the Abbey, following footpaths through the mass of trees and finding something interesting around every corner.

Now he was standing outside the old ruins of the cloisters where the monks had once strolled in peaceful prayer, and like the old Baron before him, certain he could hear their murmurings.

John Hanson approached him quietly, knowing the

boy had fallen in love with the outdoor grounds of the Abbey and rarely spent any time indoors.

And it was only now, having fled the house himself, if only to escape from the noise and distress that Mrs Byron was causing to Joe Murray and all the other servants, that Hanson finally understood the boy's consuming passion to spend most of his time outdoors and away from the house.

"Lord Byron."

The boy came out of his reverie and looked at him; a smile brightening his face when he saw whom it was. "Today?" he asked. "Do you have time today, Mr Hanson, to tell me more about the history of this place?"

"Well, it is a relief to get away from ... my papers."

The boy nodded. "Especially when the air out here is so sweet."

"The history of Newstead Abbey..." John Hanson knew it all, but — "Where do I start?"

"*Genesis*," the boy suggested. "At the beginning. Shall we walk?"

"That would be pleasant."

Hanson was still amazed that the boy, as afflicted as he was with his limp, still managed to spend every day walking for hours; for longer and much farther than more able-limbed boys of his age.

"I can only go back as far as King Henry the Eighth," Hanson said as they walked slowly through the gardens. "Newstead really was an Abbey then, the home of Augustinian monks."

"When England was Catholic?"

"Yes, but after his marriage to Anne Boleyn and the separation from Rome, the King ordered the dissolution of all monasteries and the monks were forced to leave here. The Abbey and all of its surrounding lands within the Sherwood Forest, was then occupied by the Byron family."

The boy looked disturbed. "So my inheritance of this place is all due to the dispossession of poor monks forced out of their home."

"No, my lord, the —"

"My lord," the boy said derisively. "A title that was gained through torment and dispossession! How could I ever be *proud* of that?"

Again John Hanson was amazed, not only at the boy's capacity for adult speech, rare in one so young, but also the sharp clarity of his intellect.

"No, you are quite mistaken in that, Lord Byron. You asked me for the history of Newstead Abbey, and yes, its possession by the Byrons does indeed date back to the time of Henry the Eighth, but not your *title*. The first Baron Byron of Rochdale dates back to King Charles the First."

The boy pondered for a moment. "So the Byrons already owned the land on which Newstead Abbey was built."

"Yes, and once the monastery was vacated, I presume the family decided that the Abbey, being larger, would make a more suitable home. Of course, since then a wing has been added, and many other changes have been made over the centuries."

"And Newstead *is* rightfully mine now?"

"Oh, most certainly. I can also tell you that your paternal ancestors came from Normandy and were the owners of large estates in England during the reign of William the Conqueror, the first Norman King of England in the eleventh century."

The boy was staring at him with blue-eyed incredulity.

Hanson shrugged. "If you do not believe me, I can assure you that the name of your ancestor, Ralph de Byron, can be found as a landowner in the Domesday Book, although it is written as '*de Burun*', in the Norman style of that time."

"Why do I not know this?" the boy said with wonder. "Can you tell me more?"

Hanson did not answer, deciding to ask a question of his own. "How old were you when you last saw your father?"

"I was three, but I remember him well."

Now it was Hanson's turn to look incredulous. "You remember him, even though you only three years old?"

"Yes. I'm told I have a very retentive memory, and I do remember my father. I remember how he used to sit me on his lap and laugh and play with me. Sometimes he would tell me stories about big ships with white sails. I still remember the warm love I always felt from my father when he was home, and I loved the very *sight* of him."

He picked up a small stone from one of the broken walls and violently flung it as far away as he could. "Although my mother insists that it was *me* who drove him away from our home."

"Your mother told you that?"

"Yes, my tormentor ... " He flashed Hanson a small sardonic smile. "A woman of a diabolical disposition."

Hanson did not doubt it; the woman was so overbearing that he was already feeling crushed under her constant demands. But to say such a thing to her son ...

"You? You were only a small child, so how could *you* have been responsible for his absence?"

"She says I cried non-stop from the day I was born until I was about five years old, and I believe she is right. I remember crying a lot."

Hanson was feeling concern. "Do you know why you cried so much?"

"Yes, because of this..." he pointed down to his right foot. "I cried because of the pain."

"Does it still cause you pain?"

The boy nodded. "Walking has always been a painful business for me, but I believe I have now mastered it well. Although walking *would* be a lot easier for me if I could have a special shoe."

He looked at the attorney. "Can you tell me, Mr Hanson, pray tell me ... am I rich now? Can I afford to buy myself a special shoe?"

Hanson smiled. "My dear boy, you are now the Lord of Newstead Abbey, so yes, we *can* afford to get you a special shoe."

Suddenly man and boy were both laughing, both excited at the prospect of a new and expensive special shoe, and in that moment the two became firm friends.

Later that evening, John Hanson asked himself *why* he had been so excited at the prospect of getting a new shoe to make walking easier for the boy?

Although he knew the reason why – because he was a *father*. A father of three sons and two daughters, and he was appalled by the mother's regular disregard of the boy.

"But if he were my son," Hanson thought protectively. "If he were *my* son..."

~~~

From that day onwards, John Hanson devoted himself assiduously to the boy's interests, becoming almost like a quasi-father to him, shielding the boy from his mother's sudden outbursts of rage.

"That boy will be the death of me and will drive me mad!" she raged. "How easy it is for him to go off walking and talking with you, Mr Hanson, yet with *me* when I try and talk to him — he lolls off to sleep like a weak and consumptive girl!"

She stood in a dark blue velvet dress that was too tight for her obese figure, her plump red face distorted with anger and ridicule. "And now I discover he has started writing *poems*! Poems about this place! I found pages of the stuff in his room. He should be ashamed of himself, I say, *ashamed!*"

Hanson regarded her steadily. "Do you find something particularly odious about the writing of poetry, Madam?"

"I most certainly do. It's all twiddle-twaddle and even worse than that — it's unnatural and unmanly for a boy to spend his time sitting in his room writing poetry."

"One of my own sons writes poetry," Hanson replied stiffly. "And neither myself nor his mother consider him to be unnatural or unmanly."

"Aye, but then your son is *English*. So it's to be expected, isn't it?"

She nodded her head sagely as if expecting Hanson to agree that the writing of poetry was an English vice.

"I'll not have my George growing up girlish and depraved. All poem-writers are depraved in one way or another."

"Even Robert Burns?"

"What!" she cried, advancing a few paces closer to his desk. "Don't you *dare* say a word against Rabby Burns! He is the voice of Scotland, and was a better man than you will ever be."

The woman was mad. Her contradictions of her own words were ludicrous. He could take no more of her, not today, not for another minute.

"Pray excuse me ..." Hanson moved swiftly out of the room, seeking some fresh air and some sanity.

Walking through the gardens at the back of the house he took some deep breaths to calm the disturbance of his mind caused by that *ridiculous* woman, and also wondering what caused her to be so. He had now learned that her father had committed suicide in a moment of madness, so perhaps she did suffer from some sort of mental derangement?

How else to explain the unstable way she treated her

son? Loving him one day and spoiling him with over-indulgence, and then a mood-swing into hating him the following day and rushing around impatiently to give him another whack of her "hard hand".

And then her husband ... well, he knew all about John Byron and his selfish and wilful ways ... a man who had not cared a jot about the welfare of his wife or son when he had relieved himself of the burden of life by taking poison.

And then there was the boy, the dear boy, impossible to dislike and easy to love ... a boy who had began his start in life unable to stand up to anyone, crippled as he had always been. An easy target for one and all, unable to run away fast enough or far enough to escape whatever cruelty pursued him. A boy who was so playful and affectionate with all the Abbey's farm animals, and yet amongst humans he always seemed to have a look of suspicion or shy torment in his blue eyes.

A small bird flitted onto the branch of a tree above Hanson's head, twittering away cheerily, and then flying off again into the freedom and pleasure of life.

There was something so symbolic about that small happy bird, something that tugged at John Hanson's heart as he thought of young George.

If there was one thing that *both* parents of that boy now owed to their son ... it was surely a plea for his forgiveness.

~ ~ ~

Hanson went looking for Joe Murray and finally found him in the grounds near the cloisters, his head thrown back laughing with delight as he watched the boy and a young dog rolling on the grass together.

"What's this, Joe?"

Joe was still smiling fulsomely as he looked at the solicitor. "A young pup I brought from the village for him. And look at the two of them now, did you ever see such joy in boy or dog?"

"Oh, Mr Hanson," the boy laughed, noticing him. "Come and meet my new friend. I have named him *Woolly*!"

Hanson nodded. "He's big enough for a pup. Is he a cross-breed, Joe?"

"Aye, a mongrel cur, but it was when I saw how the young master loved all the other animals on the farm that I decided he might like an animal of his own for some company. A mongrel, yes, but he was all I could get."

"I'm going to take him for a swim in the lake."

Hanson watched the excited boy limping away with the dog trotting beside him. "Can you swim?" he called out.

George looked back and laughed. "I can swim better than I can walk."

When he had gone from view Hanson looked curiously at Joe Murray. "Did you ask for the mother's permission to get him a dog?"

"No fear."

"She may not like it, and I would hate to see her venting another of her rages on the boy because of the pup."

Joe Murray shrugged, unconcerned. "She'll not get near the boy now, not with her hand nor her mouth. You saw how the dog instantly took to him, two young pups together. Let's go round to the lake," Joe said eagerly, "and see if he really *can* swim."

Hanson followed Joe's hurried footsteps round to the side of the house and the huge 'Garden Lake' where the two men stood in amazement as they watched the young master swimming strongly and joyfully, fully clothed, and the dog paddling in the water trying to catch up with him.

"Is that not a sight for sore eyes," Joe said happily. "Look at the two of them — half an hour ago they were strangers, and already they love each other. And believe me, Mr Hanson, that boy needs some affection from someone. So his own dog will be a start in that."

"But, Joe..." Hanson said cautiously, still reeling from all the rage and abuse he had taken, "if the mother does not like it—"

"Then she can lump it!" Joe said. "She can rant and rage at the boy all she likes, but she won't find it so easy to do in the future, not without some unpleasant consequences."

"What do you mean?"

"See Woolly there, he'll be protecting the boy devotedly with his life from now on, and if anyone goes near him menacingly or even shouts at him, well ..." Joe shook his head fearfully at the thought.

John Hanson smiled, somewhat cynically. "Joe, the dog is still merely a pup."

"Maybe so, maybe so, but he still has the nature of an attack dog in his blood," Joe replied seriously, and then looked at Hanson. "Oh, did I not tell you? The reason the young master immediately named him Woolly, is because the dog is half *wolf.*"

Chapter Ten

~ ~ ~

To explore all the surrounding lands of Newstead Abbey was just too far for an eager and limping boy to walk, so Joe Murray took him to the stables and showed him a sleek brown pony.

"He belongs to you now, my lord, so why don't you ride him? He's a gentle animal and sometimes a bit sedate in his pace, but it would still be quicker than walking."

The boy ran his palm down the pony's neck, but his eyes were on the larger horses. "I would prefer to ride a horse."

"No, no, Mr Hanson would never allow that – too risky for a boy so young," Joe said firmly, and then smiled, "but he has agreed to a pony."

"Does this pony have a name?"

"Aye, a fine English name, Mr Shakespeare."

The boy smiled; he had ridden on a number of Shetland ponies during his time in Scotland, but none with such a grand name.

A short time later Joe Murray stood watching with satisfaction as Mr Shakespeare and the boy rode off together at a moderate pace.

Returning to the Servants' Hall, Joe said to Nanny Smith, the housekeeper, "When I was that young, I spent all my time dreaming about running away to sea."

"And did you?" Nanny asked.

Joe shrugged. "Oh, not until I was a lot older – near on fourteen."

~ ~ ~

He had ridden no more than two miles when he met two

young girls also riding ponies and wondered who they were. The older girl, who looked about twelve, rode up to him.

"Are you aware, pray, that you are riding on *Annesley* land?"

He glanced around him, perplexed. "Is all this not part of the estate of Newstead?"

"No," she said firmly. "Newstead has three thousand, two hundred and fifty acres, and Annesley has three thousand, one hundred and twenty-five acres. So Newstead *is* bigger than Annesley, but only by a hundred acres or so." She spoke as if she had learned the numbers very carefully. "However, young man, you are now riding on *my* land."

"Your land?"

"Mary is the heiress to Annesley Hall and all its land," said the younger girl sitting on the pony beside her. "One day she will own it all."

Mary was looking at the quality and cleanliness of his clothes and knew he was no peasant or son of a tenant, so he must be —"The new Lord Byron," she said. "You see *I know* who you are."

She seemed to know everything.

He sat looking at her silently, his eyes studying every detail of her oval face. She had light brown hair and dark brown eyes and, despite her uppity manner, she was very, very pretty.

"So your estate backs onto mine," he said.

"No," she answered, "your estate backs onto mine."

"But I own mine *now*," he said, refusing to be bullied. "Yet you may have to wait years and years before you inherit yours."

The girl was struck dumb at this, unable to dispute it, so instead she laughed, and then relented; although she later told him it had been fun acting like the *mistress* of the Annesley estate.

"We have brought a picnic, would you like to join us?"

Her friendliness intimidated him more than her haughtiness and brought back his natural shyness. If he dismounted, she would see his limp, and then her friendliness might go away again. If she had not been so pretty he might not have cared, but she was ... the prettiest girl he had ever seen.

He shook his head and patted the neck of his pony. "Mr Shakespeare is not used to me yet, I should take him back."

"Why do you speak in such a funny way?" asked the younger girl curiously in her clear English voice. "You sound very different to other people we know, doesn't he, Mary?"

"My accent is Scottish," he said, and shot a challenging look at the girl named Mary. "Or dinna ye know that also?"

Mary laughed at his impertinence, deciding she liked this Scottish boy. "Well," she said finally, "my cousin and I ride our ponies out for a picnic almost every day in this warm weather ... you are quite welcome to join us on Annesley land. And we always bring delicious cakes."

He did not answer, feeling a shyness again. He turned the pony around. "Thank you, Miss..."

"Chaworth," she said. "Mary Ann Chaworth."

~ ~ ~

John Hanson realised he had stayed longer at Newstead than he had intended, and now it really was time for him to return to London and his own family. But he had no intention of being derelict in his duty of care to the young lord, and now he must face the mother with his decisions.

He dreaded the coming interview, knowing her reaction, but it had to be done. Summoning up all his courage, he rang the bell for a maidservant and asked her to tell Mrs Byron that he wished to speak with her.

That done, he returned to the seat behind his desk in the library, and waited.

She finally appeared an hour later, and as always he stood when she entered, his eyes noting the sheet of paper in her hand.

"Now, Mr Hanson," she said without preamble, "I have made a list of all the repairs that need to be done here, but surely you know that the house is just too big for George and I to live in *all* of it."

"Yes, Madam, and that's the reason why the old Baron lived solely in one wing and left the rest of the house to dilapidate."

"He certainly did. The old bugger left it to go to wreck and ruin. Now, I think the best solution is to have the wing where the old Baron lived — the *best* wing where George and I are placed now, fully repaired and refurnished to my own style and taste. And when that's done, we can plan ahead for the restoration of the whole of it."

As always, Hanson regarded her steadily. "Mrs Byron, the time has come for your son to return to school."

"What? Back to Aberdeen?"

"No, a more suitable school has been recommended."

"Recommended by whom?"

"Lord Carlisle."

"Indeed? And when did that mystery bogey-man recommend that to you?"

"In this letter, which I received yesterday." He held out the letter, and stood watching her as she read it.

"But it says here ... 'I fully agree with your recommendation of Dr Glennie's Academy in Dulwich, London...'" She glared at him. "So it was *you* who recommended this school, not Lord Carlisle."

"If Lord Carlisle had disapproved of the school, he would not have agreed to the recommendation. Mrs

Byron, your son is now a ward of the Court of Chancery, and a future Lord of the Realm. His continuing education is vital, and there is no suitable school here in Nottingham."

She stepped back a pace, as if she had suddenly heard something here that terrified her.

"Ward of the Court ... Lord of the Realm ... Is he no longer to be my son at all?"

"He will always be your son."

"And if I object ... to the school in London?"

"Do you object?"

She licked her bottom lip, confused. "I do realise that he will need to attend a school, but ... I don't want to be without my George. I live only for him."

"A house would of course be rented for you close to the school," Hanson said. "So you could visit him regularly."

"Visit him?"

"Dr Glennie's Academy is a boarding school, so he would live in."

"Lord save us, I'm going to faint!" She reached out to a chair by the desk and flopped down on it, her face stark white.

Immediately Hanson saw that she was not pretending and rushed to pour her a glass of water. She took the glass from him with trembling hands and almost dropped it. He put his own hand beneath the glass to secure it, holding it while she took two or three sips and then she sat back, looking like a woman ravaged by shock.

"It would bereave me to let him out of my care," she said. "Yes, I would be quite *bereaved*, I love him so dearly."

"You would be living very close to the school, and while you are in London the repair work and refurbishing of your wing here in Newstead could be done in your absence."

"No, no, I could never live in London again. I have too many bad memories of that place, bad memories of the time I lived there with my dear dead Johnny. And then there was also my own near-death experience of George's birth in London."

When she lowered her head and started to weep, John Hanson did not know what to think. Her reaction was not what he had expected nor prepared for. He found her mother's tears even harder to deal with than her mad rages.

He said: "Mrs Byron, would you like to adjourn this conversation and continue it later today, or even tomorrow? You look quite unwell. Shall I ring for a maid to take you to your bedroom?"

"I think that would be best," she agreed weakly. "It's only my bed that I am fit for now. Yes, please ring for one of the servants to help me."

When she had left the room, John Hanson sat for a long moment in silent reflection. He had expected tantrums and explosions of jealous rage, and he had been determined to stand up to her, because the woman was a hard-mouthed bully.

Yet now he was feeling almost as stunned as she herself had been earlier, because now he knew something else about her. Now he knew that underneath all that fury, and in her own strange way, she did love her son.

Finally he lifted his pen and began writing a letter to his wife, informing her that he would be delayed in Nottingham for some time longer.

~ ~ ~

She lay on her bed staring at the ceiling with unseeing eyes. It was all slipping away from her. She was losing all control of her son. All her care, all her love for him, was now to be counted as nothing against the power of the Court and the determination of John Hanson.

Yet, Hanson was a parent too, a father ... so surely he must have some understanding of a loving mother's feelings?

John Hanson did, and in the days that followed he attempted to make everything as easy as he possibly could for the mother, speaking to her gently at all times, his manner supportive as well as understanding.

"You are determined in your wish not to live in London?"

"I hate that place. A stinking city full of sin. And if George is to be boarded away from me there..."

She began to weep again, her handkerchief dabbing at her eyes. "I cannot be left to live on my own here in this great place," she said. "And the servants here ... well, they have not got as much as one good brain between the lot of them – and that Joe Murray is the *worst,* always going over my head and behind my back."

John Hanson looked down at his papers. "Mrs Byron, there is a rather beautiful country house in the nearby village of Southwell that could be put at your disposal, Burgage Manor. It would be a charming place for you to live in while your son is away at school."

"A country manor ... beautiful?" Her interest sharpened. "Have you seen it yourself?"

"Yes, I went there yesterday, solely for the purpose of inspecting it on your behalf."

"So when can *I* see it? This country manor?"

"We could take a short carriage ride over there this afternoon if you wish."

"Why not now?"

"Very well, we can go now, if you wish."

She jumped up. "I'll get my cloak."

~ ~ ~

Burgage Manor, a light-stoned, three-storied Georgian building with gardens, truly was beautiful, inside and out. Mrs Byron loved it.

"Oh, I could be happy here," she said to John Hanson. "Well, as happy as any broken-hearted mother *could* be without her son."

Hanson smiled. "And you need not be lonely here. Do you know, Madam, that within just a few short miles from here, live some of your relatives on the Byron side. They are all very anxious to meet you."

"Eh?" She looked startled. "So why did they not come up to the Abbey to meet me then?"

"Very few outsiders have ventured near the Abbey in the last twenty years. The Baron made lots of enemies before he became a recluse. And apart from that, most people believe the Abbey is haunted."

"Nonsense! If there were a ghost lurking anywhere in the Abbey I would have seen it. There were quite a few old ghosts in my own Gight Castle in Scotland, so I know one when I see one, and I've seen no ghosts at all at Newstead."

John Hanson changed the subject. "So, would Burgage Manor be suitable for you?"

"Oh, it would indeed. But only while George is away at school," she added quickly. "After that I insist upon George and myself returning to live at Newstead Abbey, his ancestral home."

"Of course."

"And I will want some new servants here, servants of my own selection and choice, not the ones from the Abbey. I could not trust myself to live here alone with that bunch of upstarts. I might *kill* one of them — especially that Joe Murray. The old Baron should have taken that snooty bugger with him."

John Hanson smiled, relieved to see that Mrs Byron was at last returning to her usual cantankerous self. She certainly seemed more relaxed and cheerful on the drive back to Newstead, and when the carriage turned into the courtyard and she again caught sight of the Abbey, a perplexed frown moved over face.

"Tell me, Mr Hanson, how exactly does Lord Carlisle have any connection or concern with my business or my son? He has never even seen the boy, not once in his life, so why was he selected as George's legal guardian?"

"Lord Carlisle's father was married to the Honourable Isabella Byron, daughter of the 4th Lord Byron," explained Hanson. "She was a sister of your son's grandfather."

"So ... a Carlisle married a Byron ... and she was the aunt of my dear Johnny?"

"Yes."

"And the great-aunt of my George?"

"Yes."

"It's hardly a close connection ... not as close as my own, and not close enough for Lord Carlisle to stick his nose in and start telling us all what we should do. Or does he intend to keep doing that *in absentia* as well?"

Hanson diplomatically gave no answer, but his eyes were mildly amused. Personally, he disliked the cold and austere Lord Carlisle, but he could not allow Mrs Byron to know that.

~ ~ ~

He had ridden out on Mr Shakespeare many times, but he had not encountered the pretty girl or her cousin again, probably because he had not gone anywhere near the land belonging to the Annesley Estate.

Joe Murray had warned him to "Keep well clear of Annesley, my lord. We at Newstead have nothing to do with the Chaworths, and they have nothing to do with us."

"Why?" he asked curiously.

"Oh, now," Joe said, "it's not something a boy as young as yourself should know. So we will leave old bones buried and speak no more of it.

Chapter Eleven

~ ~ ~

London, 1798-1801

The visit to the Consultant in Harley Street was enlightening.

He had taken his time inspecting the boy's foot and gave his opinion that it was not a so-called "'club foot'" at all.

"The foot is turned inwards, causing him to walk in a sloping way on the *side* of his foot," he explained to John Hanson, "unlike a club foot which turns upwards and often makes walking at all impossible."

Hanson glanced at his young charge, who was lying on the Consultant's couch, his blue eyes fixed on Dr Baillie's face, listening intently to every word he said as his right leg and foot were manipulated and inspected.

Hanson said: "The boy suffers a great deal of pain."

"Yes, now the reason for that is due to the strain on the ankle and these lower calf muscles. Do you see ... how thin the ankle and lower muscles of the leg are? Any continuous weight on them must cause a great deal of strain ... No, my diagnosis is that this affliction was caused by some sort of semi-paralysis of the foot, probably caused by some irregularity when he was still in the womb."

"Is there a cure?" Hanson asked.

Dr Baillie shook his head. "None that we know of. And even if a cure were to be discovered, I would say it is too late. The damage to the foot and ankle was done so long ago that I doubt the restoration of those muscles could ever be restored."

After a silence the boy finally spoke: "So am I to be a cripple for all of my life?"

"A cripple?" Dr Baillie now gave his attention to the whole of the boy and not solely to one of his lower limbs.

"My dear boy you have *never* been a cripple. You have been bravely walking around on a semi-paralysed foot for years, and for that you must be highly commended. Others with the same affliction have not been so determined and have allowed themselves to be carried around from one place to another."

"Will I always limp?"

Dr Baillie sighed. "Yes, I am afraid so." He suddenly smiled and tapped the boy's leg. "But we can help you to minimise the limp and make it easier for you to walk. And in time, as you grow older, people may not notice that you have a limp at all."

John Hanson knew that he would never forget the expression of surprise and elation on the boy's face at this news: and a week later, when he was fitted with his special new shoe, his delight as he stood on his afflicted foot and found he could stand and balance himself more easily, caused joyful tears to form at the edges of Hanson's own eyes.

The special shoe was an 'inner' shoe to be worn inside normal boots or shoes. The sides of the soles were built up to support his inward-turning foot, with a brace around the ankle for support.

"New inner shoes will have to be made periodically as you grow older," said Dr Baillie. "And as you do grow older, you must also ensure that you always remain slender in your physique, in order not to put too much weight on the leg."

Outside on the street, after a short walk to the carriage, the boy could not contain his exhilaration at the new ease of his walking: not a miracle, but better, much better. Now he could walk with just a slight sliding of the right foot instead of a pronounced limp.

From that day forward the boy's life in London became a happy one. He settled into his new school without any difficulty.

At the end of the first month John Hanson received a report from the headmaster, Dr Glennie:

"His reading in history and poetry is far beyond the usual standard for his age. His manner is playful and good-humoured and he is already very much beloved by his companions."

Hanson put down the letter, finally feeling reassured that the hard decision, which he had made at Newstead, had been the right one.

~ ~ ~

He spent the Christmas break from school at John Hanson's home in Earl's Court, fitting in easily with the other children who all liked him extremely, especially Hanson's youngest daughter who, at eight years old, had rather a precocious way of speaking.

On the young Lord's first shy arrival inside the house, she had circled him silently for some minutes, inspecting him from head to foot, then turning to the rest of the family, she had declared: "Well, he is a very pretty fellow, so I believe his company will be most welcome."

Mrs Byron had written to say she was "most regretful" that her son was unable to return to Nottingham for Christmas, even though it would necessitate a long journey for him there and back in the period of only one week allowed for the holiday, but her burden would be eased by the many new friends she herself had made in Southwell.

John Hanson found himself feeling very pleased and relieved by Mrs Byron's new conciliatory attitude.

But it was not to last — the New Year brought a change of tone and mood.

As the winter months progressed, the letters of complaints from Dr Glennie to John Hanson became numerous, as did the letters of complaints from Lord Carlisle — and all due to the sudden reversal in attitude of Mrs Byron, who kept journeying down to London to try and drag her son out of school during his lessons and *"get him back to his maternal home where he belongs."*

When this failed, she took lodgings in nearby Sloane Terrace and continued her demands, insisting upon taking her son out of the school at weekends, unsettling his regular routine, and causing him great embarrassment in front of his friends.

One afternoon in March, a messenger in a carriage delivered an urgent note to John Hanson from Dr Glennie, requesting him to come to the school immediately — Mrs Byron was there again causing the most unholy rumpus.

"I have written previously to Lord Carlisle," Dr Glennie wrote, *"but he offers me no help, insisting that he has had enough of Mrs Byron and her frequent letters of complaints and he requests that I now put the matter completely in your hands."*

It was clear that the amiable Dr Glennie was now almost out of his wits with the woman, and Hanson made immediate haste to the school in the carriage.

When he entered the school's hallway he could hear Mrs Byron's voice thundering away somewhere down the corridor in such a loud and audible display of temper that it was impossible for her ranting not to be heard by all the other young scholars and servants in the building.

Hanson walked quickly towards Dr Glennie's office, turning a corner to see young Byron standing in the corridor, listening to it all, and surrounded by three or four of his school-fellows who appeared to be consoling him, one with his hand on his shoulder.

As the boys all had their backs to him, they did not hear or see him approach, and it was then Hanson heard one of the friends say, "Byron, your mother is a fool."

Byron glanced in annoyance at the boy who had spoken. "I know it, but *you* should not say it!"

"Lord Byron ... "

The boys turned, broke away, and young Byron seemed very relieved to see his guardian.

"Mr Hanson, you must tell her how much I hate her scenes, how much I detes*t* all scenes made by anyone, and especially scenes made by my mother!"

John Hanson nodded. "I suggest you boys now go out to the garden or somewhere else. You should not be listening here. Go on, go on!"

The boys seemed reluctant to leave Byron, but once he made a move to leave, they all quickly followed him.

Five minutes later, John Hanson was given a small private office in which to talk alone to the fretful Mrs Byron who kept insisting innocently that she had "*not* been making any trouble!"

"I could hear you, Mrs Byron. The entire school could hear you shouting. Have you any idea of the harm you are doing to your son with this intolerable behaviour? He has his own physical infirmity to cope with, so he should not have to cope with yours as well."

"*My* infirmity? What on earth are you talking about?"

As always, Hanson regarded her steadily, but the anger in his voice was clear.

"You are unstable, Mrs Byron. You are making your son's life here at the school not only insecure, but also embarrassing and miserable. He has asked me to tell you how much he detests all scenes, especially those scenes continually caused by you."

She sniffed. "He said that, did he? I suppose he would prefer me to act like he does then — glaring at me in his silent rages with one of those *underlooks* of his."

"At least his rages are *silent*, Mrs Byron."

"Yes, dark, dark rages, full of hatred," she agreed. "Oh, if you only knew, Mr Hanson, how that boy torments me with his long dark silences."

Hanson took a seat and assumed his lawyer's face and manner.

"May I remind you, Mrs Byron, that you promised to allow your son to continue his studies without interruption. Yet you have not kept to these professions of yours, have you? And despite Dr Glennie's numerous requests, you have continued to interfere and thwart the progress of the boy's education in every way that you can devise."

"I have not! I have simply called here to *see* him, but they refused me, pretending he was in lessons."

"And so you barged into the classroom and attempted to obstruct the teacher in his task, causing not only embarrassment to your son, but also distraction to the schoolfellows around him."

"I simply wanted to *see* him, if only for a few minutes. What's so wrong with that?"

"Mrs Byron, surely you understand that it is in these early years, that all the elemental parts of learning which are requisite for a boy destined to go on later to a great school are so important."

"What great school are you talking about?"

"Harrow."

"Harrow ... but is that not also in London?"

"Yes."

"Oh Lord save us!" She lowered her head and began to weep. Out came the dabbing handkerchief. "If only you could understand how much I love him ..."

"Then surely you should have enough self-denial to

allow him to have the best start in life possible to him. But no, you are so self-willed that you truly believe your own feelings are more important than his. You treat him like a possession – no, more like a *pet* that you can love and kiss or hate and hit as you please. But no more, Mrs Byron, no more."

She sat looking at him, her mouth open, dumbfounded. His cold anger was beginning to chill her with a strange feeling of fright.

He stood up, unwilling to spend any more time with her, his expression and voice controlled and formidable.

"Your access to your son is now restricted to those times in his school holidays when he returns to Nottingham."

She glared at him. "Even at Christmas time? Because you and *your* family kept him away from me last Christmas?"

"And you know the reason for that, Madam. As soon as your son heard that you had brought that vile young woman down from Scotland to be your maid again, he begged to be allowed to stay with me over Christmas."

"May Gray said it was all lies ... what George told you about her."

"I trust you have sent her back?"

She lowered her head and nodded meekly. "I will never forgive her for the horrible things she said to George about *me* – the trollop."

Me, me, me again! Hanson was sick of it. He walked to the door. "Good day, Mrs Byron. I suggest you see yourself out, and with some quiet dignity and respect for the school if you please."

~ ~ ~

There was no sign of young Byron or his friends when he returned to the corridor, so he made his way directly to Dr Glennie's office where he found the dear man attempting to restore his equilibrium with a pot of tea.

"A cup for you, Mr Hanson? I suspect you need one."

"No, thank you." Hanson then explained the restriction of access he had imposed on the boy's mother, which would be recorded in the file.

Dr Glennie sat shaking his head. "So unusual, a mother like that. All our parents are a delight to deal with, but that woman ... so uncouth and vulgar ... and yet young Byron is quite the opposite, very polite and respectful in his manner."

Hanson sighed. "In my experience with the world, a child either becomes very like, or completely *unlike* the dominant parent. We must be thankful that young Byron has chosen to be the complete opposite of his mother."

"Yes, but I do not believe he has remained impervious. The violent disturbance to his psychology must have had some damaging effects."

"Yes, that is a concern of mine."

"A great concern," said Dr Glennie. "The woman has aged *my* heart and brain and the rest of my vital organs by at least five years from the stress of her tantrums, and that only from her visits. How must it have been for the boy to live through his tender years with her?"

"How indeed."

"She appears to possess a mind wholly without cultivation, and certainly does not possess the powers of refinement and intellect required to form the character and manners of a young nobleman, her son."

"Then you must do your best to help him, Dr Glennie, and so must I." Hanson paused thoughtfully, remembering the words of the doctor in Harley Street. "But I suspect that young Byron will find his own way of mastering any mental damage caused to him by his mother, in the same way he has been mastering his infirmity with a determination to walk as well as he can, despite the continual pain it has caused him."

Dr Glennie was not inclined to agree. "Damage to a young boy's mind is not as easy to manage or master as a malformed foot."

Hanson did not argue. "But he is doing well here?"

"Oh yes, in every way. I believe he feels this school gives him some sanctuary away from it all, and now I understand why."

Hanson turned to leave. "If there are is any further disturbance you will—"

"Send for you immediately? Of course I will."

A week later, aided by a man she had recruited to her service, an attempt by Mrs Byron to secretly abduct her son from Dr Glennie's School and carry him off to France and out of the jurisdiction of the Court, was unsuccessful.

"France! A country at *war* with England and the English!" Hanson could hardly believe it. "Did you not stop for a second to consider the danger of your mad scheme? The danger to your son as well as to yourself?"

"How many times must I tell you – he is *my* son! I am the only one who can look after him properly."

"In the way you looked after him when your maid was sexually molesting him under your roof? If it was up to me I would have had you *both* prosecuted."

Finally accepting defeat, Mrs Byron returned to her country manor in Southwell, bought herself a small dog as a companion, and sent all the bills for the dog's food to John Hanson.

PART THREE

HARROW

1801-1805

~~~

Friendship is doubly dear to one who thus for
kindred hearts must roam,
And seek abroad the love denied at home:
Those hearts, dear Harrow, have I found in thee,
A home, a world, a paradise to me.

BYRON

Chapter Twelve

~ ~ ~

The prestigious school of Harrow contained many pupils from the nobility. The sons of Dukes and Earl's and Viscounts and many young Lords themselves, studied in its classrooms.

A place of privilege, it was like living in another country; an enclosed and private domain separated from the real and noisy world outside; a male world of study and play where young adolescent boys often fell in and out of love with each other, and where the sport of cricket reigned supreme.

Now aged thirteen, and having moved up from Dr Glennie's school into Harrow, Byron found himself in the unusual predicament of having to *share* a bed in his boarding house at the school. Harrow had become over-populated by the sons of the aristocracy and so a shared bed in the dormitories was made available at half the cost.

Mrs Byron wrote to the headmaster in a fury, informing him that unless he could share a bed with a Duke or a Viscount, then *her* son, a *Gordon* – and a direct descendent of James the 1st of Scotland – must have his own bed, whatever the cost.

"He had not only his own bed, but his own *room* at the school in Dulwich," she reminded John Hanson.

"Yes, but that room was Dr Glennie's own back parlour which he made available as a private bedroom for your son," Hanson explained. "Dr Glennie, in his kindness, felt that due to the boy's infirmity, causing him to take longer to get dressed and undressed, he should be saved any embarrassment in front of the other boys by having his own room."

"And now that he has entered Harrow, has my George's infirmity *miraculously* gone away, Mr Hanson?"

"No, but he is older and stronger now, and —"

"Why are you being so mean with our money? It is not your money! Every penny of it belongs to my George, and I would be obliged if you would remember that."

John Hanson put a hand to his brow ... it was impossible to argue with her, yet he would try.

"Mrs Byron, despite Dr Glennie's good intentions ... your son has told me it was that very separation at night from the other boys at Dulwich which made him feel like an *outsider,* exacerbating his notions of inferiority, due to his infirmity. So I thought—"

"Then let him share the dormitory at night with the other boys at Harrow, but *only* the dormitory, because whatever he may have told you back then, he told me only last week that he is now so used to having his own bed, both at home and at Dr Glennie's school, that he would find it very strange to have to *share* a bed with anyone. So have it done, Mr Hanson, and have it done tomorrow!"

When she had gone, Hanson picked up his pen, deciding he had no other choice but to send a letter by messenger to the headmaster at Harrow and confirm the stipulation of a single bed for Lord Byron, whatever the cost.

~~~

Shy, at first, Byron soon began to love the company and friendship of his dormitory at night ... the fun of silly jokes played on each other, the muffled laughter, the long whispered conversations in the dark where the boys learned more and more about each other's families

— stories which Byron listened to intently – but also a subject which he personally never spoke about.

A new world, a new life, so much so that he began to leave the boy hitherto known as George Gordon far behind him, and now responded quickly and naturally when, like all the other boys, he was addressed solely by his surname of Byron.

A popular favourite amongst his friends, by the time he reached the age of fifteen, Byron was beginning to show signs of extremely good looks in his appearance, constantly causing a buzz of fevered whispers amongst some of the other Harrow boys due to his unique and inimitable habit of looking at anyone who caught his interest with one of his *underlooks* – head tilted and downcast, but blue eyes raised under black lashes, fixed on the person of interest – causing many a young Harrow boy to blush, stumble in his steps, and then spend a long and emotionally-confused night without sleep.

He was also now showing signs of physical strength, the tutors noticed – a fighter who loved to spend his spare time boxing in the school's gym — *"If the lower part of my body is weak, due to my right foot, then I shall make sure the rest of my body is very strong."*

To accomplish this aim, Byron caught the coach into town every weekend to take private lessons from the former professional Boxing Champion known as 'Gentleman John Jackson', until he was almost as good at boxing as he was at swimming.

John Hanson suspected that the true reason for Byron's determination to become a skilful fighter was solely due to his own surprising need to defend his mother.

The older he got, the more embarrassing his mother became. And now, within the hallowed halls of Harrow, her lack of dignity and her outrageous shouting at the headmaster or tutors over some imagined slight against herself or her beloved son had resulted in Dr Drury finally ordering that "*the gates of Harrow shall be barred against her. All doors shall be locked to Mrs Byron from now on.*"

The humiliation and shame she relentlessly caused to her son was something she had always been incapable of recognising. She was who she was, and nothing below a bolt of lightning striking her from the sky above would ever change her.

It was Byron who gradually changed. In his fifteenth year he violently threw himself into the occupation of defending his mother against the Harrow snoots, responding to all sneers with a quick temper and violent fists — his declaration as always — "I know it, but *you* shall not say it," causing the headmaster, Joseph Drury, to now liken him to "a wild mountain colt."

Yet with his mother's eventual barring and absence, peace reigned and his popularity soared again, and all due to his hilarious "witticisms" that could strike an opponent dumb faster than any fist.

John Hanson occasionally visited him at Harrow and regularly received reports of his progress, feeling no concern whatsoever when Byron's tutor complained of his — "inattention to business and his propensity to make others laugh and disregard their employment as much as himself."

Hanson threw down the report. What boy did not seek fun and laughter occasionally in an attempt to relieve the oppressive tedium of the classroom?

Yet it was not all fun or fighting for Byron; his personal struggle went on.

One day, from a window of the school's vantage point high on Harrow Hill, the headmaster's wife, Mrs Drury, saw young Lord Byron coming up the hill on his own, without his usual band of followers.

After watching him for some minutes, she sighed tragically and said to her husband: "There goes Byron, struggling up the hill, like a ship in a storm without a rudder or a compass."

Dr Drury joined her at the window. "That hill is certainly no friend to him."

"Why does he not use a walking stick on such occasions?" she asked. "It would make the climb up the hill so much easier for him."

Dr Drury paused, rather heavily. "That young man has great pride, my dear. If anyone was to offer him a walking stick, he might very well hit them with it."

Chapter Thirteen

~ ~ ~

The summer of 1803 was very hot. At the end of June Byron set off on his journey to spend the holiday living with his mother in Nottingham.

In his own mind he had called a truce with her. His method now was not to change her, but to *tame* her, keeping her happy with regular letters, and visiting her home of Burgage Manor as often as possible — if only to keep her away from the gates of Harrow.

The journey from London to Nottingham took just over a day, the stagecoach stopping at the regular halfway post where fresh horses could be obtained and weary passengers could partake of some dinner, followed by a night's sleep, before setting off again.

At the inn that night, he met a new friend, and both fell so madly in love with each other at first sight, that the innkeeper eventually allowed Byron to take the friend away with him.

"But only because I can see you are a true animal lover, my lord," said the innkeeper, looking pleased as punch at the two gold sovereigns Byron had placed in his hand. "And it's a good home I'm sure you will give him."

"What's this? What's this?" Mrs Byron demanded when he walked into the hall at Burgage Manor accompanied by his new friend. "You can't bring another dog in here – he'll upset Gilpin!"

"Then Gilpin will have to be upset," Byron answered. "His name is Boatswain, and his ancestors are Canadian. Is he not the most beautiful dog you have ever seen?"

Mrs Byron peered at the dog and had to admit that he was indeed a beauty – coal black in his coat with some white around his feet.

"But Gilpin won't like it!" she insisted. "Another dog roaming around his house. What breed is he?"

"A Newfoundland, a noble breed, very gentle but strong. Although a man in the coach insisted he is an Eskimo dog, a breed of husky.'

Boatswain stood looking up at Mrs Byron, his tail wagging.

"Why do you always have to get such big dogs," she demanded. "Look at him – only a pup and already four sizes bigger than my Gilpin."

"And how is *my* Woolly?"

"Oh, that wolf of yours. He's still prowling the grounds at Newstead. I did ask the gamekeeper to shoot him but the insolent man refused."

Byron gave a small laugh. "If I thought you were serious I would ask the gamekeeper to shoot *you*."

Gilpin, an irascible little fox terrier, wandered out to the hall to see what was going on, immediately turning feral at the sight of a rival in his realm; yapping and snapping insanely at Boatswain who answered him with low growls.

"I told you Gilpin would be furious!' Mrs Byron scooped up her pet while Byron laughed and led Boatswain up to his bedroom.

"Those two downstairs — two terriers together, eh Boatswain?"

Boatswain responded by lifting his front leg and devotedly offering his paw ... causing Byron to feel such an overwhelming emotion of love for the dog that tears slipped down his face as he crouched down and hugged him.

"And tomorrow," he said to Boatswain, "I will take you over to Newstead Abbey where you will meet another new friend, named Woolly."

~ ~ ~

The following morning, upon returning from a short stroll with Boatswain, Byron was greeted in the hall by his mother, her face redder than usual as she said in a low hush and rush. "George, you have a visitor. She's come over here from Swan Green at this early hour of the morning because she is so desperately eager to finally meet you."

"Who? Who is she?"

"One of your great aunts – on the *Byron* side. So go into the drawing-room now and make a good impression."

Boatswain was the first to lollop into the drawing-room, making the old lady shriek with fright at the effusion of his greeting.

"Take him away – I do not like dogs! Ohhhhh, I think he is trying to *bite* me!"

"Bo'sun, ... Bo'sun!" As soon as Byron had gathered Boatswain behind his legs, he assured the lady that his dog was merely being affectionate.

"Are you sure I am safe?"

Byron smiled. "I am certain."

She began to relax, sitting back and slowly looking him up and down. "So you are George, eh? Jack's son."

"Oh, he's a *Byrrone* through and through!" Mrs Byron cut in quickly. "Every bit his father's son."

The old lady gave an amused little laugh. "Oh, my dear, I do hope he is *not* quite so much like his father. We always used to call him Mad Jack"

"Oh ..." Mrs Byron became flustered. "And why was that?"

"Well, there was his deplorable gambling, and then of course, his notorious womanising ... and also you must have heard ..."

Byron had stopped listening, urging Boatswain to sit at his feet while he sat down in an chair and studied his great-aunt ... she was frail in her build, aged somewhere in her late seventies or early eighties, dressed to the hilt in velvet and wearing a chestnut wig, and also very disdainful in her tone and manner.

"How tall are you?" she suddenly demanded.

Byron blinked. "The last time I was measured by my tailor ... I was five feet and nine inches."

"And how old?"

"In his sixteenth year," Mrs Byron answered. "Another few years and he'll be as tall as a tree."

He flashed his mother a look, wondering why she was being so obsequious to this woman – not her usual manner at all.

His great-aunt was speaking to him again. "Now tell me, George, how fervent are you in the practice of your religion?"

When he did not immediately answer, she nodded knowingly. "Like all youth I see ... not as dedicated as you should be, and that is why I came to see you today, so I may catch and guide you while you are still so very young!"

"My George knows all about the Bible," his mother put in, looking somewhat perplexed. "As devout a Christian as I myself am."

"Indeed?" the old lady frowned, patted the side of her wig regally, and graciously accepted the china saucer and cup of tea handed to her by a maid. "And are you hoping, George, to go to Heaven or the moon when you die?"

Byron blinked again. "The moon?"

"Where else?" she looked from mother to son. "Oh, I know all you *orthodox* Christians like to talk about a place called Heaven being somewhere unseen up there in the sky, although it is beyond my fathoming why none of you have yet concluded that place *up there in the sky* must surely be the moon. After all, we talk about God being in his "Heaven" and we also talk about 'the man in the moon' and I truly believe they are one and the same person."

Byron stared at her. *And this madwoman dares to call my father mad?*

She suddenly looked at him. "Are you acquainted with the books of Ariostos?"

Byron cleared his throat and nodded. "I have read some of them."

"Well there you are then," she replied with a nod of satisfaction, "there's the proof! Ariostos clearly states that *'All things lost on earth are treasured in the moon'.*"

"But everyone knows that Ariostos wrote fiction," Byron said, but the old lady was not listening, responding to an exclamation from his mother and replying with exclamations of her own.

"And every single one of my ladies at Swan Green concurs with me," she was saying to his mother. "In fact, once a week we get together at dusk and say our prayers up to the moon and wave to our unseen ancestors. It's quite magical in the summertime, so much more so than our fusty old church."

"Pray excuse me," he murmured, standing to leave the room quickly before he might burst out laughing.

Boatswain jumped up to follow him and it was then that his great-aunt noticed his slightly uneven hurried step.

"Is that why you have a dog?" she asked. "Because of your deformity?"

Byron stopped dead ... turning to look at her. "Madam?"

She pointed to his foot. "We all know about your deformed foot, dear, it is the talk of Southwell. So is that why you need the dog, to help you along?"

Mrs Byron could see her son's eyes flashing blue fire as he responded, "Boatswain is not a guide dog, Madam, and you may also have noticed that I am not *blind*."

He abruptly left the room and his mother faced the old lady with discomfit and some annoyance.

"You should not have made any reference to his lame foot. It's a subject that torments him and always sends him into a rage."

And such was his rage, that once inside his bedroom the only way he could release his hurt feelings was to limp over to his desk and, in a storm of satirical fury, scribble down a verse —

In Nottingham County there lives at Swan Green,

As curst an old lady as ever was seen;

And when she does die, which I hope will be soon

She firmly believes she will go to the moon.

Chapter Fourteen

~ ~ ~

"The talk of Southwell? My *deformed* foot?"

Frustrated and full of bitterness he quickly left the house and made his way over to the house of the Pigot family across the Green.

In the previous years during his visits to Southwell he had made friends with Elizabeth Pigot and her brother John. Both were a few years older than him, and both were poetry fanatics. Theirs was a house that he had often escaped to, enjoying the fun when the three of them sat scribbling away in competition towards the funniest or the saddest poem they could write.

Elizabeth opened the front door, smiling and receiving him with great friendliness.

"Byron, you are back! Oh my – you are beginning to look so *grown up* these days! And oh, oh ... who is this adorable creature?"

"Boatswain."

He stood watching as she bent to fuss and fondle the dog, but his mind was seething with questions. "Is it true that I have become the *talk* of Southwell?"

Elizabeth was spared from answering by the arrival of her brother John, coming into the hall all smiles with his hand held out. "Byron, my dear fellow!"

As soon as they had shaken hands, John Pigot took his arm. "Come through to the back garden, we are just about to have some tea. Then you can tell us all your latest news from Harrow."

As soon as they had stepped into the back garden he asked again: "Is it true that I am the talk of Southwell?

John flushed a deep red. "Well..."

"Are they now saying I am deformed?"

Elizabeth followed with Boatswain, her face as embarrassed as her brother's face, not quite sure how to answer.

"They say your deformity is a curse that was placed on you as punishment for the evil deeds of the *Wicked Lord.*"

He stared incredulously at Elizabeth, but Elizabeth had not spoken ... yet it was a female voice.

Elizabeth quickly moved Boatswain aside and said formally: "Lord Byron, may I introduce you to Miss Mary Ann Chaworth."

He had already turned to look towards the direction of the voice, but the sun was glaring in his eyes, making him blink and momentarily blind.

And slowly by his swimming eyes was seen

A lovely female face of seventeen...

She had been standing by one of the rose bushes. On her head she wore a blue velvet bonnet that matched the blue velvet sash on her slender white dress, as white as her teeth as she smiled at him.

"Lord Byron and I have already met ... once upon a long time ago," Mary said to Elizabeth, and then she smiled at him. "Although, I must say, you look nothing at all like the 'Wicked Lord', which is very fortunate for you."

"Who is this wicked Lord?" he asked, confounded.

She walked closer towards him, moving like a willowy nymph. "The wicked Lord," she said, "was your great-uncle, the 5th Baron, the one you have now replaced as the Lord of Newstead Abbey."

Her eyes looked even darker than he remembered, her light brown hair was looped in coils about her neck ... and he had never forgotten her.

"I never met my great-uncle," he told her. "I know as much about him as I know about you."

"And look here, Mary," John put in anxiously, "you cannot blame Byron for what his great-uncle did."

"What did he do?" Byron asked her. "Something so bad that you feel free to insult *me* for it?"

She was standing in front of him now, a slender girl about four inches shorter than himself, her eyes examining his face. "Are you truly so innocent?" she asked. "Or are you simply pretending that you do not know?"

"Miss Chaworth," he explained, "since moving from Scotland to England, and apart from a few months in Nottingham, I have spent most of my time living in London."

"And we have not told him," Elizabeth said quickly, and looked to her brother for support. "Have we, John?"

"No, indeed no," John insisted. "And why should we tell him? He is not responsible for the long feud between your two houses."

"Feud?" Byron was even more confounded.

"I suggest," said Elizabeth, assuming a prim face and blunt voice, "that we all sit down and have some tea, during which time I think it only fair that you tell him, Mary, if only to get this terrible unpleasantness out of the way."

They all sat down at the garden table, which was already draped in a white tablecloth, while Boatswain ambled off to explore the farthest areas of the shrubbery.

After the maid had brought tea and scones and a dish of honey, Byron sat listening as Mary Chaworth told him how *his* great-uncle, and *her* great-uncle, William Chaworth, had been neighbours and great friends, until the day they were both in London playing cards.

"In a tavern called 'The Star and Garter'," Mary said

distastefully, and then went on to tell of how the two men had started to argue and then both men, each insisting they had been insulted by the other, called for a duel of their swords, instructing the landlord to immediately supply seconds, and then retired to an upstairs room to settle the matter, where the Baron mercilessly killed William Chaworth with his sword.

Byron was perplexed. "But if *both* men had agreed to the duel?"

"Yes," Mary agreed, "but in most cases it would have resulted in a sword being knocked out of the hand or a small harmless gash of blood to settle the matter, but *your* great-uncle was not satisfied with that. In his temper the Baron deliberately thrust his sword straight through William Chaworth and killed him."

After a silence, all Byron could think to say sincerely was, "I am very sorry, Miss Chaworth."

Mary's gaze and tone suddenly softened, "Still, John is right, it was not *your* crime, so you should not be held to blame for it. However, I believe the bitter feud between our two houses will go on for ever."

John Pigot gave a reassuring little laugh. "Perhaps one day you two should marry and end the feud between the Chaworths and the Byrons once and for all."

Byron half smiled, embarrassed. "That would be like a Montague seeking to marry a Capulet, so I would think not."

"And besides," Mary added, dabbing a napkin to a drop of honey on her lips. "I am much older than you."

Elizabeth was amused. "Hark the dowager! You are not as yet eighteen, Mary."

After another silence, Byron said, "Miss Chaworth, will you remember this ... I succeeded to the title and estates of Newstead, not as the heir of the 'Wicked Lord', but as his *son's* heir."

Mary smiled at this new twist on the matter. "Yes, I will try and remember that."

As the conversation continued from one topic to another, Elizabeth could not help noticing a particular frisson of interest between Byron and Mary, and it disturbed her ... He was so young and Mary Chaworth was, well ... appearing to be so very friendly with the young Lord, which was not a good thing at all.

For Byron, the afternoon which had started off so strangely hostile, finally ended when a carriage came to take Mary home and she gave her hand to him in farewell with a warm smile. "I apologise for my coldness earlier. Are we now friends?"

Byron took her hand and bent over it so low he was almost kissing it with love.

"I suppose ... we may be seeing you again?"

She smiled. "I hope so."

Elated with secret delight, once her carriage was out of sight he quickly made his excuses to John and Elizabeth Pigot, setting off for home across the Green with Boatswain trotting beside him.

"Did you *see* her, Boatswain? Did you ever see such a lovely creature as Mary Ann Chaworth?"

Boatswain barked, picking up his excitement and joining in, his tail wagging madly.

When he got inside Burgage Manor, he went straight to his room and threw himself into a chair by the window, still caught up in the rapture of Mary Ann Chaworth, feeling a quickening of his heartbeat as he remembered how delectable she had looked, sitting there, opposite him, at the table, delicately eating a scone ...

> *I longed to sip*
> *from off her lip*
> *the honey on it.*

Later that afternoon he decided to ride over to Newstead.

All the principal rooms of the house were empty but he finally found Joe Murray in the Servants' Hall, sitting at the table drinking tea with the housekeeper, Nanny Smith, while the cook was busily kneading some dough at her own table.

All stopped what they were doing or saying when he entered.

"Oh, your lordship," said Nanny Smith, moving to get to her feet, but Byron gestured for her to remain sitting.

"May I join you?"

Joe Murray's eyes almost popped out of his head. "What, here? In the servants' hall?"

Byron sat down on the chair next to Nanny Smith and looked seriously at Joe Murray. "Tell me about my great-uncle, Joe, the Baron. You knew him so well."

Joe Murray was not in the habit of tittle-tattling or revealing details about his employer or indeed anything else that went on inside the privacy of Newstead, and he exchanged an alarmed glance with Nanny Smith.

"The duel with William Chaworth, Joe, I think I am now old enough to know."

"Well, it was a duel," Joe said hesitantly, "with seconds provided and everything proper, and both men were normally the closest of friends, so no one took it with much serious alarm, and it did *not* happen the way the Chaworths say it happened."

"So what way did it happen?"

Joe laid his forearms on the table and clasped his hands together. "Well, the duel was going along in the normal way, hit for hit, nothing very disquieting, and I thought that once the tit for tat with the swords had run its course, revealing a speck of blood on one or other of them, that would be the end of it. And it would have been so, but for the tavern-keeper. He was the one truly to blame for what happened next."

"What?"

"Well, they were near to the door of the room, you see, having skipped around the room in the way gentlemen do in these things, and the Baron was just about to snap his sword at Chaworth's sword when the tavern-keeper pushed open the door and at the same time pushed the Baron forward ..."

Joe shook his head. "I was only a young man then, but I'll never forget the whiteness of the Baron's face when he saw his sword stuck into Chaworth and blood pumping down his white waistcoat like a crimson flood. A dreadful business, and from that day on the Baron was never the same man. He turned into a recluse and became very peculiar. The Chaworth family, of course, insisted that it was a cold-blooded murder and never forgave him, and the relationship between Annesley and Newstead was cut dead from that time on."

"Tell him about the sword," Nanny Smith urged. "The sword that killed William Chaworth."

"Oh yes, the sword," Joe nodded. "Many was the times I tried to remove the sword and put it away, but the Baron wouldn't allow it. He insisted on having the sword propped up by his bed and always spent the time before sleep staring at it, night after night throughout all the following years, as if torturing himself, until in the end it drove him near to madness. They were cousins, y'know?"

"Who – my great uncle and William Chaworth?"

"Oh, yes," Joe nodded. "Distant cousins."

"How distant?"

"Oh, I'm not rightly sure, but the blood of the Byrons and the Chaworths was joined some time way back in the past, so there's *blood* as well as a long feud connecting the two houses."

Byron was elated ... so he and Mary Chaworth were

not complete strangers after all – somewhere down the bloodline of history their paternal ancestors had once been kinsmen.

"Tell him about the wine," Nanny Smith urged again. "That was the strangest of all."

"No," Joe replied firmly. "I was asked about the duel and so that's all I will speak of. The Baron is in his grave now, so let the dead rest."

"Yes, tell me about the wine," Byron said curiously. "I am asking you to tell me, Joe."

After another hesitation, Joe said. "Well, it was a special bottle of wine, very costly, and before they left for London the Baron and William Chaworth intended to drink it, but when time ran out on them, the Baron said, 'Never mind, the bottle will still be here when we get back and we'll sample it then'."

Joe looked sadly at Byron. "Of course, they never did come back together, or sample the wine together ... but from the day of his return to Newstead, every evening the Baron would order that same special bottle of wine to be placed on the table with his supper, and every evening the bottle of wine was left on the table unopened, night after night for so many years. And God help the maid who forgot to put that bottle of wine on the table ... Oh, if it was not there, the Baron kicked up a terrible temper until it was brought, as if he could not eat his supper without it."

"Very strange," said Nanny Smith, shaking her head and glancing at Cook who was stood listening to every word.

After a silence, Byron asked, "Where is the bottle of wine now?"

"It's still down in the cellar where it was returned every night..." A sudden realisation struck Joe. "Of course it belongs to *you* now."

"Yes, it does, so bring it to me," Byron said. "We will

open it and we will all drink a toast to the Baron and William Chaworth, God rest their poor souls, now they are *both* dead."

"What, my lord, open it?" All in a moment Joe Murray looked petrified and excited at the very thought of opening the treasured bottle of wine. "Are you sure?"

"Of course I am sure. We either drink it or smash it to break the spell it held over the Baron for so many years."

"Oh, I don't think we should smash it," Joe said, rising quickly to his feet. "I believe that particular bottle of wine cost a small fortune when it was bought, so it would be even more valuable now."

"I'll fetch the glasses," said Nanny Smith excitedly, while Cook was busily washing the flour from her hands.

Joe came back with the bottle and a corkscrew, his face flushed. "I can't believe it is finally going to be opened. Now, are you *sure,* my lord?"

"Open it!" Byron commanded, standing and smiling when he heard the *pop* of the cork, knowing that meant no air or damp had penetrated the cork. "Now let's see if it was worth the cost and all the fuss?"

He placed a good measure of the red wine into each of the four glasses and then lifted his own in a toast: "To William Byron and William Chaworth."

He sipped first and the three dutifully followed, after which they all looked at each other and it was Joe who was the first to speak: "Well, I am not an expert, but in my opinion, it would be hard to find a more beautiful wine than this!"

Byron smiled his agreement. "And now another toast to break the long spell of the unopened bottle. "To an end to the long feud between the Chaworths and the Byrons!"

Having now sampled the wine and knowing how

good it tasted, all drank agreeably to such a fine toast.

And on that Byron left them to it. He had found out what he had wanted to know and now he was no longer interested.

"What ... my lord," Joe stuttered. "You mean you are leaving *us* to finish the bottle?"

"If you wish, and when you have finished it, throw the empty bottle as far as you can into the waters of the lake."

When he had gone, Joe Murray looked at Nanny Smith and laughed, "Only the young would come up with a simple solution like that – to *open* the bottle and put an end to it."

Chapter Fifteen

~ ~ ~

The brilliance of the blue sky, the heat of the afternoon sun, gazing over the hills at sunset – had he ever known such a beautiful summer as this? A summer of one blissful day after another, and all because of a girl named Mary Ann Chaworth.

They had quickly become an outgoing foursome, Byron and John Pigot, followed by Elizabeth and Mary Chaworth, until the pairings had subtly and gradually changed over the days to John and Elizabeth, and Byron and Mary.

Occasionally he would ride out in the mornings to Annesley Hall, her ancestral home, which was no more than two miles from the back of Newstead Abbey, although he would have ridden twenty miles, or even a thousand miles, just to see her again.

He now thought of her as *his* Mary, whose personal beauty was equally matched by her vivacious personality, so friendly and so lovable.

His Scottish accent had long faded over the years through the influence of his two English schools, yet occasionally Mary referred to him playfully as "my Scottish boy."

During their ramblings, John Pigot noticed that Byron's natural shyness had vanished, his conversation always pleasant and very droll, often containing a slight twist of satire, frequently reducing them all to laughter.

In August an invitation was sent to "Lord Byron" inviting him to a Grand Ball at Castleton Hall in the Peak District. His immediate inclination was to tear up the invitation ... until he saw the dismay of his three friends.

"Castleton Hall!" Mary exclaimed. "Oh, they have such wonderful Balls and only the elite of title and rank are ever invited."

Byron shrugged. "What would be the point? A Ball means *dancing,* something I cannot do."

Mary smiled enticingly. "But if you were take us along as your guests, *we* could do all your dancing for you."

"While I stand watching and holding up the wall? Where would be my pleasure in that?"

"We would not dance all the time, just a few times now and again; and the rest of the time we would all stay together watching the fun."

John Pigot was more interested in seeing Peveril Castle. "It has been standing there since the eleventh century in Castleton," he told Byron, "ever since the Norman Conquest. So it would be wonderful to see it. Maybe we could even have a peek inside."

"I would love to see the inside of Peveril Castle," Mary exclaimed. "Oh, Byron, Byron, *Byron* ..."

How could he resist such a request from his beloved?

And when he saw both John and Elizabeth nodding their heads eagerly, he stemmed his reluctance and agreed.

One week later the four set off in a carriage for a few days holiday in the Peak District, accompanied by Mrs Pigot as the young ladies' chaperon.

The Peak District, with its beautiful scenery of high hills was full of romance, but the Grand Ball itself was just as Byron had feared it would be, a dismal affair for him.

In the dances of the evening, Mary, in her slender blue silk dress and looking more beautiful than he had ever seen her, was continually singled out by a young man who invited her for dance after dance, while Byron sat looking on, sullen and offended – although he tried not to show it, assuming an air of haughty indifference, while his feelings of physical inferiority inwardly plagued him, cursing his damned useless foot.

Although he could now walk with only a slight limp, to dance would be as difficult for him as trying to fly to the moon.

And now it hurt, *hurt,* to see the girl he loved being led out by another to dance so gaily on a ballroom floor from which he was physically excluded.

When the orchestra finally came to the end of their musical piece and Mary returned to her seat beside him, he gave her one of his sullen underlooks and said pettishly, "I hope you like your *new* friend."

The words were scarcely out of his lips when he was accosted by an ungainly-looking young lady who rather boisterously claimed him as a "cousin" on the Gordon side, putting his pride to torture with her loud and vulgar laugh, and when the intruder at last paused to take a breath, he heard Mary's voice whispering playfully in his ear, "I hope you like *your* new friend?"

~ ~ ~

The following day they were back in accord, as friendly as ever as the four friends gave Mrs Pigot the slip and set off to explore Peak Cavern, which they had been told was "one of the wonders of Derbyshire" which ran under the ruins of Peveril Castle, high on the hill above it.

They entered the cavern through a huge natural gap in the rock, and with candles to light their way they moved slowly through a geological subterranean wonderland of crystallised formations into the Grand Chamber, which led on into smaller chambers through narrow passageways, until they reached a narrow stream which had to be crossed in a boat capable of holding only two at a time.

Mary wanted to go first, excitedly pulling Byron along

with her, while John and Elizabeth affably agreed to wait their turn until the boat returned.

As the wooden punt was pushed off by the ferryman plodding at the rear of the boat, the ceiling of rock became lower and the ferryman bluntly ordered them, to "Lie down."

They looked at each other, and then at the ferryman.

"With the rock above now so close to the water," said the ferryman, "you will have to lie down as the space between water and rock becomes very narrow."

They slowly lay down in the narrow wooden punt, facing each other and looking up at the roof of crystallised rock only a foot or so above their faces, while the ferryman wading at the stern was stooped so low that his head was below the top of the boat.

For Byron the situation was agonising, to be so close to this heavenly creature whom he had fallen in love with at first sight a few months ago, so close he could feel the warmth of her body, alone here in the candlelit darkness with no eyes watching them, not even the stooping ferryman.

In her own confusion, Mary did as she always did whenever she was mystified by her thoughts or feelings, raising her hand to touch her light brown hair at the side of her face, unaware that this innocent gesture moulded her young breasts together above the neckline of her dress, causing him to take a breath and quickly raise his eyes upwards as if entranced by the formations of the rock above them.

Then all too soon the dream was over as they returned to the Great Chamber and saw a glimmer of daylight.

Did John and Elizabeth speak to either of them when they had excitedly replaced them in the boat? Byron was not sure if they had or not, still stunned by the rapture of lying so close to her.

Mary, too, was quiet and subdued.

Eager to get out of the claustrophobic chamber where a few other people had now arrived to take the boat ride, Byron lifted the candle and took Mary's hand, bending his head and silently leading her back down the dark narrow passages until they reached the large aperture in the rock that led out to the sunlight.

There they looked at each other in silence, but neither was capable of saying a word.

~ ~ ~

From the day after they had returned from Matlock, most of their meetings were stolen ones, secret and exciting, each using a confidante to send and exchange letters. Byron used his new young valet, William Fletcher, as his messenger, and in return Mary's replies were delivered by her maid.

A gate leading from the back of Annesley Hall, near to the old Oratory, became their meeting place, from where they would go walking together through the trees, often late into the afternoon.

When the time came for him to return to Harrow he was reluctant to leave, unable to bear the thought of the one hundred long miles that would stretch between them.

Mary consoled him by giving him a large gold locket containing a lock of her hair and her picture, and he finally returned to Harrow, so deeply in love that he was unable to concentrate his thoughts on anything other than her, failing to answer the master whenever he addressed him, slouched across the desk lost in his own world of dreams.

He knew his friends laughed at him for falling so romantically in love, and all had become familiar with the gold locket he wore on a thin black ribbon around his neck.

William Harness lost patience with him one night during a game of billiards.

Byron had been winning, potting the black ball every time, but now Harness was finding his form, potting the black and hitting cannons until he was catching up on points when all at once Byron made a sound of alarm and began searching hastily for something under his waistcoat. "Good God! I have lost my —" but before he had finished the sentence he had found his hidden treasure.

Byron smiled and kissed the locket, while William Harness glowered. "Byron, you have got to *stop* always thinking about this girl of yours!"

"I can't stop," Byron admitted. "She is the world and everything in it to me. Nothing else matters."

Chapter Sixteen

~~~

The following year, when the summer vacation had ended, Mrs Byron received a letter of urgent inquiry in mid-October from John Hanson.

'Madam – Lord Byron did not return to Harrow at the beginning of September as he should have done for the Autumn term. What is the reason for this? Is he suffering from some indisposition or malady? If he is ill please inform me. I have written to his Lordship numerous times, and so has his headmaster Dr Drury, but neither he nor I have yet received any reply. Please respond by today's mail coach.

Yours etc., etc.,

She laid down the letter, her smile scornful; knowing that John Hanson suspected that *she* was to blame for her son's absence from Harrow; suspecting that *she* was the one keeping him home to indulge her possessiveness.

Well, she would soon let John Hanson know that it was her son who was indulging in his own possessiveness.

'Sir – I cannot get him to return to Harrow though I have done all in my power for six weeks past. He has no indisposition that I know of but love, desperate love, the worst of all maladies in my opinion."

Yours etc., etc.,

What she did *not* tell Hanson was the truth – that for the past six weeks she had not even seen her son because he had removed himself to lodge at Newstead to be nearer to Mary Chaworth at Annesley Hall, a short ride from the Abbey.

But she had been kept informed of all his comings and goings. Oh, yes. Owen Mealey, the steward of the estate, had been ordered to keep her informed or lose his employment; and so the steward regularly rode the twelve miles from Newstead to Southwell to tell her what was going on.

"He's been boarding and sleeping at the Abbey most nights, and in the days him and her go off riding on their horses all over the place," was Mealey's last report. "But now this past week or more, I've heard he's been invited by the Chaworths to visit Annesley Hall in the daytime and sometimes they even allow him to sleep there at night too. So it looks to me like the feud between the two houses is over and done."

"Do they appear *very* friendly?" she asked the steward. "My George and Miss Chaworth?"

"Well, I can only speak for what I see of the two of them when they are at Newstead, walking in the grounds or playing with the two dogs."

"Then speak, man, speak*!*"

"He's paying court to her, clear as day. And she's always very flirtatious with him."

"The trollop! And when *she's* not there at the Abbey, is George always with that Joe Murray?"

"No, Madam. When Miss Chaworth is not at Newstead with Lord Byron, he spends all his time alone, wandering around the place with his dogs, mostly with Boatswain though. He truly loves that dog and we all see it, and Woolly is beginning to get very jealous."

"You had better warn Lord Byron then, and quickly

too," she advised. "A wolf is not to be trusted nor offended."

Owen Mealey had laughed. "Oh, Woolly would never hurt his lordship, he's only jealous because he wants all the attention for himself."

And then Owen Mealey had laughed again. "But young Lord Byron now, he has taken up another trick that makes us all laugh when we sees it. What he does, is he takes the rowing boat out on the lake, always with Boatswain in the boat beside him. And then, without any warning, he suddenly ups and throws himself into the lake fully clothed, and Boatswain always jumps in after him to save him, dragging him with his teeth on his collar over to the land."

It was the most ridiculous thing she had ever heard. "Throws himself into the lake fully clothed? Has my George gone mad?"

"Oh no, it's his way of training Boatswain to be a life-saver, in case of any true emergency. It's a very deep lake, as you know, and old Joe Murray often goes out there in one of the boats on his own, just him and his pipe."

"So when he's not throwing himself into the lake or playing at romance with Mary Chaworth, what else does my George waste his time on?"

"I'm not rightly sure, other than Joe tells me his Lordship has no intention of going back to London or leaving Miss Chaworth. But other than that ... well, he does enjoy doing his pistol-shooting at bottles lined up on the wall and now there's also hundreds of bullet holes in the outer doors of the old cloisters where he does all his shooting practice. Joe reckons his lordship is a perfect shot now – a real wafer-splitter."

"So George is training Boatswain to save Joe Murray if he falls into the lake, and Joe Murray is training George to kill someone one day in a duel! You tell that

Joe Murray I will kill *him* one of these days!"

She had shut the door on Owen Mealey then, but she was not too displeased. Her son was abandoning both London and Harrow and giving them all the snub – as they had all snubbed *her* in the past. So let John Hanson stuff *that* under his hat and think about it!

And as for Mary Chaworth? Well, she knew something about that young miss which George obviously did *not* know. Flirtatious indeed!

~ ~ ~

They had been walking and talking for some time on Diadem Hill, overlooking her home of Annesley Hall and the green land all around it.

Today he was light-hearted and she was the one filled with gloom.

As they returned down the slope of the hill she paused for breath, leaning back against a tree behind her. The late afternoon sun was lower now, slanting its rays through the trees.

"All the birds seem to have fallen silent,' she whispered. "I can hear my own breathing."

He stood looking at her for some seconds before he bent his mouth to hers and kissed her.

She blushed at his kiss and moved gently away. "You should not have done that, and we should walk on."

"Why?"

"You know why."

Now it was he who moved to stand in her place, leaning against the tree. "I know only that I love you, Mary."

She gave a painful little sigh. "We can be no more than friends, Byron."

"Why?"

Looking at him, leaning against the tree, his head was downcast and his dark lashes cast a faint shadow on his pale face, giving it an almost feminine quality. It was such a pity that he was the most beautiful young man she had ever seen.

"This summer ... I have been absurdly childish, I realise that now."

His head remained down, only his eyes lifted to look at her with one of his *underlooks*, which unknown to him was very sexual ... the cause of her occasional heated breaths and fluttering heartbeat.

"Is it because you still believe you are too old for me?"

A tearful mist was covering her brown eyes. "It's not about age, Byron, but we must stop meeting, stop seeing each other, and you must return to London and forget our foolish summer."

"Foolish? Why .... why was it *foolish?*"

She took a deep breath and told him. "Because I am engaged to be married and he will be returning to Nottingham in a few weeks. We are to be married quite soon."

After a space of time when words were lost to him, his confusion stunned him. "So have you just been *playing* with me?"

"No! How can you even think that? My engagement to Jack was decided upon and agreed –"

"But at Annesley, in your home, your parents welcomed me – "

"Because they like you, Byron, and they know how much you like me ... " A tear slipped down her face.

After another stupefied stare, a slow suspicion came into his mind, his eyes flashing blue fire in rage. "So vengeance for the Chaworths has come at last."

"No, no," Mary said quickly, "No —"

"Not for you maybe, but for *them*, yes, yes! A way to hurt and humiliate a Byron has finally come!"

He had walked past her, but now he swung around again. "Tell me the truth — would they ever allow you to *marry* a Byron?"

She was trembling, her head lowered, but she gave no answer.

"Then damn you all."

He walked away and never once looked back, his eyes filled with tears and his heart thumping with pain. Was it all a charade? A mischievous dalliance on her part?

By the time he had ridden too fast and reached the parkland acres leading to his house, the pain in his leg caused him to dismount and to limp more slowly and more visibly — and Joe Murray was the first to see him, rushing out to offer his arm which he gratefully leaned upon and allowed himself to be helped indoors.

"My room," he said, and Joe nodded, keeping his strong old arm firmly in place for support as his young master slowly climbed the stairs, one step at a time.

In his room, he motioned to the chair by his desk, and Joe escorted him to it, but he did not sit down, his eyes resting on the poem he had written only last night with such jubilant happiness and love — *'To Mary.'*

Seeing the tears streaming down his face, Joe Murray made no comment and showed no reaction other than to take a white linen square out of the front pocket of his apron and hand it to him.

He took the handkerchief, wiped his face, handed it back, and sat down. "Thank you, Joe."

"I would suggest a drink, my lord, a glass of claret perhaps?"

"No, thank you."

"Is there anything else I can bring up to you?"

"Yes, Boatswain. Find him and send him up, will you."

Joe nodded. "Fletcher took him out for a run. I'll send the dog up as soon as they get back."

As Joe reached the door, Byron said, "One more thing, Joe ... I do not believe that she will ... but if Miss

Chaworth calls here at any time, or sends a letter, will you inform her or her servant that Lord Byron is not at home to her."

"Yes, my lord."

"And you will make sure to specifically use the name *Lord* Byron when you do so."

"Yes, my lord."

And yet, despite his determination to be proud, his crushing heartache could not be contained and later that night he slipped out of the house, mounted his horse and rode the two miles to Annesley Hall where she lived.

He drew to a halt under some trees at the back of the house.

A full moon hung low over the house. Lights from the candles were glimmering in the windows of some of the rooms, and one of those dimly-lit rooms was Mary's bedroom; he knew her chamber.

He sat on his horse in the shadows, staring up at her window and wondering what she was thinking now, what she was feeling?

He wondered if she sensed his presence, out here in the darkness? He had once revealed to her in a weak moment that although he had spent the day with her, he often rode back at night just to gaze up at her window and feel closer to her. He had loved her with all the tenderness of his young and ardent nature. His love was *more* than love, it was adoration, and it consumed him.

And yet she had been sorrowful today, dark sorrow in her eyes; and he knew her to be a dutiful daughter, who loved her mother and her home, and as an only child and the heiress to Annesley she would have to do what her parents wished, marry a husband of their choice.

And now he knew their choice would *never* be a Byron. They would never forget that William Chaworth had been killed by the 5th Lord Byron, and so would never allow a descendant of *that man* to ascend to the ownership of Annesley through marriage to their daughter.

Everything was such a confusion; his emotions and thoughts in disarray. He damned himself now for walking away from her today in the heat of his temper and shock, without knowing the answers to so many questions in his mind.

When the light in her room went out, he turned the horse around and rode slowly back to Newstead with nothing gained, and everything still lost.

On returning to Newstead he sat on the window-bench in his room with Boatswain at his feet while he stared up at the stars, the unconquerable stars, while his thoughts drifted, his emotions unbearable; first love, true love, never to find again. There was only one Mary Ann Chaworth, and he would love her forever.

The North Star was shining as bright as a heavenly torch, hypnotising his focus, watering his eyes.

> *I saw two beings in the hues of youth,*
>
> *Standing upon a hill, a gentle hill,*
>
> *Green and of mild declivity ...*

Boatswain barked and nuzzled his hand to comfort him, and his hand began to stroke the dog's noble head until the calm and silence of the stars returned, and his mind returned to Diadem Hill.

> *These two, a maiden and a youth were there,*
>
> *Gazing – the one on all that was beneath*
>
> *Fair as herself - but the boy gazed on her;*
>
> *And both were young, and one was beautiful:*
>
> *And both were young – yet not alike in youth.*

A Strange Beginning

As the sweet moon on the horizon's verge,
The maid was on the eve of womanhood;
The boy had fewer summers, but his heart
Had far outgrown his years, and to his eye
There was but one beloved face on earth ...

Chapter Seventeen

~ ~ ~

"Even if you were of a proper age," his mother said, "and even if she was disengaged, that young lady would most definitely not be *my* choice for you."

"So it's fortunate that particular choice will never be yours."

She did not like his tone, his haughty manner, his cold dismissal of her view, his obvious lack of love for *her*, his mother; it lit fire to the worst side of her nature.

He had called at Southwell not to return home, but merely to collect his post; and now her eyes narrowed as she watched him reading his letters.

"And do you know just *who* she is engaged to marry, George?"

"No."

"Well then, I will tell you whom your rival is. His name is Jack Musters, the son of the Sheriff of Nottingham at Colwick Hall. He is expected to return soon from serving in the army in Ireland, so a brute happy to oppress the Celts. And yes, they *do* say he can be a bit rough around the edges, so not a haughty aristocrat like you, George, oh no, not a bit like you."

His eyes were on the letter from John Hanson but he was not reading, unable to resist listening to her.

And she knew she had got his attention, even though he was pretending to be engrossed in his reading.

"Oh, but his other glories are *supreme*, according to the tongues of Southwell," his mother went on. "They say that Jack Musters is a superb sportsman, the pride of Nottingham. They say that he can ride faster, jump higher, fight harder, dance smoother, and play cricket better than any other man in the county."

"Good for him." He picked up a letter with the postmark: *Harrow, NW London.*

"And they also do say – according to one of our own kitchen maids – that Miss Chaworth was overhead by one of the Annesley kitchen maids, and she was talking about you, George, about *you* ... saying that although the energetic Jack could sometimes be troublesome, she would never consider marrying a lame boy who could not dance and walked with a limp ... and so they are certain the insolent brat was talking about you, George, about *you*."

After a pensive silence, he looked at his mother. "I detest you," he said, and turned and walked out of the house.

"George ... George!" She was up on her feet, her fat body rushing after him, "George Gordon Byron, don't you dare turn your back on your mother! Don't you *dare* walk out of this house ..."

But he was gone, riding away faster than any Jack Musters could have ridden, and as she stared after him, she knew she had gone too far ... although in all truth, Mary Chaworth *had* been overheard saying those words ... but it was at the time she had first met George, before she had got to know him ... Damn the trollop, hurting her George in this way, and now making her do the same.

~~~

He was riding faster than he could, harder than he could, his right foot able to sit in the stirrup but not *grip* it, using the grasp of his knee to keep his balance as he galloped on ... eventually falling off less than a mile away from Newstead Abbey.

Unhurt, save for a few grazes, he sank down on the side of the road, overwhelmed by such a strong wave of sadness and depression he found himself contemplating suicide ... his father had taken poison, so why could he not do the same?

The sound of a horse and rumble of carriage wheels in the distance made him look up and recognise his old friend and adviser, as well as an admirer of his poetry, coming along in his open carriage.

Reverend Becher, at sight of him sitting there on the side of the road with his horse standing behind him, knew at once that he had taken a fall and ordered his driver to halt.

"Are you hurt, Byron?"

"No, sir."

"You look hurt?"

"Then I must be."

"Dear, dear ..." Reverend Becher opened his side door and stepped down from the carriage. He could see that the poor horse was blown, his neck lowered, panting hard.

And then a few more steps closer revealed to him the tears running down Byron's face.

"Now, now, why so mournful?" Becher knew young Byron well enough to realise that it was no mere fall from a horse that had reduced him to this melancholy state.

He asked gently, "Would this dejection be anything to do with Miss Chaworth and the announcement of her engagement?"

Byron wiped at his face and turned his head to stare down the road, declining to answer ... leaving Reverend Becher with no other choice but to attempt to cheer him by assuming his role as pastor, quietly advising Byron of all the great blessings Providence had bestowed upon him, not only in his rank, and all the doors that rank would open to him in the future, but so many other great advantages, and the greatest is that you possess a mind and extraordinary mental powers that place you above all the others."

"Oh, my dear friend," Byron said desolately, "if *this,*" he put his hand to his forehead, "places me above all the others, then *that* —" he pointed to his foot, "places me far, far below them."

"Nonsense!" Reverend Becher knew that the bitter sensitivity of his infirmity, which haunted Byron like a curse, and probably would continue to do so for the rest of his life, had to be rationalised now with some plain talk.

"You have allowed this torment of yours to get out of proportion. It is time that you started appreciating the other blessings that Nature has also showered upon you in a kind of counterbalance. Others do not see the difficulty with your foot as you see it."

Byron looked at him. "How do they see it?"

"A *trifling* deformity, which is often hardly noticed. And when it *is* noticed, it is seen as just one very slight blemish on your beauty. Or did you think Miss Chaworth was the only one to have such prepossessing looks?"

Byron stood up, unwilling to continue the conversation, except to say: "No other female will ever efface her from my heart."

Oh the young, the *young* — how little they know! Reverend Becher smiled. "Were you on your way back to the Abbey?"

"Yes."

"Can I offer you a lift?"

"No, thank you. It's less than a mile." He caught hold of the horse's reins and led him onto the road. "Oateater and I will walk the rest of the way at our own pace."

"Oateater?" Reverend Becher smiled again. "An apt name for a horse, eh? Well, good day to you, Lord Byron, and please remember to send me some new poetry as soon as possible. God bless you."

Byron waited for the carriage to move off, then he and his horse began their slow walk down the road ... and although Reverend Becher had travelled on hoping he had given good counsel, he had no idea that his words of wisdom had not influenced Byron's depressed mind in the slightest. He had received the Reverend's words as mere pats on the head such as those given to a child — a *trifling* deformity indeed? Such a patronizing insult. Becher would sing a very different hymn about Providence if forced to spend a day walking in *his* shoes. And no patronizing words from Reverend Becher could ever wipe out the actual words Mary Chaworth had said to her maid, about not being able to consider marrying a man who walked with a limp and could not dance due to being "*lame.*"

He looked ahead of him ... and there it was, his ancestral home, looming like a huge palace against the skyline. Even in its dilapidated state in parts, Newstead Abbey was still a stupendous sight of architectural magnificence. Had not even *that* persuaded her, that he was worth waiting for, limp and all?

But no, despite what Becher had said, now he knew that she saw him as all the others in Nottingham saw him, as deformed ... and the deformed could not be loved. *He* could not be loved. So from now on he would not expect it, nor even hope nor wish for it. From now on the deformed would be transformed into the true son of Mad Jack Byron and the true heir of the 'wicked Lord', the 5th Baron Byron.

Joe Murray, always a hawk, saw him tiredly leading the horse up the leafy lane that edged the side of the front lake, and rushed out to meet him.

"Did the horse take lame?"

Byron smiled, cynically. "No, I did. I was riding too fast."

Joe Murray regarded him sternly. "Now you have

been told, many times ... a jog or a trot, but never to race."

Once seated inside the parlour, Joe insisted on tending to his wounds, dabbing a wet flannel on the graze above his eyebrow and then bending down to unstrap the outer boot on his right foot.

"Joe, you are a better mother to me than my own."

"I daresay," Joe nodded, carefully removing the boot, "but if you had said a better *father* ... now that I might have taken as a compliment."

"You have all my compliments, Joe, you are the best person I know."

Joe sighed heavily and looked at his bloodstained flannel. "I need a clean flannel and some more hot water."

While he was gone, Byron took out the letters he had pushed inside his jacket and began to read the first one, the letter postmarked from Harrow which he had opened in Southwell but had not read.

A plaintive letter from one of the younger Harrow boys, disturbed by his absence, and reminding him of some throwaway sentence he had said to him at the end of the previous term ...

'You said you shall miss me most damnably, I did not doubt it, for who I wondered will you have there to comfort you under afflictions, and who will you have to help you undress when you go to bed? Come back, Byron, we all miss you.'

He was still reading the letter when Joe Murray returned to the room. "Some good news, my lord?"

Byron shrugged. "It appears that my absence has not only been noticed, but also regretted by some of my schoolfellows."

"Indeed?"

Byron then explained to Joe the strict rules of Harrow and Eton and every other school of that class.

"At all times, the junior boys are completely subservient to the boys in the upper forms, until they themselves reach the higher classes; and from this subservience, no rank is exempt."

He raised the letter in his hand. "Hence, my young servant, who is missing me."

"Is he a gentleman?"

Byron thought about it. "He will be, one day, when he grows older than his fourteen years. But right now he is merely the very good-natured but clumsy son of the Duke of Dorset."

"It is my opinion that you *should* go back to Harrow, if only to finish your education."

Byron stared into space for so long that Joe thought he was never going to reply.

"Yes, I should go ... as far away from here as possible, and as soon as possible ... all I want now is to forget. "

Joe nodded sympathetically. "They say first love is the worst love."

After another long silence, Byron said quietly, "I shall return to London in the morning."

Chapter Eighteen

~ ~ ~

Upon his return to Harrow, many of Byron's friends noticed a marked change in him: he appeared more grown up, more subdued, and in sport he was only interested in those events that required hard physical strength – boxing as often as possible in the gym, swimming for hours in the Harrow bathing pond.

Determined to involve himself in as much physical activity as possible, he neglected his doctor's appointments without a care, as if he needed the physical pain to blot out an even deeper pain.

At other times he was very withdrawn, retiring within himself in thoughtful solitude, regularly taking himself off to a particular tomb in the churchyard at Harrow, which commanded a high view over towards Windsor, where he would sit for hours, wrapped in brooding thought, until it became so well-known as his favourite resting place that his friends called it "Byron's tomb."

One day in the autumn of 1804, under John Hanson's instructions, his doctor visited him at the school, shocked to find him immersed in a hectic game with his schoolfellows, running in his limping way across the field in the rain with the inner shoe on his right foot quite wet and his outer shoe falling off.

Byron's laughter immediately ceased when he saw the doctor approaching, beckoning him off the field.

As soon as he had reached the edge of the grass, Byron turned his fury on the doctor. "Did you have to visit me *here,* reminding all my friends of my blasted foot!"

Dr Laurie kept his calm. "Lord Byron, you have

neglected all your regular appointments with me, and so I am forced to come to you. And such thoughtless bravado as I saw out there on the field has probably caused much damage to your foot and lower leg muscles, as well as the total destruction of your shoe."

"I don't care about my blasted shoe. But I do care that *they* have now been reminded of my infirmity. I will be treated with sympathy for at least a month, not allowed to become involved in any of the games, and so will return to being an *outsider* again."

"I suggest we go to the medical room where I can attend to you, and new measurements will have to be taken and sent to Sheldrake for the manufacture of new shoes as soon as possible."

True to his prediction, Byron was given all the kind consideration so often bestowed on physically flawed beings: his name not included in the team list for games, forcing him to go to the gymnasium and punch his frustration into a boxing bag.

Well, if he was going to be an outsider in one arena, he would become an outsider in all arenas. He would become the greatest *outsider* that ever lived!

~ ~ ~

In the classroom, the pupils had been given the task of making a short speech about their favourite hero.

Byron listened to all the repeated eulogies about Nelson and Wellington, his eyes glancing at the tutor who was beginning to look as bored as he felt.

The tutor was Henry Drury, the twenty-nine-year old son of the headmaster, but unlike his father, Henry Drury was considered by most to be a pompous ass who had once called Byron a "blackguard" for knocking a playground bully unconscious in a fight.

Byron eyed the tutor with contemptuous dislike: the pompous ass may have *called* him a blackguard, but he would never make him one.

"Lord Byron."

Byron stood to give his oration. "Gentlemen, since the age of ten years old, and that would be in 1798, the year of the famous uprising in Ireland; my own hero since that time has been a man whom, like so many of ourselves, was a young aristocrat. An aristocrat now famous for always wearing a *green* cravat, even though the wearing of the colour green had been banned in his country, a country ruthlessly oppressed by the rule of England."

"Damnit, Byron – surely you are not referring to Fitzgerald!"

Byron looked at the speaker. "Yes, Lord Edward Fitzgerald, the son of the Duke of Leinster and the first House of the Irish aristocracy who sacrificed all in revolution in an attempt to free his people – "

"Lord Byron!" Henry Drury interrupted. "You were requested to give an oration on one of the heroes of our own country, not a hero of one of England's enemies."

"Ireland is not England's enemy, Ireland is England's slave!"

"Lord Byron, resume your seat!" snapped Henry Drury, and Byron obediently sat down, remaining calm amidst the uproar that followed amongst his schoolfellows, the aristocrats arguing with the non-aristocrats until Henry Drury furiously gavelled for silence.

"Lord Byron, every young gentleman is allowed at least one mistake in his thinking, and because of your young years, you must be forgiven for this one. I suggest you return tomorrow with an alternative hero. Class dismissed.

The following day, Lord Byron was again requested to stand and give his second oration.

"Gentlemen, my second hero is not an aristocrat like

many of ourselves, but an ordinary man who became a soldier and has risen to greatness."

Henry Drury sat back, glad to see that Byron had chosen the more suitable choice of Wellington as his hero.

"A man who saw the oppression of the poor people of his land strangled with starvation and poverty, while the small clutch of the French aristocracy lived in every luxury and fed themselves on the bread of Heaven. So who could blame this ordinary man for supporting the Revolution and becoming a great soldier in the cause of a Republic and the American ethos of all men being equal."

"*French* aristocracy? Good God, I believe he is talking about the damned Corsican!"

His face reverent with admiration, when Byron said the name *"Napoleon"* the classroom was again in uproar.

"Lord Byron!" bellowed Henry Drury. "You are now in great danger of being expelled!"

~ ~ ~

Later, in his father's office, Henry Drury made his case for the immediate expulsion of Lord Byron, *demanded* it.

"Lord Edward Fitzgerald sought war in Ireland against the Crown of England and Byron now names him a *hero*. England is at war with France and Byron names Napoleon a *hero* — and this from a young man who will one day have a seat in our own House of Lords! His expulsion from Harrow should be immediate."

The headmaster shook his head, unwilling to be persuaded.

Henry stared at his father, fuming. "Why not, pray? He has caused riots and confusion in my classroom and when he is not doing that, he is reducing them all to laughter with his caustic wit against *me!*"

"How many times have I told you, Henry, that young Byron at times is like a wild mountain colt, and far easier to be *led* into line and submission by the gentle pull of a silken string than the yank of any hard rope.

Henry frowned at his father. "I don't understand you, sir."

"You made a big mistake when you called him a blackguard in front of all his peers, Henry. You attacked the defender and not the bully. Now, I suggest we have no more talk of expulsion, put today behind you, and find some silken string to use in your dealings with young Byron. You will find he is very agreeable to those who are fair to him."

After a silence Henry gathered himself up and walked to the door, his face petulant. "So you will *not* consider my request for his expulsion?"

"Certainly not. That young man has some great intellectual qualities which I truly believe will one day add lustre to his title. And I want that lustre to reflect on Harrow."

The lenient smile lingered on the headmaster's face until his son had left the room; and after allowing himself a few minutes of considered thought; he went in search of his wife.

"My dear, I want you to have a little *tête-à-tête* with young Byron."

Mrs Drury, after listening to her husband's instructions, adjusted the lace collar at her throat before asking, "And if I do use the silken string approach, how will I know if I have succeeded in persuading him to step back into line?"

"Oh, you will know, my dear, you will know. Young Byron has always had what I call, 'mind in the eye'."

"And what is that, precisely?"

"The thoughts in his mind are always reflected in his

eyes."

~ ~ ~

Over dinner that evening, Mrs Drury reported to her husband about the interview with young Byron.

"Well, I used the silken string, as much of it as I could."

Dr Drury nodded appreciatively, chewing a piece of beef. "I told you so, my dear. It has always been my experience with Byron, that no matter how dark his vehemence, the least touch of a gentle hand authorised by love to guide him, always renders him docile and placated."

"He was neither docile nor placated with *me*," his wife responded.

"No?" Dr Drury put down his fork. "Was he rude?"

"Oh no, not rude. Stubborn."

"Stubborn? How so?"

"He has a lot of grievances against this school of Harrow, and although he did so with respect, he did not hold back on telling me what those grievances were."

Dr Drury was astonished. "Such as?"

"He says he will never forgive Harrow for making him hate Horace, when in his earlier years he had great love for the Latin poems of Horace."

"And those poems are thousands of years old, so how has Harrow made him hate them now?"

"By force. He insists that *forcing* the pupils to study over and over those books they have read many times can only lead to weariness and eventual dislike."

"The impudent young devil!"

"He also states that forcing the pupils to read *Prometheus* three times a year is ridiculous."

"But that's the system!"

"I told him that, and he had the temerity to say that the system must be wrong then. He said that forcing anyone to continually give the attention of their mind to the same thing day after day can only inspire tiresome dislike and eventual hatred."

Dr Drury was so flabbergasted, he sat back in his chair and thought about it, unwillingly so. Yet, was that not the same thought he often harboured in his own mind when, day after day, he was *forced* by his occupation and income to attend to the same old dreary routine as a headmaster?

He looked at his wife. "That boy is moving closer and closer to being expelled."

Chapter Nineteen

~ ~ ~

The librarian sat at his desk reading a book in the Greek language. Occasionally he looked up from his book to slyly watch the group of older boys sitting at a table near the window, all talking rather louder than they should ... all except Lord Byron ... now a monitor, and third Head Boy of the School.

He was sitting amidst the group, his elbow on the table and his head propped up on his hand, his eyes closed.

Under other circumstances, the librarian would have reprimanded the boys for talking at all, even in whispers, but as they were the only group in the library, all other tables empty, and the group had been sent in here by the master for the sole purpose of discussing their topic, he was forced to allow them to speak without any reproach.

Young Claridge, of course, was speaking the loudest, as he always seemed to do when in the company of Byron ... one moment speaking with exaggerated sophistication, and then with jesting absurdity ... and all in the vain hope of receiving a glance or a smile from his adored one.

Yet Byron just dozed on, in the dreaming world of his own mind.

The first time the librarian had even noticed Byron, *"the shy boy with the limp"* as he was referred to by most masters at that time, was two years previously, when he had been chosen by Dr Drury to give a performance on Harrow's Public Speech Day, and he had surprised everyone by giving a tremendous interpretation of *King Latinus* in Virgil's *Æneid*. And then, last year, he had again been chosen and gave another powerful performance of *Zanga* in Edward Young's *The Revenge*. His love of the power of language and his own superb command of its use was evident to all who stood and listened to him in amazement.

Now he was a senior, a leader, always surrounded by his adoring clan.

The librarian mentally noted all their names: Harness, Claridge, Edward Long, Tom Wildman, Wingfield, Lord Delaware – Delaware was one of those rebellious yet charming Americans, a son of the American Ambassador; and the rest of the group were the same regular bevy of good-looking companions whom Byron seemed to have collected around him.

All seemed fascinated by him, as if caught in some strange romantic spell, and his *limp* ... well, his limp not only seemed to set him apart from all the other boys, but also appeared to add to his strange attraction.

The librarian sighed; such was the behaviour and development of young males together in a boarding school. He had seen it all so many times before.

In such communities as this one in Harrow or Eton or any other enclosed boarding school, there is always to be found an outstanding personality... the favourite one ... and yet it had been a long time since the librarian had witnessed such a favourite amongst his peers as Byron.

And was Byron aware of it? The librarian was not so sure he was.

Although, Byron did appear, on occasions, to betray some tender feelings for the young and sweet Lord Clare, who was absent today.

However, it was all very entertaining to watch, and not altogether dissimilar to the behaviour and ethos of male-worship of the ancient Greeks in his book, to which he now lowered his eyes and pretended to read.

~ ~ ~

"Are you asleep, Byron?"

He was still sitting with his head propped on his hand and his eyes closed.

"Byron, are we boring you?" Delaware indignantly knocked his elbow. "I repeat, are we boring you?"

"Oh, I cannot tell you how much." Byron sighed and opened his eyes. "All this endless talk about *literatooor*. I was simply having a doze while waiting for one of your tongues to fall out."

Delaware pounced on him, and the laughter that followed caused the librarian to rap his ruler. "Gentleman, please!"

One of the younger boys entered the library and rushed up to the table. "Lord Byron, you have a visitor. A young lady."

The laughter immediately vanished from Byron's face. "A young lady?"

He knew only *one* young lady ... His heart began to beat furiously. "Her name?"

The boy shrugged, turning to leave. "I don't know. I was instructed to find you and tell you she is in the Visitors Room."

The boy was halfway down the corridor when Byron hurriedly caught up with him. "Did *you* see her? The young lady?"

"Yes."

"What does she look like?"

"Like a young lady."

"What colour is her hair?"

"Well, she is wearing a hat, a small red hat, but her hair hangs down her back and it is light brown."

Mary's hair was light brown.

By the time he had reached the door of the Visitors Room, he had come up with three possible reasons as to why Mary Chaworth had made the journey all the way down to London to see him, and every one of those reasons made his heart pound even faster ... until he opened the door and saw that the young lady was not Mary at all ... She was about the same age, rather plain in her looks ... and a complete stranger.

He stood by the open door and looked at her with silent curiosity, yet she seemed to recognise him instantly, rising to her feet with a nervous smile.

"Lord Byron?"

"Yes."

"Forgive me for coming without any request or warning, but I have been longing to meet you for such a long time."

"And who are you, pray?"

"Augusta."

"Augusta?"

Her nervousness seemed to heighten, her face blushing a deep pink. "You have not been told about me ... I am your half-sister ... Augusta Byron."

He did not speak for some seconds, utterly shocked, and then it slowly came to him, far back in the distant past.

"Oh ... now I recall ... my mother was my father's *second* wife, and there was some talk ... oh, very long ago ... of a child and the first wife." He stared at her, half disbelieving. "You are my father's daughter?"

"Yes."

There was an awkward silence. At length Byron, still shocked, finally said, "This is all rather unexpected for me. A sister? I thought I was alone in the world."

Augusta sat back down on her chair and clasped her hands together, head bowed as she said rather sadly:

"I was first told about you when I was five. Papa came to visit me and told me I had a new baby brother. And when he came to visit me after that, I always asked him about 'Baby Byron' but then he stopped coming, and I was told Papa had died, and no one ever spoke to me about 'Baby Byron' again ... not even when I asked."

Mournfully shaking her head, Augusta continued, "And then, in the hurry of life, from one place to another, I confess I forgot all about you, until one day a few months ago when Lord Carlisle mentioned you, telling someone you were now at Harrow."

Byron seated himself at her side and took one of her hands to clasp in both of his own, saying in a tone of much feeling, "If for no other reason, I must be grateful to Lord Carlisle for bringing you here, my dear Augusta, if indeed I may call you that?"

Augusta nodded. "And may I call you George?"

Byron smiled reluctantly. "My mother is the only person who calls me George now. I'm quite happy for you to call me Byron, as everyone else does."

"Very well," Augusta agreed. "I shall continue to call you by your title of Lord Byron."

"No, no, drop the Lord prefix – just Byron."

The next hour was a time of discovery for both of them. He learned that Augusta's mother had died giving birth to her, and she had been brought up by her grandmother, Lady Holderness, who had also died a few years later; and since then she had led the usual existence of lone females of the aristocratic class, moving around from one distant maternal relation to another – until very recently, when she had been given a permanent home in the residence of Byron's own guardian, Lord Carlisle.

"Lord Carlisle? I have met him only once, years ago, when John Hanson took me to meet him."

"He has been very kind to me."

Byron shrugged. "Then you are honoured, because *I* have not seen him since. In fact, I am certain he does everything in his power to avoid me. Why is that I wonder?"

Augusta gave an embarrassed smile. "I believe he is very frightened of your mother."

"*Everyone* is very frightened of my mother," Byron responded. "So is that why Lord Carlisle keeps his distance? In fear that my mother may suddenly pop out from somewhere and wrathfully upbraid him for something or other?"

Augusta put her hand to her smiling lips. "I should not have spoken."

Byron shrugged again. "It's no more than what I already know – she is a harridan. And you are what age now?"

"Twenty-two."

Byron sat looking at her silently, feeling a strange new emotion.

When the time came to part, both were hesitant. He asked her, "Will you visit me again?"

"As often as I can, when the household resides in Piccadilly, but Lord Carlisle prefers to spend most of his time at Castle Howard. We all leave for Yorkshire sometime soon, that is why I was so determined to come here today."

"Will you write to me?"

Augusta smiled, somewhat shyly ... "I suspect I shall find myself writing letters to you every day from now on. Would you hate it if I did?"

Byron shook his head, emotion in his eyes. "I still cannot believe I have a *sister*."

~ ~ ~

In the months that followed, true to her word, Augusta wrote to him regularly, and he immediately replied; and very quickly, through their letters, they became each other's trusted confidante; and to Augusta, and her alone, he was able to reveal his true feelings about his mother.

<u>*To The Hon. Augusta Byron*</u>

I am glad to hear, my dear sister, that you like Castle Howard so well. I have no doubt what you say is true and that Lord Carlisle is much more amiable than he has been represented to me. Never having been much with him and always hearing him reviled by my mother, it was hardly possible I should have conceived a very great friendship for his Lordship.

My mother, you inform me, has now also written to you, commending my own amiable disposition. If she does this to you, it is a great deal more than I ever hear myself, for the one or the other is always found fault with, and I am told to copy the "excellent example" I see before me in "herself".

I thank you, my dear Augusta, for your readiness to assist me in any way you can, but I do not wish to be separated from my mother entirely, for I do believe she likes me; she manifests that in many instances, particularly with regard to money, which I never want, and have as much as I desire.

But her conduct is so strange, her caprices so impossible to be complied with, her passions so outrageous, that the evil quite overbalances her agreeable qualities.

She spends most of her time in displaying the faults and censuring the foibles of others. This however is nothing to what happens when my own conduct admits of animadversion; then comes the "tug of war" – and my entire Byron family, going right back to the Norman Conquest, are upbraided! And then myself abused, and I am told what little accomplishments I possess, are derived from her, and "her alone".

Our holidays come on in about a fortnight. I have not mentioned that to my mother, nor do I intend it; but if I can, I shall contrive to evade going to Nottingham and shall spend my holiday in London

Write soon, and believe me

Ever your affectionate Brother, BYRON

Chapter Twenty

~ ~ ~

So long it had taken, and yet so soon it came, the final week at Harrow, the end of his youth.

On Speech Day, some of the finest carriages in the land rolled through Harrow's gates containing some of the most elite of England's citizens, all arriving at the school to have a good time and a good day with their sons, but not one of the milling throng had come for Byron.

Fatherless as he was and always had been, he watched the men stepping down from their carriages to smile proudly on their sons, while the mothers fluttered hugs and kisses over their precious darlings.

His own mother he had kept well away from London today, telling her that Speech Day was not until the following week.

His Guest of Honour was to be his sister Augusta, but she had written back full of sorrow and regret, because on the day she would be only midway through the long journey down from Yorkshire to London with Lord Carlisle and his family.

That his guardian, Lord Carlisle, had made no effort to leave Yorkshire on an earlier date to come and be present on this, his last official day at Harrow, did not surprise him, yet he resented it; as he also resented John Hanson for being "unable to attend" due to the unavoidable circumstances of being out of London on important business matters.

No matter: when his turn came to step onto the stage, it all helped him to give a bravura performance of *King Lear's* rage against the storm.

Ignoring all the applause, he immediately left the stage and returned to his room, sitting down to finally answer the letter he had received from his mother a few days earlier, requesting to know – now that his schooling was over – what he intended to do with his future? Would he now return to take up his inheritance and the residence of Newstead Abbey and become the Lord of all that his eyes surveyed?

He picked up his pen and wrote with the fire of a deep determination –

The way to riches, to greatness, lies before me. I can, I will, cut myself a path through the world or perish in the attempt. Others have begun life with nothing and ended greatly. And shall I, who have a competent if not a large fortune, remain idle? No, I will carve, myself, the passage to Grandeur, but never with Dishonour. These, Madam, are my intentions.

BYRON

PART FOUR

CAMBRIDGE

1805 – 1808

'Thine was the charm that bound us all.
What was the magic of thy spell?'

'To Lord Byron From His Friends.'

Chapter Twenty-One

~ ~ ~

Trinity College,
Cambridge. 1805

John Cam Hobhouse was twenty years old. He had arrived a week early at Trinity College, Cambridge. At his home in Bristol he had left behind four siblings and fourteen *step*-siblings, and even now he felt quite certain that his stepmother had not yet noticed his early departure, his absence from the sibling crowd.

The first friend he had made was Scrope Davies – whose first name rhymed with *soup* and not soap – who had also arrived a week early at Trinity, and now the two friends passed their time in watching the influx of new undergraduates arriving every day.

Both young men were highly intellectual, and both very quickly reached the same conclusion about the new arrivals: all looked mediocre and boring, and all were clothed in similar neat outfits and displaying the same apprehensive expression on their anxious *first-day-at-college* faces.

"We shall not have our minds inspired to change the world by this dreary lot," Hobhouse said with a sigh.

Scrope Davies agreed. "A glass of wine, I think, to dull our disappointment?"

Both young men were about to turn away when a new undergraduate arrived on the scene, and both stood and stared ...

"Dear God," Hobhouse said, "I do believe we have an *extrovert* in our midst."

The new undergraduate was wearing a white hat, a

grey cloak, and riding on a matching *grey* horse with a large dog trotting beside it. "He *must* be an aristo?" Scrope Davies said.

Hobhouse was too busy staring as a servant, possibly a valet, jumped down from his own horse to rush forward and assist the undergraduate down from his magnificent grey, and then removed his cloak from his shoulders.

The undergraduate was black-haired, tallish, lissom, and stunningly handsome, all of which made Hobhouse instantly hate him.

It was only when the young Adonis started to walk in their direction, and Hobhouse saw the slight limp, a smile came on his face.

"Ah, feet of clay," he murmured to Scope Davies, "so not a young god of Olympus after all."

Scrope was already walking forward to shake hands and welcome the new inmate.

Byron smiled as he responded to both men, and that smile alone made Hobhouse hate him even more.

"*Lord* Byron?" Hobhouse asked pugnaciously. "Did I hear correctly? Then how so? According to the register, there is not *one* nobleman, nor indeed any man of rank, listed to attend Trinity this year."

Byron shrugged. "I did hope to go to Oxford with some of my friends from Harrow, but there were no rooms left at Christchurch, so here I am at Cambridge. Excuse me, gentleman."

As Byron walked on, with his dog guarding his every step, and his servant carrying his bags, Hobhouse looked at Scrope Davies with narrowed eyes. "'Tis a pity he's an aristocrat."

"Why?"

"Why?" Hobhouse glared. "Because the aim of all aristocrats is not to *change* the world – but to own it."

Scrope shrugged. "Judge not without seeing the

evidence."

"I saw his flamboyant style, that was enough for me," Hobhouse declared, then raised his fist in a gesture of revolution. "To your tents, Israel! The Kings of Egypt shall not turn us into slaves!"

~~~

Once the grand opening ceremonies at Trinity were over, John Hobhouse got down to his work in the University.

He opened a Whig Club for all those students who were opposed to the present Tory government.

Lord Byron was one of the first to register his name.

"He's a Whig!" Hobhouse said to Scrope Davies. "Opposed to this corrupt Tory government!"

A week later Hobhouse opened *The Amicable Society*.

Lord Byron registered his name.

"He's amicable!" Hobhouse said to Scrope. "Is there anything our young lord is *not*?"

"Not amused," Byron told Hobhouse when he arrived late at the first meeting of *The Amicable Society* and found them all quarrelling.

"They are *debating*," Hobhouse protested.

"No ..." Byron was quite certain as he looked around the room. "They are definitely *quarrelling*, Mr Hobhouse. All are rowdily speaking over each other and many appear more furious than amicable ... so maybe you should think about changing the name of your club?"

"To what?

"To perhaps ... The *Rumpus* Society?"

"Oh tripe!" Hobhouse grunted, but Byron was already walking away as if Hobhouse and his club of quarrelling amicables were now a mere moment already discarded into the past.

"A typical aristo!" Hobhouse fumed to Scrope. "This

is *college,* for God's sake, not the mumbling House of Lords."

Yet, Hobhouse found himself to be very surprised when Scrope Davies told him the following afternoon—"Lord Byron has gone."

"Gone? From Trinity? Was he sent down? For what reason? What do you mean by *gone?*"

Scrope shrugged. "Just walked out. Had a disagreement with the Dean and then left."

"Do you know what the disagreement was about?"

"His dog, Boatswain, that big husky. According to Matthews, the Dean ordered Byron to remove his dog from his rooms, and made him read again the rules and regulations which state very clearly that no dogs, cats, parrots or any kind of birds are allowed to reside within the college."

"So, he has taken his dog back to his ancestral mansion then. That's not *gone.*"

Scrope was not so sure. "Matthews is convinced he will not come back. He says Byron loves animals more than humans. Apparently the poor fellow had tears in his eyes when the Dean ordered the dog out."

"Poor fellow? Byron is no *poor* fellow!" Hobhouse was losing patience with Scrope who was too kind in his nature for his own good.

"Trinity may not have allowed Byron to keep his beloved dog, but everything else is *given* to him on a plate. Now you and I, Scrope, you and I have to study hard here if we wish to get our degree."

"As does everyone."

"*Not* everyone, and certainly not Lord Byron. It is clearly stated in the Rules and Regulations – just as clearly as the rule forbidding cats and dogs – that all noblemen are *exempt* from the need to sit for any examinations. *No* examinations – yet they still get their degree. With an average mark, of course, but what aristo is going to care about that? Some are even gifted with Honourable Doctorates and God knows what else just for simply attending a university. Is that fair? Is that equitable? Is that *democracy?"*

"No, but unlike the revolutionary Americans who now have no king nor court, *we* live under a monarchy and not in a democracy," Scrope pointed out.

"And therein lies our pain," Hobhouse replied, walking to the door with his usual command, "*To your tents, Israel! We shall not be slaves!"*

~~~

Hobhouse did not see Byron again until a month later when he returned to Cambridge, and once again he was causing a sensation, standing by the fountain with a laughing group of students surrounding him.

Hobhouse went to investigate, and found himself laughing along with the others when he saw that Byron was holding in his arms a small bear ... and the strange young animal was clinging to Byron with his paws around his neck, frightened by the laughter.

"He's *adorable!"* a student exclaimed. "Delightful!" echoed another; but some sense and sensibility was forced to intervene.

"Now look here, Byron ..." Hobhouse had stopped laughing "You know you *cannot* bring that animal into the college, and certainly not into your rooms."

"No, Mr Hobhouse, I believe you are quite wrong in that assertion," Byron replied. "The rules state 'no dogs, cats, or birds', but the rules contain no statement disallowing *bears."*

Hobhouse grunted. "You must be mad if you think the Dean will allow you to get away with that! They will not allow you to have a *bear* from the wilds of some woods to sit with you in your rooms."

Byron smiled. "I'm hoping they will allow little Lord

Bruin here to sit with me in the *classroom*, because I think he is clever enough to be allowed to sit for a Fellowship."

This sly dig at the Fellows brought an uproar of laughter from the students.

"He is, after all," Byron continued, "a bear from an *aristocratic* household – my own. Therefore, like myself, he would obtain his degree without even being required to sit for the exams."

Unlike the rest of the laughing students, Hobhouse was not amused, storming back to the rooms of Scrope Davies and telling him all about it.

Scrope, too, found it hilarious, and therefore was completely missing the point of Byron's very clever trick.

"Do you not see what he is doing?" Hobhouse demanded. "Under the disguise of using that silly bear of his, he is challenging the Dean and the dons and the entire aristocratic class to which he belongs – *challenging* the inequitable system that makes one set of rules for the common man, and another set of rules for the aristocracy."

Scrope stopped laughing and sat up. "By God, so he is. A fellow revolutionary then?"

"It would appear so. He has even called the bear *Lord* Bruin. And he is right, there is no rule that says a bear cannot attend the university."

Scrope Davies sighed. "He will be sent down of course. Probably on the spot and told to take his bear with him. But in any event, you have to admire his defiant audacity."

"I *would* be inclined to admire him," Hobhouse conceded, "if I did not find him so annoying."

"Yes, now why is that, Hobby? Pray enlighten me? It cannot be because he is unquestionably rich, as most aristos are. No, it cannot be that, because your own father is one of the wealthiest men in Bristol."

Hobhouse, unsure of how to respond, took out a handkerchief and mopped his brow, unable to admit that he was jealous – instantly and utterly *jealous* of Lord Byron from the first moment he had seen him. It was not that he had looked like a dandy in that *white* hat, not to mention the *grey* horse to match his *grey* cloak, it was that Byron himself was so strikingly handsome – enough to make any man spit.

Hobhouse hated all handsome men, because he knew he would never be one of them. His mirror had persuaded him to give up all hope long ago. His face was a pugnacious face, and his nose was hooked, but not as bad as the beak on the Duke of Wellington. Was that the reason for the fact that, as much as he liked females, not one of them yet, in his experience, had appeared to find him attractive.

And he was still recovering from the rebuff to an advance he had made in the summer to a neighbour's daughter in Bristol; a lovely girl, walking through the garden, his hand on her back had accidentally slipped down and touched her bottom, resulting in her making the most awful din and screaming like a crazed prima donna at the opera.

But if it had been someone *handsome* like Byron making the same accidental slip, she would probably have mutely turned around and let him feel the front bit too. Women were so duplicitous. He intended to have nothing more to do with any of them and become a chaste intellectual and political revolutionary instead.

"I dislike the fact that he's an aristocrat," he said to Scrope. "And if he is *not* sent down and remains here at Trinity, we will no doubt discover that despite his clever little piece of trickery with the bear, he will have a brain as empty as an upturned bucket."

"Very few empty buckets come up from Harrow,"

Scrope said. "However, judge not until you have seen the evidence."

"Honestly, Scrope, I am getting very *tired* of that repetitive statement of yours. Did you learn that at your father's knee?"

"Every blasted day," Scrope admitted. "Not from my dear father, who is a vicar, but from my pompous older brother. Why do you think I came to Trinity to read Classics instead of Law?"

Rushing to a lecture the following morning, Hobhouse saw Byron rushing towards him in the corridor, surely going in the wrong direction? And obviously he had awoken late, because the white collar of his blouse was hanging open carelessly over his dark blue Trinity gown and his hair was untidily ruffled.

"The lecture hall is *that* way," he pointed out, and Byron nodded. "Yes, Mr Hobhouse, I know that, but I am on my way to see the Dean."

"Ah, been summoned have you, about the Fellowship of your little bear?"

"Precisely."

"Well the first thing you should do is tidy yourself up," Hobhouse advised in a fatherly tone, glancing over the white wings of Byron's open collar and the lopsided gown. "The Dean will not be pleased to see you in such a dishevelled state."

Byron smiled sardonically. "Your concern endears me, Mr Hobhouse."

Hobhouse suddenly found his mind invaded by a grave suspicion about Byron, suspecting he was not a revolutionary at all, but worse, *much* worse.

"Open collar, gown slung over your clothes, untidy hair, all in some kind of romantic disarray – the Dean will think you have just rushed in from a night in a whorehouse. Here, let me at least straighten your gown."

And in the manner of his own nanny down the years, Hobhouse quickly straightened the gown on Byron's shoulders.

Amused, Byron asked: "Hobhouse, how on earth does your mother manage to cope at home without you?"

"My dear mother is dead alas, and my *step*mother likes to pretend I don't exist, having too many of her own brats to contend with." And then unable to stop himself, Hobhouse voiced his suspicion about Byron.

"Tell me, Byron, are you one of those unconventional *Bohemians* who care nothing for rules and decorum? Your style of dress and manner of behaviour, bringing in big dogs and small bears and wearing a *white* hat, seems to suggest that you are."

"A Bohemian?" Byron laughed. "No, Mr Hobhouse, I am only what you see – a *Byronian.*"

Byron was still laughing when Hobhouse stood watching him rush on down the corridor to his meeting with the Dean, and no doubt he would be quickly rushed back out again by the Dean, ordered back down to wherever he came from, along with his silly little bear.

~~~

"Well, the verdict is in," Scrope said. "Lord Byron has been allowed to keep his bear."

"Surely not?" Hobhouse glared in disbelief. "You mean to say, *I* cannot keep a parrot, but he can keep a bear!"

"Not overnight, apparently, the bear must be lodged elsewhere, but he can be brought into his rooms during the daytime, just so long as he is *out* before the gates are locked at night."

Hobhouse couldn't believe it. "How could this happen?"

"From what Byron said to Matthews, it seems that the Dean and some of the dons scoured through all the rules and regulations, and indeed could find no stipulation whatsoever regarding the exclusion of a *bear* from an undergraduate's rooms. So you were wrong, Hobby, our Lord Byron obviously gave *microscopic* attention to the rules before bringing in his bear."

Hobhouse sat down in a chair. "Oh, it's all becoming very clear to me now ... the injustice of it all ... Lord Byron, you see, being the only aristocrat here this year, has now become one of the Dean's *pets,* and so the Dean has waved aside all the rules for the common man, and allowed his pet to keep his own *pet.*"

"It would appear so."

"It shall not be tolerated." Hobhouse jumped to his feet. "I shall organise an immediate protest." He marched to the door. "*To your tents, Israel!*"

He returned an hour later, defeated. "Not one will join me in a protest, all claiming to be too busy, idle lot."

"And now that you are back from your failed riot," Scrope said breezily, "I am off for a few hours in town, unless you care to join me?"

"Where are you off to?"

"To a club, for a few games."

"What kind of games?"

Scrope smiled slyly and shook his hand in the air. "The roll of the dice."

Hobhouse flopped down in a chair. "Oh, don't say you are a *gambler*, Scrope, pray contradict me. It is a fool's game and you will lose tons of money."

"I know, but fortunately I have tons of money to lose, because more often than not I do *win*."

"I will never understand why intelligent men gamble, even though they know they will lose a lot more than they will ever win. Why do you do it, Scrope, why?"

"For the excitement, Hobby, the *excitement.* And a wonderful relief and escape from your obsessive dislike of   Byron."

Chapter Twenty-Two

~ ~ ~

John Cam Hobhouse continued to keep his eye on Lord Byron, watching him in the same fascinated way that a child would watch a lion in the zoo.

One of his habits, which Hobhouse thought very strange, and very unlike most undergraduates, was that, according to Scrope Davies, Byron liked to take a warm bath every day, even on those days when he went swimming in the River Cam.

"He's meticulous about cleanliness," Scrope had said, "and he has not *one* but a *collection* of toothbrushes."

Vanity, vanity, all due to that young man's *vanity*, Hobhouse decided.

Yet one conundrum still remained, which Hobhouse could not fathom out.

Byron, he noticed, had a strange power of attracting friends to his side, which was almost magical. Hobhouse wondered how he did it? If he could find out *how* Byron did it, he would use that same magical power himself, because so far his list of recruits for a student protest against the corrupt Tory government remained dismally small.

And then there was that rather strange sultry *underlook* of Byron's that seemed to make even the master stutter midway through a reprimand.

Hobhouse practised his own version of the 'underlook' in his mirror, and then tried out its affect on Charles Matthews, who crumbled up laughing.

"Hobby! I thought you *hated* Byron, so why are you trying to imitate him?"

"In the hope of attracting some more recruits for my

162

Whig Club at the very least," Hobhouse admitted woefully. "And it is all thanks to Byron that my Amicable Society closed down."

"Well, yes, but I must admit, his many puns about your ridiculous *amicables* were very, very funny."

Hobhouse stood thoughtful for a moment, and then eyed Matthews. "Byron does not like me, does he?"

Matthews shook his head. "Can't stand the sight of you, Hobby. Avoids you at all costs. But only because you have been so vilely condescending to him from the first day he arrived here."

Hobhouse exhaled a huge sigh. "Well I am very glad to know that my dislike of Byron is reciprocated. It saves me the trouble of even *pretending* to be polite to him in the future."

~~~

Byron was sitting at the desk in his room, reading his post and busily dashing off letters in reply.

To The Hon. Augusta Byron.
Castle Howard
Yorkshire.

My Dear Augusta — In compliance with your wishes in your affectionate letter, I proceed as soon as possible to answer it. That you are unhappy, my dear Sister, makes me also: I sympathize better than you yourself expect.

But really, after all, I feel a little inclined to laugh at you, for LOVE, in my humble opinion, is utter nonsense, a mere jargon of compliments, romance and deceit.

Can't you drive this cousin of yours out of your head, or if you are so far gone, why don't you give the old General the slip and take a trip to Scotland. You are quite near to the Borders.

Adieu, my dear Sister, forgive my levity; write soon, and God bless you.

Your affectionate Brother, BYRON

Baffled and rejected as he had been in his own passionate love for Mary Chaworth, his only consolation now lay in the comfort of doubting that any such feelings as *love* truly existed in anyone.

He then opened a letter from John Hanson, and as he read it, all his humour and flippancy vanished, replaced by immediate anger; his hand shaking as he lifted the quill to reply:

To Mr John Hanson

Sir – After the contents of your letter, you will probably not be surprised at my answer. Mrs Byron and myself are now totally separated; injured so much by her, I now prefer the refuge of strangers.

You hinted a possibility of Mrs Byron's appearance at Trinity. The instant I hear of her arrival I shall quit Cambridge. Please convey this to her on my behalf.

Yours truly, BYRON

Only John Hanson fully understood the turbulence of his

relationship with his mother, knowing that his last visit to Burgage Manor had been the final visit – due to some petty little disagreement which had resulted in yet another explosive hurricane of her fury when her usual missiles of poker and tongs were sent flying across the room at him, the poker catching its target and hitting him hard on his *right* leg, causing him to make a hobbling hasty escape to the house of the Pigot family, who had all readily agreed to help him escape Southwell and make an instant flight down to London.

He had started out on his journey in a chaise with four horses – his mother had immediately followed in a chaise and two, determined to catch him and bring him back – a farcical action which had made all Southwell laugh for days, according to John Pigot.

No, he would *never* allow her to embarrass and humiliate him again, on that he was determined.

He lifted his quill again and wrote a hasty note to his friend, again aiming at manly flippancy, as if he was above at it all.

To Mr John Pigot

My Dear Pigot — Many thanks for your amusing narrative of the latest proceedings of Mrs Byron Furiousa. But seriously, your own mother has laid me under great obligations, and you, with the rest of your family, merit my warmest thanks for your kind connivance at my escape.

As to Mrs Byron, present my compliments to her and tell her I have not the smallest inclination to be chased around the country again, and if she appears in Cambridge I shall quit for Portsmouth and board a ship to anywhere.

Adieu — Byron.

PS: In London I consoled myself by purchasing a very young and small bear that had been stuck half-starved into the window of a pet shop with a chain around his neck, and when I looked at him, his sad eyes looked back at me as if begging me to rescue him, which I did — and now he is here with me, well-fed and studying for his M.A. at Trinity — B.

Scrope Davies appeared at the door, as cheerful as always, inviting Byron to join himself and Matthews who were heading off to a club in town for a few games of Hazard.

"A few games of Hazard," Byron said, "would be most welcome."

"Dinner first, of course."

Long after midnight, when most of Trinity was fast asleep, the three of them were still in the club, still shaking and throwing the dice, still drinking glass after glass of wine, until all were thoroughly intoxicated and Scrope Davies was the only one with any money left in his pockets.

"Come along, Scrope, you've lost a fortune. Time to go," Byron advised; but Scrope was having none of it.

"Lady Luck is just waiting to pounce on me. Another few games and you will see her appear to bless her darling Scrope."

"It's a wonder you can even *see* the dice," Byron said, his own eyes slightly glazed. "One more throw, then let it be, Scrope, let it be."

At three o'clock in the morning, Scrope was still

having "one more throw" until Byron slid onto the floor unconscious.

Matthews brought him round and helped him to his feet, but Scrope still refused to stop playing, the dice still rattling in his hand. "She's coming, Lady Luck, I know it ... I can feel her presence coming closer!"

"If we stay here watching him, he will not stop," Matthews said to Byron, "but if we leave he will soon follow us, so let's you and I go."

When he awoke the following day, Byron had no idea how he and Matthews had got back to the college the night before – all a blank. He slowly looked around him, realising he must have fallen asleep on Matthews's sofa ... and there was Matthews himself ... conked out on the floor by the fireplace.

He glanced again at the window and the daylight, and then at the clock ... it was after *one* o'clock in the afternoon! They had missed hall, and two lectures, and no excuse other than gambling and drunkenness.

He smiled – but it had been *fun!*

He made some tea and woke Matthews who, despite his sore head, also laughed at the memories of the night before.

"Poor Scrope, I wonder if he's back in his rooms now, or locked up in the debtor's prison?"

They went to check, staring with disbelief when they saw Scrope Davies – in bed, and a ceramic bowl next to his bed filed to the brim with banknotes.

"One thousand pounds!" Scrope grinned tiredly. "I told you she would come. No matter how hard she tries to deny me, Lady Luck has always found me *irresistible."*

Byron thought it hilarious, especially in view of the fact that — "Scrope, who would ever *believe* that you are the son of a vicar?"

"And an Eton scholar!" Scrope reminded him. "An

Eton scholar who has just cleaned out a Cambridge nightclub, haha!"

Chapter Twenty-Three

~ ~ ~

Upon his first arrival at Trinity, and having been allotted '*Super*-excellent Rooms' on No 1 staircase in Newark Court, Byron had instructed John Hanson to meet all the bills for his purchases of new furniture, china plate and crystal glasses, as well as a new four-poster bed which had been delivered and fitted up in his bedroom.

Added to which, he had asked Hanson to send him regularly from London *'four dozen bottles of wine, one dozen bottles of port, same of sherry, claret and champagne.'*

After leaving Harrow, and spending a long hot summer with some of his friends down in London, he had determined to change his life, his mind and his mood when entering Trinity – gone forever was the self-conscious invalid, and in his place stood the self-respecting aristocrat.

"I feel as independent as a German prince who coins his own cash," he wrote to Augusta, *"or a Cherokee Chief who coins no cash at all, but enjoys what is more precious – freedom."*

Even so, the duality of both characters often invaded his nature, sometimes withdrawn and silent in his own form of interior depression; but more often vivacious and happy, and his inimitable wit and flippancy of phrase was now renowned as the *spice* of all dinner parties.

One of these dinner parties had just ended; the two

169

last companions were leaving Byron's rooms when John Hobhouse appeared at the open door, standing to stare with surprise at the luxurious and elegant furnishings ... a dinner table which had been laid out in the best style for eight or ten people ... the best plate and crystal ... and even the apartment itself seemed to be, in Hobhouse's opinion, more fitting for the Dean than an undergraduate.

A servant was busily gathering up the glasses while Byron remained sitting at the table, twirling the last inch of wine in his glass, before looking up and seeing Hobhouse.

"Mr Hobhouse," he said sarcastically. "What a delight."

"I'm looking for Scrope, I thought he might be here."

"No, tonight I believe he and Matthews are at the gaming club."

"They did not dine with you?"

"No."

"No, and I know the reason *why* they did not dine with you." Hobhouse sauntered further into the room. "Scrope has told me all about it."

Byron sat back in his chair. "Told you all about what, pray?"

"About all these undergraduates constantly forcing themselves into your rooms and into your company, fighting each other over which one received your dinner invitation and which one did not, doing everything possible to get into your favour and good graces, and all for a reason not very admirable."

Byron frowned. "Such as?"

"Good God man, can't you see that the intention of these leeches is to *live* off you? Saving their own money while they eat your dinners and drink your wines and think themselves so clever while feeling the richer for it."

Byron smiled. "I'm glad to hear it, Mr Hobhouse. I consider myself fortunate that the attorney in charge of my Newstead estate has given me a very large yearly allowance, so why not share it?"

"And *that* is the reason," Hobhouse continued undeterred, "why Scrope Davies, Charles Matthews and Edward Long no longer attend your dinners. All true and honourable gentlemen who are now *refusing* to join the beggars who are shamelessly taking advantage of your generosity."

"No, I think you are wrong, Mr Hobhouse..." Byron sat forward and looked at the all the cards on the table, "everyone who has dined here tonight has left me a dinner invitation in return."

"And what a bargain that will be for them!" Hobhouse scoffed. "You feed them like a king and they will feed you like a servant in return."

Byron was puzzled. "How so?"

Hobhouse sat down at the table and used his softer, 'older-brother' tone. "Scrope has told me that you never eat meat, is that correct?"

"Correct. I never eat animals ... except, perhaps a small piece of fish now and again."

"Why is that?"

"I have to keep a meticulous guard on my weight."

"Indeed?" Hobhouse was disappointed. "So it's really all due to *vanity* then?"

"No, it's really all due to the fact that I cannot put too much weight on my right leg."

"Oh, I see ..."

Hobhouse looked sheepishly apologetic, and Byron smiled mischievously. "Although I must confess, Mr Hobhouse, I *do* possess a great deal of vanity."

"So, no meat – a cheap dinner for them in return for a banquet – and Scrope tells me that you also drink very little wine?"

"On the contrary, sometimes I drink *copious* amounts of wine until I cannot see straight; but, in general, I prefer soda water."

"So a *very* cheap guest indeed." Hobhouse sighed, and then sat gazing around him, fixing his eyes on a very large mirror across one wall.

"That's an uncommonly large mirror," he said curiously. "Was it here when you came, or did you have it fitted?"

"No, it was here when I came, and when I first moved in I thought some of my friends had grown very attentive and tireless in coming to see me, but I soon discovered that their main reason for coming so often was to see *themselves* in my mirror."

While Hobhouse did likewise and sat gazing appraisingly at himself in the mirror, Byron stood and lifted a clean glass from the trolley. "A glass of claret, Mr Hobhouse? Or is the interrogation now over?"

Hobhouse was startled. "I am not interrogating you. I am merely advising you on behalf of Scrope and the others, because *they* claim to be too fond of you to risk offending you."

"But not you." Byron questioningly held up the wine decanter.

Hobhouse nodded. "Oh, very well ... but half a glass is all I can manage. I still have some studying to do tonight and my mind is quite dulled by the subject."

"Then you should not eat meat."

Hobhouse half smiled. "Are you hinting that I am fat?"

"No, I am voicing my belief that all red meat weighs down the body and has a lethargic effect on the mind, slowing it down. Another reason why I never eat it."

"To help you study?"

"To help me *write*." Byron smiled. "Did Scrope not tell you? I'm a poet."

"A *poet?*" Hobhouse could not restrain his grinning sneer. "Oh, my dear Lord Byron ... putting aside your professed *vanity* for one moment, I must warn you of the many rival poets you will find here in Cambridge. Some are excellent, none are great, and, in fact ... I must confess that I have my *own* literary ambitions in that field."

Byron twirled his wine again, a sardonic smile on his face. "So *you* are one of my poetic rivals then, Mr Hobhouse?"

"I'll be your main rival," Hobhouse took a slug of wine and smacked his lips, "when we leave here and reach the time of seeking to get published."

"I am already published."

"What?" Hobhouse sat staring while Byron stood and moved over to his bookshelf, lifted down a slim volume, and handed it to Hobhouse. "This only arrived yesterday, so you are the first I have shown it to."

Hobhouse gazed at the dark blue cover of the book in his hand, *Fugitive Pieces*: *A Collection of Poems* by *George Gordon Byron*.

"My friend John Pigot thought they should be published and took them to Ridge in Newark, the only publisher in Nottingham, who readily agreed to publish, a hundred copies to start," Byron explained. "But now, that's the only existing copy left."

"Oh I say ..." Hobhouse was stunned. He opened the book and began to glance through the pages ... "Why is this the only one left? Has it sold out?"

"It has not sold even *one* copy to the public, and never will. As soon as John Pigot had sent this copy to me, Reverend Becher, our pastor, descended upon the publisher and requested to buy a copy, and as soon as he had read the book, he returned the next morning and insisted on buying all the remaining ninety-seven copies, and then promptly *burned* the lot in Ridge's fireplace!"

"Why?" Hobhouse was puzzled. "Are your poems that bad? Poorly written? What?"

"No, they were *not* poorly written. It was just one poem that Becher objected to – my favourite poem which was entitled '*To Mary*'. Becher claimed it contained passages of immoral lewdness and declared me to be a most 'profligate sinner' as well as insisting that my poem was as near to 'smut' as a poem could get. Yet I know that I have never written a word of smut in my life! I write *truth*."

Hobhouse could see Byron was grieved. "Nothing wrong with a bit of smut," he said. "Far better than all that flowery nonsense."

"It was *not* smut," Byron insisted, "it was love."

Now it was Hobhouse who was grieved: it seemed Byron, who was two years younger than him, had already experienced love and he still had not. Nevertheless, he was impressed.

He quickly leafed through the pages of the book until he found the poem "*To Mary*" his eyes widening as he read certain verses.

"Can I borrow this? he asked. "I would like to read the entire book."

"Yes, but keep it safe and bring it back without any creases or thumb marks. It is my only printed copy."

"You are very different to my earlier opinions about you."

"To your earlier *prejudices* against me."

"Quite so," Hobhouse agreed. "Although I blame *you* for making me hate you."

"How?"

"First of all – that *white* hat! And the grey horse to match your grey cloak. And then when I learned you were an aristo, well ..."

Byron laughed hilariously as Hobhouse listed all his

snap prejudices.

"Then when you turned up with that *bear*... good grief, I thought you must be hopelessly mad as well as empty-headed." Hobhouse looked around him. "By the bye, where is your little bear?"

"Gone."

"Ran away?"

"No." Byron sighed. "Bruin and I truly *adored* each other ..." He then told Hobhouse of the vicious poem written by Hewson Clarke, a failed poet now studying at Emmanuel College, pointing out how cruel it was to have a bear lodged in a college room by day and a nearby stable at night.

"What hurt me the most," Byron confessed, "is that Clarke, under the guise of being my friend, has dined here many times and seen how *well* I have always treated Bruin, and how much Bruin loved me, allowing only me to hold him."

Byron refilled his wine glass. "But when I neglected to respond to a few of Clarke's dinner invitations, only through forgetfulness and a full diary, he writes this vicious poem about myself and Bruin and sends it to *The Satirist* so all Cambridge can read it."

"So you sent the bear away?"

Byron's expression was dismal. "I had to, reluctantly, because I could see Clarke's point, even though he had turned out to be such a fake friend and turned on me like that."

Byron shrugged. "And now Bruin is on his way down to Newstead in the care of my valet, hopefully to spend the rest of his life more happily in the company of my servants and plenty of green gardens to play in."

Hobhouse's face was grim. No matter how much he had privately laughed at the ridiculousness of Byron having a bear for a pet, Scrope Davies and others had told him that no bear on earth could receive as much love and tender care as Byron expended on his pet.

"Can I see Clarke's poem?"

"I might have torn it up ... but I might still have it ..." Byron went into his bedroom, and returned holding an open copy of *The Satirist*.

"I *will* tear it up, after you have read it. Although I have to say—" Byron added angrily, "Clarke has made a very grave mistake, because there is no greater satirist in all of Cambridge than *myself,* and Clarke will find that out in the very near future."

"No greater satirist in all of Cambridge?" The cynical expression was back on Hobhouse's face. "One cannot make such a claim without showing some proof."

"All right, maybe I overstated," Byron conceded, "but here's a thought – while you sit reading Clarke's poem, I'll sit here and spin off a few satirical lines in reply, and then *you* tell me if you think it will hit my target?"

"Very well," Hobhouse agreed, "but be prepared, my opinion will be an honest one."

"Anything else would be an irritation." Byron removed a quill and ink and some paper from the bookcase and sat down and began to write rapidly, while Hobhouse lifted the magazine and began to read Hewson Clarke's poem:

> *Sad Bruin, no longer in woods thou art dancing,*
>
> *With all the enjoyments that Love can afford;*
>
> *No longer thy consorts around thee are prancing,*
>
> *For other thy fate — thou art slave to a lord!*

Hobhouse read on, considering the poem to be nothing more than jealous drivel and threw it down. "Now, let me see what you have written about Clarke."

Byron handed over his sheet of paper and Hobhouse read:

Poor Clarke, still striving piteously 'to please',

Forgetting doggerel leads not to degrees.

A would-be satirist, a hired buffoon,

A monthly scribbler of some low lampoon.

Condemned to drudge, the meanest of the mean,

And furnish falsehoods for a magazine.

Devotes to scandal his menial mind;

Himself a living libel on mankind.

Before Hobhouse could read the next verse a knock came on the door, immediately followed by two inebriated undergraduates who casually strolled in.

"I say, Byron, is there any more of your delectable claret left?"

Hobhouse furiously jumped to his feet. "How dare you walk in here without invitation or a call to enter!"

He moved solidly towards them. "If you want claret so badly then supply it yourselves why don't you? Instead of constantly leeching off Lord Byron and taking advantage of his foolish generosity. Out, I say, *out!*"

The two undergraduates backed out quickly and Hobhouse slammed the door in their shocked faces. "Ingrates!"

Behind his back Byron was smiling, thinking Hobhouse a very strange and amusing fellow. For all his talk of revolution for the common man, he spoke in a very top-drawer way. He said *'boke'* instead of 'book', and *'thaht'* instead of 'that'.

As Hobhouse turned back to the room the door opened again, and one of the students poked his head inside. "Lord Byron, pray believe, we intended no offence —"

"*Out!*" Hobhouse turned and slammed the door

again.

When he turned around, Byron was still smiling. "Do you know, strange as it now seems to me, I think I am beginning to *like* you, Mr Hobhouse."

Hobhouse shrugged. "Call me Hobby. All my other friends do."

"Oh, so now you wish to become my *friend*?" Byron gazed tiredly at all the dinner and party invitations lying on every surface of his room. "Mr Hobhouse, I already have more friends than I can cope with."

"I can see that, and that's why I intend to give you my help in alleviating that problem."

From that night on, Hobhouse became known as *"Byron's Bulldog"* — always there to snarl and come between Byron and anyone who tried to push their attentions upon him, guarding him from all the leeches and the infatuated lovelorn and sending them all on their way with short shrift.

Byron's laugh, when he was told by Scrope Davies of Hobhouse's new nickname, was so hilarious it gave him a mischievous idea.

"Oh, good grief ..." Hobhouse exclaimed a few days later when Byron entered his rooms to introduce him to his latest pet — a small bulldog.

Unaware of his new nickname, Hobhouse asked, "Why a bulldog? Could you not have found a breed of dog more appealing in looks?"

"Beauty is in the eye of the beholder." Byron lifted up the small dog and playfully hugged him. "I chose him because he looked such a friendless animal, rather like myself when I was a small boy."

Hobhouse looked at the bulldog disdainfully. "And is this beast of yours going to be another lord like your bear, *Lord* Bruin?"

Byron shook his head. "No, once again I was thinking of myself when I came up with a name for this young beast, whom, I may add, is a breed of dog much derided and greatly misunderstood, in the same way the poem to my Mary was misunderstood and wrongly deemed unfit to be read. So, Hobby – say hello to Smut."

"*Smut?*" Hobhouse's disdainful expression was replaced by a howl of laughter.

Chapter Twenty-Four

~ ~ ~

<u>*To The Hon. Mrs Augusta Leigh.*</u>

My dearest Augusta — so you have finally captured and married that cousin of yours and become Mrs Leigh! An officer in the 10th Dragoons indeed. My congratulations! I wish you both all the happiness that Life can provide, and look forward to celebrating with you both soon.

Adieu my dearest Augusta. Write soon, and don't forget to love me too.

Your affectionate Brother —BYRON

He sealed the letter and then looked up with a smile at Hobhouse. "What I find so wonderful about having a sister, is that I know she is bound to love me, come what may, simply because we are related by our blood."

Hobhouse lowered Byron's copy of the *Æneid* from his eyes, his expression flat. "She is only your *half* sister."

"So? We still share our father's blood. That's reason enough for us to love each other."

"Is it? I have fourteen half-siblings, all my stepmother's children, and all of whom share my father's blood, yet not one of them feel *bound* to love me."

"No? Do you love any of them?"

Hobhouse shrugged. "No ... Yes. Well, I'm quite fond of my full brother Benjamin ... he's a nice enough fellow and we get along whenever I'm in Bristol ... but the rest of them? My step-siblings? I keep forgetting their *names*, and I always get their faces mixed up. Every year she produced a new one and they all looked the same to me, and then I was shunted off to school before the last ten were born and now I don't even bother *trying* to remember who is who and which is which."

"So how do you communicate?"

"If it's a female I say *'Hello, Sis,'* and if it's a male I say *'And how are you, young man?'* It never fails, and they never suspect that I don't actually have a clue who the heck they are, other than being one or other of my half-blood relations."

Byron pondered. "But in her letters Augusta always tells me that she loves me, and always signs off at the end — 'Your loving sister'."

"That's nothing more than traditional, the normal form for females in letters. They write it whether they mean it or not."

"Do they?" Byron was sad to hear it. Augusta had become his rock, the receptacle for all his private confidences, the one person he felt he could trust, his one and only *blood* relation ... apart from his mother who was a stranger to love in any form.

"And now that Augusta is married —"

"Well I don't know the girl do I?" Hobhouse cut in. "But if she is like other females that I *do* know, then her mind will be consumed completely by her new husband, a new place to live, how many babies she hopes to give birth to – and her younger half brother will be the *last* thing on her mind. Grow up, Byron. You have said yourself that love is a fallacy for the foolish."

Byron was sinking into a gloomy mood. "I said it was a *misleading* notion."

"Same thing. Here today and gone tomorrow. A myth. Is that what the girl in your sinful poem did — mislead you?"

Before Byron could answer Scrope Davies walked in on the conversation: "Girls? The *very* subject I have been thinking about. Now here's my suggestion."

Scrope sat down. "I suggest that before we go for our little summer holiday in Brighton, we stop off for a few days in London, have a few games in the clubs, and then at the end of each night, after plenty of champagne, we avail ourselves of some *horizontal* refreshment."

He looked at Hobhouse and then Byron. "Yes? No? Good idea?"

"Do you mean prostitutes?" Byron asked.

"No, I mean courtesans, *London* courtesans, *classy* courtesans who know how to treat a man. Surely you didn't think I meant the type of prostitutes that walk the streets here in Cambridge? Who would touch one of *them?*"

Hobhouse replied in a serious tone: "Those prostitutes who walk the streets here in Cambridge, are now beginning to cause a lot of trouble between the townsmen and the gownsmen."

Scrope Davies frowned. "How so?"

"Oh, did you not hear? I thought you knew everything, Scrope. Some of our undergraduate gownsmen have been verbally abused over it."

"Over *what?* Don't drag it out, Hobby, just tell."

"Well, in order to protect the undergraduates, the University has been given its own yeomanry force who now have the right to patrol the streets at night, as well as the authority to arrest and send up for prosecution any prostitute found walking near the college walls, and this has caused many of the whores to move on and ply their trade elsewhere, which has made some of the local young townsmen very annoyed."

"Disgusting! Let them all go to hell in the same cart for all I care," Scrope replied. "Now does this not *prove* that London is the only place to go for some clean feminine fun?"

"Clean feminine fun?" Hobhouse looked at Byron. "I think it's a devilishly good idea. What else are young gentlemen to do, living in this all-male world as we do? It's not normal. And if it is respectable young *ladies* we must wait for – then all we are allowed is one kiss on the cheek before her parents are demanding a lifetime of marriage in return."

Scrope laughed and stood to slap Hobhouse on the back. "Well said, Hobby, well said. Are you in, Byron? Or do you intend to remain chaste?"

"Chaste?" Hobhouse scoffed. "This is a young man who has already been accused of being *a profligate sinner!*"

"Really?" Scrope shot a surprised smile at Byron. "And are you?"

"A sinner, yes," Byron confessed placidly, "but not a profligate one."

Chapter Twenty-Five

~ ~ ~

Once again he was standing still in the darkness, standing alone in one of the cloisters around the quadrangle, gazing up at the ever-present stars. His first year at Trinity was a day short from being over, and now he was looking back over the past year.

What a night of stars! The rooms all around the courtyard were filled with Trinity men, most of enormous intellect and culture and study, but did they also *see* the magnificence of the stars out here above their windows?

He had made many friends here at Trinity, and few were as mercenary in their friendship as Hobhouse had inferred. Many friends ... but his two closest, and his two favourites were Edward Long and John Eddleston.

He had known Edward Long at Harrow, although not well, and yet it had been a wonderful discovery on that first day for both of them. Finding an old and familiar face amongst new strangers was a comforting relief. He and Ned Long had been rival swimmers at Harrow, and continued to be rival swimmers here at Cambridge.

Though the River Cam did not have a very translucent wave, it was fourteen feet deep where they often went to dive and swim, and where there was a stump of a tree at least ten or twelve feet deep, embedded in the river, around which Ned often clung to and wondered aloud – "How the devil did I come here?"

Poor Ned, he had found it hard here at Trinity, hating the life of study – *"scarce difference to the classrooms at Harrow – the same old Prometheus!"* he would say in a despairing voice, preferring to spend his time listening to music or playing his own flute or violoncello.

"*You are the only reason I stay sane here,*" Ned had once said to him; and yet, even then, Byron had not realised the melancholy thoughts or the state of real depression that Ned was sinking into.

Not until the day he had agreed to accompany Ned on a visit to his uncle's house, where Ned, strolling into the hall, noticed a pistol lying on the hall-table and immediately picked it up and – without knowing whether the pistol was loaded or not – fired it against his head, leaving to chance whether it might or might not be loaded.

The shock of possibly being a witness to seeing his friend blowing his brains out, had forced him to tell Ned — "You should leave Trinity and go wherever you want to go, and be whoever you want to be."

And Ned had done that, yesterday, left Trinity to go straight into the Guards and join the British Army on the battlefields abroad. A young man in search of death – a young man who was not considered by others at Trinity to be fun or cheerful company – yet Byron had loved him.

Leaving the cloisters behind him and wandering out to the Great Court, he propped himself against the ledge of the fountain and watched the waters tremble and shiver as Trinity's great clock chimed out its heavy chimes in the darkness.

And then there was his other favourite, John Eddleston ... he too was now gone ... and tonight Trinity felt very empty without the two of them.

He had been introduced to Eddleston by Ned Long, due to Ned and Eddleston sharing a deep passion for music, but there the similarities in their tastes and status ended.

Eddleston came from a poor family of low birth and

was aged only sixteen, yet somehow his pastor had managed to get him a music scholarship at Trinity of one shilling a week as well as his board and education;– and all due to his beautiful voice. In the Cambridge choir Eddleston not only sang with the beautiful silver voice of an angel, but also *looked* like one in his red gown and white surplice.

Yet outside the choir, John Eddleston was a lonely boy who clung shyly to Ned Long for company – the *haut* of the upper-class system being as strong in Trinity as anywhere else in the wider world. And his was a situation that Byron sympathised with, having himself once been a lonely boy living with his mother in rented rooms in Aberdeen.

"But we never had a *maid* as you did," Eddleston had said. "My sister's a maid now, in one of the big houses."

"He's so lonely here," Ned had said one day to Byron, "do you mind if he joins us?"

Byron had looked down at the young boy standing alone in the courtyard, and recognised yet another poor friendless animal *in* need of rescue. And so the three of them had gone to swim in the Cam, and from that day on they did so much else together: riding, swimming, laughing: walking along the Backs and taking Smut along to join in the fun, never tiring of each other's company.

And they had often dined together in the evenings, just the three of them, followed by Ned and Eddleston listening to music or playing it, while he engrossed himself in reading *The Life of Lord Herbert of Cherbury:* a poet and philosopher who was of particular interest to him – because at the age of 15, he had married his cousin Mary, then aged 21, and lived happily ever after — "*notwithstanding the disparity of years betwixt us.*"

And *his* own Mary had still not married Jack Musters,

so why the long delay? Was there still hope?

The Trinity clock chimed the quarter past the hour, the waters of the fountain trembled and shivered again, and then all was very quiet.

Love was so sweet, in all its forms.

Byron was not sure exactly when he realised that young Eddleston had fallen in love with him, yet it was a *pure* love that all young boys living in a male-dominated world knew. He had suspected it – the red hot blushes on the face were the sure give-away – but it was not until the day that Eddleston had shyly presented him with a small friendship ring, that he knew it for sure.

It was a gold ring with a pink Cornelian stone in the shape of a heart, which the boy must have had to save up hard from his weekly shilling to buy, but it was the expression on his face, when he gave it, that touched Byron's heart the most ...

> *He offered it with a downcast look,*
> *Fearful that I might refuse it,*
> *I told him when the gift I took*
> *My only fear would be to lose it.*

He glanced down at the ring on his hand, so very small he was forced to wear it on his smallest finger.

And then, just a week ago, Eddleston had also announced that he was leaving Trinity, weeping his eyes out as he did so. His father had decided that college was all well and good for the rich boys, but now that he was no longer able to work, then his *son* must quit college and get a job in order to bring some money into the family. Employment had been found for him as a clerk in a Mercantile House.

Byron sighed deeply: *Yesterday* had been such a sad day ... saying farewell to the two of them, Ned Long and

John Eddleston, knowing neither would be returning in the autumn term, leaving him with that mad and more sophisticated group of friends, Charles Matthews, Scrope Davies and Hobhouse – and talk of the blasted Devil!

"Ho, Byron!" Hobhouse called. "Is that you there?"

Scrope and Matthews were arm in arm, laughing and slightly drunk coming across the court towards him.

"So gloomy, and all alone?" Matthews observed. "Oh, my dear Hamlet, is something not right in Denmark?"

"You should have come with us," said Scrope. "We've had a capital time, with lots of champagne, just in rehearsal for our holiday, you know?"

Scrope and Matthews propped themselves each side of him, on the ledge of the fountain, and within minutes he was laughing with them, still unconsciously touching the ring on his small finger, which Hobhouse's hawk eyes saw.

"Now look here, Byron," he said, his voice slightly slurred. "This is not Harrow you know, so we can't allow you to carry on as if you were *still* at Harrow. That was a boy's school, sir, a *boy's* school."

"I know that."

"Oh, do you? Then I beg your pardon."

Scrope and Matthews laughed. "Hobby is more drunk than he knows," Matthews whispered in Byron's ear.

"I mean, I do honestly and very sincerely *mean,*" Hobhouse continued, "that you allowing young Eddleston to give you a ring to wear on your hand is not on, not acceptable."

"Why not?" Byron protested. "I loved that dear boy."

"And Edward Long – did you *love* him too?"

"I totally adored Ned. And it's my sorrow that he's gone now."

Matthews was grinning slyly. "Still, I imagine you had very little left to learn when you came up here from

Harrow, eh Byron?"

"What do you mean?"

"All that study of the ancient Greeks?"

"All my special schoolboy friendships were *pure* passions of the heart," Byron insisted. "And so were my friendships with Ned Long and John Eddleston!"

"Friendships? You have just told us you *loved* them."

"Yes, because that's what friendship is – love without its wings."

"What? Say that again," Hobhouse demanded. "That sounded rather *poetic*."

"Friendship is love without its wings," Byron repeated. "In the case of *true* friendship it is."

"You know, I honestly cannot think of any reply to that," Hobhouse admitted. "No reply at all."

"Then *don't* reply," Scrope advised.

"Say nothing at all," Matthews suggested, which confused Hobhouse.

"What is the point of *saying* nothing? It makes no sense."

Scrope linked his arm through Byron's, grinning wickedly. "Are you looking forward to our trip to London, By? All those lovely courtesans just waiting for us."

Byron looked from Scrope to Matthews, and Matthews put his palms up. "No good looking at me, I'll be coming along on the trip but I won't be entertaining any courtesans, not even if they came free."

"Why not?" Byron asked.

"I am not attracted to females, never have been, never will be."

"There now, you see, Byron ..." Hobhouse pointed a finger at Matthews. "*There* now is why you cannot go around wearing rings given to you by *boys,*" Hobhouse warned. "People may think you are somewhat like Matthews there – odd!"

"I think *you* are odd," Matthews retorted, and was laughing again.

"No, no," Scrope Davies drunkenly wagged a finger in the negative. "Hobby is what the psychologists term as being homo-*social,* as indeed are many men, myself *not* included."

"Homo-*social?* What the devil is that?" Hobhouse asked.

"Homo-socialism," Scrope explained, "is men who prefer their friends to be *men,* and indeed often feel great love for their male friends, and only truly feel comfortable in a social sense when in the company of other men; but when it comes to *sex,* then, and only then, are they interested in women."

Hobhouse was astounded. "Did your brother the lawyer tell you that, Scrope?"

"No, my other brother the psychologist told me that, Hobby."

"And on that, gentlemen," Byron said, standing to leave, "I'm off to bed. See you all in London next week."

~~~

Upon reaching Southwell, Byron had made up his mind to stop feigning indifference, and come right out and ask John or Elizabeth Pigot just what was going on in relation to Mary Chaworth? Was she marrying Jack Musters or not? And why the delay?

Although he did realise that he had no right to ask anyone about her, especially since before returning to Harrow he had sent her a note saying all he wanted to do was to *forget* her.

Something he still found impossible to do.

As soon as he had stepped down from the carriage outside Burgage Manor, he saw John Pigot bounding across the Green towards him.

"Byron, dear fellow! I have some good news. Ridge

says he will publish your book if that one poem to Mary is removed. Otherwise he sees no point in publishing if the local vicar keeps burning the books. No chance of any re-orders with that going on."

"No, forget *Fugitive Pieces*," Byron replied. "I am preparing a new collection without any amorous stuff in it, and all immaculately chaste."

"George!" His mother stood at open door beaming, her arms held out to him. "Come to your dear mama, George!"

Byron glanced at John Pigot, quickly flashing up his eyes, and then walked up the short path and allowed her to hug him. "Are you well, Mother?"

"George ... have you grown taller?"

"I don't know."

"I'm sure you have – another inch taller at least. That will be from your *Gordon* blood. Few of the Byron men were much above medium height."

"Shall I come back later?" John Pigot called.

"No, no, come in now," Byron insisted. "I'm sure my mother will be delighted to sit us down with some tea."

Mrs Byron did not look at all delighted in not having her son all to herself, and John Pigot wished Byron had not insisted on his going in. Mrs Byron terrified him, especially now that she *knew* he had helped her son to escape from her the last time he was home. And she was a woman who never let a grudge pass until she had exacted some kind of *revenge*.

Once inside the drawing-room, John sat down in a chair, uncomfortable and embarrassed, and then completely mortified by her callousness when Mrs Byron – before her son had even sat down – said to him gravely: "George, I have some news for you."

Byron looked at her. "What kind of news?"

"Take out your handkerchief first, you will want it."

"Nonsense."

"Take out your handkerchief, I say."

"Why?" And then a worried look. "Has something happened to Boatswain or Bruin?"

His mother sighed. "Take out your handkerchief."

Byron glanced impatiently at John, and then took out his handkerchief to humour her.

"Mary Chaworth is finally married ... to Jack Musters."

John saw a peculiar expression, impossible to describe, pass over Byron's face, which had turned very pale.

"Of course," his mother continued, "Jack Musters has now taken the name of Chaworth in order to claim her inheritance, so in future Mary will be known as *Mrs* Chaworth."

"Mary married." Byron shoved the handkerchief back into his pocket and affected a careless manner. "Is that all?"

"Why, George, I expected you to be *plunged* into grief!"

Byron made no reply, and then turned and walked out of the room. "I need to collect my luggage."

Rather than be left alone in the room with Mrs Byron, John jumped up and followed him. "I will help you to carry it in."

If he had delayed a minute John would have missed him. Byron had ordered the driver to return the bags to the carriage .

"Are you leaving?"

"Yes."

"Where are you going?"

"Straight to London."

"But Byron—"

Byron quickly hugged him and said, "Goodbye, dear friend, I'll write to you from London."

And then he was in the carriage and banging for the

driver to be off.

John stood and watched the carriage rolling away, knowing how deeply his friend was affected by this news of Mary's marriage, so definite now, so final.

If it had been left up to him, John thought, and if he had been *allowed* some time beforehand, he would have broken it to Byron more gently.

John slowly turned to look at the open door of the house, knowing Mrs Byron was sitting in there waiting for her son to return with his baggage ... should he go in and tell her Byron had gone?

John decided on safety over bravery and ran back as fast as he could to his own house, bolting the door behind him.

"If Mrs Byron comes knocking," he warned his mother and Elizabeth, "don't answer, don't answer."

"Why ever not?" his mother queried. "Is Byron not home from Cambridge yet?"

"Yes, and fled again. She told him about Mary Chaworth before he had even sat down."

"Oh that *silly* woman – she is her own worst enemy," Mrs Pigot said with despair – and then rushed out to the back gate to bolt that also.

Chapter Twenty-Six

~ ~ ~

The four friends had arranged to meet on Friday evening at Gordon's Hotel in Albermarle Street.

It was understood that each may arrive at the hotel at differing times during the day, so the official time for all to join up was at seven o'clock in the evening, in time for their first London dinner together.

By eight o'clock Byron had still not arrived.

"We may as well go in and dine," Scrope Davies suggested. "If Byron arrives when we have eaten, he can always get something at the Cocoa Tree Club."

At the end of their meal, leaving the Dining Room, Scrope Davies walked over to the desk and asked the Hotel Manager, "Has Lord Byron checked in yet, do you know?"

"Lord Byron?" The manager appeared surprised. "Lord Byron has been residing here for almost a week, since last weekend I believe. And your name, sir?"

"Scrope Berdmore Davies."

"One moment."

The manager moved to flick through his list of messages. "No ... no, the only message I have here from Lord Byron is for a Mr John Cam Hobhouse."

"That's me," said Hobhouse, coming over to take the message, glancing at Scrope and Matthews. "What the devil is Byron up to?"

Hobhouse read the short note. "He's at the Cocoa Tree Club ... he says he will meet up with us there."

"Then lead on, Hobby, lead on," Scrope said. "The dice will be getting very hot by now."

Inside the club, with its dim lights, and filled as

always with young gentlemen and their belles, they eventually found Byron in the gaming room, standing at one of the tables and surrounded by a group of other players as he excitedly rattled and shook the box of dice and then a twisting— "*throw!*"

Joining him, Scrope and Matthews were grinning, while Hobhouse was frowning.

"Last night I threw fourteen mains running," Byron told them, "and carried off all the cash on the table. This now is my eighth throw."

"Byron, why are you doing this?" Hobhouse asked. "You don't even like gaming."

Byron threw him a careless, defiant smile. "Well now I love it, Hobby. I love the excitement and the rattle and dash of the dice, and the glorious uncertainty – not only of good luck or bad luck – but of *any luck at all!*"

"Something has angered and upset him," Hobhouse said quietly to Scrope. "I know that 'damn them all' expression of his."

Scrope was not listening, too eager to get in on the game himself. "Move over, Byron, the *expert* gamester has arrived!"

Hobhouse and Matthews left them to it, going to the outer room and taking a table where they ordered a magnum of champagne and sat listening to an exquisite black girl with an exquisite voice singing moodily about "*my precious lo-v-e ...*"

Byron joined them a short time later, still smiling carelessly, "I have left it off for a while, without being much of a winner or a loser."

"Where's Scrope?" asked Matthews.

Byron grinned. "You won't see much of Scrope tonight. He's in there, red hot, rattling and throwing and *winning!*"

Hobhouse shook his head despairingly. "I just don't understand it, this gambling game. It's not the money for you, the excitement is not caused by the money you may win, so what is it?"

Byron poured himself a glass of champagne. "I've told you, Hobby, it's the excitement of the thing that pleases me, because it's always there."

He sipped his champagne, his eyes on the beautiful singer. "Women, wine ... all can sate now and then, but every cast of the dice keeps the gamester *alive*. Besides, a man can game for ten times longer than he can do anything else."

"Get sated with women!" Hobhouse retorted. "Chance would be a fine thing. We haven't even started on *that* game yet!"

Byron grinned. "Not you, Hobby, but I have been in London for a week. That reminds me ..." He looked around the room, "where's my blue-eyed Caroline?"

He beckoned over a waiter. "Where's my blue-eyed Caroline?"

"Miss Cameron went upstairs to rest while you were in the gaming room, my lord. Shall I send for her?"

"Pray do. I would like her to meet my friends here."

"No, *don't* send for her," Matthews cut in, and looked with annoyance at Byron. "This is supposed to be a chums holiday, By. It was agreed that any women would be restricted to bedtime hours only."

"True." Byron smiled at the waiter. "Will you ask Miss Cameron to go to the hotel and wait for me there. She can rest in my room."

The waiter bowed, and moved off, much to Hobhouse's consternation. "I thought we were all going to Madam Durville's together. So who is this blue-eyed Caroline?"

"Oh, she's adorable and I'm already half in love with her," Byron confessed. "We have been inseparable since our first night together."

"Inseparable?" Hobhouse asked. "You mean ... in the

daytime as well?"

"Of course. I was here on my own, so why should we separate in daytime when we enjoy being together so much?"

"Good grief." Hobhouse was appalled. "And have the two of you been ... " he nodded, "you know ...?"

"Making love?" Byron prompted, and laughed. "Oh, it is a den of iniquity down here, Hobby, are you sure you want to stay?"

"Well have you?" Hobhouse demanded.

Byron laughed again, and looked at Matthews who appeared very amused by Hobhouse's reaction.

"I did as you asked, Hobby," said Byron, changing the subject, "and booked a box at the opera for tomorrow night, although I had to pay a full year's subscription for the box, so I hope you enjoy it."

"What!" Matthew's amused expression changed to one of pain. "Do we *have* to go to the opera so soon? I think I forgot to pack my dress suit."

A young lady arrived silently at the table and whispered something in Byron's ear. She was dressed very beautifully in a blue velvet outdoor costume and a small velvet blue hat on her auburn hair.

Hobhouse stared at her inquisitively. She was no more than eighteen years old, a vision of loveliness, and looked as innocently-sweet and refined as an earl's daughter.

"Oh, yes ..." Byron took his hotel key from an inner pocket of his jacket and handed it to her, then the girl slipped away as quickly and as silently as she had arrived.

Hobhouse was astounded. "I say ... is that ..."

"My blue-eyed Caroline, yes."

"She's very ... sweet," Hobhouse opined, the champagne softening his mood, "Very delectable indeed."

"Isn't she though," Byron smiled. "Sweet and gentle, the only type of female I like."

"She's still a whore," Matthews said realistically. "No matter how sweet and gentle she is."

"There's no such thing as perfection, Charles," Byron agreed good-humouredly. "All beauty has its flaws."

"*Gentlemen!*" Scrope Davies arrived at the table, flushed with excitement and holding up a wad of banknotes. "The rest of our holiday will be paid for by Lady Luck and the hottest gaming table in the Cocoa Tree club. So let the night begin!"

~ ~ ~

The following evening, as they prepared to go to the Opera, Matthews knocked on Byron's door in a fluster. "I *did* forget to pack my dress suit, what will I do?"

Byron eyed him suspiciously. "Do you *want* to go to the Opera?"

"Of course I do! I love the opera, especially when it's my old friend Amadeus."

"You did not seem very eager last night."

"Simply because I was not sure if I had packed my dress suit. Now what will I do?"

"The hotel manager is bound to have some spare suits and stocks for such an emergency. Go down and ask him if he can help you."

"That's a thought." Matthew nodded. "You three better not head off without me."

Later, in the hotel lobby, Matthews finally joined them, dressed in a magnificently fashionable, if somewhat exaggerated, shirt and leather stock-cravat, his head held high and looking as haughty and puffed-up as the Prince of Wales on a night out.

They proceeded to the Opera House to enjoy Mozart's *The Marriage of Figaro,* where Matthews sat in the box with his head held in the same haughty upright position throughout.

Byron kept glancing at Matthews, at the stiffness of his head. It was a very handsome head, but either he was so entranced in Mozart that he lost all interest in those whispering to him, or he was expressing a sense of immense grandeur due to sitting in a box.

During the interval, Matthews took a glass of wine from the tray and decided to take himself outside for some air.

"Is Matthews all right?" Hobhouse queried. "He's looking quite flushed in the face."

"He always looks like that when he's listening to Amadeus," Scrope said.

"I think I'll go outside too," Byron decided. "Are either of you coming along?"

"What – stand around outside as if we are in Fop's Alley, no thank you!" said Hobhouse.

Byron carried his glass outside to where Matthews was standing against a wall, his head in the same upright position and staring straight ahead as if in a dream.

"They say Mozart's music *can* do that to you," Byron said, standing beside him.

"Come round," said Matthews, "come round so I can see you."

"Why should I come round? I'm standing right beside you. All you have to do is turn your head."

"That is exactly what I can *not* do! Can't you see the state I'm in?"

Matthews pointed to his buckram shirt collar and the inflexible leather stock-cravat under his chin.

"I'm near strangled up here! Damn that hotel manager and his emergency clothes."

Byron's laughter was so hilarious he could not contain it, even when they had returned to the box. And after whispering to Scrope and Hobby about Matthew's predicament, both took one look at their friend's stiff upright head, and doubled up in muffled laughter, until they all had to quit the box and leave the Opera House.

"As *I* am the one who has suffered tonight," Matthews insisted, yanking off the rigid stock and loosening the string of his shirt collar. "I think *I* should be the one who chooses where we go for supper."

"So where?"

"A friend has told me about this wonderful little place on the Strand. It's called *The Hat House*. Quick, hail that cab!"

On the Strand, stepping out of the carriage and entering the glass lobby of *The Hat House,* Byron looked through the glass at the other diners, and then at Matthews in disbelief – "You are jesting!"

"No," Matthews assured him seriously. "And it costs only a shilling extra for the privilege."

"The name of the place should have warned us," Scrope said.

Hobby and Byron wearily agreed; the name *should* have warned them, as one of Matthews' oddities was that he liked to dine with his hat on, and often boasted of the sheer *comfort* of his head being covered at meal times – something that breached all etiquette of society – except when they dined in each others private rooms at Cambridge, when Matthews always dined with his hat on.

"I'm not eating with my hat on!" Hobhouse declared. "It would be like going to the Opera without my shoes on."

Scrope Davies held up his palms.. "Gentlemen, please, I beg you to consider – poor Matthews has suffered great discomfort tonight with his neck being strangled throughout the entire first half of the opera, so the very least that we, his *friends*, can do to make up for that, is to allow him to dine in public with his damned hat on."

Scrope turned to Matthews. "Will this be the first time you have done it in public, Charles?"

"The very first time," Matthews replied exultantly, "and I can hardly wait for the *thrill* of the experience at last."

Scrope nodded. "In we go, gentlemen, in we go."

"And to think," Byron muttered to Hobhouse as they were led to a table, "I could now be back at the hotel making love to my blue-eyed Caroline, instead of participating in this absurdity. However, here goes ..."

He slapped his top-hat further down on his head, sat down at the table, and lifted the menu.

Chapter Twenty-Seven

~ ~ ~

In 1807, *Hours of Idleness,* Byron's second collection of poems was published by Ridge in Newark, and also by Crosby in London.

Crosby's advance editions had been sent out to reviewers and Byron waited with nervous anticipation for the verdict of the reviews. In all else in life, in his love for Mary, in his early love for his mother, all had resulted in rejection, but now – through his poetic writings – the affection he had so long craved from as far back as his childhood days would hopefully now come to him, along with a recognition of his worth as a poet.

The first shock came a few days later when an old friend from their school days in Aberdeen, sent him a letter warning him that a most bitter attack was being prepared for him in the next edition of the *Edinburgh Review.*

> *"I have seen the proof of the critique. You know the system of the Edinburgh gentlemen is universal attack. They praise none that are not already established with the public and therefore also established in their own esteem."*

Byron could not understand it – why? It was not that his poetry was bad, he *knew* it was not, at least no worse than many others they had praised, so why were they selecting him, of all people, for such unfavourable criticism – or an *attack,* as his friend named it?

Then, strangely, and in a kind of panic, his worst

fears were the effect of such a review on his mother. However much *she* criticised him, she always appeared to find it unbearable when others did so. He had to warn her ... but not directly.

Instead he wrote to Reverend Becher who, despite the burning of his earlier poems, had remained in touch by regular letters and continued to encourage him as well as urging him to "refine your writings in a more *chaste* way."

"My Dear Reverend Becher,

I am happy that you still retain your fondness for me and you approve of my latest poetic collection, and although I had hoped that the public would allow me some share of their *praise also, I have heard that I am of so much importance that a most violent attack is prepared for me in the next number of the Edinburgh Review, but I am aware of it and hope you will not be hurt by its severity – nor my mother, whom I know always reads the Edinburgh Review.*

Please warn Mrs Byron and tell her not to be out of humour with them. Pray assure her that it will do no injury to me whatever, and I beg her mind will not be ruffled. They defeat their object by indiscriminate abuse, and they never praise anyone except those who are above their criticism.

Believe me, most truly, BYRON

When he read over the letter, he wished he felt more sanguine and careless than he was pretending. A failure now with his first publication, would be a failure forever. All other publishing doors would be shut to him in the future.

In the days that followed he found himself shrugging it all off and becoming more optimistic. Maybe his friend in Edinburgh had exaggerated? Maybe it was all a jest so that he would be relieved and even *more* delighted than he would have been when the review turned out to be an excellent one?

He was glad of the mental diversion when Scrope Davies and Matthews came to collect him for a swim in the Cam.

Bereft as he was now of Ned Long and John Eddleston to swim with, Scrope and Matthews had decided to take their places, laughingly boasting that within a few weeks both would become such serious swimming rivals to Byron that they possibly might even take the crown from *"the best swimmer in Cambridge."*

They had been swimming for no more than ten minutes when Byron noticed something very wrong with the way Matthews was traversing the water, and swam over to him.

"You are swimming with too much *effort* and labour and holding yourself *too high* out of the water. If you swim into any obstacles or come to a difficult pass you will be in trouble. Lower your eyes and lower your head."

"No, can't get my head wet," said Matthews, revealing yet another oddity. "Shoot over to the bank and get my hat will you?"

"What is it with you and your damned *head?"*

"Have you won any of the prizes at Trinity? Have *you* already won the Downing Prize?"

"No," Byron said, knowing that Matthews, being five

years older than himself, was already an intellectual supremo and one of the finest scholars in the place.

"So now you understand why I always protect my head – my *brain*. One must, you know, if the mind is where all the work is done."

"And one must learn to *swim* properly if one is in deep water," Byron chided. "Now here, let me swim beside you and show you in what ways you are doing it wrong."

"Oh, very well," Matthews agreed, "but not without my hat on. And if my head or my hat gets wet I will blame you for that, Byron."

Byron let his hands circle the water as he grinned teasingly at Matthews. "When you are making love to whomever you make love to, do you keep your hat on?"

"Only if there is a hole in the roof and it's raining. Now stop being personal and go and get my hat."

~~~

A few nights later, when the three friends called into Byron's rooms to join him for dinner, they found him in a such a state of agitation and rage, Scrope wondered if Byron had been challenged to a duel and was eager to get it done and over with, not knowing how else to account for the fierce anger in his eyes.

Challenges and duels in response to the smallest slight or insult were a fairly regular occurrence at Cambridge, and sometimes young men were killed, although most were only slightly injured in arm or leg.

It was Hobhouse who recognised a copy of the *Edinburgh Review* in Byron's hand and instantly knew that the devils had done their worst.

"What do they say?"

Byron held up the article and read:

> "*It is a sort of privilege of poets to be egotists,*

particularly one who piques himself (though indeed at the ripe age of nineteen) as "an infant bard"...

"And then, as to my *poems*, they say –" Byron read out — "*Viewing them as school exercises, they may pass.*" And the rest is just a litany of dismissive condescension."

Byron flung the review down in disgust.

Hobhouse felt for his friend; all three did. Byron's pride had been wounded to the quick, and his ambitions humbled. He had been so delighted by the praise in a few minor publications, but now he was writhing under the sneers of the highest.

And Hobhouse understood, even more than Scrope or Matthews did, that Byron's disposition would make him feel such condescension ten times more acutely than any other young poet.

Unlike others, who had loving families and hordes of relatives to comfort and support him in a crisis, Byron from childhood had always journeyed through the world alone, had always stood alone, without the roof of a single relative to receive him, save for a mother who gave him more grief than comfort.

"And do you see ... *do you see* ..." Byron pointed to the article now being read jointly by Scrope and Matthews — "They seem to believe that I am some sort of *Richard the Third* character, hobbling around on a club foot while scribbling puerile poetry!"

Hobhouse shook his head, silently enraged, while thinking it would be difficult for any sculptor or painter to imagine a subject of more incensed beauty than the face of the young poet now so alive and on fire in the burning energy of this unfair attack.

"I did warn you about that publication," Hobhouse

told him. "Their reviewers are brutal and give no quarter to newcomers."

"No *quarter!*" Byron snapped. "I shall give *them* no quarter in my reply."

"Best to ignore it," Scrope Davies advised. "Silent contempt is always best."

"No, Scrope!" Byron was insistent. "So many of these reviewers, who have never written a stanza or a book in their lives, sit on their backsides pontificating in judgement on the work of others, revelling in their power to praise or condemn. How mighty *their* egos! And what have *they* written — other than pompous and condescending cock-twiddling reviews on the shortcomings of others!"

"Oh, I say ..." Matthews looked at Scrope. "I did not know Byron possessed such a blazing temper, did you?"

"Other writers may be destroyed by them, but I intend to fight back!"

"If you write a letter in reply to their review of your book they will laugh at you," Hobhouse warned. "And they will be thrilled to know they have annoyed you, it will merely add to their own sense of importance."

"A letter? I have no intention of lowering myself to write those whores a letter," Byron said. "I intend to *ridicule* them in verse — in another book! That's the only way I can be sure the bastards will be forced to read it — to *review* it."

He cleared them all out and started to write straight away, while his rage was hot — fair criticism was acceptable, personal attacks on the author's age or anything else was not.

"So how to start my satire? By making clear my position, my stance ...

Prepare for rhyme — I'll publish right or wrong:
Fools are my theme, let Satire be my song.

Hobhouse returned, too worried to stay away.

"You are turning into my shadow, Hobby," Byron snapped. "Oh very well, stay, *stay* if you must, so long as you don't attempt to try to put me in a good mood because that would be impossible."

"It's your *anger* I'm concerned about," Hobhouse replied. "I would hate it to overwhelm you and get you into trouble."

"I don't give a damn about trouble. I've played it safe for too long, pretending to nod in praise when others acclaim drivel and rubbish. Now, right or wrong, I'm going to do what is expected of me and become a *rebellious youth* – a poet with an alternative voice to the usual poems about flowers in May."

"That's what I am afraid of," Hobhouse said, and then more gently, "Listen now, why don't you take some time to calm down, to reflect, to —"

"No! I do this now or I do *away* with myself! If I'm not a poet as they say – then what am I? What will I *ever* be if they stop me now? A limping idiot for others to deride and with nothing more to my name than a useless title."

Hobhouse was mature enough to realise that this was more than just a tantrum in response to wounded pride, this cut went deeper, much deeper.

He said quietly, "Have you always wanted to be a poet?"

"No, like most boys I wanted to be a *soldier*, to ride out and fight and win battles and all those other things which I soon learned would be impossible for me to do because of *this*." He slapped his right thigh. "But there is nothing wrong with my hands or my head or my heart – and I did not choose to be a poet – poetry has always *invaded* me and my mind without me ever wishing it."

"Then write," Hobhouse said, placing a calming hand on his shoulder. "Write, and keep on writing, until you prove the critics wrong."

Byron nodded. "I shall attack the critics through the bards they praise and praise, no matter how dull the poetry, whether the critics be bribed or be paid with high dinners, publishing and reviewing has always been a whoring game."

He looked at Hobhouse. "Which poet do the critics praise most, yet you dislike?"

Hobhouse gave it small thought. "Oh, it has to be William Hayley. I'm sure they only keep praising him because he's so rich and has influence in the higher echelons."

"Hayley? I agree! He sends me to sleep too."

Byron picked up his quill and began to write furiously: —

   "Behold – ye whores! – one moment spare the text,

"No, no!" Hobhouse exclaimed, looking over his shoulder. "You cannot call the critics *whores,* not in writing."

"Why not?

"At the very least, it's rude."

Byron looked at him. "Hobby, what other word, less rude, is there for prostitutes?"

"I only know one other word," said Hobhouse, "and I only know *that* because it is the word the townsmen use when referring to the street prostitutes here in Cambridge."

"So, what is it?"

"Tarts."

"That will do."

Byron's pen began to fly across the page —

   Behold! –ye tarts! – one moment spare the text
   On Hayley's last work, and worst – until his next.

Whether he spin poor couplets into plays,

Or damn the dead with purgatorial praise,

His style in youth or age is still the same,

For ever feeble and for ever tame.

And once Byron had begun, Hobhouse knew there was no stopping him, not until Francis Jeffrey, the reviewer of the *Edinburgh Review,* was slaughtered in two pages of satirical rhyme. And then he returned back to the highly-praised dull writers:

Another epic! Who inflicts again

More books of blank upon the sons of men?

Hobhouse left him to it, knowing Byron would continue to write throughout the night with no thought of sleep.

~ ~ ~

Ten days later, the first unfinished draft of Byron's manuscript of *English Bards and Scotch Reviewers* gave much laughter to his friends.

Although Hobhouse was very surprised at his poetic lampoon of Wordsworth:

Now comes the dull disciple of thy school,

That mild apostate from poetic rule,

The simple Wordsworth, framer of a lay

As soft as evening in his favourite May.

Thus, when he tells the tale of Betty Foy,

The idiot mother of 'an idiot boy';

A moon-struck, silly lad, who lost his way,

And, like his bard, confounded night with day;

So close on each pathetic part he dwells,

And each adventure so sublimely tells,

That all who view the 'idiot in his glory'

Conceive the bard the hero of the story.

"*His favourite May* ..." Scrope Davies laughed. "Although that particular month does seem to feature a lot in Wordsworth's poems."

"Of course, it will never be published," Hobhouse said. "No publisher will touch it."

"Not even a *brave* publisher?" Byron asked.

"There's no such thing," Scrope said scathingly. "Publishers are interested only in *profits* and regard their authors as no better than servants. None will take a chance on having an author ruin their reputation by publishing something as inflammatory as this."

"I think a *small* brave publisher might take that chance," Byron said"

"Well, even if you do send it out," Matthews advised, "I would not use your own name, I would use a pseudonym."

"Such as?"

They played around with pseudonyms for a while, until Hobhouse finally suggested, "How about *Anonymous.*"

~~~

Later that evening, at Byron's dinner table, when they had consumed three bottles of claret and all were feeling more tranquil, Hobhouse felt bound to say, "Poor old Wordsworth and his Betty Foy though. I thought you liked him, Byron."

"I did, but only mildly so; until when I was in London after leaving Harrow, I was introduced to a very eminent gentleman, who told me that he was —"

"Wait!" Scrope interrupted. "Is this a true story?"

"Yes."

"About Wordsworth?"

"Yes."

"One I can pass on?"

"Yes."

"Then pray continue."

"And this eminent gentleman told me he was such an admirer of Wordsworth," Byron continued, "that he invited the poet to dinner – whereupon Wordsworth – for all his talk of equality, turned out not to believe in it so much when it came to *conversation* – no equal shares. No, from one course to the next Wordsworth talked and talked, holding court like a king with a courtier, until by the time the bill was presented to this gentleman to be paid, he eventually left the table as *wordless* as when he had arrived. He told me he had not read another *word* of Wordsworth since."

Scrope and Matthews collapsed with laughter, but Hobhouse wanted to know more. "Come on, Byron, the story has no weight unless you tell us who that eminent gentleman was?

"That eminent gentleman was, and still is, Lord Harcourt. I met him when I went to collect my sister at his home in Portland Place."

Chapter Twenty-Eight

~ ~ ~

Ridge of Newark nervously declined to publish the manuscript of *English Bards and Scotch Reviewers*, as did Crosby of London.

"Then I will publish it myself," Byron decided. "I will prepare the finished text for a printer and pay him for his service, and then I will give the books to a bookseller in London to distribute and sell in return for the usual commission. That's what many other successful writers have done."

Later that year, Byron and his friends returned to London for a few weeks in the summer, staying at Dorant's Hotel off Piccadilly.

Byron had a particular reason for choosing a hotel in Piccadilly. He loved the area with all its shops, hotels, coffee houses and clubs. Its main glory though, was *Hatchards* Bookstore, a place he frequented often when in London and had spent a fortune within the store, as well as those fifty or sixty books he had ordered by post to be sent to him at Cambridge or Newstead.

The following morning he rose early and left the hotel as soon as all the shops had opened, too eager and too curious to wait any longer to see how his satire *On English Bards and Scotch Reviewers* was selling in the most prestigious bookstore in England, or even if they were stocking it.

It had been printed and distributed by James Cawthorn of London but he had not yet received a report from Cawthorns to tell him how well or *unwell* the book was doing, nor had he seen any London newspapers, although he was preparing to wince and shudder at *their* reviews, if indeed they bothered to review the book at all.

He strolled into Hatchards, which was fairly empty at this time of the morning, as casual in his browsing of the bookshelves as he had been in previous visits, browsing here, browsing there ... until finally he saw it – *On English Bards and Scotch Reviewers* – but only *one* copy of it ... just one lonely solitary copy. He blew out his breath in bitter disappointment.

He picked up the book and pretended to be casually browsing through it, while glancing sideways at the store assistant who was standing nearby, ready to assist; a young man he had not encountered in the past.

"This book ..." he said to the assistant, "the author is anonymous. How very strange. Do you have an idea who the author is?"

The young man swiftly glanced sideways left and right, as if wondering if he should tell. "Not for certain, sir, but there is a rumour going around that the author is Lord Byron of Newstead and Rochdale.

"Indeed? Lord Byron? Have you read it?"

"I have, sir," said the assistant, smiling. "I thought it very funny."

"Funny? How so?"

"Well, it is written with great wit, sir, and not in the *usual* poetic way."

"And yet you have just one copy?"

"Yes, sir, that's because —"

"*Lord Byron!*" The manager of the store came walking towards him with his hand held out, a smile beaming on his face. They had met numerous times before and were well acquainted.

"Well done, my lord, well done! The entire first edition of a thousand copies has sold out. We have sent to Cawthorns to supply more as quickly as possible." He looked at the book in Byron's hands. "That is my *own* copy. I was forced to put it there until we receive more, although *you* cannot buy it," he laughed. "It is there just to show our customers that we do stock it and will be getting more in if they wish to order it."

Byron was amazed. "How did people learn that I was the author?"

The manager waved the red-faced assistant away and lowered his voice: "Notwithstanding our precautions, you are pretty generally known to be the author. Whether that is due to some loose-tongued person at Cawthorns, I do not know."

"And you say it has sold out?"

"Yes, and all within three weeks since delivery. It seems that one gentleman bought and read it, told a friend, who then told another – until now it seems that all London wants to read it. Everyone thinks it is very funny, but my own opinion is that the book accords with the view of the public at large and you are saying what most people dare *not* say – that some of our most successful authors are sitting on their pinnacle of fame because cronies of the Literati have placed them there, and have *kept* them there."

He pretended to cough with a slight "ahem" and spoke behind the hand covering his mouth. "I fully agree with you about *Hayley*. But now, I have heard some more good news which I am only too happy to share with you."

"*More* good news?" The shock was dissolving and Byron was beginning to feel the first thrills of his success ... a thousand copies sold!

"This news will delight you," said the manager, clapping his hands together and looking delighted himself. "The Princess of Wales has read *English Bards* and was quite overwhelmed by it, declaring at a dinner party three nights ago in St James's Palace that it had '*the fire of genius*' in it."

Byron was stunned, floating on invisible wings all the way back to the hotel, although he presumed that his feet *must* have touched the ground or people would have stopped to stare at him floating along.

He went straight to Hobhouse's room and roughly shook him out of his sleep. "A thousand copies have sold, Hobby, a *thousand!*"

"What?" Hobhouse's eyes were blinking furiously. He looked at the clock. "Oh, good grief, it's only ten o'clock! Damn you, Byron. You know I never wake before noon on a holiday!"

"Did you hear what I said, Hobby? A thousand copies have sold."

"Of what?"

"My *boke* – English Bards."

"What? Oh, good grief ... a *thousand* copies. Oh, my head ..."

"They are asking for a second printing as soon as possible!"

"Well now, this is unbelievably wonderful!"

"Isn't it though?"

"I give you my congratulations, dear friend, congratulations, and well *deserved* I say." Hobhouse pushed back the bedclothes to sit on the side of the bed. "Have you told Scrope and Matthews?"

"Not yet," Byron grinned, "but I imagine they will be as eager to celebrate as I am."

~~~

When Hobhouse and Matthews were ready to return to Cambridge, Byron and Scrope Davies decided to remain in London a while longer – Scrope because he wanted to get back to the gaming tables, and Byron because he had become involved again with the "blue-eyed Caroline."

"Are you mad?" Hobhouse demanded.

Byron grinned. "No, well ... perhaps I could be a bit

maddi*sh*. And 'ish' means only very slightly."

"So when do you intend to return to Cambridge?"

"In a week or two."

"Good, because this is your final year and only a fool would neglect his studies and sacrifice his degree for the sake of a female."

"Hobby, I will be back at Cambridge in a week or two, I promise."

When a month had passed and still no sight of Byron at Cambridge, Hobhouse complained to Matthews: "He's as unreliable as a woman, as fickle as the wind, and all his promises are as uncertain as tomorrow's sun."

Two months later, Hobhouse was so alarmed at the news reaching Cambridge about Byron, he sat down in anger and wrote a stern letter of remonstration to him.

Dear Byron,

The story of your continued relationship with Miss – (I forget her name) – is all over Cambridge. I did not much wonder at it, considering yourself to be too frequent in the caresses of the first pretty girl which you chanced to light upon.

This life you have lately adopted – those nightly vigils and daily slumbers, that habit of agitating your mind and body in the pernicious exercise of midnight gambling, were they not enough, together with that total want of fresh air and healthy exercise, are enough to weaken and exhaust your frame.

It is because I have a regard for you that I have frequently wished to see you have done with such deleterious practices, so imprudent when practised by any one but especially by a person of your advantages.

I learn from Scrope that you have given up the dice. To be sure you must give it up. For you to be seen every night in the clubs with the vilest company in town! Could anything be more shocking? Anything more unfit? I speak feelingly on this occasion. You shall henceforth be "non ignara mali miseris"

I suppose it is no longer your intention to return to Cambridge. I shall never again have the pleasure of seeing you – nothing could be more unexpected by me

I am going to Eton this evening with Tavistock until Sunday, by which time I will be gratified to receive one line from you.

Farewell, and believe me,
Yours most sincerely
John C. Hobhouse

This letter of rebuke from Hobhouse had a sobering effect on Byron who, without more ado, broke off his relationship with Caroline Cameron, and returned to Cambridge.

Chapter Twenty-Nine

~ ~ ~

In the spring of 1808 Francis Hodgson commenced his residence at Cambridge as a Fellow and a tutor of King's College.

He had been a close friend of Scrope Davies at Eton during their schooldays and now at Cambridge the two quickly resumed their old friendship. Yet within a very short time the friend that Hodgson became the most intimate with was Byron, the youngest of the exclusive group of four.

Francis Hodgson was the one friend Scrope Davies had always insisted upon visiting during their regular visits down to London, where Hodgson also spent many of his vacations, continually engaged in literary pursuits, and where he had first met Byron.

Although six years older than the young poet, and having published two volumes of poetry himself, the attraction of Hodgson and Byron was instant and mutual. A love of history, of philosophy, and above all, poetry, were enough in themselves to provide endless subjects for discussion.

There were many points of resemblance in their characters and enough of a difference to produce harmony. Added to which both were high-spirited and warm-hearted, and genial in company; but both were also equally subject to periods of melancholy and depression in their private thoughts – a trait which each recognised in the other.

And yet, unfathomably to Hodgson, having read Byron's *Hours of Idleness* and secretly nicknamed him *'the poet of pain'* was his amazement at Byron's propensity for laughter and his inclination to see the funny side of everything.

No subject, no situation so dire enough to cause glum faces in the others, ever ended without Byron seeing the funny side and eventually reducing them all to his own hilarious laughter.

And now Hodgson was here, at Cambridge, and Byron's delight was enough to cause Hobhouse to say grumpily to Scrope Davies – "Anyone would think it was the Second Coming of Christ instead of a mere tutor."

"You dislike him solely because he is handsome, but now that you mention Christ," Scrope said seriously, "I think you should know, because I don't think you would have detected it in London, Hodgson is a very religious and *Christian* young man."

Hobhouse was astounded. "Religious?"

"Oh yes, his father and grandfather were both Reverends of the Church, and I believe Hodgson intends to take Holy Orders himself in the future."

"Then I doubt he will have much time for us," Hobhouse said more cheerfully, "because *we* are all avowed atheists – including Byron."

"You think so?" Scrope was not so sure. "At times I have found myself suspecting that Byron is not so avowed in his atheism as he pretends to be."

"Oh, nonsense. Why would he pretend to be something he is not?"

"Possibly to please Matthews," Scrope shrugged. "You know what a publicly-avowed atheist Matthews is. And Byron has such affection for Matthews, and such respect for his intellect, that he hates to disagree with him, especially on a subject that Matthews feels so fervently about."

Hobhouse gave a small, sneering laugh. "Do you honestly think that Byron, of all people, would *pretend* to be an atheist for the sole reason of not hurting

Matthews?"

Scrope's face was still serious and thoughtful. "I think Byron would pretend to be anything rather than hurt one of his friends."

"I thought you told me recently that Hodgson had been made an assistant Master at Eton?"

"I did, last year, but before his first year as a Master was up, Hodgson was offered this post at Cambridge, and so here he is."

"How old is he?"

"A year older than me, twenty-six."

Scrope suddenly looked at Hobhouse and laughed with amusement. "Cheer up, Hobby, I doubt the company of your blue-eyed boy has been snatched away from you completely."

"Oh, tripe! As if I would care," Hobhouse growled. "His company is more a nuisance than friendship. Do you know, Scrope, he is now driving me mad with his constant demands that I learn how to *swim*."

~ ~ ~

As the months passed Hobhouse slowly became as fond of Francis Hodgson as Scrope Davies and Byron, considering him to be a wise and kind-hearted fellow of great learning, who allowed others to hold their own opinions without any attempt to change them. He was also very good company with great humour and, in many ways his turn of wit was very similar to that of Scrope Davies.

During those same months the friendship of Byron and Francis Hodgson became even closer, with Hodgson becoming his younger friend's *mentor* in all things, not just poetry and academics, but some of his most private confidences, including his unhappy relationship with his mother.

"I can still remember, even though a small child," Byron said one night after they had shared dinner, "my first feelings of pain and humiliation were given to me by my mother. The coldness with which she received my caresses in infancy, and her frequent taunts about my infirmity wounded me so much that one day, although I did not answer her, I bit straight through a china saucer with my teeth and broke it."

Hodgson, for the life of him, could not even begin to understand how a mother could make taunts about an impairment in a child *she* had given birth to.

Yet now he was beginning to understand the affectionate enthusiasm with which Byron had thrown himself into his boyish friendships at Harrow, and why he still corresponded regularly with those friends as if they were treasures he did not want to lose.

"It's true," Byron admitted, "the affection of my friends means everything to me, and my affection for them can never be challenged. But love ..." he smiled ruefully, "love is something I no longer hope for or even want. Affection is my utmost."

"But why?" Hodgson asked with puzzlement. "You are still so young, and one day you will meet a young lady whom you will fall in love with and who — "

"No, no," Byron insisted, "that will never happen, because I have already met her, the love of my life, but now she is married to another – a man who can hop, skip and jump like a ballet dancer."

Hodgson detected the sarcasm in Byron's voice, but as he too had been crossed in love by a female only a few months earlier and was still feeling sore-hearted about it, he felt sympathy, and decided it was time to open another bottle of claret as they talked on.

So Byron confided to him about his all-absorbing love for Mary Chaworth.

"All my poetry is about her," Byron said quietly. "All

and any tenderness or light in the sentences comes from the very soul of my feelings for *her*. She was and still is my *beau idéal,* my first and favourite, and will remain so until the last day of my life."

Hodgson compressed his lips together, fighting back a smile, certain that Byron was being over-romantic and over-dramatic about his love for the girl; not knowing that in the years ahead Byron was to prove him wrong by flinging a halo of his love and his genius around her, immortalising his "Mary" in some of the greatest works of poetry ever written in the English language.

~ ~ ~

In the summer of 1808 Francis Hodgson accepted Byron's invitation to spend a few days with him and Hobhouse at Newstead, fairly relishing the opportunity to see the bedrooms where kings of old had slept in the past; while Hobby was more excited about the prospect of a good hunt in the Sherwood Forest with a long gun in his hands.

As soon as they entered the house, Joe Murray greeted Byron with a sorrowful face.

"It's bad news, my lord, but sadly I have to tell you that I believe we have lost Sydney."

"Sydney? Are you sure?"

"Well, no, I can't be sure for certain, but I believe we must now accept that he *has* perished, somewhere in your rabbit warren, for we have seen nothing of him at all for the past three weeks."

As the sorrowful conversation between Byron and his servant continued, Hobhouse and Hodgson glanced at each other, both feeling very uncomfortable indeed.

As soon as Joe Murray was out of earshot Hobhouse remonstrated with their host:

"Now look here, Byron, this has put Hodgson and myself in a very difficult position. Tomorrow morning we were hoping to go out on a hunt and shoot bullets into as many foxes and rabbits as we can find, but how can we do that now – faced as we are with you and your household all lamenting over a rabbit who died *naturally* in his own warren?"

Byron sighed. "You don't understand. Sydney was not one of a thousand wild rabbits, he was our pet, and a long-standing beloved member of this household. And he was *more* than just a rabbit, he was a *character*, and with a personality not dissimilar to my own."

Hobhouse and Hodgson looked at each other and burst out laughing. "You mean he was a poetic rabbit? " Hobby laughed.

"No, he was very shy," Byron responded, "but if you are going to laugh about it –" Byron's petulant expression suddenly changed to absolute delight as the sudden din of barking brought Boatswain racing up to him, jumping up and almost knocking him backwards.

"Boatswain!"

As the two men stood watching Byron and his dog lovingly devouring each other, Hobhouse said to Hodgson, "You see how quickly Sydney is forgotten? Now you are seeing the *real* Byron. He's exactly the same with women; his heartbreak over one immediately vanishes as soon as another just as pretty comes into view."

"That's not true, Hobby, and you know it." Byron straightened, but his hand was still on Boatswain's head.

"Boatswain, you have my permission to ignore Mr Hobhouse for the duration of his stay here, have nothing to do with him ... but I want you now to say hello to Mr Hodgson."

Still panting excitedly, Boatswain looked up at Hodgson, and then lifted his paw to him.

Hodgson did not respond, because his eyes were fixed

in fear on a second dog that was standing silently further down the passage, a dog that had the look of a wolf about it, and his eyes were staring balefully at Byron's back.

When Byron again bent his head towards Boatswain the second dog growled and charged, sinking his teeth into Byron until the ripping sound of his breeches being torn out made him yell out with shock.

He turned and stared at his attacker with disbelief. "Woolly!"

Woolly was cautiously backing away now because Boatswain had turned to face him with a low growl, and then Hodgson and Hobhouse jumped back as pandemonium erupted in a dog-fight that brought Joe Murray and Fletcher running into the hall, both carrying pokers.

"My God," said Hodgson, his hands clinging fearfully to Hobhouse's arm, "what are they going to do with those pokers?"

Byron grabbed the poker from Fletcher's hands and bravely managed to pull Woolly's head back until he had inserted the poker between his snarling teeth, while Joe Murray did the same to Boatswain.

Fletcher quickly took over from Byron again, and he and Joe, still holding onto the pokers, pulled the two dogs away in opposite directions, one towards the front of the house and the other towards the back.

"Until they calm down," Joe said to Byron, "But I have *warned* you about Woolly's jealousy."

When the dogs had gone, Byron turned to his two friends, his eyes wide with incredulity. "Did you see that? He tore the backside out of my breeches!"

Neither man answered, still in shock from the violence, Byron looked backwards and put his hand to the torn parts of his breeches. "I never thought I would see the day ... since I was ten years old that dog has loved me, but now I am twenty years old, he has decided to *eat* me."

"You will have to have him shot," Hobhouse snapped. "And have it done quickly."

"Have him shot?" Byron stared. "Don't be silly, Hobby, why would I do a cruel thing like that? I'll sort Woolly out in my own way."

Francis Hodgson was immensely relieved when the housekeeper arrived, full of apologies for the behaviour of the dogs, and offering to show them up to their rooms.

She delayed only to hand Byron a small towel to cover the area of his body where his breeches were torn, but he refused it.

"I don't care who sees my backside, I need to go and talk to Woolly."

As they followed the housekeeper up the stairs, Hodgson quietly asked Hobhouse, "Is it always like this here? A madhouse of dead rabbits and fighting dogs?"

"Oh, this is just the beginning," Hobby replied. "You have not met his *bear* yet. And then there's Smut, his bulldog. He also lodges here now."

"And *Apropos,*" Nanny Smith said. "That's another small bulldog he rescued from God knows where. He really must stop doing it."

When they had reached the landing she turned and gave them both a reassuring smile. "Now you really have no need to worry. The animals are usually very calm and content. It's only when his lordship first arrives home that they get too excited. And you should know, if he has not already told you, that he and Woolly have been together since they were both very young pups, his lordship was only ten at that time. And he brought Boatswain home when he was still at Harrow and only fifteen."

"How do the two dogs get along when Byron is not

here?" Hobhouse asked.

"No rivalry at all, but these days Woolly prefers to keep to himself in his favourite spot in the old cloisters."

At the open doors to their adjoining rooms, Nanny finally advised them, "Now take time to relax and catch your breath before washing and changing for dinner, which should be ready in about an hour."

She looked at Hodgson. "In the meantime, is there anything in the way of refreshment I can send up to you?"

"Oh yes," Hodgson answered quickly. "A glass of brandy would be greatly appreciated."

"Brandy?"

Hodgson nodded. "Just a large one."

Nanny Smith smiled. "And the same for you, Mr Hobhouse?"

"Yes please, but make mine a very *large*, large one."

~~~

Considering the strange and disappointing beginning of his visit to Newstead, Francis Hodgson was delightfully surprised by the wonderful time that followed.

After a long and sumptuous dinner that night, Byron decided it was too late and too dark to show Hodgson around the huge house, and suggested they take their wine into the library.

Hodgson immediately noticed that the bookcases around the library walls were all filled to capacity with books, and after only a few minutes of browsing he quickly realised he was looking at a treasure-trove of some of the finest books of antiquity ever printed.

Here was a room, he thought, where a man who was also a scholar could relax and feel at home. A large fire was burning in the marble fireplace, the leather armchairs gleamed from regular polishing and the wooden tables glowed in the flickering lights of the flames and candles.

Boatswain, who had sat quietly by the table throughout dinner, also accompanied them into the library, sitting himself down peacefully in front of the fire, while his eyes kept devoted surveillance on every move his master made.

They drank and relaxed and talked late into the night, and as always there were bouts of laughter. Only one dark shadow was cast over the night, and that was when Byron, holding a glowing candelabra, escorted them up to their rooms and deftly used it to light the candles inside the two bedrooms.

"Oh, one thing I must tell you," he said to Hodgson. "If you wish to go downstairs during the night, don't be alarmed if you look over your shoulder and see the ghost of a monk in black robes following you."

"What!" Hodgson almost jumped out of his skin. "You mean ... this house has *ghosts?*"

"Only one," Byron assured him. "The Friar."

"The Friar?"

"Yes, I know he is the Friar because of his black robes whereas all the other monks would have worn brown. But if you see him," Byron warned, "say naught to him as he walks around, and he will say naught to you."

"You have *seen* ... this ghost?"

"Many times. He walks from room to room and from hall to hall. I may be the lord of Newstead by day, but the monk is the lord by night."

"My God, this is worse than the dogs!" Hodgson had started to shiver, until Hobhouse walked through the open door of the bedroom carrying a candle that he held close to Byron's face so that Hodgson could clearly see the laughter in his eyes.

"He pulls this prank on everyone," Hobhouse said impatiently. "*He* thinks it's funny, but no one else does. Go to bed, Byron."

A sudden sound from the dimly-lit landing made Hodgson jump with fright and Byron laugh. "It's only Boatswain. He always sleeps in my room when I am home."

Hodgson was still feeling unnerved; as a spiritual man he believed in the everlasting life of the spirit. "So are there, or are there not, *ghosts* in this place?"

"You will sleep as sound and as safe as a babe surrounded by hushing angels," Byron assured him.

And Hodgson did.

When Hobhouse woke him the next morning to get ready for their early-morning shoot, Hodgson felt as refreshed and as peaceful as if he had slept in the arms of God himself.

And from then on it was all fun. After a delicious breakfast of ham and eggs and black coffee, followed by the priming of the guns, Hodgson and Hobhouse were about to set off with the gamekeepers when Byron came rushing out to them, still wearing his nightshirt.

"Take Boatswain with you."

To Hobhouse, this was an unusual request. "Why so?"

"I want to spend some time alone with Woolly. I'll take him over to visit my mother. Even Woolly shrinks into timidity in her presence."

"Are you still certain you will not come with us?" Hodgson asked.

"Me? Shoot a poor animal?" Byron looked disgusted.

"And yet you would not hesitate to shoot a man if called out in a duel," Hobhouse retorted wearily. "Such hypocrisy! Come along, Boatswain, come along."

The dog looked reluctant, until Byron gave him the order to "Go!" Yet even then, it was Francis Hodgson that Boatswain chose to trot beside.

"You see, Hobby, even Boatswain is wary of you!" Byron said laughing.

"As if I care," Hobhouse growled back. "Say a prayer I

don't shoot him by accident."

Byron was so confident that Hobhouse would not harm a hair on Boatswain, that minutes later he sent *Smut* and *Apropos* to join them, watching the two small bulldogs galloping away like scamps.

Joe Murray came out to join him, draping a dressing-gown over his shoulders.

"Woolly is fine now, back to normal," Joe said. "But you have to remember that he is an *old* dog now, and prone to be cantankerous in his moods. Do you think it wise to take him over to your mother's?"

Byron smiled and turned back to the house. "I wouldn't dare go over there without him, Joe. If I have Woolly with me she will get rid of us quickly, but at least she will be unable to complain to all Southwell that I did not visit her while in Nottingham."

"What I cannot understand," Joe said with puzzlement, "is how she always *knows* – even from twelve miles away – that you are here on a visit?"

Byron agreed. "That is puzzling, isn't it?"

"And it's become even more puzzling to me," Joe said, "since you told me that you always travel well clear of Southwell on your journeys down here. So how does she always *know*? And know so quickly?"

"The answer is obvious," Byron realised. "We have a traitor in our camp. One of the maids perhaps?"

"No, never." Joe was certain. "But I'll not rest now until I find out who. And if and when I do find out, do I have your permission to dismiss that person on the spot?"

"You do. If it is someone employed at Newstead then they work for *me,* and not my mother. So let any dismissal of yours in my absence be a lesson to others."

~ ~ ~

Later that morning, when Hodgson and Hobhouse

returned from their shoot, they eventually found Byron on the waters of the front lake, reclining in a boat and reading a book, with Woolly by his side, while allowing the boat to drift about wherever it may.

"He often does this," Nanny Smith said. "Sometimes he stays out there reading for hours, but I'll call him in now, and once you two have changed out of your hunting clothes, all three of you can sit down to a nice luncheon."

After lunch Byron was eager to take Hodgson to meet his beloved bear.

"Hobby is still afraid of Bruin, but he is the gentlest bear in the world," Byron assured Hodgson, and ducked into the kitchen to collect a tray of Cook's biscuits.

Arriving at Bruin's compound, Hodgson saw that it was quite a grand affair for an animal. The bear had his own wooden hut to sleep in, as well as a tree house, and all kinds of oddments to play with.

As soon as Byron entered through the door of the compound's wiring, the tray of biscuits was knocked out of his hand as the bear jumped on him with a growl and brought him to the ground.

Hodgson was immediately alarmed, but Hobhouse merely sighed with exasperation. "Those two always greet each other with a scrap. I find it exhausting just to watch them."

Byron and Bruin were now wrestling together on the ground, and Byron was laughing. "It's just our way of making love," he said to Hodgson, and then imitated Bruin's growl and the two were wrestling again.

"He's a strange animal, is he not," said Hobhouse.

Hodgson had to agree. "I must admit, this is my first sight of a *real* bear. I didn't know they could be so playful."

"I was referring to Byron," said Hobhouse. "Have you ever met anyone like *him* before?"

Hodgson had to laugh, and was equally surprised at the sudden meekness of Bruin when Byron took him by the paw and slowly walked him over to the wiring where his two friends stood. The bear was only as high as Byron's elbow and Hodgson saw he was still very young.

"Bruin, say hello to Mr Hodgson." Byron pointed, and Bruin sniffed Hodgson through the wire.

"Do you like him, Bruin, do you like our Hodgson?"

Bruin dropped down on all fours and found one of the biscuits scattered over the ground, picked one up in his mouth, brought it back and offered it to Hodgson who was utterly amazed.

"Take it," Byron said, "take the biscuit or Bruin will think you don't like him."

Hodgson slowly took the biscuit. "I'm not expected to eat it, am I?"

"No, but don't throw it away until after we have left."

"Don't ask him to give *me* a biscuit," Hobhouse said. "I wouldn't touch a biscuit that has been in a bear's mouth!"

Bruin had already lolloped away to fetch another biscuit, lolloping back and offering it to Hobhouse, who backed away in disgust.

"Me, Bruin, give it to *me.*" Byron bent down and took the biscuit from Bruin's mouth with his teeth and promptly ate it."

"Oh, good grief, did you really *have* to do that!" Hobhouse was appalled.

"I did it to protect his feelings from being hurt by *you*. If you dislike animals so much, Hobby, then why on earth do you keep coming here?"

"To shoot them of course! Not to share food with them."

Byron was not listening, because now he and Bruin were dancing together in a waltz, and Bruin being a bear and Byron having a limp, made it a very funny spectacle for Hodgson to watch; although he could see the dance was something that Bruin and Byron had obviously done many times before.

Even Hobhouse was laughing.

When the dance ended, Bruin threw back his head and made a low gutteral roaring sound in the back of his throat. "He wants to dance on," Byron said, and the two of them danced around inelegantly again.

"When I found him," Byron said over his shoulder to Hodgson, "he had been discarded because his owner's intention was to train him as a 'dancing bear' for a travelling circus, but poor Bruin proved so clumsily inept he was discarded and put up for sale. So here you see –*two* bad dancers together."

Before leaving the compound, Byron lost himself in a long affectionate bear hug with Bruin, while Hodgson and Hobhouse listened to Bruin purring like a contented kitten.

"He's adorable," Hodgson said as they walked away, and then looked back to see that Bruin had climbed up into the tree to stare after Byron as he departed.

"Ah, he's still watching you," he said, but Byron did not look back. "It will upset him if I do," he said, "but once we are out of sight he will gather up all the biscuits and eat them, and then go into his house for a short sleep to recover from his exertions."

"Wrestling and dancing with a bear ..." Hobhouse shook his head. "No observer would ever believe that you are a Cambridge man, Byron."

Byron looked at him sharply. "I'm not a Cambridge man, Hobby, I'm my own man and I live by my *own* rules."

Hodgson laughed. "Yes, Byron, I think the Dean would agree with you there."

~~~

That afternoon Hodgson finally got his wish to be shown around the rest of the Abbey. "It will take at least an hour," Byron warned him, "but you may as well see it now before the builders arrive."

"Builders?"

"Yes, in another few weeks this place will be filled with workmen making improvements to the house in readiness for my living here after I leave Cambridge. And then, come January, when I reach my majority at twenty-one, there will be no more having to go hat in hand to John Hanson, no more needing the approval of Lord Carlisle or the Court of Chancery – I will legally be a *man* who answers to no one."

"Apart from your mother," Hobhouse said. "Will you not be allowing her to live here with you when you take up full residence?"

"Yes ... yes ... I will be duty-bound to do that," Byron replied, "but I have already come up with a solution." He smiled mischievously. "Come outside and I will show you."

When the three were standing outside the front of the Abbey, Byron said: "As you know, the house is built in a square with a courtyard in the middle..." He pointed towards the far corner of the South-East wing at the *back* of the house.

"That wing there – I intend to have refurbished in the grandest style for my mother. She has already told me that she wishes to have a *green* damask drawing-room and a *red* velvet bedroom, and have them she will – including her own dining room and staircase and gardens and everything else."

He turned round. "But my own private apartments will be there — " he pointed to the opposite end of the front of the house, "in the North-West wing – with all the rooms and corridors and the length of the Abbey between us. I won't even be able to hear her when she's thundering abuse at one or other of the servants."

Hodgson could still not help feeling somewhat sad about the relationship between Byron and his mother. His own mother had died when he was fifteen and he still had tender memories of her, and still possessed great love for her.

They moved back inside and up to the first floor of the house and walked along the length of the gallery leading to the Grand Drawing Room, which was seventy foot in length and forty foot wide.

"Now you see why we did not relax in here last night," Byron said to Hodgson. "It's far to big for companionship."

"You could use it as a ballroom," Hobhouse said. "It's certainly large enough."

Hodgson's eyes were moving over the oak-panelled walls and oak girders on the ceiling, finally staring at each of the three magnificent long windows that lighted the length of the Drawing Room. On the walls hung portraits of Henry the Eighth and Queen Catherine Parr and other royals.

"And you say *kings* have stayed here?"

"So I am told, and so they must have," Byron replied, taking them on to show Hodgson *'King Charles The Second's Bedroom'* in which a portrait of His Majesty still hung on the wall. The State four-poster bed was huge with hangings of French tapestry at each corner post; and on the bed itself was a coverlet that Byron said had been worked on by Mary Queen of Scots.

"That's the only thing in this room that I like," Byron said, "the coverlet embroidered by our own Queen Mary of the Scots"

"It's all very interesting," Hodgson said as they continued their tour, "and despite its age it has a strange and peaceful charm about it. Last night I slept like a babe in arms."

Byron smiled. "It was a house devoted to God and prayer for many centuries. Perhaps that's why it always feels so peaceful here."

Byron then took them along the Western corridor, which led to his own apartments, remote from all the other rooms in the house.

"This is where we dined last night," Hodgson said, a little confused because they had been walking around the square of the building until he did not know where he was.

"Yes, in my own private dining room; and then we went down a few steps, and then up another few steps into the library."

Hodgson nodded. "And all so confusing."

Byron opened a door to reveal a stone spiral staircase and led them up to a door that opened into his dressing room, which had another door on the far side opening into his bedroom.

"This part is all very secret, isn't it?" Byron grinned.

Hodgson stood looking around the bedroom with some puzzlement, his eyes moving from the dressing table on which there were the usual toilet accessories; the desk over by the window on which ink and pens and a sheaf of papers lay; the four-poster bed and the rest of the furniture ... it was only a very moderately-sized apartment, and certainly smaller than the bedroom he himself had slept in the night before.

He said curiously to Byron: "Of all the large bedrooms you have to choose from, why did you choose this bedroom for yourself?"

Byron smiled. "The window. It has the best view in the house ... take a look."

Hodgson moved over to the wide oriel window and instantly understood ... From here, he had a perfect view of the calm blue lake, clear as crystal, its borders overhung with water-loving trees, disturbed only by the sound of the waterfall.

And beyond, was the boundless grandeur of Sherwood Forest, above which towered a number of green hills ... and further afar off he could see the turrets and spires of the distant town ... all of which, viewed from the window by day was truly enchanting ... and by night, under moonlight, this landscape would obviously possess a haunting beauty ... a perfect window for a poet to stand at night and allow his mind to wander and be inspired.

He turned and looked at Byron, who was smiling slightly, as if knowing his thoughts; but just as quickly in his usual way, Byron's manner became flippant as he pointed to his dressing-room: "Now *that* is the room where the Friar slept in the monastery days. The 'guardian of the Abbey who refuses to leave', and many a night he strolls through that wall of my dressing-room to join me at the window and gaze out."

Hodgson stared at him.

"He has no ill intent, and his spirit towards me is good and kind. I have no fear of him."

Hodgson was still staring. "I thought you said there were no *ghosts* here!"

"I did not say that – Hobby did."

"Because it's true," Hobhouse said irascibly to Hodgson. "Despite what he says, I know for certain that if there were any ghosts here, Byron would be the *first* to run out of here in fright."

Byron laughed his amused laugh, and then led the way down to the cloisters.

"That's the *main* thing I shall miss about Byron when we leave Cambridge and go our separate ways," Hobhouse muttered to Hodgson as they followed down the stairs ... "that peculiar laughter of his."

"Peculiar?"

"Yes, as if all the world's a comedy and everyone in it

is absurd. Haven't you noticed? The way he turns *everything* into a jest?"

"Well, not everything ..."

"You must admit though, he is seldom serious for long."

Hodgson turned away and pretended interest in a painting on the staircase, surprised at Hobby's lack of insight. It was true that Byron was excellent company and often in a laughing mood with his chosen friends, just as he was often distant and silent with strangers. But it was also true that his vulnerability to depression and melancholy, so deep-rooted in his nature, was often profound and pervasive. The fact that he made no attempt to reconcile these two sides of his personality was, in Hodgson's view, what made Byron such an *original*, and potentially great poet.

Later that evening, dressed for dinner and tired of waiting around, Hobhouse wandered up the secret staircase to Byron's rooms and found him in his dressing-room, shaving.

"Good grief ... what are you doing?" Hobby said in shock, because Byron was not shaving his face, but the front of his hairline on the left side of his brow.

"Just half an inch or so," Byron responded, unperturbed, "and just on this left side."

"But why?" Hobby could not comprehend it. "Most males are terrified if their hairline recedes a fraction, but you are deliberately receding yours! So why?"

"To make me look older and less pretty, but more to look *older* than anything else."

"And how long, pray, have you been doing that?"

"Since I was sixteen or so. From the first week I met my Mary. Did I tell you she was older than me?"

"That was back then, so why are you still doing it now?"

Byron smiled as he rinsed the razor in the bowl. "I

stopped for a while, during my last term at Harrow. But when I was preparing to go to Cambridge I started again, knowing I would have to compete with *highbrows* like yourself, Hobby."

"You're mad."

"Have you noticed what a fine high brow Matthews has? They say a high brow proves intelligence, and Matthews has proved that, has he not?"

"Matthews is only intelligent in an *academic* sense. In all other ways he's a fool, and so it seems are you."

"Matthews is not a fool in *any* respect. So why would you say he is?"

"Because I know him better than you do," Hobhouse shrugged, and then despairingly shook his head. "I'm surrounded by mad men! I have one friend who likes to wear his hat, even at dinner, to cover his high brow, and another friend who shaves part of his hairline to make his brow higher. And then there's my other friend, Scrope – *he* don't care how high or low his hairline is, because he's always too busy gambling."

"What about Hodgson?" Byron grinned. "I doubt you could find much fault with him."

Hobhouse found a lot of fault with Hodgson at dinner later that evening, because the man absolutely refused to join in his jolly mockery of Byron's vanity in shaving his hairline.

Francis Hodgson lifted his glass and sipped his wine, no longer fooled by it all, and thinking it very sad that throughout their stay here, poor Hobhouse had kept up his usual jibing and cutting sarcasm in an effort to conceal – possibly even from himself – his love for Byron.

Oh, not in a homoerotic way, of that Hodgson was certain, but it was *love* nevertheless ... an emotion so alien to Hobhouse that he was clearly finding it very hard to understand and cope with ... another poor soul who had never encountered the emotion of love in his home or boyhood years.

Chapter Thirty

~ ~ ~

Later that summer, Byron graduated with his M.A. degree and was preparing to leave Trinity College for the last time. Hobhouse had already left and had held his celebration the night before, but there were still a few engagements for Byron to fulfil in the following days.

On his way out, he remembered he had to write replies to two letters before he became too busy or too intoxicated to do so — returning to his desk and dashed off two notes.

My dear Augusta, — I return you my best thanks for making me an uncle, and I forgive the sex this time; but the next must be a nephew.

As you ask, I do not know that much alteration has taken place in my person, except that I am grown somewhat taller.

I hope you are quite recovered. I shall be in town soon, and will call, if convenient for you.

As always, your affectionate brother – BYRON

Embarrassment was his main sentiment as he began his second reply, to Elizabeth Pigot, his Southwell friend and regular correspondent, whose letters he had woefully neglected to reply to for some time.

My dear Elizabeth,—"Better late than never, pal," is a saying of which you know the origin, and as it is applicable on the present occasion I hope you will excuse its conspicuous place on the front of my letter.

My friends (with the exception of a very few) are all departed, and I am preparing to follow them but I remain till Monday to be present at two concerts.

On Monday I depart for London. I will quit Cambridge with little regret, because my life here has been one continued routine of dissipation, out at different places every day, engaged to more dinners, etc., etc., than my time here would permit me to fulfil.

I have been awkward in my habiliments of late for want of practice. Got up in a window to hear the oratorio at St Mary's, popped down in the middle of the MESSIAH, tore a woeful rent in the back of my best black silk gown and damaged an egregious pair of breeches. Mem. — never tumble from a church window during service.

Adieu, do not remember me to anybody in Southwell.

Yours etc, BYRON

~ ~ ~

On Sunday Mrs Byron, as usual, attended the morning service at the church in Hucknall, where she frequently spent most of her time silently admonishing God for a whole host of things she thought He could have done a whole lot better.

But today, on this glorious sunny Sunday, she was

more than thankful to Him for her son's graduation and becoming a Cambridge scholar. Now he would return to live in Nottingham and restore his mother to her rightful place as the mistress of Newstead Abbey.

"Praise the Lord!" she answered loudly in response to the vicar's prayer.

On leaving the church, at the door, she rebuked the vicar for the organ being out of tune, but very mildly so; and then she took a short walk around the church's front garden to inspect the roses, smiling and speaking graciously to everyone who crossed her path, except for a few village folk whom she ignored.

Then she returned to her carriage and headed back home to prepare for her afternoon tea-party in the garden.

As always, she dressed very carefully when entertaining visitors, wearing her finest damson silk gown, followed by a buff-coloured Duchess of Devonshire wide-brimmed hat in order to protect her face from the sun. The sun always coloured her cheeks the same red as the roses.

At two o'clock precisely, all her ladies arrived on time, for none would dare to be late, although all were wonderingly curiously as to Mrs Byron's 'special reason' for hosting this gathering.

There were ten ladies in all, seated around a large circular table in the centre of the lawn, and once all had their tea-cups in their hands and before they had a chance to sample from the platters of delicious-looking cakes, they found out the reason for this special event.

Mrs Byron, they now knew, had gathered them all together so they could sit comfortably and listen attentively while she sang out the praises of her noble son.

"A Cambridge scholar! Is there any other mother on this earth who would not feel as *proud* as I do today?"

"Oh, certainly," all agreed, and kept on agreeing, well they had to: she was, after all, the mother of their Lord of The Manor.

"My George has such a good heart. A very *kind* heart."

Even silently, none could disagree with that, for they had seen no evidence to the contrary.

"And his talents are *great*. One day he will be a *great* man."

"Are you referring to his poetry, Mrs Byron?"

"His poetry? Why, that's nothing more than a *leisure* pursuit! A mere diversion from his more serious ambitions. No, I am referring to his potential talents as a *legislator*. You know, of course, that in January when he reaches his majority of twenty-one years, he will be officially taking his seat in the Palace of Westminster, in the House of Lords?"

Mrs Pigot sat sipping her tea, thinking how mortified with embarrassment Byron would be if he could witness this outrageous display of boasting from his mother. And knowing them both so well, she could not help wondering why Mrs Byron never revealed any of these motherly feelings of pride to her son.

Chapter Thirty-One

~ ~ ~

Now that his Cambridge days were over, Byron spent most of August and September busily organising the renovations to Newstead Abbey, occasionally escaping the noise of the workmen by trips down to London to spend time with Scrope Davies in the clubs; although now he was always a spectator at the gaming tables and never a player.

During one of these evenings, while he was standing at one of the tables viewing a game, Byron noticed a gentleman carefully watching him. He was tall, fair-haired, very handsome and exquisitely dressed, aged somewhere in his late twenties or very early thirties.

Sipping a glass of champagne, he appeared to be observing every detail of Byron with the eyes of a scrutineer.

At the end of the game, Byron said quietly to Scrope Davies, "That gentleman over there has been watching me very attentively. Do you know who he is?"

Scrope looked around, and grinned, "That's 'the Beau'! George Brummell. A gaming friend of mine."

Seeing he was being talked about, 'the Beau' approached them with a stern face. "Scrope, pray grant me a formal introduction to your friend."

Scrope was happy to oblige, and did so very formally, "Mr George Brummell, allow me to introduce you to my dear friend, Lord Byron."

"*Lord* Byron?" Brummell smiled. "Ah, that explains it. Tell me, Lord Byron, who is your tailor?"

Annoyed at being questioned in such a challenging way by a stranger, and one who had *demanded* an introduction, Byron responded by giving a condescending smirk as his eyed flicked over Brummell's coat. "Why? Are you in *need* of a good tailor?"

A second or two of silence before Scrope and others who had been listening, started laughing.

"Byron, did I not just tell you that Mr Brummell is also known as *Beau Brummell,*" said Scrope. "The high priest of men's fashion. And whatever style the Beau wears, every other man in London wants to copy."

"Do they indeed, do they really?" Byron was not prepared to be impressed.

Beau Brummell was smiling, unwilling to take offence, because Lord Byron was not only an extremely handsome young man, but also his condescending response reminded Brummell of himself.

"I was merely admiring the superior cut of your coat, Lord Byron. It fits you perfectly, so my compliments to your tailor."

Brummell's good-natured response disarmed Byron. "Thank you, I will convey your compliments to him."

"So who is he?" Brummell persisted. "Your tailor?"

"Schweitzer and Davidson."

Brummell laughed. "I knew it! I knew that coat was cut by one of *my* tailors. Only Schweitzer or Davidson could cut a coat that superbly. Did you know they are also patronized by the Prince of Wales?"

Byron showed his surprise. "No mention of that has ever been made to me."

"No mention of any other clients is ever made to anyone." Brummell said. "They serve only a very *select* clientele."

Byron smiled. "Including you, Mr Brummell?"

"And *you,* Lord Byron."

After a brief thought, Brummell said, "May I offer you a glass of champagne?"

Byron turned to Scrope who had already lost interest in the conversation and was back at the table watching the game.

Byron agreed to a glass of champagne. "Why not."

Walking to the outer room, a young man rushed up to Brummell with a beaming smile on his face — "Oh, Mr Brummell, how *fortunate* for me that you should be here tonight. May I ask your opinion of my new coat?"

"Coat?" Brummell's gaze travelled over the ill-fitting construction. "Coat? For heaven's sake, my dear fellow, don't misapply names so abominably. It is no more like a coat than like a cauliflower — if it is, I'll be damned!"

Brummell walked on, leaving the young man stunned with dismay.

When they sat down at a table, Byron had a rueful smile on his face. "I think you have just destroyed his evening."

Brummell shrugged. "It's very irksome being famous. Every gent from here to Islington think they have a right to accost me for my opinion on whatever concoction they are wearing."

"Forgive my ignorance," Byron said with some puzzlement, "but *why* exactly are you famous?"

Beau Brummell smiled. "Well, my fame only extends to the borders of London," he confessed, "but here in the city I cannot walk the streets in any peace. I design clothes for the male body, Lord Byron, my *own* male body that is, but as soon as my tailors make a garment in accordance with my design, and I then *wear* it, every young gent in London wants their own tailor to copy it."

A waiter arrived at the table and poured the champagne.

Byron glanced down at his own dark blue jacket. "Are you hinting that I have copied one of your designs?"

"I never hint. Some fools can never reach the conclusion of a hint. I am *saying* that either Schweitzer or Davidson thought one of my designs would be very suitable for you. And they know I am very selective about *who* wears one of my designs. In your case, I approve."

Byron looked at him steadily. "Because I am titled?"

"Not at all. My best friend for years has been the Prince of Wales, so your title would hardly impress me. How tall are you?"

"Five ten."

"There, you see!" Brummell sat back with a satisfied sigh. "It's a fact, y'know, that the average height of most men in England is five foot *five* or *six*. I myself am six foot tall, so all my designs take my height into consideration when drawing the lines." He took a quick sip of champagne. "So it absolutely galls me when I see all these squat five-foot-sixers trying to look good in one of my designs. It's just *not possible!"*

Byron smiled and then began to quietly laugh, thinking Beau Brummell to be one of the most absurd men he had ever met. What other man would spend his time in the exciting atmosphere of a nightclub, talking about *clothes.*

And yet the subject went on ...

~ ~ ~

Byron returned to Newstead on a night in late October, just before midnight. The sky was clear, the stars were out, but an icy wind was blowing, shivering the trees.

Having heard the carriage, Joe Murray came down the staircase to greet him. "It's a cold night, my lord, but the fires are lit in all the main rooms and in your bedroom. Will I get you some refreshment?"

"Some hot tea would be nice, and a few crackers, nothing more. I dined like a king in London."

"Oh, and Mr Hobhouse is here. He arrived yesterday."

"Hobhouse – here?"

"I believe he is still up, reading in the parlour."

Byron was delighted and entered the parlour to find Hobhouse ensconced very comfortably in an armchair before a huge fire, reading a book.

"Hobby, I do believe that you are beginning to enjoy our country ways here at Newstead." Byron threw off his cloak. "What brings you?"

"Oh, good grief ... *what* are you wearing?" Hobby was staring in disbelief at Byron's skin-tight yellow leather breeches.

Byron looked down at his breeches. "Wonderful, aren't they? This leather is as fine and as soft as silk."

"You look like one of those outrageous London dandies. Whatever made you buy them?"

"Not what – whom."

"Whom then?"

"Scrope's friend, Beau Brummell. As it turns out, we share the same tailor. And according to Mr Brummell, Schweitzer and Davidson may be the best for coats, but when it comes to a perfect cut for *breeches*, one really *must* go to John Weston's in Bond Street."

"But why *yellow?* And why so tight? Good God they are indecent! Nature has been very good to you but there is no need to flaunt your manliness."

Byron laughed and sat down in a chair. "I doubt I will be wearing them around Nottingham, but it was fun wearing them in London. Brummell insisted on taking me to Weston's where they measured me and had the breeches delivered to my hotel two days later."

"Brummell." Hobby shook his head. "Next you'll be wearing starched collars up to your ears. Scrope has told me all about Mr Brummell, and Matthews absolutely *detests* him."

"Does he? Matthews? Well, yes, I think I can understand why Matthews would find a man like

Brummell rather tedious."

"I'll tell you precisely why. According to Scrope, Brummell takes at least two hours every morning washing and pampering and putting on his fine clothes before he sets out to breakfast amongst London's *Haut Ton*, who all adore him. Followed by a change for the afternoon's tea parties, then another change of finery for the evening's socialising. He has no other occupation whatsoever, apart from gambling at the clubs every night. As Matthews says – how can any intelligent man live like that? What is the point of such a vain and *vacuous* life?"

Joe Murray brought in the tray of tea and as soon as he had left, Byron took the opportunity to change the subject to something more interesting.

"So, Hobby, what brings you? You can't have just wandered up here all the way from Bristol."

Hobby sighed. "From Surrey this time. I regret to say that my father and I have had another frightful row."

"What about?"

"Religion again, and politics. With him being a devout Unitarian, it infuriates him that I have now declared myself to be an atheist. He insists he '*will not have it!*' Nor does he approve of me being an ardent supporter of the Whigs in opposition." Hobby sat back and gloomed. "To be honest, I doubt if he and I will ever be capable of getting along."

After a silence, Byron asked, "And Bristol, how is life for you there?"

"Oh, awful! Crowded. You know I have eighteen siblings?"

"Eighteen? Did you not once tell me that you had *fourteen* siblings."

"Fourteen *half*-siblings, and four full, making eighteen in all."

Byron's mind was boggling at the very thought of it,

and it showed.

Hobby explained: "My father had five children by my mother, and then after she died and he remarried, he sired a further fourteen with my *step*mother."

"And you are the eldest of a total of nineteen?"

"Yes." Hobby shrugged gloomily. "The house in Bristol is big, but not big *enough*. Always so crowded and noisy with the children, not to mention their nursemaids and nannies and the rest of the servants. At times it really is unbearable. And the most damnable thing of all ... after I graduated and went home expecting applause and praise, my stepmother stood in the hall staring at me as if trying to remember who I was."

Byron was silent, feeling sorry for his friend. Their situations were similar yet completely dissimilar. Both had an unsatisfactory relationship with their parent. One felt alone in a crowded family, and the other truly was alone. The main difference was in their attitude to it all: Hobby loved constant companionship, whereas he personally needed periods of total solitude.

"You can always come here, Hobby, any time you wish." Byron said. "As you can see, I have more than enough rooms to spare."

"Oh, my dear fellow, I *do* appreciate that, but I will not impose on you, nor will I take advantage of our friendship. Apart from that, a solution is at hand. The reason my father and I were in Surrey was due to him now having leased a huge house there, an absolute mansion of a place, Whitton Park, in Richmond. The entire family will be moving there in a month or so, and I, of course, shall be living in the garden."

"The garden?"

Hobhouse nodded. "There is a very nice cottage of six rooms at one end of the parkland and my father has agreed that I can have it as my own personal residence.

Are you drinking that tea?"

Byron had forgotten the tea. He felt the teapot, which was now lukewarm. "Would you prefer a glass of brandy, Hobby?"

"I certainly would."

Byron stood and moved over to the drinks cabinet, bringing back a decanter of brandy and two glasses and poured liberally.

"But my main residence now shall be in London," Hobhouse continued. "As soon as I leave here, I intend to rent myself an apartment of rooms there. And when I do, you will be very welcome to lodge there, Byron, whenever you are in London ... or are you still addicted to hotels?"

"Very much so. Although John Hanson keeps complaining about the enormous extravagance and insists that if my trips to London are to continue, then I must give up the hotels and rent an apartment instead."

"Understandable."

Byron sighed. "But I *love* hotels, Hobby, the hustle and bustle and excitement. And the freedom – during the past few weeks I have stayed at four different hotels, moving from one to another every few days."

"That's mad. Why did you do that?"

"For the fun of it! Different rooms, new bars of soap, different staff, different waiters rushing up to you helpfully with their shining silver trays."

Hobhouse shrugged. "You're still such a child in many ways, Byron. That's why you love dancing with bears and swimming with dogs."

Byron thought back to his childhood, and changed the subject to politics — a subject, as Whigs, they both completely agreed upon. The English political system was so overtly corrupt that one did not even have to be a radical to be against it.

Hobby agreed. "The other day I heard a politician

saying to my father —'The English people are a menace, and so they *must* be contained, for the sake of England."

Byron frowned. "Who was he, this politician? Tell me his name and I shall lampoon him to disgrace in my next satire."

"Then he says to my father – 'I shall vote with them tonight though. I think it does us good to yield a point or two to the people now and then'."

They talked late into the night, reluctant to leave the warmth of the fire and the cosy companionship of the parlour. Byron, as always, spoke about his wish for the freedom of Ireland, while Hobhouse spoke of his own *new* determination.

"It was seeing the children, my siblings, and how innocent the smaller ones are, and how well they live, with every need supplied ... so if and when I *do* become a politician, my first and main ambition will be to try and get legislation for the abolition of child labour. Some other way will have to be found to help the poorer classes survive without having to send their children out to work in factories, and most as young as only six or seven years old. A child should be allowed to be a child."

"Yes ..." Byron agreed, and as he always did whenever the subject of childhood was mentioned, he felt a sudden tiredness coming over him.

The fire had died down to red embers by the time they eventually stood to go to their rooms. "Hardly worth my while going to bed now," Hobhouse said with a yawn. "I promised Mr Mealey the steward that I would go fishing with him at dawn."

Byron grinned. "Hardly worth your while going fishing either, because you never catch anything."

"Perhaps not," Hobby huffed, "but when I do finally catch my first fish, I shall make *you* eat every bit of it in a humble pie."

PART FIVE

A love lost

The heart will break, but broken live on.

BYRON

Chapter Thirty-Two

~ ~ ~

The *'Invitation'* arrived a few days later while Byron and Hobhouse were sat at breakfast.

Joe Murray carried it in, an uneasy expression on his face as he placed it on the table.

"This has just been delivered, my lord, by a servant from Annesley Hall."

"Annesley ...?" Astonished, Byron looked at Joe, and then down at the thick square of cream vellum on which his name was written in black ink ... so, yes, it was unquestionably for him.

Hobhouse saw Joe Murray's apprehension and also saw that Byron's face had turned quite pale. "What is it?"

Byron slowly unsealed the square and removed a thick, cream card, his voice quiet as he read: "It is ... a cordial invitation to Lord Byron and guest to join Mr and Mrs Chaworth of Annesley Hall for an evening of Music and Dinner on Wednesday, 2nd of November, at five o'clock ..."

"So? That's nice."

"No, it is not nice, Hobby, it's ... it's very surprising."

"Why so?"

"It's from my Mary." Byron looked in some confusion at the square cover and card, "Well, it certainly was *written* by Mary, I know her handwriting better than my own."

"Perhaps she assisted her mother in sending out the invitations," Joe suggested. "I would take from it nothing more than that. And no doubt there have been many others from the gentry invited as well."

Hobhouse sat back. "And cut off from the rest of the world as we are here at Newstead, it will be pleasant to have a jolly musical evening in the company of others for a change. I say we go, Byron."

Byron peered curiously at the card. "I don't see *your* name on this invitation, Hobby."

"Yes you do ... it says "guest" and am I not your only guest here at the moment?"

Byron glanced at Joe Murray, "Thank you, Joe."

Joe nodded and left the room, closing the door behind him.

"I can't go, Hobby, I can't see her again. She is still the love of my life."

Hobhouse sighed impatiently. "No she is not. She is someone you had a very youthful passion for at one time, but then she married, and that was the end of it."

"Was it indeed?" Byron looked at him. "And what would *you* know about it?"

"I know that first loves never last because they are always based on unreal romanticism. And I'm quite sure that if you do accept the invitation and she *is* there on the night, you will soon realise what a fool you have been to have kept her on a high pedestal for so long."

"You say this – *you,* who have never been in love."

"Oh yes I have," Hobby insisted. "I had my own first love when I was fifteen. It lasted no more than six days but it took me weeks to forget her. And then last Christmas I saw her again, all grown up and hard-faced, and my only emotion was relief that I had been too young at the time to propose my suit to her."

Byron was no longer listening, his mind going back to the days of his youth and the love for Mary Chaworth that had so engulfed him, remembering every day and night of it so clearly, because he still often allowed his mind to think of her.

"What you don't understand, Hobby," he said quietly,

"is that my misery, my love for that girl was so violent, so truly passionate, that I honestly doubt if I could become so attached to anyone else in that way again."

"Oh, tripe! You have had associations with others since then; pretty girls whom you seemed to find *very* delightful. Remember your blue-eyed Caroline?"

Byron frowned. "Yes, but those others, I didn't *love* any of them. I have only ever loved one, and that is Mary Chaworth. And those others ... they never affected my *senses* in any way, not in the way Mary always did."

"And what way was that?"

After a brief silence Byron said: "When I was away from her, I could not sleep, I could not eat, I could not rest, and all my energy was devoted to enduring and counting the hours that had to pass before we could meet again. "

"You were a young fool back then."

"And not much wiser now ... I still recollect every word we said to each other, every detail of her face, the way I loved her flirting laugh ... the pages of poetry I would write about her. As Plato said – *'At the touch of love everyone becomes a poet.'*"

"He also said, 'Love is a serious mental disease,'" Hobhouse replied. "Plato was no fool."

Byron looked down at Mary's familiar handwriting on the card.

"This invitation ... if Mary did not wish to see me again, she would not have allowed her mother to include me on the guest list."

"Or perhaps she is so happily married to her husband that she knows your presence would be a matter of complete indifference to her."

~ ~ ~

Indifference was not the sensation Mary Chaworth experienced when Lord Byron's arrival was announced at Annesley Hall.

Her first sight of him, when he was led into the drawing-room, accompanied by a "Mr John Cam Hobhouse" quite startled her emotions. Four years had passed since she had last seen Byron, and those years had made a significant change in his appearance and manner.

The passionate and over-emotional youth of her memory was now an elegant young man who had been educated at Cambridge. The early good looks of his boyish features were now heightened and had refined into an uncommon masculine beauty, and yet his manners had subsided into that tone of gentleness and self-possession which more than anything, in her opinion, marked the true gentleman.

Byron too, was noticing the slight changes in Mary. Not yet twenty-three, he thought her even more beautiful a woman than the lovely girl he had once known so well. He saw her wonderful dark eyes, her masses of light brown hair intertwined in coils around her slender shoulders, her full rosy mouth and her lovely body.

When she held out her hand in greeting to him, he bowed over it and could feel it trembling at the touch of his own, and the troubled expression in her eyes when she looked into his seemed to speak of sudden and futile regrets. It was not what he had expected.

He had expected her to be as indifferent to him as Hobhouse had predicted, and he had determined in return to be very nonchalant in his manner towards her, and converse with as much composure as he could contrive; but now all his valour was shaken and his plans fallen like dust.

The rest of the evening was like a dream, a sad and bewildering dream where no one else seemed to matter to either of them.

There were fourteen seated to dinner: Mary at one end of the table, and Jack Musters at the other, with six guests sitting facing each other down each side. Mary's mother was seated to the right of Jack Musters, whereas Byron had been seated to the right of Mary

Occasionally, each spoke politely to the person seated on the other side of them, but to each other across their corner of the table neither said a word; yet their eyes constantly met over the tureens and flickering candles and lingered silently.

Byron later wrote to Francis Hodgson:

> *'I was determined to be valiant, and converse with sang froid; but instead I forgot my nonchalance, and never opened my lips even to smile or laugh, far less to speak, and the lady was almost as absurd as myself, which made both of us the object of more observation than if we had conducted ourselves with easy indifference.'*

And no one had observed them more than Mary's husband, Jack Musters, who knew all about Lord Byron's earlier attachment to his wife, and resented it even more now that he had met him, but later he intended to bring out his winning card.

Yet it was strange ... even Hobhouse was puzzled ... for Mary and Byron to sit so close and not exchange even one word with each other.

And Mary was acting very oddly indeed, Jack Musters noticed, fiddling with her cutlery but eating nothing. And on those rare occasions when Jack did meet her eyes, her glance was icy.

Byron's calm composure remained dignified throughout. Even during the musical entertainment when dinner was finally over and Mary Chaworth sat on the seat beside him, he appeared to be listening calmly to every note, while Hobhouse watched him, and worried, and wondered.

Only at the end did Hobhouse see Byron's composure put to a trial – when the baby daughter of Mary Chaworth was brought into the room by her smiling husband.

At the sight of the child Byron started involuntarily, and Hobby saw the difficulty he was having to conceal his emotion – but he managed it, even going so far as to kiss the infant's cheek.

After that he was eager to leave, and so was Hobhouse; both saying their goodnights to one and all, and agreeing to visit again, although Hobhouse knew a further visit was now *never* going to happen.

Mary stood at the door and once again Byron was bowing over her hand.

She watched him walk away towards his carriage and saw that his steps were quick and light, amazingly quick in view of the affliction of his right foot.

A few moments later, at the door of his carriage, he turned and looked back at her, and slowly raised his hand in farewell.

She raised her own hand, watching as the carriage disappeared down the avenue, and thinking sadly, very sadly, how stupid she had been to marry Jack Musters – the marriage was not a happy one; it had been difficult from the start.

And then she thought of Byron, two years younger than herself and still a very young man, but his composure and manner and looks were everything any female would admire.

Her mind went back to the past, as it had so often done of late, thinking of Byron's natural tenderness, his gentleness, not only with her, but even the smallest animal in need of care. It brought a sting of tears to her eyes, because gentleness and tenderness were two things that Jack Musters was incapable of.

She stood for some minutes staring into the empty space where his carriage had been ... one of the things she had never forgotten about Byron, and now after tonight she knew she never would forget, were his beautifully expressive eyes ... and the colour, that light shade of pure blue ... beautiful ...

~ ~ ~

Inside the carriage Byron sat silent and spoke not a word to Hobhouse, his eyes fixed on the dark window, until he finally said, "Do you think she is happy?"

Hobhouse had not a clue whether Mary Chaworth was happy or not, other than she had spoken very little throughout the evening; but this hopeless attachment of Byron's had to be brought to a firm and final end.

"I think she is very happy," Hobhouse replied. "She has a husband and a child and seemed to me the very picture of contentment."

"Did she," Byron said flatly, and continued staring at the dark window, feeling his old heartbreak returning as his mind wandered.

I've seen my bride another's bride,

I've seen her seated by his side.

I've kissed, as if without design,

The babe which ought to have been mine

And showed, alas, in each caress

Time has not made me love any less.

That night Byron did not sleep at all. He sought to

relieve his mind by occupying his thoughts in writing his letter to Francis Hodgson about the night's event, and the absurdity of he and Mary not speaking a word to each other across the table or at any other time. "*You will think all this great nonsense, and if you had seen it, you would have thought it still more ridiculous ...*" finally ending his letter on a more serious note of despair:

'What fools we are! We cry for a plaything, which, like children we are never satisfied with until we break it open; though unlike children, when it is broken, we cannot get rid of it by putting it in the fire.'

The following day Hobhouse could see Byron wandering around the estate in lonely walks, wishing for no other company but Boatswain; and even when they did meet up and converse, Hobhouse could see that Byron's mind was not there, not fully present or paying much attention, if any at all.

All Byron's thoughts were of Mary, knowing she would expect him to follow etiquette and send a note to Annesley in appreciation of the evening's musical entertainment, and later that afternoon he complied and wrote a short letter to her mother.

Yet the impulse to communicate with Mary personally and privately was overwhelming. To speak to her at last, not with eyes, but with *words* – words to tell her ... tell her all ... the thoughts of his mind and the feelings of his heart ... to lay them in bare truth across the page, and if she laughed at him because of his words, then that would be her choice, and nothing would be lost, because she was already lost to him.

He dipped his pen in the ink and began to write, as he

always wrote — rapidly, with fire in his soul, and in the language of poetry.

Well, thou art happy, and I feel
That I should thus be happy too;
For still my heart regards thy weal
Warmly, as it was wont to do.

Thy husband's blessed – and 'twill impart
Some pangs to view his happier lot:
But let them pass — Oh! how my heart
Would hate him, if he loved thee not!

When late I saw thy favourite child,
I thought my jealous heart would break;
But when the unconscious infant smiled,
I kissed it for its mother's sake.

Mary, adieu! I must away:
While thou art blessed I'll not repine;
But near thee I can never stay;
My heart would soon again be thine.

Away! away my early dream
Remembrance never must awake;
Oh! where is Lethe's fabled stream!
My foolish heart be still – or break.

He sought out Fletcher and asked him: "In the past,

Fletcher, do you remember ... the letters you used to deliver to Miss Chaworth?"

Fletcher, a young man himself, involuntarily gave a grin, a very wicked grin. "Aye, I do, my lord."

"And the servant you trusted at that time, is she still there, at Annesley?"

"Aye she is, my lord. I know that because my wife has often seen her in the town and passed a few friendly words with her."

"Your wife?" Byron had forgotten that Fletcher had married one of the maids. "Would your wife agree to take a private letter to Annesley and pass it to that servant."

Without hesitation Fletcher nodded. "For *you*, she would, my lord."

~ ~ ~

During dinner Byron spoke to Joe Murray about Boatswain.

"He seemed unusually lazy today, Joe. Very slow in his walk, tottering along as if he was as old as Woolly. Also his bark sounded very croaky. Does he look unwell to you?"

Joe thought about it. "Well, he did get a vicious attack from a fox a few weeks ago, a mad vixen she was, gave him a bite on his leg, so I reckon Boatswain ventured too near to where the vixen had her cubs."

"Damn foxes," Hobhouse said. "And *you* think it's cruel for us to shoot them, Byron."

"He could have a sore throat," Byron said to Joe. "That's the only explanation for his croaky bark. I think you should send for the vet to come and take a look at him."

~ ~ ~

Late in the afternoon of the following day, Byron rode over to Southwell to see his mother. He was quietly anxious about the coming interview with her, knowing she would be upset and would probably throw a tantrum, but it had to be faced, had to be done. He had made his plans and now he wanted to execute them as quickly as possible.

"What, what?" she said when he told her his decision, jumping to her feet, her eyes wide and bewildered, her hand moving to her heart. "When did you think up this nonsense?"

"Mother, please, sit back down and listen, that's all I ask, for you to *listen.*"

He walked over to the drinks cabinet near the drawing-room window, took out a decanter of whisky and a glass and poured her a good measure.

She stood staring after him, watching every move he made, her face turning stark and pallid as she realised he must be serious, because he had never approved of her drinking and he had never poured her a glass of whisky before. Not until this day.

"This decision of yours ... this *nonsense*, it's all due to your visit to Annesley the other night," she said accusingly.

He turned and looked at her. "How did you know about that?"

"I know everything about you, George," she boasted smugly. "Very little goes on at Newstead that I *don't* know about."

"Oh yes," he said with an uncaring sigh, "the traitor in my camp. I had forgotten about that."

"Gossip," she said, quickly correcting herself. "I learn everything through all the women's gossip in the village, although I suppose most of it is untrue."

She sat down again. "But *Annesley* – the butcher, the baker and even the candle-maker knew there was a special dinner and musical evening being held there three nights ago. My only surprise is why they did not also invite *me* as well as you?"

He put the glass in her hand and stood by the fireplace.

"Mother, I have to go away, I *need* to get away from England. In two months from now I will be twenty-one and will have reached my majority, and from that day forward no one will be able to tell me what to do or *not* do – not you, not John Hanson, and not the Court of Chancery. I will be a free man, free to do as I please and go where I wish. So let us get that fact settled first and foremost."

"If you need to get away from England, George, why not go up to Scotland? You've said many times that you long to visit the Highlands again."

"No, I need to go *far* away from here, as far away as I possibly can, and for a long time."

"No, no," she said with a groan, a horrible sensation of impending disaster making her entire body tremble. "You will be drowned or murdered or something terrible will happen to you, I know it, I know it!"

"You are being silly now. How can you know it?"

"In the same way I know that we Scots have second-sight. And there have been times of late, George, when I have had nightmares of you going away, and always in the dreams I know I will never see you again."

She gulped at her whisky but her lips felt thick and numb. "If you go away – far away, I *know* I will never see you alive again."

"That's superstitious babble. I have had dreams too but, unfortunately, *none* of them have come true in reality."

She jumped to her feet, her breath panting, looking at him like a stricken animal, and then her expression turned murderous, full of loathing. "It's that Mary

Chaworth! It's because of *her* you are going away! What did she do the other night, eh? Did she flutter her eyelashes and give you one of her flirting laughs; the hussy! And she a married woman now!"

The tirade went on and on and there was no reasoning with her, no acceptance of his insistence that Mary had acted throughout like the perfect lady that she was.

He returned to Newstead in a state of agitation, and became even more agitated when Joe Murray told him the vet had just left, after declaring Boatswain to be very ill.

"He reckons it must have been the bite Boatswain got from the fox," Joe said. "He made me chain him up in the barn and said I was to make sure that *you* did not go near him, my lord, and you were to stay well away from him."

"Me? Stay away from Boatswain? Don't be ridiculous!"

He turned and walked hurriedly towards the back of the house with Joe Murray scurrying after him. "No, my lord, you must stay away from him. The vet said his illness is dangerous to humans!"

"And did he say what that illness was?"

"Not to me, but he explained it all to Mr Hobhouse."

"And where is Mr Hobhouse now?"

"I believe he is up in his room, my lord."

Byron had not missed a step in his hurry out to the barn where he found a "DO NOT ENTER" paper pinned to the door.

"The vet wrote that notice," Joe told him. "He said we were to put Boatswain's dish of food and water near enough for him to reach, but not for any of us to enter or touch him in any way."

Byron entered the barn to see his beloved Newfoundland dog lying in the corner, his front paws out in front of him ... and then, lifting his head and seeing his master, Boatswain gave a small croaky bark.

"Ah, Bo'sun ... Bo'sun ... hello boy, hello ... what's amiss with you, eh?"

Joe Murray watched his lordship kneeling down before the dog; one hand gently stroking his head while the other held the paw that Boatswain had lifted to him in his usual greeting.

"Oh dear, oh dear ..." Joe whined in fear, and went rushing back inside the house to fetch Mr Hobhouse.

When Hobby reached the barn, he remained safely by the door. "Byron, come away, please, Boatswain has rabies."

"Rabies?" Astonished, Byron looked at Boatswain, slumped and languid and appearing too tired to move a muscle.

"That vet must be mad! Does this poor sick dog look like a rabid beast to you? Does he look furious or about to attack anyone? Is he scratching or biting his own body?"

"No, but ... the vet *did* say it was rabies. He has to be kept quarantined and you really *must* come away from him now."

Byron stubbornly refused. "I'll stay until he's asleep at least. I'm not leaving him like a friendless animal with no one willing to care for him – and I do *not* believe he has rabies."

When the veterinary doctor returned the following day, he cleared up any confusion by explaining to Lord Byron that there were two types of rabies: the *furious* type, where dogs turned mad and brutal, and the *paralytic* type, and it was this second type that Boatswain was showing signs of now.

"Do you see – his lower jaw has already dropped since I saw him yesterday, hanging open and he is unable to close it, poor thing. This will soon be followed by his inability to swallow at all, leading to a drooling of his spittle and a foaming around his mouth. So let me warn you – no human must touch the dog's mouth at this stage, because his spittle contains infection of the disease which could lead to madness and even death in a human"

Byron could not believe it. "Are you saying my Boatswain is *dying?*"

"Oh, most certainly, your lordship. In another few days the paralysis will spread from his jaw to his throat, and then to all his other muscles, after which he will go into a coma and die."

Byron was so anguished by this calamity, and Hobhouse was so distressed at seeing his beloved friend so hurt, he took his gun and set out to find and shoot the vixen who had infected Boatswain.

Joe Murray told him the area where the fox's attack on Boatswain had taken place. "She needs to be shot," Joe said, "else she'll be attacking other animals and even the deer in the park will be in danger before she dies in madness herself."

"What about the other animals?"

"No fear there, Mr Hobhouse. The vet has inspected them all and he says there are no signs of contagion and all are well, even Woolly. But he's so old now he rarely ventures outside his favourite spot in the old cloisters. And the two bulldogs, Smut and App, well they spend all their time at the front of the house, too wrapped up in playing with each other to bother with anyone else."

In the following days Hobhouse and the gamekeepers shot every fox on the estate they could find; while Byron spent most of his time in the barn, taking care of Boatswain.

It was a distressing ordeal that lasted ten days, during which time Byron constantly and lovingly wiped the dripping spittle from the dog's lips with his own hands, using a succession of small cloths he had cut up for the purpose. Not even the vet could stop him from doing it, nor the anxious appeals from Hobhouse or Joe Murray.

"I have no cuts or scratches on my hands," he insisted irritably, "so my bloodstream is safe from infection. No! I will not leave him to die alone."

As the maids and other staff were very reluctant to go into the barn at all, fearful of the "mad" dog inside, Joe Murray and Fletcher took it in turns to carry in the numerous bowls of water which Byron used to wash his hands, and all thought it a blessed relief when, after a paroxysm of fits in the final stages of his madness, Boatswain finally lapsed into a coma and died.

Byron had shed all his tears by then, and he too was glad to see that Boatswain's suffering was over.

"I need a bath," he said tiredly to Joe Murray. "I need to sanctify myself in a bath of hot water and a large bar of soap. As for this barn, arrange for it to be burnt down as soon as possible. I never want to see it again."

"And do you want Boatswain's body to be burnt in it?" Joe asked.

"Of course not. I want him buried in the garden, near to *my* side of the house. Come, I will show you where. I have already chosen the spot."

Later, when Fletcher and Robert Rushton carried the bath of hot water into his room, assisted by two maids, Byron nodded and waved a hand for them to leave, eager to immerse himself under the water.

When they had left, Byron was about to pull off his shirt when he saw one of the maids still standing by the open door, silently watching him ... Susan, an attractive young girl with strawberry blonde hair whom he had occasionally and flippantly flirted with.

Now he looked at her blandly. "Yes?"

When she did not answer, her eyes glowing like lights, he said, "You should leave and close the door behind you, Susan, unless it is your intention to see me naked?"

Susan Vaughan still gave no answer: she loved and had been suffering a passionate fervour for Byron for a long time, and now she wanted him to know it.

Byron recognised the expression on her face and instantly became flippant with a half smile, "Oh, if I was not so exhausted."

Susan smiled and continued to glow at him, and under other circumstances he would certainly have been tempted, but not now, in his loss and bereavement for the most lovable friend he had ever known.

He bent down to test the temperature of the water with his hand. "Pray close the door behind you, Susan," he said without looking at her, and she slowly stepped over the threshold and closed the door quietly behind her.

As soon as he was bathed and dressed again, Byron sat down at his desk to write a letter to Francis Hodgson.

> *Newstead Abbey, Notts*
> *Nov. 18th 1808*

My dear Hodgson — Boatswain is dead. He expired in a state of madness after suffering much, yet retaining all the gentleness of his nature to the last, never attempting to do the least injury to any one near him.

> *Hobhouse sends all sorts of remembrances. But, in the words of Gaffer Thumb, "I can no more."*
> > *Believe me, dear H, yours – Byron.*

Boatswain was buried in the garden of Newstead Abbey. Above where his body lay, Byron had a four-sided white marble obelisk built as a landmark, and in tribute to him, engraved with Byron's own words.

On this spot

Are deposited the Remains of one

Who possessed Beauty without Vanity,

Strength without Insolence,

Courage without Ferocity,

And all the Virtues of Man without his Vices.

This praise, which would be unmeaning Flattery

If inscribed over human ashes,

Is but a just tribute to the Memory of

Boatswain, a Dog,

Who was born at Newfoundland, May, 1803

And died at Newstead Abbey, November 18

1808

~~~

Joe Murray thought it a very grand monument to be placed over the coffin of a dog. "Better than a king would have," Joe said, and then almost choked on his ale when Byron told him that the other sides of the monument had been left blank – in readiness for himself and Joe.

Joe stared at his lordship, and then at Mr Hobhouse. "Is he being serious, Mr Hobhouse?"

Hobby nodded. "I believe he is, Mr Murray."

Joe contemplated for a moment, scratched his head, shrugged his shoulders, and then looked at the serious face of his young lord.

"Lord Byron," he said, "there would be no greater joy and honour for me at the end of this life, than to have you buried beside me when we are both dead, but I don't like the idea of being buried in the same tomb as a dog ... fact, I don't like it at all."

When Byron gave no answer, Joe added hesitantly, "Well, if I was *sure* his lordship would come along and lie there with me, I should like it well enough, but I would not like to lie alone with the dog."

Byron looked at Hobhouse and both smiled, and Joe was relieved to see it was all a jest. "And it's good to see you smiling in your old way again, my lord, oh, indeed it is."

Yet, later that morning, Joe found that his lordship's affection for him was not to be set aside so lightly.

"I am so glad now," Byron said wistfully, "that only a few months ago I had Boatswain's portrait painted. If I had not done that, his image would not now be hanging on the wall here in Newstead allowing me to see his noble face again, and remind me of all our happy times together. So it is my wish to do the same with you, Joe."

"Do what with me?"

"Have your portrait painted. Pray humour me, Joe, and agree to sit for it."

"What a palaver ..." Joe complained a week later when he was forced to sit on a chair for hours in his best clothes while the distinguished artist, Thomas Barber, painted him. "It's *ancestors* and *family* that gets painted and hung on a wall, not a mere servant."

"And you are the head of my household *family* here at Newstead," Byron replied. "Sit still, Joe."

"Folks who come to Newstead, I mean *gentry* folk, will think I've raised myself above my station when they see my picture hanging on the wall. It's not done, my lord, it's not *done.*"

"It's done,' the artist said. "Do you want to take a

look, Lord Byron?"

Byron got up from his chair and walked across the room to look at the painting – and loved it. "It's *you* exactly, Joe. Come and see!"

Relieved to get up from the chair, Joe ambled over to view the painting, and was not much impressed with what he saw.

"Well?" Byron asked.

"Well, to those that know me, it can't be *me,* can it," Joe said dismissively, "not without my pipe."

"Your pipe?" Of course – that was the only flaw. Whenever Joe was not working, he always had his pipe in his hand. "So why did you not *bring* your pipe with you?"

"I didn't know as if I should, my lord."

"Go and fetch it now." Byron looked at the artist. "Can you add it, without him having to sit again?"

"Yes ... I will redo his hand and somehow include the pipe."

When his favourite pipe was added to the portrait, Joe looked a lot more satisfied with it. He was even more pleased when his lordship spared him any further discomfort and embarrassment by taking the painting away to his own wing and hanging it on the wall of his dressing room – away from the casual eyes of visitors who may think, as a servant, that Joe had acquired airs above himself in the ranks of life.

"That's my only complaint, my lord, but other than that...." Joe stood admiring his own image more and more as he looked. "Well, I think I still make a very handsome-looking fellow for my age. What say you, my lord?"

Byron smiled. "And what age is that, Joe?"

"Almost seventy – too old to be still looking so good," Joe said, and Byron laughed.

In truth, Joe had the looks of a strong and a rugged

mastiff, but as Byron gazed at the painting again he saw
only a beloved old man who was very dear to him.

Chapter Thirty-Three

~ ~ ~

Mrs Byron was delighted to sit for her portrait, pleased as punch at her son's suggestion, and then spoiled it all by flirting disgracefully with the artist throughout the first sitting.

Byron was embarrassed, the artist was embarrassed, yet still her black eyelashes fluttered up and down during her sporadic eruptions of girlish giggles.

For the first time in his life Byron saw his mother as a *woman,* and it repulsed him, sending him across the Green to the Pigot's house where he found Elizabeth in the parlour sitting with her sewing box. John was still at his university up in Edinburgh studying medicine.

"I have made you a purse," Elizabeth said, showing him the black velvet purse with a cord string. "For your coins ... you said you needed one."

"I do ... but I did not expect you to sit down and make me one." Byron felt very moved by this act of friendship.

Elizabeth lifted her needle and continued her sewing. "Are you still writing verse?"

"No, I have not done a *stitch* of poetry in months." He noticed a strange yellow stone in her sewing box, picked up the stone and looked at it. "What is this?"

"Oh, that ... " Elizabeth made a face. "A gypsy woman came by the other day and said it was an amulet that I should keep if my wish is for a happy life."

Byron smirked at such nonsense. "And all due to the magic of this stone?"

"Apparently so. She said if I kept the stone it would ensure that I would never fall in love, and therefore my life will be happy."

"*Never* fall in love?"

"That's what she said. It will turn the heart to stone."

"Then it's just what *I* need," He slipped the stone into his pocket, "because I am determined to *never* fall in love again."

Elizabeth looked at him silently.

"Here," he said, slipping the ring off his small finger, "you may have this instead in fair exchange."

Elizabeth took the ring, and sat gazing at the small pink cornelian heart in its centre, surprised that Byron should be wearing – and now giving to her – such a cheap little ring.

"Thank you," she said, and put the ring in her sewing box.

Mrs Pigot arrived with a tray of tea and the conversation became more genteel and formal.

~ ~ ~

By the time he returned to Burgage Manor the artist had left and his mother was in a jolly mood, until her new little terrier dog jumped onto her lap and it reminded her of something that had been annoying her.

"What's all this I hear about you erecting a six-foot marble obelisk over Boatswain? It's the most ludicrous thing I have ever heard – a grand funereal monument for *a dog!* And as well as making everyone in the town doubt your sanity, it's also a complete *waste* of good money."

"I'm just glad Boatswain did not get ill and die while I was away on my travels ... that would have broken my heart completely."

"Stop that! I want no more of *that* nonsense!" she said angrily. "George, you are *not* going away! I will not allow it. I forbid it! And I have already written to instruct Mr Hanson to refuse you the money to fund it. Lord save us! – Only last week you told me you were five thousand pounds in debt from all your high living!"

"Not to mention all *your* high living," he replied. "Mother, there is no need to worry. When my Lancashire property is sold in a few months it will bring me *sixty* thousand pounds at the very least. A King's ransom and ten times over."

"Oh, now you are beginning to sound like your father! *He* used to say the same sort of thing to shut me up about his gambling. And *he* deserted me and went running off to the Continent too! You are a *Byron* through and through George, just like ..."

Her tirade went on until every Byron back to the start of the earth was condemned under her vitriolic censure. He finally turned to leave the room without answering a word in response, detesting her acrimonious scenes and refusing to be drawn into her long passions of fury.

It distressed him; his dislike of his mother; and he wished it was not so. He wished she would make it easier for him to like her more, and dislike her less, but he could only feel fondness for her from a distance, and during long periods of absence away from her.

He had been back at Newstead only a few hours when one of her servants delivered a letter from her, filled with apologies for all of the hurtful things she had said to him, which *'I ever so sincerely regret now.'*

She wanted him to come back to the Manor so she could explain to him personally how distraught she was at his talk of going abroad to be drowned or killed, and because she was certain that if he went away she would never see him alive again, and that would break her heart because she ever so sincerely loved him.

He finished reading the letter, feeling only annoyance and frustration. This is what she did! What she had *always* done, ever since he was a child. Acted horrid and hard and vulgar, and then in a swift change became kind and meek and loving, until you didn't know where you were with her, or whether she loved you or hated you. Now he didn't care which, but that was not the answer.

He felt that he *should* love her, because she was his mother, and somehow he had to try to get on better with her, if only because it was his duty and responsibility to take care of her in the future, in her old age, and that could only be accomplished if he could learn to have more patience and tolerance.

He did not go back to Burgage Manor, but later that night in his bedroom, he sat down at his desk and answered her letter:

Dear Mother, — If you please, we will forget the things you mention, I have no desire to remember them.

I am furnishing the house more for you than myself, and I shall establish you in it before I go on my travels. I am now fitting up your green drawing room and red bedroom and the rooms over as sleeping rooms.

If I do not travel now, I never shall, and all men should one day or other. I have at present no connections to keep me at home; no wife, or unprovided sisters, brothers, &c. I shall take care of you, and when I return I may possibly become a politician. A few years' knowledge of other countries than our own will not incapacitate me for that part. If we see no nation but our own, we do not give the rest of mankind a fair chance:—it is from experience, not books, we ought to judge them.

When your rooms are ready I shall be glad to see you; at present it would be improper and uncomfortable to both parties, and it will be better for you to reside at the manor for a while longer.

I have already arranged for my will to be drawn up from the moment I am twenty-one. And (in case of any accident) I have taken care that you shall have the abbey and manor for life, besides a sufficient income. So you see, my improvements are not entirely selfish. I shall place my property and my will in the hands of trustees till my return, and I mean to appoint you as one. From Hanson I have heard nothing – when I do you shall have the particulars.

Yours &c — BYRON

What he did *not* tell her, was that he had also set up a Trust to provide an annuity for Joe Murray, ensuring that Joe would have a regular pension for the rest of his life, should any accident – or worse – prevent his own return to England.

He read over the letter, smiling as he read ... *at present it would be improper and uncomfortable to both parties ...*

It would indeed be improper and *very* uncomfortable, especially now that he was allowing one of the maids to sleep in his bed at night, the pretty Susan with her passionate eyes.

And now Susan had come into his room and was leaning her soft body over his shoulder, asking him if he could feel "the rocking" of her heart?

Chapter Thirty-Four

~ ~ ~

On January 22nd 1809, on the day he reached his majority and became twenty-one years old, Byron hosted a huge party for all the farm tenants and employees of Newstead. It was an event all had been looking forward to with anticipation of a good feast, and Lord Byron did not let them down. Oxes and pigs were roasted, fish were grilled, vegetables simmered, and benches and tables laden with every kind of pies and cakes as well as numerous barrels of ale were provided in plenty in the Stone Room.

Byron joined in the fun by accepting and eating a plate of fried ham and eggs, declaring it to be delicious, and then slipped out of the house where he was violently sick.

"Why did you do it?" Joe Murray remonstrated. "You know your body is not used to digesting animal meat."

Looking sickly and pallid, Byron agreed, "Never again, Joe, I will never eat the meat of any animal again ... although it *did* taste delicious at the time ... I think I'll go back to bed for a while."

He had fully recovered later that evening when all his friends arrived for a party in the Great Drawing-Room, which had been turned into a ballroom. He had not invited any of the local gentry, as that would have required him to invite Mary and her husband, and the very sight of Mary again would ruin it for him.

By ten o'clock, dinner over, the dancing was in full swing and Byron was happy to see John Hanson and his wife happily waltzing around the room, as were two of Hanson's daughters – both being swirled around by

Thomas Wingfield and Tom Wildman, two of his friends from Harrow.

Yet all had to agree that *Mrs Byron* was the belle of the ball!

She had prepared her repertoire for this night carefully, eager to ensure that everyone had *'the loveliest time'* and insisted that her son halt the orchestra and announce the entertainment she had prepared for one and all.

Byron did so without embarrassment, turning it into a comedy act, announcing grandly "Ladies and Gentlemen, for your entertainment tonight ... "*Miss Kitty Gordon of Gight!"* ... and holding her hand high, he led her like a queen up to the orchestra, lifting the train of her dress and arranging it on the floor behind her like a diligent courtier.

"Oh good grief ..." Hobhouse whispered to Matthews, "Byron must be as drunk as a lord."

Matthews, Scrope Davies and Hobhouse, stood laughing at Byron who was indeed a handsome if comical sight. His coat of burgundy velvet over a white shirt with lace collar and cuffs was splendid, but it was what he wore on top of his black hair that was so comical.

On his head he now wore the gold coronet studded with pearls, which John Hanson had escorted from the bank-vault in London to Newstead. The coronet was officially Byron's now that he was of age, so he walked around wearing it tilted on his head in a form of aggrandised humour.

"Look at him,'" Hobhouse said. "He's all velvet and lace and mischief."

"Hush now," Matthews urged. "His mother is about to bawl our ears into deafness with a song."

Yet all were stunned into astonishment when the orchestra quietly played again and Mrs Byron sang to the music a poem written by Scotland's greatest poet, Robert Burns ... and she sang it beautifully:

> *'My love is like a red, red rose*
> *That's newly sprung in June:*
> *My love is like the melody,*
> *That's sweetly played in tune ...*

At the end of the song she was supposed to step down but, flushed with delight by the tumultuous applause, she followed it with another song by Burns that had everyone clapping in time to the music.

> *'John Byron, my jo, John,*
> *When we were first acquent;*
> *Your locks were like the raven,*
> *Your bonnie brow was brent;*
> *But now your brow is bald, John,*
> *Your locks are like the snow ...'*

"Byron, I didn't know that Robert Burns knew your father," said Scrope Davies, very impressed; until Byron quietly replied, "The name should be John *Anderson* not Byron, she's been changing it for years."

The song ended to more applause and Mrs Byron revelling in it, insisting on entertaining them all with one more song.

"*A sweet ballad this time*," she announced ... and as she began to sing again the orchestra caught her key and tune as she sang Burn's beautiful *'Afton Water'* —

> *"Flow gently, sweet Afton, among thy green braes,*
> *Flow gently, I'll sing thee a song in thy praise;*
> *My Mary's asleep by thy murmuring stream,*
> *Flow gently, sweet Afton, disturb not her dream..."*

By the time she started the second verse Byron had left the room, knowing that every verse would include the words "My Mary".

He wandered down to the servants' hall where the household staff were having their own party, wondering how *they* were getting along in their celebration?

He found them all seated down each side of the long table with Joe Murray sitting in the top seat – and so inebriated from all the wine that he had drunk, Joe was also singing – a very ribald and loose song, despite being in the presence of the female servants.

"Joe!"

"Oh, my lord! Many happy returns of the day to you!" Joe smiled. "I was just singing an old Navy song in your honour."

"You were in the Navy?"

"Oh, indeed yes," Joe said proudly. "At the age of fourteen I was sailing the wild seas as a cabin boy and steward to the captain of a King's ship. It was my job to keep his uniform and other clothes in ship shape. Oh, great days ... great days ... now here's another Navy song for you that all our crew used to enjoy ..."

Joe launched into the song that contained so much wayward wickedness it shocked all the female servants who swiftly put their hands over their ears, while it made Byron and the male servants laugh so hilariously it caused Nanny Smith to accuse his lordship of "encouraging Joe in his naughtiness."

At the song's end, his lordship proudly announced to all present that he was now promoting — "Our own naval hero and former cabin boy, Joe Murray, to the rank of *Lord High Admiral* of the Great Lake in front of Newstead Abbey!"

The laughter and clapping was thunderous and Joe Murray was twitted on his new title for weeks afterwards, much to his annoyance and frustration, because he could not remember a single thing about that night once he was sober again.

In the ballroom, Hobhouse was drinking champagne while sitting at a side-table with John Hanson; and as it was just the two of them, Hobby ventured to discreetly ask the attorney a question about a private matter that had been troubling him for some time.

When Hanson sat silent for a moment and did not immediately respond to the question, Hobby explained quickly — "You see, it's so terribly shocking, that at times I find myself wondering if it is true or not."

"Oh, yes, it's quite true," Hanson answered, his expression grave. "Although I am very much surprised that Lord Byron should have told *you* about it. It was a matter that caused him great shame and distress at the time, *and* I may add, it caused great distress to myself also. I wanted to *prosecute* that vile young woman."

"Byron gave me no actual details, you understand?" Hobby said with a tinge of embarrassment. "Other than the briefest information. He was in one of his dark moods at the time. He said that he believed his experiences at that time contributed much to his later periods of depression and melancholy."

"Yes, I believe that is also very true." Hanson's face saddened as he thought back.

"Shortly after he was eighteen," he said, "I met Lord Byron one evening in London for dinner. He was very melancholy on that night also, and referred back to that time of living with May Gray and having acts of sex forced upon him. He said he felt that the innocence of his childhood had been stolen from him, depriving him of the normal silly happiness of childhood and juvenile development that others boys had enjoyed. He sees it as the sole cause for why he often feels, in his mind, so much *older* than his friends."

Hobhouse was much affected by this. "And yet he is

the youngest of us all ... Oh, poor Byron ... I did not realise ..."

"And I believe it is also the reason why he loves his animals so much," Hanson added. "Not only because he believes he can trust them more than humans, but because he can enjoy being childish in the way he so often *plays* with them."

Hobhouse sat alert when he saw Byron coming back into the ballroom, pausing to pass on something very funny to Matthews and Scrope Davies, causing them to erupt with laughter.

"Pray don't tell Byron that I have spoken to you about this," Hobby said quickly. "I would hate him to think I doubted his word or betrayed his confidence."

"But you did doubt his word, Mr Hobhouse. His very *private* word."

"I simply found it too shocking to fully believe because he was then only a child of nine or ten." Hobby said fretfully. "And I have not betrayed his confidence in any way, because he told me that you were the only other person who had full knowledge of it."

"I would be very dismayed to find that his lordship has put his trust in someone who does not trust *him*."

"Then be assured, Mr Hanson, that of all the people in this world, Byron can trust *me*. My lapse in speaking to you was due to my natural inclination to be cynical about everything. You know what Byron is like – a complexity of contradictions: one day he loves having company, the next day he hates company and wants to be alone. He says he would never eat animal meat, yet today he says he *did* eat animal meat."

"And, according to Joe Murray, was violently sick afterwards."

Hobhouse glanced towards Byron again. "He would be mortified if he knew I had approached you about that frightful business in his childhood. It would spoil his celebration completely – and look how *happy* he is tonight!"

Hanson leaned forward and saw Byron walking towards them, the laughter still on his face. "Oh, thank goodness he has taken his coronet off instead of wearing it slanted like a court jester!"

"I think he was merely trying to take the 'pomp' out of it all," Hobby said.

"Yes ... and I can tell you another reason why he is happy tonight," Hanson said, smiling, "because he thinks that now he is twenty-one he will be free of *my* iron hand restraining his spending, and from now on it will be himself telling me what to do ... Am I correct, Lord Byron?"

"Correct about what, Mr Hanson?" Byron sat down on the chair next to Hobhouse and looked from one man to the other.

"Your happiness at finally being free of my complaints and restrictions on your spending."

"I am absolutely *delighted to* be free of you at last, Mr Hanson. You are the most miserly lawyer in all Christendom."

Hanson laughed. "And yet I believe you told my wife earlier this evening that you wish to retain me, and that you absolutely *refuse* to have anyone else?"

Byron sat back and sighed ruefully. "Women are such gossips."

Chapter Thirty-Five

~ ~ ~

In April 1809, Byron's plans to go abroad were nearing completion.

His rented London apartment in St James Street was no farther than a short walk from the rented apartments of Scrope Davies and John Hobhouse.

"You were not serious about going abroad, were you?"

Hobhouse had waited until they had returned to Byron's rooms after having lunch in Mayfair before bringing up the subject again.

"I have always been serious about leaving England." Byron was standing by the window, his hands in the side pockets of his breeches, gazing down at the street below. "Why? Have you been doubting it?"

"Yes, because you usually never know your own mind for more than ten minutes."

"Don't exaggerate, Hobby. I usually know my own mind very well."

"So where are you planning to go now? Is it still to India?"

"No, Asia Minor."

Hobhouse could not help smiling, because he still did not take any of it seriously. Ever since the night they had visited the Chaworths at Annesley Hall, Byron had often talked about going away and leaving England as soon as possible, yet here he still was – still *talking* about it. Well, let him talk on if it helped to console him.

"Why did you change your mind about India?"

"It would take too long to get the requisite papers for India. The Foreign Office has advised me that because I am a 'Lord of the Realm', I must be given British protection while I am in India, and that means official letters have to be sent to the British Consulates in Bombay and Bengal, and confirmations received back, and all that nonsense and nuisance would take at least a year. I can't wait that long."

"You have been communicating with the Foreign Office?" Hobhouse's brows puckered. "You mean you *are* serious about leaving England?"

"I have to, Hobby. I can't get my mind right here. I have to find a way of getting over her and putting the past behind me once and for all. Apart from that ... it will be fun to travel and see some of the rest of our world."

"Fun to travel – on your own?"

Byron took a step away from the window and stood for a moment looking at his glass-fronted bookcase crammed with books. "I just want to see places and learn things ... widen the scope of my mind through *reality*, not books."

Hobhouse's face had turned ashen. "But ... but only a month ago you officially took your seat in the House of Lords! I thought you were prepared now to start casting your votes in the House and maybe work to bring change and do great things to help England."

"I don't want to do great things to help England!" Byron snapped. "I want to do *something* to help Byron!"

After a silence, Hobby asked, "So when will you make your maiden speech in the House?"

"When I'm *ready* to do so. When I have something worthwhile to speak about."

Byron shrugged and returned to the window, again looking down at the people walking along the street.

Hobhouse refused to be deterred. "As a sworn-in Peer of the realm you *have* to do your political duty by casting your votes in the Upper House. And as you are so fond of quoting Plato, let me remind you that Plato said *'one of the penalties for refusing to participate in politics, is that we end up being governed by our inferiors."*

After a long silence, Byron shrugged, "I know, but still ... let me do some living first."

~ ~ ~

Hobhouse was passionate about his Whig politics, but that was not the reason he was objecting so strongly to Byron leaving England for a number of years. His objections were less to do with the necessity of another opposition vote, and more to do with himself.

How was *he* to enjoy life if Byron was not around? All that wit and vivacity and laughter? From the time their friendship had started at Cambridge life had daily become more pleasant, more amazing. True, it had also become more amusingly *absurd,* because Byron never failed to see the ridiculous in most things, hence so much laughter ... Scrope loved him, Matthews adored him, and quite a few young men at Cambridge had fallen hopelessly in love with him, because that was the strange *spell* that Byron cast.

One only had to observe Joe Murray and the rest of the staff at Newstead to see their absolute and genuine devotion to him. He was not like others, not of the norm. He was different, but not in any way that one could put their finger on and understand it. He was just *Byron.*

"Why don't you come with me, Hobby?"

Hobby came out of his silence and stared. "Go with you?"

"Yes, why not? It will be fun, and twenty-three is too young to be occupying yourself solely with politics."

Hobhouse was at a loss for words, because he knew it was impossible. "My father would never allow me to go wandering over Europe ... half of it is at *war*. The place is blood-soaked! Have you thought of that, Byron – that you will be walking through a war zone?"

"I will be sailing direct to Malta and by-passing the war zones."

"But why go to Asia Minor – the Ottoman Empire? My God, don't you know? They say the Turks are utterly barbaric."

"That is why the Foreign Office insist that I wear the red military coat of a British officer at all times while I am there. It will ensure my protection on sight apparently. Also I will be given papers with the Royal Seal."

"The Royal Seal – why?"

"The Foreign Office has requested me to bring back my opinion of the Turks, especially the pashas."

"The *pashas*?" Hobhouse could scarcely believe it. "Don't you know that a pasha is a Turkish officer of high rank, or a military ruler of an entire province?"

"Of course I know that."

"Then why go? Why allow the Foreign Office to *use* you? Because that's what they are doing! Can't you see the danger?"

"Oh yes," Byron smiled, "and that's the attraction and the excitement."

"Irrespective of the fact that you might get killed?"

"Oh, heigh-ho," Byron shrugged indifferently. "I often felt suicidal when I was younger, so now I will have a chance to see what it *really* feels like to totter about on the edge of the cliff."

Hobhouse's face was now grave as well as ashen. "Byron, this is not something to jest about."

"Oh, it is, Hobby, it *is,*" Byron insisted. "Because I will not be in any danger. The Turks have no quarrel with us, and I will simply be an appreciative Englishman going to visit the great Constantinople."

"And if you get killed by a group of rogue bandits?"

"Then if it must be so, pray let my blood be spilled on the soil of Greece."

"Greece?" Now Hobhouse was feeling utterly confused. "Byron, what the devil are you talking about? You have me all in a jangle – and I am truly not in the mood for one of your Byronic bamboozlements!"

Byron looked at Hobhouse very seriously. "Think back, Hobby, think back to all the years we have spent in classrooms studying ancient Greece in every aspect; it's language, it's philosophy, it's *literature.* And then, at Cambridge, all the study for our degrees? So wouldn't it now be truly wonderful to physically *go* to Greece and see where it all happened? Where *they* all lived ... Sophocles, Socrates? Plato?"

When Hobby sat staring at him but did not answer, Byron continued, "Because that is where I am truly going, Hobby, where I shall be travelling and living for some time, maybe for years – in *Greece.* The trip to Constantinople and Turkey was not originally in my plans, but now it will be just a short visit, and that's all."

"Because of the Foreign Office?"

"A small service to my country, nothing more."

After another silence Byron asked again, "Will you come, Hobby?"

Hobhouse shook his head regretfully. "I told you, my father would never allow it, nor would he agree to *fund* it."

"I thought he was one of the richest men in the country?"

"He is, very rich, but he will never pay for something he does not want, and I don't have sufficient funds of my own. No, Byron, I cannot go, but neither can *you* go on your own. It's a wonderful scheme but a wild one, which I think you should abandon for the time being at least."

"I won't be entirely alone. Fletcher, my valet, has petitioned to accompany me, and Matthews says he might come too, as far as Greece."

"Matthews? You told Matthews all about it before you told *me?*" Hobby was outraged. "You asked him first?"

"Yes, and I've asked you today and I'll be asking Scrope tomorrow, although I know *he* won't want to leave Brummell and the clubs to go riding across Greece."

Hobhouse stood up in a huff of indignation. "Do you think we are all as free and as careless as you? Matthews might *wish* to go with you, but financially he can barely exist as it is, never mind finding the money to go to Greece."

Byron was visibly surprised. "I have never had the impression that Matthews was short of money."

"No, because he is a dignified fellow, but he is an *academic,* for goodness sake. Everyone in academia lives on a pittance, including the tutors. Why do you think he now always uses your empty box at the opera? Because he loves the opera but usually cannot even afford to buy a ticket for standing room in Fop's Alley. And do you remember that night we all went to the opera and Matthews pretended he had forgotten to pack his opera suit and so had to borrow one from the hotel manager?"

Byron remembered. "The night he was almost strangled by that inflexible stock around his neck?"

"Yes, he had to wear that borrowed monstrosity because he did not actually possess an opera suit of his own, but was too proud to admit it."

Byron was thoughtful. "Poor Matthews ... but he must possess one now, if he uses my opera box."

"He does, because I had one made for him and pretended it was an opera suit my brother had ordered and never worn. He would never have accepted it as a gift. He's a very proud and brilliant young man, but he will not be going to Greece with you."

Byron sighed. "Then I must go on my own."

"We cannot allow you to go on your own with only a valet for company. All three of us will be up in arms if you even *attempt* it."

"Don't be silly, Hobby, I'm not a boy anymore."

"And are you forgetting that you have an impediment?"

"What impediment?"

"You have a lame right foot."

In the silence that followed, Hobby felt an immense sadness flowing through him, touching his very soul, knowing he had said the very worst thing it was possible to say to Byron.

Byron's response was flippant; he even accompanied it with a half-smile. "Oh, I'm sure I would have remembered in time, Hobby, but thank you for reminding me."

"I did not mean to say that," said Hobby, a little ashamed.

"Why not – it's true. I'm just surprised that you would think it is something that *I* could forget."

~ ~ ~

The problem with Byron's right foot came up again later that night, but in a completely different context, during dinner with Beau Brummell.

Hobby had been dismayed to learn that he was not included in the invitation. "It's a private dinner for two," Byron told him. "The Beau writes that he has something *very important* to tell me."

"Probably the name of his new courtesan," Hobby sneered. "You know it's all around town about him and Harriette Wilson."

"Who is she?"

"An aristocratic young lady of fallen repute. Hardly a suitable companion for a close friend of the Prince of Wales."

Byron smiled. "Hobby, you are so *correct* about everything."

"Yes, I usually am," Hobby replied grumpily as he walked to the door. "So please bear *that* in mind when you are reconsidering this wild travelling scheme of yours. Personally, I had enough of the ancient Greeks in school."

Beau Brummell was dressed as resplendent as always when Byron met him in one of the smaller dining rooms of the Argyle Rooms.

"I hear you have now officially taken your seat in the House of Lords," Brummell smiled. "So I have ordered the very *best* champagne in your honour."

"I doubt that you ever order anything other than the best champagne, Beau, even for just swilling your teeth after brushing them."

Brummell laughed. "Oh, you know me so well! Seriously though, this is even *better* than the best."

"Seriously though," Byron asked as he sipped his first glass, "what is this very important thing you wish to discuss with me?"

"Fabric," Beau said, his manner turning serious. "You know fabric and its various qualities is one of my most serious passions."

Byron instantly felt his mood turning blue. "You invited me to dinner to discuss *fabric?*"

"Fabric is extremely important," Brummell's face remained serious, "especially in your case."

"Oh?"

"I have been thinking over some of your difficulties, especially when you are required to wear white stockings for balls and other grand affairs. Is that a difficulty for you?"

"In what respect?"

"Well, at these functions, one cannot wear anything else but white breeches and white stockings. It is *de rigueur*, is it not?"

Byron's second glass of champagne was almost full. He knocked it back in one gulp, deciding that if he got drunk very quickly, it might make this conversation a lot more agreeable. He moved his hand to help himself to a third glass of champagne but Brummell's hand restrained him.

"Don't be alarmed. I am not here to embarrass you. I like you extremely, Lord Byron, and that is why I simply wish to help you."

"Then pray get to the point," Byron said stiffly. "If your point is that you have noticed when wearing stockings my right ankle is somewhat thinner than my left."

"Exactly my point – and that is where design and *fabric* will provide the solution."

Before Byron could stop him Brummell had lifted a small flat case from the floor and took out some sheaves of paper covered in charcoal drawings. "I recalled you telling me recently that as a small boy all your daydreams were militaristic."

"As are the dreams of most of us. Every small boy wants to at least *play* at being a soldier."

"In this case I was thinking more of the *Hussars*," Brummell said. "Now, what do think of this?"

He laid one of his drawings flat on the table so Byron could see the lines of a pair of straight full-leg trousers down to the ankle.

"Now if these were tailored in the correct fabric, then I believe these full-length trousers could be adopted as formal wear for balls and grand functions, instead of breeches and stockings. That would save you from having to stand by the window-drapes in order to hide your right ankle behind the velvet."

Byron half laughed at the audacity of it." I was probably *looking* through the window."

Beau met his eyes and did not answer.

"Well, maybe I was doing what you say," Byron conceded, "but it would have been unconsciously and not deliberately."

"So in wearing this style of formal full-leg trouser, that self-consciousness relating to your infirmity would be gone. And see here ..." Brummell pointed to the ankle end of the trousers — "If an elasticised black strap was added to the bottom end of the trousers, it could go between the heel and sole under the black shoe and not be visible."

"Why would a strap be needed?"

"To perfect the line of the trousers, the line. Nothing is more important than the *line* of any garment."

Brummell's eyes returned to the drawing. "The strap would also prevent the trousers from wrinkling or riding up, especially when you are on horseback or getting in and out of carriages ... I was thinking of suggesting the addition of a strap to the Hussars, but I suppose I will have to suggest it to the Prince of Wales first, so he can pass it on as *his* idea."

Byron was looking at George Brummell with a new understanding. Not only was he the most perfectly dressed man in all London, but now Byron was realising that when it came to clothes, Brummell had the keen and serious eye of a true artist, a creative genius of style and design.

"Beau, you are a genius," he said smiling.

Brummell nodded, acknowledging the fact. "I think the full-leg trouser should become the fashion for everyone instead of tight white breeches and stockings and dainty black pumps on our feet. After all, we are men of business, men around town – so why should we go out in the evenings dressed like *ballet dancers?*"

Byron laughed. "I have never worn dainty black pumps in my life, for obvious reasons."

"Scrope Davies tells me that you have the talent of a fine poet."

Byron shrugged. "A small talent, perhaps."

"Shy about it, eh?" Brummell grinned. "I have no hesitation in saying that I am a fine poet myself ... a poet in *cloth.*"

And indeed he was. Throughout the evening and dinner Brummell advised Byron that his full-leg trousers in summer should be in nankeen, a heavy twilled cotton. "No under-foot straps would be needed for them, the fabric will be heavy enough without them." And for winter, he advised, "the fabric, of course, *must* be merino wool."

They drank three bottles of champagne between them, rendering them both happily inebriated.

"Tell me, Lord Byron –"

"Please, drop the lord prefix, it's too formal and uncomfortable amongst friends."

"Oh good, because I intend to make you feel *very* uncomfortable. Is it true what I am told that it was you, *Lord* Byron, you, sir, when still at Cambridge, who gave myself and my friends an unflattering name that has now stuck – *'the Dandy set'?*"

Byron laughed guiltily. "And is it true what I am told that you, *Beau* Brummell, you, sir, always insist on your shoes being polished with *champagne?*"

"Aha, a little jest of mine – champagne is sticky, is it not?"

"I don't know – I've never wasted it on my shoes."

"Glad to hear it, because the only thing champagne is capable of *polishing* is the tongue."

It was long after midnight when Byron returned to

his rooms, champagned thoroughly, and full of good humour with his valet, Fletcher.

"I've seen him once, Mr Brummell," Fletcher said, "and to me he looked like a god. Tallest young man I've ever seen, and handsome as they come."

"Brummell, a god? Now let us not lapse into idolatry of heathen images, Fletcher. No, in my modest opinion, Beau Brummell is simply a fine man who is devoting his life and talent to the sole pursuit of *elegance.*"

Byron fiddled drunkenly with the buttons of his buff waistcoat. "Did you know, Fletcher, that it was Beau Brummell who got rid of woollen vests and created the modern waistcoat for us gents?"

"No, I did not know that, my lord."

"Oh yes, he did ... good and decent fellow that he is. And do you know *why* he considered the modern waistcoat to be so necessary to us gents, Fletcher?"

"I'm sure I have no idea, my lord, apart from an extra layer on the chest in cold weather."

"To hide our braces"

Now that his waistcoat was off, Byron placed his thumbs inside his braces and flicked them.

"No *young* man of style today would ever wear a belt around his waist, bagging up his waistline like farmers and mill workers."

"But some gents do prefer the belt," Fletcher said, "if only to pull in the fat on their waistlines."

"And this 'Y' woven into the back of the braces, d'you see, Fletcher?" Byron stood sideways and looked at his back in the mirror. "That is to ensure a correct fit and make certain that the straps do not slip loosely over the shoulders and ruin the *line* of the coat on top of it."

Fletcher's face was in a state of marvel. When Joe Murray was training him up to be his lordship's valet, he had never told him any of these things.

"The tailors do not tell Beau Brummell how a

garment should be cut," Byron said. "He tells them how it should be cut."

"Aye," Fletcher nodded. "I've heard it said that one visit from Mr Brummell can make a tailor famous."

"And tomorrow, Fletcher, he will be accompanying me to my tailors and assisting me in the choice of *fabrics* for my new trousers, and I think you should come with us and get measured up as well."

"Me? Why do *I* need to be measured up?"

Byron sat down on the bed and looked up curiously at his valet. "Do you not wish to look your best when we go travelling abroad?"

"Travelling Abroad?" Fletcher took a step back. "You mean ... you've now rightly decided to take me along with you?"

"I think I will *have* to take you along with me ..." Byron looked dismally down at his right shoe, "otherwise how will I ever get my right shoe or boot on or off without your help?"

Fletcher was delighted as he knelt down and untied Byron's right shoe and removed it, and then began to carefully manoeuvre off the special shoe worn inside it, until he could not restrain himself from saying excitedly, "You'll not mind me saying I hope, my lord, but this afflicted right foot of yours is now my *favourite* foot of the two."

Byron looked at his valet, and began to laugh, until he thought it so funny he fell back on the bed in laughter. "You are so absurdly comical at times, Fletcher, I think you will make a fine companion for me when we go abroad, I honestly do."

Chapter Thirty-Six

~ ~ ~

It took yet another two months, until the first week in June, before Byron had finally completed all his arrangements; received all the necessary papers; and had his bags packed in readiness to leave England.

His mother hated the idea of him going abroad as much as she had always done, and had used every contrivance possible to prevent him from going, but all had failed; and now she was filled with a sense of fatalism and began to weep endlessly.

"If you go abroad now, George, I know I will never see you again, I know it ... I've had a premonition."

He responded with an irritable gesture. "This premonition of yours is all down to your old beliefs in the Calvinistic doctrine of predestination – God foreordaining all that will happen to us. How can you believe that when even Jesus said we all have *free will.*"

"It's nothing to do with God," she said weeping." It's all to do with my Scottish second-sight." She thumped her chest. "It's something I feel in *here!*"

"You have second-sight in your chest?"

She glared up at him with fury. "It's no laughing matter, George, no laughing matter at all! Oh, I know you think it's fair and grand to go wandering off abroad like a noble vagabond in search of adventure, but what about *me?* What about all the years I've suffered and sacrificed bringing you up? And am I now to be left here like a worn-out old ornament gathering dust on a shelf?"

"I am leaving you here to do what you have always said you *wanted* to do – become mistress of Newstead

Abbey."

"And when you come back?"

"You will remain here and continue as mistress. I will live in my own apartments in the north-west wing."

There was no stopping his going away, and she eventually came to accept it, weeping all the time.

He begged Nanny Smith and the other servants to take care of her, to be kind to her, and to do their best to ignore all her tantrums. All promised him faithfully that they would.

Two days before Byron was due to leave Newstead for London, Joe Murray knocked, and then entered his room with a surprising statement: "It's Mr Hobhouse, my lord, he's just arrived."

"What? Hobby? *Here*?"

Joe nodded. "Will I take him into the parlour?"

"No, no, no," said Byron, jumping up from his seat "He's probably come all this way just to say farewell to me. Oh the dear fellow ..."

Joe Murray followed at a slower pace as Byron went rushing down one staircase after another until he reached Hobhouse standing in the hall ... looking like he had not slept in a week ... and surrounded by travelling bags.

"Hobby?"

"I'm coming with you," Hobhouse said tiredly. "I can't let you go on your own, not amongst the Turks, it's too dangerous."

Byron stared at him, not quite comprehending. "What about your father? Did he agree? Did he *fund* you?"

"Oh, that's all taken care of," Hobhouse shrugged. "And I'm sure my *step*mother is very glad to get rid of me. She really does *not* like my father to be reminded of my mother."

"What about your papers?"

"I don't need papers. You are the one who needs all that nonsense, due to being one of His Majesty's nobles. Although King George is now so mad he wouldn't know who you are from Adam; nor himself from Adam either. This country is going to the dogs, Byron, it really is."

Byron was smiling, and then his delight overcame him as he affectionately hugged his dear friend. "Hobby, Hobby, *Hobby* – you will not regret it. It will be fun and interesting and afterwards you may even find yourself writing a *boke* about it!"

"Actually," said Hobby in his usual top-drawer accent, "that's exactly what I plan to do, write a *travel boke*."

Byron's laughter filled the hall, causing Hobby to smile with puzzlement, wondering why Byron found that so amusing – writing a travel book was a very good and *valid* reason for going abroad.

The humour continued throughout dinner, infecting Hobhouse who was now almost as happy and as excited as Byron at the great adventures and new experiences waiting for them in foreign lands.

Then, utterly exhausted from his long journey, and the previous nights of poor sleep, Hobby retired to his room and finally sank down into the comfort of his bed with a feeling of great relief and peace ... and it was strange for him to realise, as he lay thinking, how he had often felt more at home here at Newstead than in his stepmother's house. But then, cut off as it was from the rest of the world, Newstead Abbey was indeed a place of true harmony with all of the green pastures that surrounded it, a place of quiet and tranquil peace ...

The racket that awoke him the next morning was so loud and horrid, so full of menace, he jumped out of his bed in a state of confusion – someone below was being murdered – and Mrs Byron was screaming ... although her words were too far away to understand.

He quickly pulled on his clothes and grabbed a heavy brass candlestick to fight the intruder, running downstairs until he passed Nanny Smith and two of the maids in the hall near the back of the house, clumped in a group together, and all were weeping.

"What?" he asked Nanny, but she merely wiped her eyes and silently shook her head.

He passed quickly on until he realised the screaming was coming from the garden, where he saw ... to his astonishment ... Byron running distractedly through the grounds in his limping way, head bent and hands clapped over his ears, while his mother chased after him screaming vilely — *"You want to learn! You want to learn! You ungrateful lame brat! If you go, I pray you come back as ill-formed in your mind as you are in body!"*

"Mrs Byron, Mrs Byron!" Hobhouse was utterly appalled. "Mrs Byron, please stop that!"

She turned on Hobhouse in fury. "And you are no better! *You* are probably the one who encouraged him in all this nonsense of going abroad! Well you had no right to do that, Mr Hobhouse, because he is my son, *my* son, so how dare you —"

Hobby rushed past her, in pursuit of Byron, finally finding him leaning against a tree in the small dark copse of trees near the Monks' Pond.

As Hobby approached him, Byron quickly turned his head, as if ready to run again, but seeing who it was, remained where he stood, his breath heaving, and the expression of anger and hurt on his face was one that Hobby had never seen before.

"Now you know the reason why I loathe her."

"I didn't know that you did." Hobby spoke to him calmly for some minutes, but Byron shook his head angrily.

"It is to *her* false delicacy at my birth that I owe the

infirmity of my foot; and yet, for as long as I can remember, she has never ceased to taunt and reproach me with it."

"That is frightful," Hobby agreed.

"Anything else she says," Byron continued, "all the abuse and fury that comes out of her mouth at times, I always ignore and never argue a word back to her in response – but I cannot bear it when her abuse becomes so personal!"

They talked for some time, until Byron had resumed his composure, wiping the tears from his face, before they began a slow walk back to the house.

"What happens now?" Hobby asked.

"I go abroad tomorrow, as planned."

"No, I mean, what happens when we get back to the house and you and your mother come face to face again?"

Byron shrugged. "As always, I will act as if nothing unpleasant has been said by her, and she also will act as if nothing unpleasant has been said by her. It's the only way we can survive together, and the quickest road to peace. Although I should warn you, she will probably now start weeping copiously about how hard her life has been, how *badly* John Byron treated her, until everyone feels sorry for her – including *me.*"

"But if you keep allowing her to get away with it, she will keep on doing it," Hobby said. "Why don't you stand up for yourself and lash back at her?"

"I can't lash back at her, Hobby, no matter what, I cannot do it."

"Why not?"

"Because ... as she keeps telling me ... she is my mother."

After a brief silence Hobby sighed woefully. "It seems you and I have the same problem."

"Do we?" Byron looked at him curiously. "Which is?"

"We are both *gentlemen,* brought up by our schools to be nothing less than gentlemen in action and words. And on top of that, we are both *Cambridge* men ... future pillars of society and all that ... can't let the standards of our Alma Mater down by shouting at women, not at *women.* One must always remember they are the weaker sex, the gentler sex ... no matter how loud they shout or how vilely they treat us ... Oh, God, am I really parroting such nonsense?"

Byron smiled. "Hobby, you really are ridiculously confused at times."

Hobby was about to answer when he saw Mrs Byron coming along the path towards them, her head drooping slightly and looking somewhat ashamed ... "George ... Oh, George, I'm ever so sorry for what I said ... it's just that my heart is so broken..."

Byron's response was stiff and cold. "Mother, if you please, we will forget it now. I have much to do today in preparation for my travels and many things still to attend to."

"But I am *cut to shreds* at the thought of you going so far away from me, George, cannot you *understand* that?"

Feeling somewhat embarrassed, Hobhouse quickly moved on and returned to the house, leaving them behind to speak together in privacy.

Joe Murray met him at the rear door, shaking his head in disgust at it all.

"It beats me how his lordship always manages to have the patience of a saint with that mother of his," Joe said sourly. "She will hold him there now talking for a while, making her excuses, and then it will all be dropped and forgiven and not another word spoken about it. You wait and see."

And Hobhouse waited and saw, a short time later, Mrs Byron coming back down the path looking much mollified by the conversation with her son, linking his arm possessively as they returned to the house.

"I believe she has persuaded him not to go," he said to Joe Murray.

Joe smiled cynically at the notion. "And I believe you don't know his lordship as well as I do, Mr Hobhouse. She can *say* what she wants, but he always *does* what he wants. And that's how it has always been."

Hobhouse was not so sure, not until Byron told him later: "I have promised to write to her regularly, and come back as soon as possible, and she, poor soul, believed me."

"You mean you are *not* going to write to her regularly?"

"Oh yes, I will do that. It's the coming back as soon as possible that's ridiculous, because I intend to stay away for as long as possible."

"And is she reconciled to you going now?"

"She appears to be. At least, more so than she was earlier."

Yet when the morning and moment of her son's departure came, Mrs Byron stood mute and gave no response to his farewell to her; watching with tearful eyes as the carriage rolled away with George and Mr Hobhouse inside it ... followed by the trap containing Joe Murray, Fletcher and the young page, Robert Rushton.

She turned to Nanny Smith. "Why has he taken Joe Murray and Robert Rushton with him? What need has he of them?"

"They're going only as far as London. The boy has never seen London so his lordship thought it would be a treat for him, and Joe too, because they will all be staying in a hotel, and Joe Murray has not been inside a hotel for forty years or more, and then no more than once."

"So my George is indulging them? With no care for the *expense* of it all!"

She turned back inside, muttering her regular complaint: "That boy will be the death of me and will drive me *mad*."

This annoyance was increased when she received a note from Byron, now in London, informing her that he was taking all his servants with him to Cornwall and would then send them back – "*except Fletcher, who has been acting so feverishly excitable that I intend to dump him in the sea as soon as we reach Falmouth*."

It seemed an age until his next letter, which arrived a week later.

Wynn's Hotel
Falmouth, June 22nd, 1809

Dear Mother – I am about to sail in a few days, probably before this reaches you.

I have paper in plenty. You shall hear from me at the different ports I touch upon; but you must not be alarmed if my letters miscarry. The Continent is in a fine state – an insurrection has broken out in Paris, and the Austrians are beating Bonaparte – the Tyrolese have risen ...

Mrs Byron was sitting up in bed as she read the letter, while Nanny Smith hovered about the room, pretending to adjust the curtains ... waiting to hear the news.

"He tells me, Nanny, that the Continent is in a fine state – *war* everywhere. Is that a way to console one's mother?"

And then she saw a postscript written on the back of the page —

PS: Pray tell Mr Rushton that his son is well, and doing well. So is Joe Murray, indeed better than I ever saw him; he will be back in about a month.

I ought to add the leaving of Joe Murray to my regrets, as his age, perhaps, will prevent me seeing him again. Robert I take with me; I like him, because like myself in the past, he seems like a friendless animal.

"He is now taking his page with him too – abroad!"

"Is he?" Nanny clasped her hands together with utter delight. "Oh, young Robert will be over the moon! Seeing all those *foreign* places and he still only fourteen. He's a very lucky lad."

Mrs Byron "Hummphed"– and then looked scornfully at Nanny Smith: "Pity he doesn't dump Joe Murray in the sea, instead of Fletcher."

Nanny again adjusted a fold in the curtain, hiding her smile ... Mrs Byron's long-held jealousy of old Joe was fair ridiculous.

~~~

Before leaving London, a sumptuous send-off dinner for Byron and Hobhouse had been hosted for them by Charles Matthews, an act which deeply moved the two men, both knowing that Matthews did not have money to squander.

Once the dinner was over and the wine had been flowing for some time, Matthews and Scrope Davies amused themselves and Hobhouse by making merry fun of Byron's main reason for leaving England – his secret love for Mary Chaworth – secret to all but his closest friends.

"If he *'cannot love but one',*" Matthews supposed, "I

presume he means only 'one at a time', because he seems a pretty general lover to me."

"Especially with one of his maids at Newstead," Hobhouse said. "The girl follows him around like a sick chicken."

Byron took all the laughter and jibing without any offence, sad to be leaving his friends, but glad to be finally getting away, not only from Nottingham but also Annesley Hall, which held so many reminders for him.

And now they were in Cornwall, waiting for the Malta packet boat, only to be eventually told that it would be delayed for several weeks.

"So are we to hang around Falmouth until then?" Byron's impatience was unrestrained, until he was told that the packet for Lisbon in Portugal was leaving the following morning.

"Then we will sail to Lisbon instead. What say you, Hobby?"

Hobby did not care where they went, just so long as he was with Byron – having come to the conclusion some weeks previously that "*friendship*" was the only real happiness in this world." And of all his friends, Byron was the best.

Joe Murray took the news of the change of ship and destination with some gravity.

"The hold-up of the Malta packet must be due to this lamentable weather," Joe said, eying the sky. "Looks to me like there could be a storm brewing."

Byron looked up at the clear blue sky and brilliant sunshine, and then looked at Joe as if thinking him unhinged.

"Have I become colour-blind overnight, Joe, or does that sky consist of only one colour – blue!"

"Ah, but a seafaring man can hear and smell the winds *beyond* the sky, and don't forget, I was once in the Navy."

Joe stuck his hands in his pocket and kicked moodily at a stone on the grass. "Perhaps it would be wise if I was to go with you, my lord ... just to see you safely across the water like ..."

A moment later they heard Fletcher shouting excitedly to Robert Rushton *"We're going to Portingale!"*– and Byron realised the only lamentable thing in Joe's mind was that *he* was not going abroad with them.

"I mean, fair to say, my lord, I have been looking after you, off and on, since you were a lad of ten, so only natural I would have my concerns now about your welfare ... in the coming storm ..."

Byron was looking at Joe with one of his under-looks, a slight smile on his face.

"How would Newstead manage without you, Joe?"

"Hard to say ... but I don't think it will fall down or lose a roof or owt like that."

"And the staff?"

"Have Nanny Smith to instruct and guide them. A good old bird is Nanny. And don't forget, your own mother is there now to rule the roost ..." Joe suddenly shuddered.

Byron remained silent as he contemplated Joe, while Joe gazed wistfully across the sea to the horizon. "Long time since I've been on a ship ... more than fifty years now ... I have my little rowing boat on the Newstead lake, but that's not the same as having the strong planks of a ship's deck under your feet."

The following morning the cutter boats were busily ferrying the passengers out to the ship, *HMS Princess Elizabeth,* amidst a hullabaloo of shouts and pandemonium as their baggage was loaded with them.

There were two officer's wives, a few children, two or three maids, and two army subalterns going to join the British troops in Portugal.

The last cutter rowing out to the ship contained Lord Byron's party of five, which included old Joe Murray.

~ ~ ~

As soon as they were all on deck, a young midshipman, whose age could not have been more than thirteen, approached Byron and gave a bow.

"Good morning, your lordship. Captain Kidd requests that I escort you to his cabin to be introduced."

"Captain Kidd?"

Byron looked at Hobhouse, and Joe Murray, and even Fletcher was smiling, all trying not to laugh.

"Captain Kidd?" Byron said again. "Is that truly his name? The same as the famous pirate?"

"Aye, sir," the boy nodded, "but our Captain Kidd is not a pirate."

"I should damn well hope not," Hobhouse said. "Or we may all never see England again."

"Or our purses," said Joe Murray.

"Or the liquor in our trunks," said Fletcher. "They say Captain Kidd the pirate was very fond of liquor."

In the end they were all laughing, and the boy turned up his eyes: he was used to this, and probably would have to go through it all again when he was sent to address the two soldier passengers.

"I say," said Hobhouse suddenly, "this Captain Kidd is no relation to the *pirate,* is he? A grandson, perhaps?"

"No, sir. The other Captain Kidd was hanged before he could spurt a spawn."

The group erupted in further laughter, to the puzzlement of the boy. "That's what our captain says about him."

The innocence of the boy alerted Joe Murray. "Lad," he said gently, "is this your first voyage?"

"Nay," the boy shook his head, "I've been out once before."

"And how far out did you go?"

"Same as now – Lisbon, but the natives call it *Lisboa*."

"Then on this voyage, lad, you keep your eye on *me*," Joe said kindly, "because I'm an old sea-dog that can help and advise you if any time you find yourself in ship-trouble, and don't want to catch the attention of the captain."

"Aye, sir, thank you, sir."

"And your name?" Byron smilingly asked the boy. "It wouldn't be Francis Drake, would it?"

"No, my lord, it's Mayfield ... midshipman Harry Mayfield"

"Then lead on, Mr Mayfield, lead me on to your captain."

"And you, young Harry," said Joe Murray, "you do remember what I said to you – any seafaring trouble and you send for *me*."

Two days later it was young Harry who was laughing his head off as he watched the old sea-dog, Mr Murray, stumbling along the deck, his face as yellow as jaundice; while the rest of his party were confined to their cabins with bad seasickness; even the young lad with them, Rushton, was too sick to move.

All sick – all except Lord Byron who enjoyed the rocking and rolling of the ship and seemed to have been born for a life on the water.

He was now coming along the deck. *"Roll on blue ocean, roll!"* Byron laughed at the boy, who laughed back and asked him:

"Did you never want to be a sailor, my lord?"

Byron sat down on the railing between the pegs of the mizzen shrouds.

"No, Mr Mayfield, I was never destined to be a sailor of any rank, but my grandfather was a Naval Officer in the Royal Navy and rose to the rank of Admiral."

"Admiral?"

Yes, Admiral John Byron, my father's father, who was known to every sailor in his time as 'Foul-weather Jack'."

"Why so?"

"Because no matter how fair the day, or how bright the sun, as soon as Admiral John Byron commanded and took a ship out from port, the weather *always* turned foul. I'm told some sailors deserted their posts and jumped ship rather than sail with him."

"He must have been a good sailor though, if he was made an admiral."

"He must have been," Byron nodded, "because he succeeded in circumnavigating the world on his many voyages, and Captain James Cook gave some beautiful place the name of '*Byron Bay*' in his honour."

"Captain James Cook?" the boy almost spluttered. "The great explorer?"

"Yes, the same."

Young Harry's face was full of wonder. "And Byron Bay, where is that?"

"Oh, some place in the Antipodes. I'm told it is in the north-west section of New South Wales."

Byron looked up at the flapping sails. "This wind is good, because it will get us there faster."

"And it's a warm wind."

"It is, Mr Mayfield, a warm June wind."

Young Harry liked Lord Byron, and liked him more with each day that passed – yet Harry also found him as strange and unfathomable as the dark depths of the sea beneath them. For as friendly and playful as his lordship could be in daytime – at night he always preferred to remain alone and aloof.

He never joined the captain in his cabin for dinner, nor even stayed with his friends, but always took himself up on deck to sit alone, leaning against the mizzen shrouds, often humming a tune to himself as the stars twinkled above him, his eyes constantly following the track of the moon across the sky.

Young Harry Mayfield knew this, because he often slyly and secretly watched him, and often desperately wondered what Lord Byron was thinking about as his eyes calmly contemplated the stars and the slow path of the moon in the sky.

PART SIX

"Of Albania, it may be said, they (Lord Byron and John Hobhouse) were almost the discoverers of it, so little was known of it in England, or even in Western Europe, previous to their journey."

John Galt.

Chapter Thirty-Seven

~ ~ ~

September 1809
Newstead Abbey,
Nottinghamshire.

This now – this thing that kept torturing her in the middle of the night and most of the day – was it really the Scottish second-sight? Or a premonition? Or nothing more than a devoted mother's fear for the life of her son?

She pulled herself out of the bed and held on to one of the four posts, her breathing deep ... This conviction, within her, that she would never see her son alive again, why was it so strong?

She sat in the darkness, listening to the silence. The silence of the great mansion of Newstead Abbey, her son's ancestral home.

That rankled: the fact that it was not *her* home also. No, when her son had inherited the title of Lord Byron at the age of ten, Newstead Abbey had become *his* ancestral home, and his alone. And she, his mother on the Gordon side, was now merely and legally her son's tenant.

What she needed now was a glass of whisky, but she knew her bedside bottle was empty.

If only she had the nerve to open her door and walk down the long dark corridor to the library where she had another bottle hidden behind the Bible.

She took a step to move, then hesitated. No, she did

not dare – not even with the light of a candle would she dare to walk around Newstead Abbey alone at night, and all due to the fright put into her by son.

She did not believe in ghosts, but once he had returned from university in Cambridge and they had moved in here to live in this mansion, George had convinced her that Newstead Abbey – at one time a monastery – had its own ghost.

"If you wish to go wandering along the corridors during the night," he had said to her, "don't be alarmed if you look over your shoulder and see the ghost of a monk in black robes following you."

Nonsense, all nonsense!

Yet George had insisted – "He walks from room to room and from hall to hall, and refuses to leave because he was once the Friar of this Abbey. The Caretaker. So if you see him, say naught to him and he will say naught to you."

Ridiculous!

Yet George had continued to warn her ominously: "*I* may be the lord of Newstead by day – but the *monk* is the lord by night.*"

She was certain he had made it all up, just to keep her away from his wing of the house and his bedroom, convinced he was sleeping with one of the maids. Yet no matter how many times she had attempted to go up there at night and catch him out, she had faltered in her steps, so great was the fright he had instilled in her.

She slowly moved her body back under the sheets and eiderdown, laying back tensely in the darkness, wondering why, after he had *promised* to write to her regularly, she had not received a word from him since he had boarded his ship at Falmouth three months ago.

~~~

The following morning she was fast asleep when Nanny

Smith came into the bedroom to awaken her with a cup of tea.

"What? When?" she asked in alarm, her eyes dazed with sleep.

"It's ten o'clock, Madam."

"Ten o'clock?" Mrs Byron pulled her cumbersome body up on the pillows and asked her usual first question: "Is there a letter today?"

"No, Madam."

"No letter?"

"No, Madam."

Och, then I don't want to get up at all! Would it be a great sin, Nanny, if I stayed in my bed and gave no bother to life today ... I'm that weary ... worrying about my George."

"And why so?" Nanny said comfortingly. "He's a young man now, full of energy and strength, and he's no fool either, not by a long shot."

"So *why* has he not written to assure me he is alive and well then?"

"I'm sure I don't know, Madam."

"And *where* is Joe Murray? He was going with him only as far as Cornwall, and then coming back to Newstead. It doesn't take almost three months to journey back from Cornwall."

Nanny Smith was now certain that his lordship must have taken old Joe abroad with him. If not, and the two of them were stuck somewhere in England, Joe would have sent them a note.

"Well, we don't know how long it takes to get from Cornwall to Nottinghamshire, do we, Madam? No one has ever done that journey before, not anyone from Newstead."

"Were you *born* stupid?" Mrs Byron asked vindictively, her eyes murderous. "You drive me mad, Nanny, always making excuses for everyone."

She reached for her teacup and drank thirstily. "I'll not spend another night worrying without sleep. No, so there's only one thing for it! Have one of the maids bring up my breakfast – and a *good* breakfast, mind, three eggs and four sausages – and then you get my bags packed in readiness for my journey down to Cornwall."

Nanny Smith blinked. "Cornwall?"

"Aye, Falmouth. It's the only way I can find out if he boarded his ship or not. Or was he press-ganged into the Navy. We are at *war*, and that kind of thing is happening all the time – press-ganging young men onto the ships so they can help the Navy fight the French."

"And if you learn that he *did* board his ship, what then?"

"Then I'll follow him in a ship over to Malta. That's where his ship was going, wasn't it? Malta?"

"I'll have your breakfast sent up."

Nanny returned to the Servants Hall shaking her head in despair as she spoke to Cook.

"She's been following him everywhere since he was a boy. Jealous of everyone and anyone who goes near him. But if she follows him to Malta and finds him there, he'll go crazy at the first sight of her. I'm sure it was only to escape from her that he went abroad in the first place."

Cook was smiling. "She won't be going anywhere when she sees *that*." She nodded towards a letter on the kitchen table. "The steward brought it over from the lodge no more than a minute ago."

Nanny stared towards the letter. "Is it from him, Lord Byron?"

"It must be. It has his wax seal and a foreign frank on it."

Chapter Thirty-Eight

~ ~ ~

Lisbon, July 16th, 1809

*Dear Mother – we are two weeks now in Portugal
and I am very happy here, because I loves oranges,
and I talks bad Latin to the monks, who understand
it, as it is like their own, – and I goes into society
(with my pocket-pistols), and I swims in the Tagus,
all across at once, and I rides on an ass or a mule,
and I swears in Portuguese, and have got bites from
the mosquitoes.*

His mother laughed, knowing he was mimicking the
voice of a small child on holiday ... such a pity those
days of his childhood were gone now, those days when
she had full control of him. Now she had no control at
all.

 She read on:

*When the Portuguese are pertinacious, I say
CARRACHO! – which is the great oath of the
grandees, that supplies the place of "Damme", – and
when dissatisfied with my neighbour, I pronounce
him AMBRA di MERDO! With these two phrases, and
a third, AVA BOURO, which means "Get an ass", I
am universally understood to be a person of degree
and a master of languages. Tomorrow we start to
ride 400 miles as far as Gibraltar, where we embark*

for Malta.

She squinted with puzzlement through the papers in her hand, then up at Nanny Smith – "Do you see what he has done, Nanny? He *did* write to me as soon as he reached foreign soil, but then he didn't take the time nor the trouble to *post* the letter, like any good son would do! No, he's just added paragraphs here and there as he went along, without a thought or care for causing such cruel worry to his dear mother."

"At least you know now that he is safe," said Nanny, but Mrs Byron was not listening.

<u>Gibraltar - August 11th</u> – I sent my baggage, and part of the servants, by sea to Gibraltar, and travelled on horseback to Seville (one of the most famous cities in Spain). I had orders from the governments, and every possible accommodation given to me on the road, as an English nobleman in an English uniform is a very respectable person in Spain at present. The horses are remarkably good, and the roads far superior to the English roads without one toll or turnpike. You will suppose this when you know I rode through this parching country in the midst of summer, without fatigue or annoyance. I am going over to Africa tomorrow; it is only six miles from this fortress.

<u>August 13th</u> – I have not yet been to Africa – the wind is contrary, but I dined yesterday at Algerciras with

Lady Westmoreland where I met General Castanos, the celebrated Spanish leader in the late and present war. Today I dine with him. He has offered me letters to Tetuan in Barbary for the principal Moors.

<u>August 15th</u> – I have sent Joe Murray and young Rushton back by sea. Pray show the lad kindness, as he is my great favourite. Say this to his father, who might otherwise think he has behaved ill.

I hope this finds you well. Believe me,

Yours ever, BYRON

"So he *did* take Joe Murray with him – that uppity old upstart! What need had he of him, when he has Fletcher as his valet now?"

"His lordship has always been very fond of old Joe." said Nanny.

"Yes, *too* fond! Anyone would think they were related!"

The following day a second letter arrived with the Gibraltar frank on it, which Mrs Byron opened before she realised that it was not addressed to her.

Gibraltar, August 15th 1809

Mr Rushton,

I have sent Robert home with Mr Murray, because the country, which I am about to travel through, is in a state which renders it unsafe, particularly for one so young. I allow you to deduct five-and-twenty pounds a year for his education for three years, provided I do not return before that time, and I desire he may be considered as in my service.

Let every care be taken of him, and let him be sent to school. He has behaved extremely well, and has travelled a great deal for the time of his absence. Deduct the expense of his education from your rent.

Yrs etc., BYRON

Mrs Byron was aghast. "Since when did he start writing direct to our *farmers?* And since when did he start allowing tenants to withhold their rent in order to educate their sons?"

She folded the letter and handed it dismissively to Nanny Smith. "Have that delivered to Mr Ruston, and tell them to say Mrs Byron opened it by mistake."

"Robert's father?"

"Yes, him. He'll be dancing a jig around his haystack when he reads that."

~ ~ ~

Joe Murray, accompanied by Robert Rushton, finally arrived back at Newstead.

Mrs Byron greeted the old servant with great pleasure, eager to hear all his news.

Joe told her all he could, but it was not enough for Mrs Byron who wanted to know more and more, until Joe finally concluded that – apart from some early seasickness – he and the boy had "the time of our lives!"

She could see that with her own eyes; both looked as tanned and as healthy as she had ever seen them, which annoyed her.

"I don't want to know about *you!*" she declared irritably. "I only want to know about my George."

"I can only tell you so much, because from a port in Spain myself and young Robert were sent on a ship with some of the baggage up as far as Gibraltar," Joe said. "And when we finally met up with them there, Fletcher told me that his lordship spent most of his time riding across Spain *singing.*"

"Singing?"

"Aye, and Fletcher said his lordship often sang the same song – in a good voice, mind – and when Fletcher asked Mr Hobhouse what song it was, Mr Hobhouse told Fletcher it was the *roryto* from the *Messiah*. So a hymn like."

"The *oratorio* from the Messiah, you fool." Mrs Byron reflected with some surprise on this.

"Although I'm not a bit surprised," she said with a sniff of pride. "My George was always reading his Bible when a boy, and then at Cambridge he was always popping down to London and the Opera House."

She peered at Joe, suspiciously. "Is that all you have to tell me? Is that Gibraltar a safe place for a young nobleman to be?"

"Well, his lordship is fearless of all danger," Joe replied. "And if I may say, foolishly so. At Gibraltar he was still determined on going among the Moors, and I didn't like that at all, and I told him so."

"Is Mr Hobhouse not advising him sensibly?"

"Aye, he is," said Joe, lighting his pipe, "as best he can, that is. But sometimes his lordship ignores his friend's advice, and in consequence Mr Hobhouse just keeps on travelling beside him. As loyal as Boatswain he is."

"What do they do in the evening in that Gibraltar place?"

"Mr Hobhouse usually went off to his room to write passages for his travelling book, while Lord Byron amused himself outdoors flirting with the Spanish peasant girls and making them laugh."

"Flirting with the Spanish girls? So his riding across

Spain must have helped him to forget Mary Chaworth then."

"Oh, I wouldn't be so sure about that." Joe sucked on his pipe. "From what I've seen, he only *flirts* with them for fun."

Mrs Byron stood for a moment in silence, thinking of George's father – an incurable *flirt* with women *he* was – even after they were married.

"Still," she said, her face frowning with disapproval, "I don't like the thought of my George flirting with females, and certainly not with females of the peasant class!"

Joe sat up, realising his mistake, and sought to quickly remedy it. "Oh, it was all just harmless banter from what I saw, but at Gibraltar there were one or two very *high-class* young Spanish *ladies* of the *gentry* who gave his lordship a lot of respectable attention."

"Did they now? And how did my George respond?"

"He gave them a lot of respectable attention back. And one day I heard him say he thought the Spanish ladies were the most charming in the world."

Mrs Byron did not like the sound of any of it. Her plan was that one day, when she herself was much older, George would marry a young lady of very high rank – one *befitting* the title and coronet of a *Lady Byron* – not some foreign Spanish piece who could not even speak proper English.

She rushed back to her room and sat down to write a hasty letter to George, warning him –

I hear you are quite charmed with the Spanish Ladies. For Heavens sake have nothing to do with them! They make nothing of poisoning both Husbands and Lovers if they are jealous of them or they offend them. And the Italian ladies do the same. So I beg you, have nothing to do with any foreign females.

PART SEVEN

"'Tis pleasing to be schooled in a strange tongue
By female lips and eyes — that is I mean,
When both the teacher and the taught are young,
As was the case, at least, where I have been."

BYRON

Chapter Thirty-Nine

~~~

Nanny Smith said: "Well, it is late October now, Madam, so small wonder that the weather is getting colder and you're beginning to feel it. Will I bring a wrap to put around your shoulders?"

"Ye English!" exclaimed Mrs Byron impatiently. "Why must you always talk about the *weather* when you prefer to avoid a subject? I said I was feeling cold with *dread* because I have not had a letter from my George for months now, months! Did I not say that, eh? Did I not?"

"Aye, you did, Madam."

"And what has that got to do with the weather, pray?"

"Only that the post is very much like the weather in many ways, unreliable at the best of times. And the post from *foreign* countries to here ... " Nanny shook her head with misgivings.

"He promised he would write to me regularly. Now *why* has he not done that if he is fit and well?"

"I'm sure I don't know, Madam."

Nanny was feeling weary with the hum-drum of it all, having to endure this same old routine again and yet again – and all because of some stupid superstition in Madam's mind that she would never see her son alive again.

When Nanny returned to the Servants' Hall she glowered at Joe Murray. "If a letter don't come soon then Susan will have to take over my duties with her ladyship, because I can take no more of her dreads."

There was relief all round when a letter arrived a few days later. Mrs Byron devoured every word:

Malta, September 15, 1809

Dear Mother —Though I have a very short time to spare, being to sail immediately for Greece, I take this opportunity of telling you that I am well.

I have been in Malta for three weeks, where I met a most extraordinary woman, whom you have doubtless heard of, Mrs Constance Spencer Smith, of whose escape the Marquis de Salvo published a narrative a few years ago. She has since then been shipwrecked and her life has been so fertile in remarkable incidents, that in a novel of romance they would appear improbable.

She excited the vengeance of Bonaparte by her part in some conspiracy; has several times risked her life; and she is not yet twenty-five. She is here, on her way to England to join her husband, being obliged to leave Trieste by escaping from an Inn late at night dressed in male clothes. Bonaparte is even now so incensed against her that her life would certainly be in danger if she was taken prisoner a second time.

Since my arrival here, I have scarcely had any other companion, as she insisted on my company at all times. I have found her very pretty, very accomplished, and very eccentric. I developed a passion for her, but it was merely a Platonic one, and thus I broke no commandments, not even when she begged me to elope with her to Venice. Yet in the end she still managed to beguile me of my very valuable yellow diamond ring.

You have seen Murray and Robert by this time, and received my last letter. I have touched at Cagliari in Sardinia, and at Girgenti in Sicily.

Yours ever, BYRON

As always, Byron's letters to his mother were written in the way of the traveller, his news restricted solely to the everyday trivia, sights, gossip, and scandals which he knew she would enjoy reading; but beyond that, he told her nothing more.

What Byron did not tell his mother was that while in Malta, he was again encouraged by English naval and diplomatic intelligence to travel into Turkey as an innocent tourist and bring back an account of how the political wind was blowing with Ali Pasha who claimed to be an ally of the English in the war with France, but was he? And would he remain so?

An Englishman going into Turkey would be viewed with the usual Turkish suspicion and scrutiny, but a young English Lord of the Realm, possessing papers with the Royal Seal, would be greeted with great civility.

Also, while in Malta, John Hobhouse's cynical mind was beginning to puzzle over *why* the English diplomats in Malta were so very keen for *Lord Byron* to go into Turkey, and to go there straight away, before setting foot in Greece itself? What difference did the timing of Lord Byron's travels here or there make to them? Byron had agreed in London that he would go into Turkey, but why did it have to be the very *first* place he went to from

Malta?

Hobby voiced his reservations to Byron. "I don't think we should go into Turkey at all. They are reputed to be utterly barbaric – and as for Ali Pasha, I'm told that every place he has conquered in battle, he has left behind pyramids of decapitated heads belonging to the Greek soldiers who fought to resist him."

"Oh, that was long ago," interjected Sir Alexander Ball, the Governor of Malta, in whose house they were dining. "Ali Pasha is more mature now, a man of sixty, and more civilised. He also claims to be a great friend to the English, so you will be quite safe."

Byron sat back and sipped his wine, more inclined to agree with Hobby. He had left England to visit Greece, especially *Athens* ... the ancient seat of his heroes. So Turkey could wait.

After that, Hobby was allowed to see very little of Byron, due to his company being courted very selectively by either Sir Alexander Ball or Mrs Constance Spencer Smith, a young woman whom Hobby did *not* like. Not only was she *obsessed* about defeating the French, she was also – for a married woman – too flirtatious with Byron, and too assiduous in her need to constantly seek out his company, uncaring of her reputation: a very strange way for a *lady* to behave, in Hobby's opinion.

Their evenings at dinner were now also joined by a man named George Forresti, son of the British Consul in Malta, who also pressed them to go direct to Ali Pasha.

"Although you will have to go a small part of the way over land," he said. "Most of our Navy ships cannot pass through the Ionian Islands."

"Why is that?" asked Byron.

"Because the Ionian Islands are all in the hands of the French. Have been for a number of years now."

"And, you know," said Sir Alexander Ball, sitting forward at the table and speaking directly to Byron, "it is such an obstacle – such a major *obstacle* to the British interests in India having that route blocked off from us. But Napoleon is keeping a tight grip on them, Corfu, Cefalonia, Santa Maura, and all the other Ionian islands, because he knows that whoever rules the Ionian Islands, dominates the sea routes to the East. And it is trade in the *East* which hopefully will provide England with much of its prosperity in the future."

George Forresti nodded in agreement. "And that is why, Lord Byron, it would be a great service to England if you could visit Ali Pasha and pay him your respects as an English nobleman. If only to reassure him of England's friendship."

Byron looked at Hobby, and then from one man to the other – the man from the Consulate, and the man from Government House – not quite comprehending.

"What does Ali Pasha have to do with the Ionian Islands and the trade routes to the East?"

"His province is on the coast, overlooking the sea routes from the Ionian Islands. As our ally, he keeps us informed of all movements of the French ships. That is why both sides court him, and why any small thing you can do to help us retain his friendship would be most valuable."

The following afternoon, taking coffee in the sunshine outside one of the coffee houses near the seafront, Byron and Hobhouse discussed it, and Byron's mind was still firmly fixed on Athens.

"So what difference would a few months make to the alliance with Ali Pasha? My respects to him will be as courteous in January as they would be now in September, so why the rush?"

Hobhouse pondered. "I think they may simply want you to get it done and over with, so they can send a report to London and then sit back and relax, having *proved* to their employers at home that they do occasionally carry out some work now and again, out here in this sunshine."

Hobhouse sipped his coffee. "In any event, I think we should quit Malta, because you are becoming far too susceptible to distractions that are not in our itinerary, such as gallanting most nights over at Mrs Fraser's house with Constance Spencer Smith."

Byron laughed. "Do I detect a hint of jealousy, Hobby, because it is not *you* whom Constance is courting?"

"She shouldn't be courting anyone. She's a married woman."

"Our friendship is perfectly chaste. I find her eccentricity very amusing

"Ah, there you are, Lord Byron!"

Byron looked up at George Forresti, the man from the Consulate. "Good afternoon, sir."

"I say, are you gentlemen aware that there is an English brig leaving Malta first thing in the morning? The brig is to convoy a small sail of about fifty merchant ships to Patras, the chief port on the western side of the Morea. But I'm quite sure the captain would be only too happy to give you berths and drop you off at Preveza if you wish?"

"Preveza, where is that?"

"Albania. As a matter of fact, Lord Byron, if you were to get off ship at Preveza, the journey overland to pay your respects to Ali Pasha would be quite short, just four or five days travelling through the most beautiful mountain scenery. And I doubt there will be another ship leaving Malta before next week."

Byron was very tempted by the idea of being amongst mountains again. "The hills and mountains of Aberdeen were once my closest friends," he said wistfully. "The receptacles for all my thoughts."

"We may as well go and get it over and done," Hobby said resignedly. "We've seen enough of Malta anyway and should travel on." He gave a cynical smile to Mr Forresti. "And what a happy coincidence that there is a ship leaving tomorrow that will take us."

Forresti nodded. "At seven o'clock tomorrow morning the ship will sail out, so be down at the docks in good time," he advised. "The ship is the *Spider*. And may I say again, Lord Byron, what an absolute pleasure it has been to meet and dine with you here in Malta. And I have no doubts that Ali Pasha will have the same sentiments when you enter his palace in Tepeleni. Most certainly he will."

"Thank you, sir."

"Oh, and of course the same to you, Mr Hobhouse. You will take very good care of our young lord now, won't you? And happy sailing." He doffed his hat. "Good day, gentlemen."

Later that evening Sir Alexander Ball called on Lord Byron, bringing with him a servant who presented to Byron two magnificent British military red uniforms with gold epaulettes, and then handed to him one of the finest sabres Byron had ever seen, carved in gold and silver with pearls on the handle.

"I must impress on you, Lord Byron, that you will be entering the unknown world of Albania and the palace of Ali Pasha as an official envoy of His Majesty and the United Kingdom."

"An *official* envoy?"

"No other type of envoy would be allowed inside the palace, but you will be given a very good welcome I am sure."

Hobby was also provided with two more uniforms carrying the epaulette of a lieutenant. "Why is it so important for us to wear military uniforms anyway, and such *grand* ones?"

"Because the Turks have great respect for wealth and rank and are also very impressed by the of *show* of both, and especially by Ali Pasha who is constantly being courted by the French in *their* magnificent uniforms."

He turned to Byron. "All we ask is that you pay your respects to the Vizier, my lord, but while doing so, please try and impress on Ali Pasha the importance of remaining an ally to Britain."

"And this ... " Byron was admiring his beautiful sabre. "You know we shall be venturing down to Athens once we have been to see the Pasha, so where and how do I return this sabre?"

"The uniforms you may keep to wear on your travels afterwards, as they will afford you much protection in this time of war; but the sabre you must remove and present as a personal gift to Ali Pasha from yourself."

Hobby was frowning. "This all sounds like some sort of mission to me – an *intelligence* mission perhaps?"

"No, no, not at all." Sir Alex rebuffed the suggestion with an uncomfortable smile. "More of a *diplomatic* mission, and one which we are certain Lord Byron will carry out perfectly."

~~~

The following morning, some hours after the *Spider* had sailed away from Malta with Lord Byron and John Hobhouse aboard, Sir Alexander Ball and Mr Forresti from the British Consulate were very much relieved.

"I do believe," said Sir Alex to Forresti, "that as soon as Ali Pasha meets Lord Byron, his poor perverted mind will be unable to concentrate on anything else."

"Well, he is a beautiful and very personable young man," Forresti replied, "and it is well known that Ali Pasha has a certain predilection for handsome *youth*. Was it wise for us to send his lordship into such personal danger?"

"All for king and country, old boy, all for king and country. Now, shall we have our morning coffee?"

Three days after the *Spider* had sailed out of Malta, an English naval force of almost two thousand men, consisting of the 35th and 44th regiments, all under the command of Major-General Sir John Oswald, also set sail from Malta across the Mediterranean, following the same route as the *Spider*.

Chapter Forty

~ ~ ~

The *Spider* had set them ashore at Preveza, and since then Byron and Hobhouse had been riding for three days up through a rugged mountain terrain, reputed to be filled with violent robbers and cruel banditti.

At Preveza, the British Consul had provided them with a Greek soldier named Vassilly to escort Lord Byron and act as his interpreter; a dragoman named George to be both soldier and guide, and a number of extra male servants, as well as five additional saddle horses and a *sourgee* to look after the horses.

A Greek priest who was on his way to petition the Pasha, very politely asked if he could be allowed to travel with them.

Byron readily agreed, believing the priest would provide some interesting conversations on the journey. "Some Greek Philosophy perhaps?" he said to Hobby.

Hobhouse disagreed cynically. "Orthodox Religion would be my guess."

"From a priest? Oh, how clever of you, Hobby, but even *priests* are interested in more than one subject."

In the days that followed they discovered that the priest *did* have only one subject – *robbers* – constantly describing in a terrified voice every detail of how the banditti in these hills and mountains carried out their carnage.

"They hide behind the trees, and watch in silence until their victims come close, and then they rush out with their knives and guns and kill and steal everything. They have nothing, except what they can steal. Their clothes are rags, their faces are savage; they have no hearts, only cruelty."

He turned to Byron, saying with even more gravity: "And if it is a *rich* man they see, they take him prisoner and send out for a ransom, and when the money comes they still keep him prisoner and send out for more ransom, and if no more comes, they kill him."

"Lord Byron has papers of protection from the British Government," Hobhouse said haughtily. "So *we* have nothing to fear."

The priest shrugged, "So what use are your papers to them? They cannot read."

By the third day Hobhouse was becoming increasingly irritated by the warnings of the priest, and relieved when Vassilly, their Greek guard, told him they were nearing a village.

Hobhouse, Vassilly and the priest rode ahead of the group while Byron preferred to ride behind with the baggage and servants, speaking to them and the dragoman in ancient Greek, making them laugh at some of the words he used, which they did not understand, because they spoke only *modern* Greek.

"And it's *all* Greek to me," laughed Fletcher. "Oh, crikey, here's the rain!"

The novelty of the rain soon became a hindrance as it poured down in torrents, making the ground muddy and slippery for the horses.

Hobhouse was now more irritated by the rain than the priest, because the village that Vassilly had said they were "nearing" had still not been reached after half an hour's ride up a long pass through the hills, and when they eventually did reach the village the evening was setting in very dark, and the torrents of rain had now turned into a fierce thunder-storm.

Only then did Hobhouse look back and see that Byron and his party were nowhere in sight.

"They will come soon," Vassilly assured him. "The rain makes them slow."

After they had dismounted, Vassilly led Hobhouse and the priest stumbling through a narrow lane to a miserable hovel that was to be their home for the night. The room was half full of maize, the floor was of mud, and there was no outlet for the smoke from the fire but through the door.

Hobhouse gave Vassilly money and despatched him into the village to procure eggs and a few chickens so a meal could be cooked and ready for when Lord Byron and his party arrived.

An hour had passed, and still no sign of Byron. It was seven o'clock and the storm had increased to a fury. The roof of the hut shook under the clattering torrents and gusts of winds. The thunder roared without any intermission; the echoes of one peal had not ceased to roll in the mountains before another tremendous crash burst overhead.

Hobhouse, in a panic, ran down the lane but still no view of Byron. Vassilly appeared at his side and pulled him back to the hut, warning there was danger in the storm, great danger.

"But Lord Byron and the others are still *out there*!" Hobhouse yelled, and became even more distressed when he saw some of the other villagers running to and fro into each other's huts, visibly showing their fear and alarm at the intensity of the storm.

Vassilly kept assuring him that Lord Byron's servant guides knew every part of the country and they were certainly taking cover somewhere.

"Taking cover *where?* Every tree on those hills is constantly being struck by lightning!"

Vassilly could say nothing in reply because now the whole sky above the village was lit up with lightning as if in a perpetual blaze.

Hobhouse was becoming desperate. In England, a storm will pass, but here it went on and on, increasing in violence and fury.

Having heard there was a priest with the Englishman, some of the women, terrified and weeping, came to the door of the hut and begged the priest to come and pray with them in their homes, which the priest did; after which Hobhouse could hear even the *men* of the village crying out loudly for God to save them and their families.

"We must *do* something," Hobhouse told Vassilly. "We could light some fires on the hill above the village so Lord Byron can see the flames and find his way to us in the dark."

Vassilly pointed out the futility of this suggestion. "No fire will light in this rain. And can you not hear the mudslides tumbling down over the hillsides and the stone boulders crashing down from the mountains? We must stay here and try to keep ourselves safe."

"And you call yourself a *soldier*," Hobhouse snapped with contempt, and then ran outside, uncaring of the torrents drenching him to the skin until he had reached the outskirts of the village where he fired his two pistols, one after the other, in the hope that Byron would *hear* the shots and know he was trying to contact him and from what direction; but all to no avail.

By eleven o'clock the storm had not abated, and Hobby's exhaustion after the long day's ride finally left him with no other option but to lay down on his mat in the hut, wrapped in his cloak, but sleep was out of the question: every pause in the tempest was filled by the barking of the dogs, and the shouting of the shepherds in the mountains.

A little after midnight a man, panting and pale, and drenched with rain, rushed into the room and, between crying and shouting with a profusion of gesticulations – communicated something to Vassilly in Greek of which Hobhouse understood only that – "They have all fallen down! A bad accident has taken them all. We saw the dead horses rolling down the slopes by the light of our torches."

Hobhouse was so distraught, all his thoughts and emotions during this time were lost to his memory afterwards, unable to recall one dreadful moment of it, until some hours later – when he looked up and saw Byron entering the hut, like a vision in a dream ... Yes, it *must* be a dream ... because the limping Byron was helping Fletcher into the hut instead of the other way round, both dripping wet.

"He's hurt his leg – give me a hand here, Hobby."

Hobhouse was still stunned. "We were told you had all fallen down and ... there was a bad accident."

"The only accident was the falling of two of the luggage horses which regrettably we lost, poor beasts," said Byron tiredly. "What time is it?"

Hobby pulled out his fob-watch and peered at it. "Almost three o'clock."

Three in the morning, and now that the storm had eased off considerably, some of the village women arrived with bowls of steaming soup while the Greek priest stood with his hands held high, thanking God for sparing the lives of all of them.

"Not all of us," said Byron, and then told Hobhouse they had lost their way from the commencement of the storm, possibly only three miles or so from the village, and after wandering up and down in total ignorance of their position, they had been forced to take shelter by some Turkish tombstones for fear of the lightning striking any of the trees.

"If it's three o'clock now, then we were amongst those tombstones, exposed to the storm for *nine hours,*" Byron said. "And the servant-guides – far from assisting us – only made matters worse by running away! George the dragoman fired off both his pistols to try and stop them, causing Fletcher to scream out in terror, certain the shots were from banditti coming to kill us in the darkness. That's when he jumped up, and immediately fell over, and hurt his damned leg."

"I didn't mean to hurt my leg and cause you a nuisance," Fletcher said peevishly. "I was trying to *see* who made the shots."

Hobhouse said crossly –"You're an idiot, Fletcher. Thank God you are not *my* servant, as I would soon show you some shots."

"Hobby, move over and let me share your mat. My own is still with my luggage somewhere back down the slopes."

"Have it all to yourself, I'm not tired," said Hobhouse generously, standing up and moving over to sit on a wooden box in the corner of the room, watching as Byron made no protest and lay down in his wet clothes and immediately fell asleep in front of the dying embers of the fire.

Hobhouse looked over to where Fletcher was now lying on a mound of maize, also asleep.

The priest and Vassilly took shelter in some of the other huts of the village, but Hobhouse stayed where he was, no longer tired in any way, his body and mind animated with the adrenaline of relief. His friend was safe and alive. Nothing else mattered now, not even sleep.

By eight o'clock the next morning, with the offering of money in recompense, Hobhouse had gathered a party of the male villagers together to go back down the slopes and retrieve the lost luggage, and they did so, but not one man of them would take any money in payment afterwards.

"They don't want you to pay them," Vassilly said. "It will be enough to thank them."

Chapter Forty-One

~ ~ ~

The court at Tepeleni was enclosed on two sides by the Pasha's palace, and the other two sides by fortress walls.

Byron had dressed as requested and furnished, in a scarlet tunic with gold epaulettes on each shoulder. As soon as his horse reached the walls, the gates were thrown open to him.

"Welcome, welcome, Lord English!" cried a sentry. "The Vizier has been expecting you, and now you come, praise Allah."

Byron glanced at Hobhouse in some surprise. "How did he know we were coming?"

"Yes, how the deuce *did* he know?" Hobby was frowning. "We didn't know ourselves until seven days ago. Perhaps Malta sent him a dispatch by sea."

"Then why did Malta not send *us* by sea?" Byron said. "It would have saved us a lot of plodding up and over mountains."

"Lord English ..."

They were bowed and beckoned to ride their horses in to the square of the courtyard, and from then on "*Lord Byron*" was received with great deference, respect, and welcome."

The Vizier's personal "Secretary" informed Lord Byron that he was to be lodged "in a house" within the palace compound, and led him to an apartment of several rooms, where he and Hobhouse entered a large chamber of silken sofas of red and gold cushions, with a gallery above the chamber containing two rooms for sleeping – the first place of grandeur they had seen in Turkey.

"His Highness," said the Secretary, "sends to you his

regrets that he is not here to greet you. He is with his army at Illyricum, but he knows you are arriving to visit him and now he is on his way back."

"There really is no need for His Highness to return if he is with his army," Byron said politely, but his words were airily waved aside by the Secretary who insisted, "It is the *wish* of His Highness to return and meet you, Lord Byron, and the war he is fighting at Illyricrum ... " the Secretary shrugged, "it is a very *little* war."

Byron smiled at the absurdity of such a statement, and the Secretary appeared very pleased at what he thought was approval.

"Now you must rest. Everything you wish is at my service. His Highness has instructed, if tomorrow he is not returned, you are to be given horses and some guards for you to ride out and see the fine palaces of his sons."

Next morning they rode out on the Vizier's horses with a large guard to the palace of his son, Vely Pasha, a man with long black hair, somewhere in his late thirties, dressed in flowing robes and wearing a beaming smile.

He treated Lord Byron like royalty, insisting he inspected a parade of his special guards, although Vely Pasha broke all etiquette of British royalty by continually throwing one arm around Byron's waist as he walked beside him, and using the other to keep secretly squeezing his hand, in the way an Englishman would escort his lady-love; increasing Byron's embarrassment and Hobby's disapproval.

Politely declining Vely Pasha's many invitations to remain for a few days at his palace, Byron rode back to Tepeleni to be told that Ali Pasha had now returned.

"His Highness," said the Secretary, "sends to you his heartbroken regrets that he cannot invite you to dine with him, Lord Byron, or to share his repast at any time, because this is the time of *Ramadan*, a very important time for all Moslems."

"Then please convey my own regrets and respects to His Highness," Byron replied, relieved and tired out after his day visiting the Pasha's son.

"His Highness," said the Secretary, "invites you to attend upon him in the morning, when I will come for you."

"Please tell His Highness that the honour will be mine."

The Secretary, using the Turkish method of greeting or farewell, placed his right hand on his heart and inclined his head to the side in a slight bow, and took his leave.

"You *amaze* me, Byron," said Hobby when they were alone. "I did not realise that you could act the diplomat to perfection!"

Byron gave an aristocratic sniff, which he knew would infuriate Hobhouse.

"Hobby, you must remember that I was schooled at *Harrow,* and all my schoolfellows were either Dukes or Viscounts, so one soon learns the drill, whereas *you,* poor soul, were unfortunately schooled at the less prestigious Westminster."

"I've told you! There was no room for me at Eton!" Hobby responded furiously. "And *Eton* was my choice, a far superior school to Harrow!"

"And so you chose dear *little* Westminster?"

"Which in truth is a far better school than both of them! And *we* were not made to scrub our bodies raw every morning either. Is that why you are so very *obsessive* about your own personal cleanliness?"

"Oh, enough of this schoolboy quarrelling," laughed Byron. "Hobby, you take my bait *every* time!"

"And everything is so amusing to you, isn't it? Honestly, Byron, there are times when you drive me *mad!"*

"Oh, be careful, Hobby, because now you are beginning to sound like my mother."

"Then I do beg your pardon," Hobhouse said petulantly. A moment later he brightened slightly: "What do you think they will send us to eat?"

"Food, I hope."

At sunset the drum was beat in the yard and the Albanians, most of them Turks, went to prayer; and then, at last, food was brought to their chamber.

"Moslems," said the Secretary, "never eat food during the daylight hours of Ramadan. It is a time of fasting until sunset."

The dining table in their apartment was large and circular and made of silver, about a foot high from the ground, meaning they had to eat like Turks and sit on mats on the floor. Their meal was brought to them on one large circular platter which was placed on the table; a concoction of cuscus grains and vegetables mixed with pieces of roasted lamb.

It looked and smelled delicious, but the fact that Turks appeared to have never heard of knives and forks, meant they were required to eat with their hands.

Hobhouse took out his penknife and began to spear pieces of the lamb into his mouth appreciatively, while Byron was happy enough picking out the vegetables with his fingers, and Fletcher merely scooped up what he could in his hand and ate ravenously from his palm.

"I never would have come if I had known I'd have to eat food like this," Fletcher complained, eating non-stop. "What I would love now is a nice plate of English bacon and eggs. Best food in the world is English food."

"*And* English distinctions between all classes," Hobhouse said in his top-drawer voice. "Those distinctions that are so rigorously observed in England, that is."

When Byron and Fletcher kept on eating, Hobhouse

continued: "I say in *England,* because I believe there is no country in the world where all the gradations of *rank* are so uniformly observed and kept separate."

He speared another piece of lamb into his mouth, and continued grouchily, "I mean, you have to agree, Byron, that there is nothing that implies familiarity, and, at least, temporary *equality,* so much as *eating* together. It's true there are various ways in which a lowly man may rise, but *until* he has risen, he must be content to consort with those of his own station."

Byron had heard enough, responding with some impatience. "Don't be ridiculous, Hobby, and please don't insult my valet. Fletcher has been married less than a year, and yet he has left his home and wife behind in order to give his service to me on this journey."

"And it hasn't been an easy journey either," Fletcher said in a tetchy tone.

"No, it has been *far* from easy," Byron agreed. "We have been stuck out in torrential storms for nine hours, threatened with non-stop bolts of lightning, have slept in huts with no chimneys and then in cowsheds with no windows, and now we are in a silk and satin palace. So if Fletcher can share all our difficulties with us, why cannot he at least share our food tray?"

"It's just not *done,* Byron. Not in England anyway. Servants never sit and eat in the same *room* as their betters, let alone eat from the same tray."

"But it obviously *is* done in Albania, otherwise the Secretary would have led Fletcher away to the servants' quarters. Don't be such a snoot, Hobby, we are not in England now, so it will be part of our education to follow the Oriental way."

Fletcher looked apprehensively from one man to the other, wondering if their argument was about to get worse or calm down.

Hobhouse gave one of his usual shrugs. "Well, you are the captain and I a mere lieutenant, so I suppose I will have to abide by what you say." He looked at Fletcher. "No offence intended to you, Fletcher, but it really is not done."

"No offence taken, Mr Hobhouse," Fletcher replied, cheerful to know his master had taken his side. "And it would be hard for me to eat with Turkish servants, now wouldn't it, Mr Hobhouse? Me not understanding a word of their language."

Byron regarded him thoughtfully. "Fletcher, is the spare uniform ready for me to wear?"

"Aye, my lord, it is."

"Good, because the one I wore today is very dusty from all the riding. Can you make sure the spare one is sponged and spotless. On behalf of England, I would hate to make a shabby impression with His Highness tomorrow."

~~~

The following morning, an officer of the palace arrived to escort them to the Vizier. They left their apartment accompanied by Vassilly and the Secretary who, to Byron's astonishment, had dressed himself in his shabbiest cloak for the purpose.

"When we have distinguished guests at the palace," explained the Secretary, "it is very bad for me to look as rich as my master, so I always dress very humble on such occasions, to please His Highness."

When Lord Byron was announced at the door of the Vizier's chamber, Ali Pasha greeted him standing: a great compliment from a Mussulman, as Vassilly later told him, for a Turk of consequence never rises to receive any one but his superior.

The inside of the chamber was spacious and richly decorated, with a marble fountain bubbling water in the centre of the marble tiled floor.

Ali Pasha was not tall, but very fat, with white hair and a long white beard. His high turban, made of fine gold muslin, had many folds and was brooched at the front with diamonds. The long dagger he wore at his waist was also studded with jewels. He had a pleasing face, fair and round, with quick blue eyes that had none of the gravity of other Turks.

He greeted Lord Byron with a smile of delight, and bid him to come and sit beside him on a sofa covered in cushions of red and gold silk, whereupon the first thing he said was *"εύμορψω παιδι,"* and the Secretary translated, "You are a beautiful boy."

Byron was slightly indignant. "Pray tell the Pasha I have reached the age of manhood."

The Pasha looked surprised that his compliment should be rebuffed and said— *"εύμορψω παιδι "* which again was translated by the Secretary, "You are a very *brave* young man."

And so it went on. "Why, at so early an age, have you left your country?"

"To come and meet so great a man as Ali Pasha."

At the Secretary's translation, the Vizier looked delightfully surprised. "The people have heard of me in England?"

Byron nodded. "The Pasha's name is a very common subject of conversation in my country."

Due to the need of translation, the conversation was a question and answer affair, until the Vizier began to look very pleased and happy, reaching out one of his rough brown hands and touching Byron's hair.

"Even if I had not been told, I would know you are a young man of very high birth."

How did he know?

"Because," the secretary translated, "you have small ears, silky hair, and smooth white hands."

Byron laughed, and the Vizier laughed with him and spoke to the Secretary who translated, "His Highness says your teeth are like white pearls."

"Because he uses red toothpowder and brushes them morning, noon and night," Hobhouse said sarcastically.

The Secretary did not translate, because the Vizier only had eyes and ears for Lord Byron.

"And is your name George also?"

Byron nodded. "My name is George, yes."

The vizier then wanted to know more about Lord Byron's family, and for the first time in his life Byron felt very grateful to his mother for all her ranting about the Byrons right back to the conquest by the first Norman King of England.

"King Norman?" asked the Vizier. "He is your first ancestor and he also was a king?"

The conversation became somewhat confused with the Pasha's language changing from Turkish to Greek and back again; but when it was *Greek*, Byron more or less understood him, and became even more confused.

He turned his head to Hobby sitting by his side and whispered, "He seems to believe I am a nephew of King George of England. Who told him that?"

"The same people who informed him you were coming here," Hobby answered with cynical softness. "Let him keep on thinking it, I implore you."

"His Highness," said the Secretary, "would like to show you something of great interest. Please follow him."

Byron and Hobhouse stood and followed Ali Pasha over to a window where he showed them an English telescope.

"Very good, very fine," said Ali Pasha. He put the telescope to his eyes and looked through it, as if showing Byron its purpose, and then he jumped back with a small laugh of glee and handed the telescope to

Byron, urging him to look through it.

"You see that party of Turks riding along the banks of the river towards Tepeleni?"

Byron saw them. "Yes."

"That first man you see on the road is the chief minister of my enemy, Ibrahim Pasha, and he is now coming over to me, having deserted his master to join the stronger side."

He addressed this with a smile to the Secretary, desiring him to interpret it to Lord Byron.

"Is he the one you have just been at war with?" Byron asked.

"Yes, at Berat ..." and seeing what he thought was Lord Byron's interest in warfare, Ali Pasha took him by the arm and led him over to a far corner of the chamber, where he proudly showed to him a mountain Howitzer gun, and then also a strange-looking long gun which the Vizier seemed very proud of.

It looked like a fowling gun to Byron, or what Fletcher called "a duck-gun," but he pretended great admiration.

Ali then showed Byron some pistols; and took down a gun that was hanging on the wall, and said it was a gift from the King of the French.

"Napoleon?" Byron and Hobhouse looked at each other – both were admirers of Napoleon the man.

Ali Pasha smiled, confirming it was from Napoleon Bonaparte himself, and Byron and Hobhouse took a closer look at the gun. It was a short rifle, with the stock inlaid with silver and the handle studded with diamonds and jewels.

Byron was impressed, admitting that it was indeed a very handsome present.

Ali Pasha made a face, and jabbered away in Turkish to the Secretary, who translated, "When the gun came from King Napoleon, it had only a common stock, and all the ornaments have been added by his Highness, to make it look more like a royal gift."

"The King of the French is very meagre," said the Vizier, and then with eyes laughing, he slowly ran his palm admiringly down the red sleeve of Byron's arm and touched the sabre on the side of his belt. "The English always send me handsome gifts."

Byron was determined to hold onto the sabre until the very last minute, simply for his own protection. He was now slightly disturbed by the way the Vizier had run his hand down his arm in such a familiar way.

"King George," he said quickly, "treasures me with great affection, and sends to His Highness Ali Pasha his royal gratitude for the protection of my person while I am in Albania."

Ali Pasha's manner and demeanour completely changed now that he was reminded who this young man was – a *lord*, and a nephew of the King of the mighty English – he instantly became more deferential and obsequious.

"You are now my *son*," he declared. "And while you are in Albania I will be your *father*. You will come to no harm in the territories of Ali Pasha."

Byron was relieved when the meeting was over, only to be told by the Secretary that His Highness wished to have many more meetings and conversations with him.

The Pasha spoke in Turkish again and the Secretary said, "Lord Byron, you told his Highness you were very interested in Greek antiquity, yes?"

"Yes."

"Yes, so His Highness wishes me to tell you that there is, within the neighbourhood of Tepeleni some remains of antiquity—a *paelo-castro*—as all pieces of old walls or stone carvings are called in Albania. He will order horses and a large guard for you to ride out and see them this afternoon if you wish."

"I would like that very much," Byron agreed.

"Is there anything else you wish?"

"Only to ask permission to take our Albanian attendant Vassilly with us at all times," said Byron. "He is our interpreter as well as our friend."

Ali Pasha was surprised at this, asking where this Vassilly was now.

"He is standing outside the door of the chamber," said Byron.

Ali ordered the Secretary to bring Vassilly in.

Vassilly entered and, although showing proper respect, he showed no embarrassment or was bowed in any way by Ali's command.

Placing his right hand on his left breast Vassilly answered all of Ali Pasha's questions in a firm and fluent manner.

Ali spoke to him in Greek, and Byron listened: "Why did you stay outside the door and not come in to see me? You know, Vassilly, I would have been glad to see you again."

Vassilly merely inclined his head, but did not reply.

"You must attend to the Lord Byron and his friend with great care," Ali instructed. "If any harm comes to them, you know, Vassilly, that I will cut off your head."

"He is a beast," Vassilly said angrily when he accompanied Byron and Hobhouse back into their own apartment. "He is not the good man he presented to you. When I was a small boy, he was already a grown man, and many times I saw him coming out of his father's cottage with no cloth in the elbows of his coat. He had *nothing* then. He *was* nothing. Now all people call him 'His Highness'!" Vassilly made a gesture indicating it made him feel sick.

Byron and Hobhouse liked Vassilly and questioned him further.

"He was then known as Ali-Bey," said Vassilly, "and

he used to come with parties to our village in the night and steal all our flock. He made himself master of one village, and then another, amassing money and increasing his power. He put himself at the head of a large number of Turks whom he paid by plunder. He was then nothing more than a great *robber*."

Byron said: "I did not realise you were acquainted with him."

"Yes, I am acquainted with him very well!" Vassilly snorted. "Many times I came down with the men of our village and broke his windows with shot, and when we did, Ali did not dare to step out of Tepeleni for fear of our men."

"And yet now you all bow to him," Hobhouse said curiously. "So what did he do to the men of your village to change them?"

"He did nothing to our men. He made friends with our chief, saying he wanted peace, and persuaded him to come to Tepeleni for peace talks. But as soon as our chief arrived here in Tepeleni, Ali Pasha roasted him alive on a spit. After that, we all submitted. Those who resisted Ali were burnt, hanged, beheaded. He is a cruel enemy."

"And Napoleon Bonaparte?" Byron asked. "Does Ali truly dislike him as much he says?"

Vassilly was puzzled by the question, shaking his head. "No dislike. When speaking of the King of the French, Ali always calls him — 'my brother in France'."

When Vassilly had left them to ensure the horses were ready, Byron stood thoughtful for some moments before speaking to Hobhouse.

"We must not get involved in any domestic issues here, Hobby. But in relation to our own country, I think we can safely conclude that Ali Pasha is playing a double-handed game with both the English and the French."

"And with *you*, Byron. All those compliments about your hair and your hands and how you are now his *son*. All poppycock. Whenever you were not facing him, I saw him looking at you very *leeringly*. I would not trust him an inch."

"Nor should our Foreign office."

Chapter Forty-Two

~ ~ ~

Later that evening, as the sun set into the shadows, and bright fires were lit all around the courtyard, Byron and Hobhouse listened to the beating of drums and the voice of the "muezzin" once again calling the Turks to prayer from the minaret of the mosque attached to the palace.

The chanter was a boy, and he sang out his hymn in a loud melancholy recital, which sounded to Byron like — *"La illahhh—illahhh—Lhah, Mohammed resul illahhh!"*

His curious mind being interested in all things, Byron once again sought out Vassilly and asked him the meaning of those words?

"The word is not 'Illah' but *Allah,"* replied Vassilly, "and he is saying — *'There is no God but God, and Mohammed is his prophet'."*

It still sounded like *"Illah!"* to Byron who was content to stand and listen to the boy chanting a long repeated recital, while Vassilly interpreted all his words: *"God most high! I bear witness there is no God but God! Come to prayer! Come to the asylum of salvation!"* And at the end of each recital, ending with the words — *"Ya houuuuuu...."* the last notes of the boy's *"hou"* ringing on for long seconds.

"Ya-hou" said Vassilly, *"*meaning— *'He who is.'"*

"Oh," Byron nodded. "Similar to the Jewish word *'Yaweh'* and the Christian *Jehovah*."

Vassilly, although an Albanian, was not a Moslem, and found it strange that Lord Byron should be showing such a warm interest in the practices of the Moslems, and asked him why.

Byron smiled, but did not answer the question, asking instead – "Is Ali Pasha a Moslem?"

Vassilly shrugged. "He is, but not a *good* Moslem."
He pointed – "There you see the good ones."

Byron looked to the open gallery where a number of
men were kneeling on cushions, employed quietly in
prayer, some with only a slight movement of their lips,
others muttering in low voices, while around them other
men were playing cards or smoking hookah pipes.

"Many of the Albanians are not Moslems," Vassilly
explained, "but no Albanian, however irreligious
himself, will ever be seen to sneer at the devotions of
others. And to disturb a Turk at prayer would, in most
cases, lead to fatal consequences. That is why you see
those men at prayer remaining undisturbed by the other
men around them."

Yet *all* of the Albanians in Ali Pasha's compound were
proud to be *soldiers,* Byron later discovered.

Now that the sun had set and the day of Ramadan
fasting was over, a huge feast was prepared for all; and
once the food had been eaten, the night was filled with
the perpetual carousal of skirted men with long flowing
hair dancing around the fires in the courtyard, singing
about the glory of being soldiers in the army of Ali
Pasha.

Byron stood in the shadows watching them in
fascination for a long time, until Vassilly arrived at his
shoulder and spoke to him quietly:

"Ali Pasha has sent a request for you to visit him in
his chamber."

Byron reluctantly drew his gaze away from the
blazing fires.

"At this hour?"

"He has prepared honey-coated dates and sweets and
sugared sherbet to share with you."

"And Mr Hobhouse?"

"No. You alone."

The smirk was back on Vassilly's face. "The Pasha has

a harem of three hundred wives, but tonight he is very restless for more of the company of 'the young Lord Byron'. He wishes you to come and sit with him on his sofa and smoke a hookah pipe with him as you talk."

Byron turned his gaze back to the fires and the dancing soldiers, his eyes noticing two young Turkish boys of no more than sixteen, kissing like lovers. It reminded him of his boarding school.

"I must warn you," Vassilly advised, "that tonight Ali Pasha's hookah pipe may be less innocent than usual. It may contain opium, which will quickly make you very dreamy."

Byron's smile was sardonic. "I don't need opium to make me dreamy. I'm a poet."

His gaze returned to the men dancing around the fire, continuing to stare at them in silence for a time, as if transfixed by them.

Childe Harold at a little distance stood

And viewed, but not displeased, by the revelry,

Nor hated harmless mirth, however rude;

In sooth, it was no vulgar sight to see

Their barbarous, yet not indecent, glee,

And, as the flames along their faces gleamed,

Their gestures nimble, dark eyes flashing free,

The long wild locks that to their girdles streamed

While thus in concert, they half sang, half screamed –

"Tambourgi! Tambourgi!"

Vassilly's voice again interrupted his mind's flow, "Lord Byron, what will I say to the Pasha?"

Byron shrugged, and then turned away from the courtyard and began to walk towards his apartment within the palace. "Say to him that Lord Byron has retired for the night, but he will be very happy to talk with His Highness tomorrow morning, in the company of his lieutenant, Mr Hobhouse."

Vassilly placed his right hand on his left breast and smiled as he bowed in acquiescence. "It will be my pleasure, Lord Byron, to take your reply to the Pasha."

Byron placed his right hand on his left breast and responded in the same manner, with a bow of "Goodnight" to Vassilly.

He then entered his apartment to see Hobhouse in his nightshirt, preparing for bed, and pulling on his *nightcap*.

"Hobby!" Byron could not stop himself from laughing at the sheer *Englishness* of it – so different to the dancing warriors he had seen outside.

"Hobby, it may be the first rule in cold English boarding schools that wearing a nightcap in bed is essential to good health, but *not* here in Albania, and not in a warm climate."

"I'm *not* wearing it against the cold!" Hobhouse replied grouchily, pulling the nightcap further down over his ears. "I'm wearing it to try and block out that frightful racket outside! How on earth is a man supposed to *sleep* with all that clamour going on?"

"What I think," said Fletcher, just as grouchily, "is that if they celebrate like this every night after getting some food at the end of a long day of fasting, then they must all end up worn out and exhausted when their month of ramazani is finally over."

Hobhouse looked at Byron. "You were out there long enough. What *is* that awful brouhaha they keep shouting?"

"*Tambourgi! Tambourgi!*" Byron grinned. "I believe it is a war cry."

"Oh, good grief ..." Hobby said in exasperation.

"What is the point of hooting war cries at bedtime! I tell you, Byron, the sooner we get out of this place the better. The soldiers are bad enough, but that Ali Pasha – he is definitely round the twist!"

Chapter Forty-Three

~ ~ ~

Preveza, November 12, 1809

My dear Mother — I have now been some time in Turkey: this place is on the coast, but I have traversed the interior of Albania on a visit to the Pasha.

The name of the Pasha is Ali, and he governs the whole of Albania, Epiris, and part of Macedonia. His son, Vely Pasha, governs the Morea, and has great influence in Egypt; in short, Ali Pasha is one of the most powerful men in the Ottoman Empire.

The next day I was introduced to Ali Pasha. I was dressed in the full suit of a British staff uniform, with a very magnificent sabre. The Vizier received me in a large room paved with marble; a fountain was playing in the centre. He received me standing, a wonderful compliment from a Mussulman, and made me sit down on his right hand. His first question was why, at so early an age, I left my country? (The Turks have no idea of travelling for pleasure). He then said he desired to send his respects to my mother, which I now present to you.

He told me to consider him as a father whilst I was in Turkey, and said he looked on me as his son. Indeed, he treated me like a child, sending me almonds and sugared sherbet, fruit and sweetmeats twenty times a day. He begged me to visit him often, and at night, when he was at leisure, but after coffee Hobhouse and I retired to our own apartments.

His Highness is sixty years old, very fat, and not tall, but with a fair face, light blue eyes, and white beard. His manner is very kind, and he possesses that dignity which I find universal amongst the Turks. But his appearance shows nothing of his real character, for he is a remorseless tyrant, guilty of the most horrible cruelties, and so good a general they call him the Moslem Bonaparte. Napoleon has twice offered to make him King of Epirus, but he prefers the English interest, and told me he abhors the French.

He is of so much consequence that he is much courted by both sides. Bonaparte sent him a snuffbox with his picture on it. Ali said the snuffbox was very well, but the picture on it he could dismiss, as he neither liked it or the man. I saw Ali Pasha three times in the days following when our conversations were of war and travelling, politics and England.

Byron put down his pen, his face thoughtful ... "I'm writing this letter very *generally* to my mother, Hobby, but is it not strange that as soon as we arrived back here at Preveza, we learned that while we were keeping Ali Pasha employed in entertaining us in Tepeleni, an English squadron from Malta was fighting the French, and now all the Ionian Islands are under *English* rule, securing for Britain all the coveted trading sea routes to the East?"

As soon as they had returned to Preveza they had learned this from the English Consul, and only then did it dawn on them *why* they had been rushed from Malta to Tepeleni and Ali Pasha — to act as unwitting decoys while another '*little* war' was taking place behind the Pasha's back.

"It's certain they *used* us for that purpose," Hobby agreed. "Not as envoys but *decoys*. God, when I think how sly and duplicitous those diplomats in Malta were, it *offends* me. If Ali Pasha had found out sooner, *we* might have been killed."

Hobby suddenly smiled cynically at Byron. "That was probably the *true* reason why Constance Spencer-Smith was courting you in Malta. She must have known that once she suggested the two of you eloping together, it would make you leave Malta on the next ship – which would take you straight to *Albania* and Ali Pasha."

Byron shrugged, refusing to give Hobby the satisfaction of an agreement.

He said: "Ali was very delighted with the gift of his magnificent new sabre though. That should hold his alliance to Britain for a while."

"His alliance is not so important now," Hobby realised. "Not now the British have taken the Ionian Islands from the French. In fact, I would say that Ali Pasha has lost most of his leverage and bargaining power."

"But not *all* of it. Don't forget, the French are still holding Corfu."

Hobby shrugged. "For a week or two at the most. According to the consul here in Preveza, the English

naval force took one island after another with rapid
speed, so Corfu will soon fall to the English."

"Better it should fall to neither, and be given back to
the Greeks."

Byron dipped his pen into the ink and continued the
letter to his mother —

*Yesterday, the 11th November, I bathed in the sea;
today is so hot that I am writing in a shady room of the
English consul's house, with three doors wide open.*

*Two days ago I was nearly lost in a Turkish ship of
war, owing to the ignorance of the captain and the
crew, although the storm was not violent. Fletcher
yelled for his wife, the Greeks called on all the saints,
the Moslems on Allah; the captain burst into tears and
ran below deck, telling us all to call on God.*

*The sails were split, the main-yard shivered, the
wind blowing fresh, the night setting in, and our only
chance was to make Corfu, or else (as Fletcher
pathetically termed it) "go to a watery grave". I did
what I could to console Fletcher, but finding him
incorrigible, wrapped myself up in my Albanian capote
(an immense cloak) and lay down on deck to await the
worst.*

*I have learnt to philosophise in my travels; and if I
had not, complaint would have been useless. Luckily
the wind abated and only drove us onto the coast of
Suli, on the mainland, where we landed, and by the*

help of the natives, proceeded here to Preveza again; but I shall not trust Turkish sailors in the future, though the Pasha had ordered one of his own galliots to take me to Patras. I am therefore going as far as Missolonghi by land, and from there have only to cross a small gulf to get to Patras.

Fletcher's next letter to his wife will be full of marvels. One night we were lost for nine hours in the mountains in a thunder-storm, and since then he has been nearly shipwrecked. In both cases Fletcher was sorely bewildered, from fears of famine and banditti in the first, and then drowning in the second event. When we were lost in the mountains his eyes were often hurt by all the lightning, or crying (I don't know which), but are now recovered.

I am going to Athens to study modern Greek, which differs much from the ancient, though radically similar. I have no desire to return to England, nor shall I, unless compelled by absolute want and Hanson's financial neglect, but I have much to see in Greece.

Fletcher, like all Englishmen, is very much dissatisfied. He has suffered nothing but from cold, heat, and vermin, which those who lie in cottages and cross mountains must undergo, and of which I have equally partaken with himself; but he is not valiant, and is constantly afraid of robbers and storms.

I have no one to be remembered to in England, and wish to hear nothing from it, but that you are well, and a letter or two on financial business from Hanson, whom you may ORDER to write to me.

Address to me at Mr Strane's, English Consul, Patras, Morea. I will write when I can, and beg you to believe me,

Your affectionate son, BYRON

~ ~ ~

"Your *affectionate* son ..." Mrs Byron must have read the letter a hundred times after its arrival, and when she was not reading it, she was carrying it around with her.

In the second week of December, another letter arrived at Newstead Abbey, but this one was addressed to *John Cam Hobhouse, Esq.*

"It's the strangest thing," said Nanny Smith to Mrs Byron, handing her the letter. "That's the third letter for Mr Hobhouse that's come here in the past few weeks."

"Very strange," said Mrs Byron, examining the sealed letter front and back. "I have the other two put aside to enclose with my next epistle to George, but now this third letter ... there's something urgent here, something amiss ... I think I'll open it."

Mrs Byron broke the seal and removed the letter from it's cover, squinting as she began to read; and then craned forward and bent her head closer to the letter, unable to understand or believe what she was reading.

"Lord save us! I don't believe it!"

"What is it?" Nanny asked.

"This letter ... it's from Mr Hobhouse's *father* ... he

wants to know why his son has not been home for six months, why he has not answered his letters, why he has chosen to spend so much of his time living at Newstead Abbey, and does he intend to show some favour to his own family by returning home for the Christmas period?"

Nanny put a hand to her face. "Gracious, does he not know his son went abroad half a year ago?"

Mrs Byron squinted through the letter again. "Obviously not, else why would he be sending letters to him here at Newstead?"

She sat up in a flurry. "Nanny, those other two letters that came for young Mr Hobhouse – in that drawer there, bring them to me – I mean to find out what on earth is going on!"

When the two letters had been read, Mrs Byron sat back, hesitated, and looked at a distance for some time.

"Well?" Nanny asked, avid to be told.

"Well," said Mrs Byron, "it seems our young Mr Hobhouse left his family home in June, and then went abroad with Lord Byron without informing his father or indeed any of his family of his intentions."

"You mean ... he just went off without telling anyone?"

Mrs Byron nodded. "And I foolishly thought that young man to be so *sensible*. Mind you," she added caustically, "it took them long enough to notice his absence. When did that first letter come – three weeks ago! A full five months since they had last seen or heard from him."

"Is his father very angry?"

"I'm sure I couldn't say," Mrs Byron replied. "He writes like a schoolmaster."

She stood up and moved over to her writing desk.

"But I will have to write back to him now and tell him the truth of the situation. And then I will have to write to my George and tell him also, for I'm sure *he* doesn't know the truth either."

Chapter Forty-Four

~ ~ ~

"Hobby, you wretch, why did you not tell me!"

Byron had been in Athens for ten weeks when he received his mother's surprising letter.

Hobhouse shrugged, embarrassed. He took the letter from Byron's hand and read only the first few sentences relating to himself ...

It is very odd that Mr Hobhouse left England without informing his Father, and his Father did not know where he was till lately.

Hobhouse sat down and Byron listened silently while Hobby let it all out, the frustration, the anger, the dislike of his stepmother who was *always* finding fault with him — "especially when she sees my father showing me some affection."

At the end of it all, Hobby looked at Byron woefully. "What should I do?"

Byron's solution was simple. "Go back home, shoot the step-dame, and reconcile with your father."

Hobby half laughed. "Byron, please, give me a serious answer."

"Then let's start with a serious question," Byron said seriously. "Do you truly believe your stepmother dislikes you because you are your mother's son?"

"Yes."

"And that's the only reason?"

"Well, she has always been very ambitious for my father to show preference to *her* children above my mother's."

"And by running abroad without a word or a by-your-leave to your father, you Hobby, *you*, poor soul, have been playing right into her hands."

Hobby was puzzled. "Why? How?

"You are your father's first-born *son*; the legal heir to his fortune and estates ... unless he legally *disinherits* you of course. And if he was to do that, your sisters by your mother have no claim, being females, which only leaves your younger brother Benjamin standing in the way of your stepmother's children inheriting it all. Her eldest male at least."

Hobby was so utterly astounded he could not speak for a few moments. "That aspect of it never occurred to me at all! Not once. I was certain her dislike of me was *personal*."

Hobby was smiling, cheering up. "I suppose I should go back, if only to stop my father worrying."

"Yes, go back and stop the rot, Hobby, and reconcile with your father as quickly as possible."

"Would you not consider it a nuisance though, cutting short our time here and returning to England sooner than planned?"

"Me?" Byron stared at him. "I'll not be going back with you, Hobby. No. Now that I am here in my beloved Greece I shall stay here for another year at least, maybe longer, maybe for ever."

"So what will you do – on your own here – without a travelling companion?"

"I shall study modern Greek, and possibly even Italian, although being fluent in Latin will make learning Italian less difficult for me."

Byron sat back, sighing romantically. "I love the Italian language, that soft bastard Latin that melts like kisses from a female mouth..."

"At least I won't have to listen to any more of your poetry when I go back," Hobby said, returning to his old mocking manner. "But I don't need to *rush* back, do I?"

"Soonest ended, soonest mended," Byron shrugged. "And when you do eventually inherit your father's fortune one day, Hobby, and you are very, very rich, I shall come to you for endless huge loans which I shall *never* repay."

"Why not?"

"Revenge for mocking my poetry."

Later that evening they went out for a farewell dinner in the heart of Athens, and strolling back homewards, Byron was silent and sad.

Hobby asked him if his sadness was due to his departure back to England, but Byron shook his head.

"My sadness, Hobby, is for Greece itself. I came here expecting to find the Athens of my ancient heroes, but instead I found a *Turkish* Athens where the people of Greece are oppressed minions and judged inferior to their Turkish rulers."

He paused and gazed up towards the Acropolis and the Parthenon to where they had both climbed together so many times and had stood to marvel at the thoughts they invoked.

"When you think," said Byron, "of all of the great things that Greece has given to the world ... democracy, philosophy, drama, science, *medicine* ... every doctor starts his career with the Oath of Hippocrates ... and yet what has the world given back to Greece? Not one helping hand against its oppressors."

Hobby agreed completely. "Of course, when we came here, we did not realise that the Greeks — "

"Will have to throw the Turks out one day!" Byron said. "And if the Greeks don't do it with haste, then I wouldn't care if the French came and helped them to do it, because the English never will."

~ ~ ~

There were periods during the following weeks when Hobhouse found himself worrying about Byron remaining alone in Athens; but then as the months passed he had to admit, if only grudgingly, his admiration for Byron's singular determination to stay away from England for as long as possible.

While in Malta, on his homeward journey, Hobhouse received a letter from Byron telling him that he was leaving their lodgings at Signora Macri's house, and was now *"retiring to live in a convent,"* which gave Hobby a shock, until he read on:

> *"It is a monastery, but it is called a convent, and you know I do have an affinity with monasteries and their isolated solitude, having lived so long at Newstead Abbey with my black-robed Friar occasionally drifting in to my rooms to see me ..."*

It irritated Hobby that Byron still insisted his friendly ghost of a black-robed Friar had been a real and constant visitor at night in Newstead.

> *"The location is perfect — I see "Hymettus" before me, the Acropolis behind, the Temple of Jove to my right, the Stadium in front, the town to the left — how's that for picturesque?"*

Nevertheless, retiring to live in a *monastery* ... Hobby hoped that Byron was not also retiring into one of those long periods of solitary dark moods of his, when all he wanted was to be alone with his thoughts and his poetry.

A month later, upon reaching England, and emotionally reconciling with his father, who was very glad to see him again; all of Hobby's anxieties about Byron were wiped away completely when he received a second letter from him.

Capuchin Convent, Athens.

My dear Hobhouse, — I am most auspiciously settled in the Convent, which is more commodious than any tenement I have yet occupied, with room for my SUITE; and it is by no means solitary, seeing there is not only "il Padre Abbot'" but his "schuola" consisting of six "Ragazzi" all my most particular allies. These young gentlemen, being almost my only associates, it is but proper that their character, religion, and morals should be described.

Of this goodly company three are Catholics and three are Greek, which I have already set to boxing matches, to the great amusement of the Father, who rejoices to see the Catholics conquer. Their names are Bethelemi, Guiseppe, Nicolo, Yani, and two anonymous, at least in my memory. We have nothing but riot from noon till night.

My friend is Nicolo, who, although only seventeen, is my Italian master, and we are already very philosophical. I am his "Padrone" and his "amico" and the Lord knows what besides. It is about two hours since he informed me he was most desirous to follow HIM (that is me) over the world.

I am awakened in the morning by these imps

shouting "Venite abasso" and the Friar gravely observes it is more "bisogno bastonare." Besides these lads, my SUITE — to which I have added a Tartar and a youth to look after my two new saddle horses, — my SUITE, I say, are very obstreperous, and drink skinfuls of Zean wine daily, which tastes like red champagne.

Then we have several Albanian women washing in the "gardino" whose hours of relaxation are spent in running pins into Fletcher's backside and laughing boisterously about it. In short, what with the WOMEN and the BOYS and the SUITE, we are very disorderly. But I am vastly happy and childish, and shall have a world of anecdotes for you.

I am learning Italian, and this day translated an ode of Horace "Exegi monumentum" into that language. I chatter with everybody, good or bad; but my lessons, though very long, are sadly interrupted by scamperings, and eating fruit, and peltings and playings; and I am in fact at school again, and make as little improvement now as I did then, my time being wasted in the same way."

Hobhouse could not help smiling. Byron may now be approaching the age of twenty-two, but when it came to fun and playing, whether it be with animals or monks, he was like a child, a veritable *child*.

Hobby read on:

I wish you were here to partake of some of the waggeries, Hobby. You don't know what a good companion you are until you are gone. But then you are so very crabby and disagreeable at times, that when the laugh is over I rejoice in your absence. After all, I do love thee, Hobby, you have so many good qualities, and so many bad ones, it is impossible to live with you or without you.

Your ever, etc, etc., BYRON

Hobhouse was about to fold the letter when he saw more words hastily scribbled on the inside of the letter's wrapper, and noticed the abrupt change of tone to one more serious.

P.S: — I hear Ali Pasha is in a scrape. Ibrahim Pasha and the Pasha of Scutari have come down upon him with 20,000 Gegdes and Albanians, who have retaken Berat, and threaten Tepeleni. His son Adam Bey is dead. Vely Pasha has gone off suddenly to Yanina, and all Albania is in an uproar. The mountains we crossed last year are now a scene of warfare, and there is nothing but carnage and cutting of throats.

Chapter Forty-Five

~ ~ ~

The fifth of April in 1811 was a Friday, and by the afternoon it looked like yet another day was to pass without Mrs Byron receiving a letter from her son. She had not heard from him for over six months and her impatience, which a few months ago had turned to fury, had now collapsed into a desperate fear.

Her premonition that she would never see him again had come back to haunt her, more forceful and blood-rushing in her petrified certainty of it now.

The last she had heard *about* him was in response to a letter she had written to young Mr Hobhouse – that rat who had made a poor pretence of not abandoning her George and leaving him all alone in a foreign land, insisting it was George who had refused to return.

Well, all sins must be paid for eventually, and young Hobhouse was now paying for his. He had returned to England quick enough to please his father, but his father, for all his reputation of being a kind man, was clearly also a tough man, a man of *business,* who had insisted that his son serve in a militia regiment in Ireland for a year, as penance for the distress he had caused to his stepmother and the rest of his family.

And now it seemed that young Hobhouse had not heard from George for a long time either, other than a short note received some months ago, saying he had left the monastery in Athens to go travelling into the Morea, where he had caught a serious attack of malarial fever, had been very ill for weeks, but had fully recovered and was now returned to Athens.

She stood up and began to pace up and down the room. It was important not to give in to her fears; not to send her blood rushing through her again and leaving her faint. She turned to the window and looked at the beautiful day outside, calm and warm and yellow with sunshine. The green grounds of Newstead always looked lovely in the spring and summer, the Upper Lake glistening at the front; the Garden Lake at the side, and constantly the soft rippling of all the waterfalls.

She decided to distract herself by reading the latest newspaper that old Murray had brought back from the town this morning, taking it outside to the garden where she could breathe in the calming fresh air as she read.

The news on the front page was just more of the usual. The English, under Lord Wellesley, had taken Mauritius from the French, one of its most important colonies, now under British rule and with little loss of life.

It failed to hold her interest. She stopped squinting at the newspaper and sat thoughtful, beginning to wonder suspiciously about the postman ... could he have been holding onto her letters out of spite? She had given him a telling-off a few times and he had taken it meekly enough, but you never knew with people these days.

An age later, a full three days, Robert Rushton picked up some letters that the postman had delivered to the Hut and brought them to her – four letters – and all from George. The surge of relief racked her into a fit of weeping until Nanny Smith calmed her with a cup of tea, followed by a small brandy. After which, she read each letter ravenously.

Athens, January 14, 1811

My dear Mother, — I seize the occasion to write to you as usual, shortly but frequently, as the arrival of letters here is very precarious. I have received at different intervals, several of yours, but generally six months after date; some sooner, some later. I have lately made a few small tours of some two hundred miles into the Morea and Attica etc., and am returned down again to Athens where I am beginning to mix in English society. Lord Sligo, an old friend of mine from Harrow, is now here and we go together to the various dinners and balls and enjoy a bit of harmless foolery with the ladies.

More important news is that I have now (in imitation of Leander to his lady in Greek mythology) swam across the HELLESPONT from Sestos to Abydos, (from Europe to Asia) something even Alexander the Great could not do in 480 BC. The rapidity of the current is such that no boat can row directly across, and it is known to have the most dangerous nautical conditions in the world for mariners and navigators.

I am told by the Greeks that I am the first man in the world to have swam it. My first attempt failed due to the very strong currents and the massive waves smashing down, trying to suck me under, but the second time I was as determined as Leander and swam the four miles of the turbulent strait in one hour and ten minutes.

Of this, and all other particulars, Fletcher,

whom I am sending home with papers etc., will apprise you. I will not find that Fletcher is any loss, unless it is by having less confusion than usual in my wardrobe and household.

Besides that, Fletcher's perpetual lamentations for beef and beer, his contempt for everything foreign, and his incapacity to learn even a few words of any language, like all other English servants, is an encumbrance. I do assure you the plague of speaking for him, the comforts he required (more than myself) the pilaws (a Turkish dish of rice and meat) which he could not eat, the beds where he could not sleep, and the long list of calamities such as the constant want of TEA!!! would have made a lasting source of laughter to a spectator. After all, the man is honest enough, and in Christendom, capable enough, but in Greece! Lord forgive me.

The climate here is very hot and I am bronzed, but poor Fletcher is now a walking CINDER.

It is probable I may steer homewards in spring. At present, I do not care to venture a winter's voyage, even if I was tired of travelling, which I am not; as I am so convinced of the advantages of looking at mankind instead of reading about them, and the bitter effects of staying at home with all the narrow prejudices of an islander, that I think there should be a law amongst us, to set our young men abroad, for a term, among the few allies our wars have left us.

Here I see and have conversed with French, Italians, Germans, Danes, Greeks, Turks, Americans, etc., etc., and so I can judge the countries and manners of others. When I see the superiority of England (which, by the way, we are a good deal mistaken in many things) I am pleased; and where I find England inferior, I am at least enlightened.

I have a famous Bavarian artist painting views of Athens for me. I hope on my return to lead a quiet, recluse life, but God knows and does best for us all; at least so they say, and I have nothing to object, as on the whole, I have no reason to complain of my lot. I am convinced, however, that men do more harm to themselves than ever the devil could do to them.

I trust this will find you well, and as happy as we can be; you will, at least, be pleased to hear that I am so, and

Yours ever, BYRON

PART EIGHT

DESOLATION

"Few people understood Byron. Some mistook his reserve and silence for pride or superiority, but I knew he naturally had a kind and feeling heart, and there was not a single spark of malice in him"

John Pigot.

Chapter Forty-Six

~ ~ ~

The *Volgate* frigate was a friendly ship, apart from one passenger who remained remote and kept his distance from everyone.

A young gentleman who was extraordinarily handsome, but who had appeared rather bad-tempered when boarding the ship, speaking to the sailors in a very haughty and aristocratic manner as he warned them not to damage his luggage.

Of course, when they learned his name was 'Lord Byron', they completely understood and forgave him. All aristocrats were born and bred to behave in such a manner.

Lost in his own world and thoughts, Byron was feeling too sad and disconsolate to inflict his company on anyone. The very thought of engaging in empty social chit-chat with the other passengers, all strangers, drove him to the farthest end of the deck where he spent hours staring down into the water.

Bad news, bad news; heartbreaking news that had reached him in two letters only days before he had left Athens ... taking his mind and his heart back to Trinity College, and the days of his youth.

Edward Long, his friend at Cambridge who had left college to join the army, had been drowned off the coast of Lisbon, when his ship the *HMS Prince George,* a troop transport carrying his regiment to the Peninsular war, was in a night collision with an American brig, with all lives lost.

Byron was plunged into the deepest grief. Ned Long, dear Ned, who had once snapped a pistol at his own head in the hall of his uncle's house, had been only a week past his twenty-first birthday when the collision of the two ships happened. The letter had come from his father, asking Byron to write an epitaph for his son, but no matter how many times Byron had attempted to write one, his tears prevented him from completing it.

The second letter had not consoled, but added violently to his sadness. A letter written in a childish hand with poor spelling, from John Edleston's sister, telling him that her brother had died of tuberculosis.

Edleston, Edleston, *Edleston* ... the sweet boy who had given him the cornelian ring, the young chorister who had sang like an angel in the choir at Trinity ... younger even than Ned Long ... both so young, and now both were dead.

The waves below his gaze were rolling gently as his tears fell, remembering now the way he had so carelessly passed on Edleston's little cornelian ring to Elizabeth Pigot. How could he have done that? And so carelessly?

His hands gripped the rail of the deck determinedly. As soon as he got back to Nottingham, the first thing he would do was go to Southwell and get that cornelian ring back from Elizabeth. She would give it, he was certain, because she had not seemed to care much for it when he had given it to her. And then he would put it safely amongst his treasures, in memory of John Edleston.

Byron returned to his cabin feeling a desperate need to speak to Hobby, his guide, philosopher and friend, whose companionship he would *never* wish to lose.

Volgate, frigate, at Sea,
June 19th, 1811

My dear Hobhouse, — in the gentle dullness of a summer voyage, I shall converse with you for half an hour. I think I may as well talk to you now, as you can't answer me, and excite my wrath with your unfeeling and impertinent observations, at least not for three months to come ...

During the voyage Byron spent his time writing to all of his friends; to Scrope Davies – now a Fellow at King's College, Cambridge, and at weekends in London still gambling for high stakes in the company of Beau Brummell.

And then a letter to Charles Matthews ... dear brilliant Matthews who had sent them off on their travels with such a kind and extravagant dinner, although he could ill-afford it.

And then, finally, he even wrote to his book agent, Robert Dallas.

Volgate, frigate, at Sea,
June 28, 1811

Dear Mr Dallas, — after two years' absence, I am retracing my way to England. I have, as you know, spent the great part of that period in Greece and Turkey, except for two months in Spain and Portugal, which were then accessible.

I don't know that I have done anything to distinguish myself from other voyagers, other than my swimming across the Hellespont from Sestos to Abydos.

My Satire, "English Bards" it seems, is in its fourth edition, a success rather above the middling run, but not much for a production, which, from its topics, must be temporary, and of course be successful at first, or not at all.

At this period, when I can think and act more coolly, I regret that I have written 'English Bards', though I shall probably find it forgotten by all except those whom it has offended.

If you are in town in or about the beginning of July, you will find me at Dorant's Hotel, Albermarle Street. I have an imitation of Horace's "Art of Poetry" ready for Cawthorns, but don't let that deter you, as I shan't inflict it upon you. I never read my rhymes to visitors. After a few days I shall quit town for Nottingham, and I shall send this the moment we arrive in harbour, that is a week hence.

Yours sincerely, BYRON

The Reverend Robert Dallas was a clergyman who was busily trying to add to his meagre income in support of his family by working part-time as a book agent, and was often away from home and parish rushing over the country collecting manuscripts from aspiring poets and taking them down to London, but all of them so far had failed to find a publisher.

It was not until he read Lord Byron's "*On English Bards and Scotch Reviewers*" that he knew that here, at last, was some *real* poetic talent.

He had written to Lord Byron at his seat at Newstead Abbey, but it seemed that his own title of "Reverend" had put Lord Byron off, sending a polite but negative response.

Dallas could not give up. He had a house full of small children, but very few parishioners, and his living as a pastor was not enough to keep his wife and family well-clothed or well fed. He needed extra money, a *lot* of extra money, but as he had been reared solely for service in the church, as well as a small amount of Law, he knew not what else to do.

His only passion, outside of the church, was books; but few publishers were interested in cheap novels that were bought solely by females of the lower or middle classes because that's all their pockets or taste could rise to – with the exception of the author Walter Scott, whose Scottish tales were now being read by *both* sexes of the upper class.

And the upper class was where all the money was to be found; money to *buy* as many books as they wished, regardless of cost. And that's where the difficulty came in, because the upper class had their *standards*, and would not read anything that was not written with a perfect command of language and in perfect prose or beautiful poetry.

Poetry was their favourite, because it allowed them to *quote* lines or passages at their social dinners and gatherings. And despite his lordship's letter in which he modestly deprecated his work, Byron's Satire had been a great success with the upper class and was now in its *fourth* edition – a bestseller for Cawthorns.

Dallas could not give up, not on the brightest new talent to appear for years; so he had written to Lord Byron again, informing him (quite truly) that he was a distant cousin on the Byron side through marriage, and again requesting an interview, which his lordship had surprisingly granted – "*On the condition, Reverend Dallas, that you do not try to convert me to some religious sect or involve me in any discussion on metaphysics. In such matters I deny nothing, but doubt everything."*

Oh, the joy, the *joy*, when Lord Byron, with very little persuasion, had agreed that Dallas could become his literary agent; but the joy was short-lived, because at that same interview Lord Byron had also said that he was about to go off to Greece and the Levant for a number of years, and possibly may never write another word again.

~~~

Arriving at his London hotel in late July, due to his ship being diverted to the Nore, Byron found Reverend Dallas waiting to see him. It was a great inconvenience to be met with business at this early stage of his homecoming, yet Byron tried to hide his annoyance, inviting Dallas up to his room, determined to get rid of his visitor quickly.

"I now realise I have chosen an ill time to call on you, Lord Byron, but I must confess I am most anxious to read your latest work. Indeed, my excitement has kept me awake these last two nights."

Byron was unpacking his bag, taking out papers, and Dallas's eyes lit like fire on what looked like a manuscript; surprised when Lord Byron pushed that aside and took out another sheaf of papers, which he handed over.

"I wrote to you about this," Byron said. "Although I have changed the title to *Hints from Horace*."

Dallas clutched the manuscript to his chest. "I shall take this back to my lodgings and read it immediately. No doubt you will still be here over the next few days?"

"For a week or two, but I would like you to get *Horace* in train at Cawthorns as soon as possible. There are still some corrections to be done, Rever — do you mind if I continue to call you *Mister* Dallas?"

"Oh, by all means, Lord Byron. I have no objection

whatsoever."

Byron gave him a small smile of apology. "I feel uncomfortable discussing business with a man of the church, and you may find that many publishers will probably feel the same."

"Then thank you for being so honest and telling me so, Lord Byron. I shall use the appellation of 'Mister' in future and reserve my revered title solely for my church duties, which are spare and few, and my old curate enjoys taking care of most of them."

Byron looked silently at Dallas for a long moment, seeing a man in his early forties who appeared as nervous as a fourteen-year-old, and yet at the same time as harassed as a man with the weight of the world on his shoulders.

Dallas glanced down at the manuscript he was holding. *Hints from Horace?* An ancient name that did not stir his interest for big sales one bit. His eyes moved to the other manuscript which his lordship had carelessly thrown on the table. "Is that something else you may have written while abroad?"

"No, no, that's nothing worth troubling you with," Byron shrugged. "It's something I wrote merely to pass away the time when I could not sleep at night in Greece."

"May I read it?"

Byron hesitated; all he truly wanted right now was to get rid of the man. "Well, if you wish – but pray do not embarrass me by showing it to anyone else. It's something I wrote for my own indulgence, nothing more, and it is very experimental in its style."

Dallas lifted the manuscript and flicked the pages to see its length, deciding that Lord Byron must have had a lot of sleepless nights in Greece, because the manuscript was quite long for a piece of poetry.

But who was he to complain? It was written by the

author of *English Bards* so that should elicit some immediate interest from better publishers than Cawthorn's, and might even lead to a contract.

Later that evening in his lodgings, Robert Dallas sat down and began to read the manuscript which Lord Byron had regarded so dismissively ... *Childe Harold's Pilgrimage* ... the story of a young aristocrat (hence the "e" at the end of Childe to denote his rank) who had been spurned in love and sought to forget the girl by travelling to faraway lands filled with sun and romance and war.

As he read, Dallas began to realise that he was holding something very special in his hands. *This* was very different to the poetry of Wordsworth or Southey – *this* was poetry about a foreign world of which the English people knew absolutely nothing about.

Land of Albania! Let me bend mine eyes
On thee, thou rugged nurse of savage men!
The cross descends, thy minarets arise,
And the pale crescent sparkles in the glen.

Now Harold felt himself at last alone,
And bade to Christian tongues a long adieu;
Now he ventured on a shore unknown,
Which all admire, but many dread to view.

Dallas poured himself a second glass of wine and read on and on—

Here woman's voice is never heard: apart
And scarce permitted, guarded, veiled, to move,

She yields to one, her person and her heart,
Tamed to her cage, nor feels a wish to rove;
For, not unhappy in her master's love,
And joyful in a mother's gentlest cares,
Blest cares! All other feelings far above!
Herself more sweetly rears the babe she bears.

In marble-paved pavilion, where a spring
Of living water from the centre rose,
Whose bubbling did a genial freshness bring,
And soft voluptuous couches breathed repose,
Ali, a man of war and woes;
Yet in his lineaments you cannot trace,
While Gentleness her milder radiance throws
Along that aged venerable face,
The deeds that lurk beneath, and stain him with
Disgrace.

It is not that yon hoary lengthening beard
ill suits the passions which belong to youth:
Love conquers age -- so Hafiz hath averred;
So sings the Teian, and he sings in sooth -
But crimes that scorn the tender voice of Ruth
Beseeming all men ill, but most the man
In years, have marked him with a Tiger's tooth.

Oh, such *derision* for an old man seeking a young lover! Byron's scorn was almost palpable. "*ill suits the passions which belong to youth."*

Engrossed, Dallas read until it was dark and he finally reached the end of the first canto of *Childe Harold*, and never before, he concluded, had he read a poem of such rare and original talent.

Most poets followed the established models in poetry, but not Lord Byron.

Dallas was so excited he had to stand up and walk around the room, then sat down again, lifting the manuscript and staring at the pages ... this was more than an epic poem of one hundred written pages, it was an exciting adventure story, but written in verse, not prose.

Attached to the back of the two cantos were some shorter poems relating to the story, and clearly, if ever published, these shorter poems, about Greece, were to be included with *Childe Harold's Pilgrimage*.

Dallas had read no more than the opening two lines of the first poem when he was forced to catch his breath at the romantic beauty of it.

> *Maid of Athens, ere we part,*
> *Give, oh, give me back my heart!*

Unable to sleep that night, and anxious because Lord Byron seemed more concerned about sending *Hints from Horace* for publication and disregarding *Childe Harold's Pilgrimage* as unworthy, Dallas sat down to write a letter to his noble client.

In Childe Harold, you have written one of the most delightful poems I have ever read. If I wrote this in flattery, I should deserve your contempt, but I have been so fascinated with Childe Harold that I have not been able to lay it down. I would almost pledge my life on its advancing the reputation of your poetical powers, and on its gaining you great honour and regard...

As soon as he had breakfasted, Robert Dallas decided he would deliver the letter personally to Lord Byron's hotel, with the instruction that it be taken up to his lordship immediately.

"I'm very sorry, sir," said the hotel manager when he arrived at Dorant's, "Lord Byron is no longer in residence."

"No longer ... but he told me only yesterday that he intended to stay here for a week or two."

"That was his intention, sir, but he had to leave yesterday evening to return to his seat at Newstead Abbey in Nottingham."

"Oh? Do you know the reason?"

"Yes, sir. He received an urgent dispatch requesting him to return as soon as possible because his mother is believed to be seriously ill."

~~~

Throughout his journey to Nottingham, Byron could not help wondering if his mother truly was ill, or if she was playing in another of her own melodramas to get him home more quickly?

He had brought her back a shawl made of silk threads, and a large bottle of Ottar of Roses, which he had been forced to smuggle in and hope his trunk was not inspected by the customs men. So if she was truly feeling unwell, the perfume would soon cheer and restore her.

When he finally reached Newstead, as soon as he had stepped inside the front door, Joe Murray came rushing to meet him, but there was no smile of welcome on Joe's face, and no words from his mouth either, but his pallid, sorrowful expression said all.

Shocked, unable to comprehend it, Byron stood in the hall, silent, motionless, until he turned and slowly walked up the staircase to her room, where Nanny Smith found him hours later, still sitting in the dark beside his mother's bed.

She endeavoured to comfort him in his dark silence. "It was sudden, my lord, she felt no pain."

"What caused it?"

"She just collapsed. The doctor said it was a stroke. She lay here unconscious for the past few days, and then died in her sleep this morning."

When Nanny returned to the servants' hall, Joe Murray looked at her sharply. "You didn't tell him what she was doing when it happened – shouting in fury at the upholsterer? Now is not the time to tell him such things."

Nanny had a peculiar look on her face. "I can't get my mind off the strangeness of it. She spoke so many times of her premonition that she would never see him again, and she was right, but not in the way she imagined."

Fletcher was crying at the table, sniffing and wiping a hand over his face; not because of the death of Mrs Byron, but because of the white shock he had seen on his master's face.

"It's a bad homecoming for him," Fletcher said. "This may drive him away again."

Joe Murray went up to the bedroom of death, pulled up a chair and sat beside his lordship.

"She knew," Byron said quietly. "She knew she would not see me in life again. She kept telling me, begging me not to go ... I shall never dismiss anyone's premonitions again, not even my own. But where ... *where* does that knowledge come from?"

Joe said: "I've always believed that messages sometimes come to us from afar, but from *where* afar, I don't know."

A long silence hung about the room.

"I did not love her," Byron said softly, "but I should have been kinder to her."

"And she should have been kinder to you," Joe replied with quiet honesty. "Regrets at a time like this are natural, but it does not mean they are true or right."

"Yet now I realise ... we can only have *one* mother, and she was mine."

"Peace be with her," Joe said.

~ ~ ~

A full ceremonial burial in the Byron vault at Hucknall Church was to be her final resting place. Byron ordered black mourning coats, hat bands and gloves for himself and the male servants, and then he wrote the inscription to be engraved on the plate of her coffin, reminding all of the one fact that she was so proud of: her noble Scottish ancestry.

Catherine Gordon Byron

Mother of George Gordon Lord Byron

And lineal descendant of the Earl of Huntley

And Lady Jane Stuart, daughter of

King James 1st of Scotland

Byron was comforted by a long letter sent post-haste from Cambridge, from one of his very dear friends, Charles Matthews, assuring him that he and Scrope Davies would be there the following Monday to be with him at his mother's funeral, and would stay awhile with him at Newstead in the days that followed.

Hobby did not know yet, due to being away with his regiment in Ireland.

On Monday morning, another letter arrived, sent post-haste from Cambridge, from Scrope Davies, the writing somewhat shaky, informing Byron that their dear friend, Charles Matthews, would be unable to travel to Newstead for Mrs Byron's funeral, because he had drowned while swimming in the River Cam on Saturday morning. Matthews had gone to swim alone and had become entangled in a deep bed of grassy weeds on a bend in the river ...

> *"Had you or I been there, Matthews would now be alive. Hart saw him perish – but dared not venture into the grassy weeds to give him assistance. Had you been there – neither would have been drowned. My soul is heavy – I can do nothing – I walk around in despair – His body was found 12 minutes after he had sank –*

Another shock, a double horror. Byron could no longer sustain himself under it all. He collapsed in grief and was too ill to attend his mother's funeral.

Chapter Forty-Seven

~~~

My dearest Davies, — Some curse hangs over me and mine. My mother, whose age was only forty-six, has lain a corpse in this house, and one of my best friends is drowned in a ditch. What can I say, or think, or do? I received a letter from Matthews written to me the day before he died. My dear Scrope, if you can spare a moment, do come down to me — I want a friend. Matthews last letter to me was written on the Friday, and on the Saturday he was dead.

In ability, who was like Matthews? What will our poor Hobhouse feel? Come to me, Scrope, I am almost desolate, left almost alone in the world. I had but you and Hobhouse and Matthews, let me enjoy the survivors whilst I can. Write or come, but come if you can, or both.

Yours ever, BYRON

Scrope Davies replied by return of post.

My dear Byron — Heaven's vials of wrath have poured down on us. The consolation, my dear Byron, which I am able to give you, must be trifling indeed, but such as it is — you shall receive it — for on

Wednesday or Thursday next I hope to see you at Newstead.

I was going to say something in memoriam about Matthews – I cannot. Do write an epitaph for him – You, and you alone, are capable of doing him justice. His admiration of you was unbounded.

God bless you, and give you strength to overcome all your calamities –and believe me, ever your friend

Scrope Davies

When Scrope did not arrive on Wednesday or Thursday, or the days after that, Byron dragged himself out of Newstead and went to Cambridge to see him, which only added to his own wretchedness.

My Dear Hobhouse, — From here at King's College I write from Scrope's rooms, whom I have just assisted to put to bed in a state of outrageous intoxication. I think I never saw him so bad before, or in such very low spirits. I wish to God he would grow sober, as I fear no constitution can long support his excesses of late. If I lose him and you, what am I? Hodgson is not here, but expected soon.

We all wish you here, and well, wherever you are, but surely better with us. If you don't return soon, Scrope and I intend to visit you in quarters. Good night — Yours ever, BYRON

Finding himself forced to leave Cambridge due to the number of people wishing to call and pay their respects to "Lord Byron" on the death of his mother, Byron left Scrope Davies in the care of Francis Hodgson and returned to Newstead, where he put on a brave face and was polite to all; his decorum faultless.

Yet beneath his politeness he considered all the platitudes to be sheer hypocrisy, because he knew that few of them had liked his mother, if any at all.

In the empty days between these visitors, he spent most of his time wandering alone, either in the grounds or through all the silent rooms of the house. Never before had he realised just what a large and *lonely* place Newstead Abbey was. What other home would take at least *one hour* to walk around?

So many vast and empty rooms, so many stairs leading to here and there and everywhere. So much *silence*. A home built for many monks, not just one man. He stood in the centre of the Great Drawing Room and looked around him, pondering ...

> *An enormous room without a soul*
> *To break the lifeless splendour of the whole.*

Still no letter from Hobby.

His sister Augusta wrote to him every day, but she could not travel to Newstead to be with him, due to giving birth to her third child.

Three ladies came to call, claiming to be friends of his mother. Yet they gossiped so much with each other about the previous owner of Newstead *"the Wicked Lord"* that he was forced to excuse himself and seek solace by speaking to Hobby again.

Newstead Abbey

My dear Hobhouse, — My dwelling you already

know is a house of mourning, and I am really so much bewildered with the different shocks I have sustained, that I can hardly reduce myself to reason by the most frivolous occupations. I can neither read, write, nor amuse myself, nor anyone else. My days are listless and my nights restless. I seldom have any society, and when I have, I run out of it.

At this "present writing" there are in the next room three ladies, and I have stolen away to write this grumbling letter to you. I find I have no method in arranging my thoughts, which perplexes me strangely.

I have lost her who gave me being, and some of those who made that being a blessing. I don't know what lies beyond the grave, yet if there is within us "a spark of that Celestial fire", Matthews has already "mingled with the gods".

In the room where I now write, (the Blue Room) did you and Matthews and myself pass some joyous evenings in wine and conversation and laughter? And here we will, in the future, drink to his memory, which though it cannot reach the dead, it will soothe the survivors. I can neither receive nor administer consolation; time will do it for us.

In the interim, let me see or hear from you, if possible both. I am very lonely.

My dear "Cam of the Cornish" (Matthews last expression about you) may God give you the happiness that I wish you may attain.

BYRON

At last, at last, a reply from Hobby finally came; from some out-of-the-way place in Ireland, although Hobhouse was now truly endeared to the country of Ireland and its people. The Irish understood loss and personal sadness, and saw no shame in expressing it.

Enniscorthy, Wexford.

My dear Byron — After various efforts to write about my own concerns, I still revert to the same melancholy subject. Nothing is more selfish than sorrow.

Matthew's great and unrivalled talents were observable by all. His kindness was known to his friends. Three days before his death he told me he had heard from you. On Friday he wrote to me again, and on Saturday — alas, alas, we are not sticks or stones — such a death and such a man — I wish Scrope had not been so clear in the horrid details of how it happened.

I strive to forget my lamented friend, and you must do the same. But do not, my dear Byron, do not write so sadly; every line of your last letter wrings my heart. I wish I were there to console you about your mother. Despite everything, I believe she did love you. And she would be grateful to know now that you feel her loss.

Pray continue to employ yourself in the literary way. Occupation, and especially occupation of that sort, will be most useful to you in your present affliction.

If you go down to London you will be overwhelmed with compliments in Town. Ward told me that Richard Brinsley Sheridan had mentioned "English Bards" to him in terms of the highest praise.

> *ever my dear Byron*
> *Your affectionate friend*
> *John Cam Hobhouse.*

Byron had no interest in praise for *English Bards,* and yet for some perverse reason he found himself lifting down a book by Wordsworth; a book he had scarcely read, because its title had appeared so repellent to him in his younger days, but was now strangely interesting ... *Intimations of Immortality.* It was a poem that had been criticised savagely at the time, and Byron knew that he himself would probably criticise it also, yet he wondered now what Wordsworth had to say? Did he believe there was such a thing as immortality after life on earth?

He sat down in an armchair and began to read..

There was a time when meadow, grove, and stream,

The earth, and every common sight,
To me did seem
Apparelled in celestial light,
The glory and the freshness of a dream.
It is not now as it hath been of yore; -
Turn wheresoever I may,
By night or day,
The things that I have seen, I now can see no more.

Our birth is but a sleep and a forgetting:
The Soul that rises with us, our life's Star,
Hath had elsewhere its setting,
And cometh from afar:
Not in entire forgetfulness,
And not in utter nakedness,
But trailing clouds of glory do we come
From God, who is our home:

"*Our birth is but a sleep and a forgetting ...*" So what Wordsworth is saying, Byron realised, was that the beginning of life, was the forgetting of Heaven ... "*The things which I have seen, I can see no more.*"

Heaven lies about us in our infancy!
Shades of the prison-house begin to close upon the
growing Boy,
But he beholds the light above and whence it flows,
He sees it in his joy.

The Youth, who daily farther from the east must travel,
still is Nature's Priest,
And by the vision splendid
Is on his way attended;
At length the Man perceives it die away,
And fade into the light of common day.

Byron read on and on, until he reached a verse that reminded him so much of his own feelings now, and of Matthews' drowning, even to the word "grass", it brought tears spilling from his eyes.

Though the radiance which was once so bright
Be now for ever taken from my sight,
Though nothing can bring back the hour
Of splendour in the grass, of glory in the flower;
We will grieve not, rather find
Strength in what remains behind.

He had been wrong, so very *wrong* about Wordsworth. Young and foolish and angry – in *English Bards* he had lampooned a great poet ... so now his error must be atoned for.

He found pen and paper and wrote to James Cawthorn, ordering the immediate cessation of all further printing of *English Bards*, and any copies still in stock MUST be destroyed, the cost of such to be invoiced to the author.

He had published the book himself, paid all costs, and still held the copyright. Cawthorns were just the printer and distributor. They could even keep all of the profits; he did not want a penny from that book – not a farthing from that *damned* book.

He found Fletcher and gave him the letter. "I want you to take the carriage and go to London immediately, and deliver this to James Cawthorn himself. Tell him I also want a letter given to you, to bring back to me, confirming the cessation of all further printing."

Fletcher was always glad of a trip down to "Lunnun" but was his lordship forgetting something? "When I get there, where do I sleep?"

"Stay at Dorant's. I have an account there, and the manager knows you. Then as soon as you arrive, deliver this by hand to Mr Cawthorn, and *wait* for his written reply, even if you have to wait all day."

"Can I take Sally with me?"

"Sally?"

"My wife," Fletcher reminded him. "She's never been in an hotel, and it would be a large shame to waste the space in those big beds the hotels have in their rooms. And *and* ..." Fletcher added, "she did not have my wedded company for almost two years when we was abroad."

Byron looked at him steadily. "Did you tell your wife you had a mistress in Athens?"

"What?" Fletcher took a step back in alarm. "You wouldn't tell her, would you, my lord?"

"This minute I will – if you don't get a move on and attend to my business, *without* your wife."

~ ~ ~

Once Fletcher had left, and his mind more rational now, Byron sat down and wrote out his new will. In the previous will he had bequeathed everything to his mother, so now there must be changes.

Apart from some smaller bequests to Joe Murray, William Fletcher, and Nanny Smith, he instructed that, in the event of his own death, the rest of his possessions and his estate were to be bequeathed to his three closest friends, John Cam Hobhouse, Scrope Berdmore Davies, and Francis Hodgson.

Chapter Forty-Eight

~ ~ ~

He had spent a long time walking in the morning sun, returning to his habit of spending most of his time out of doors. There was a time when he left the house just to get away from his mother's noisy voice; now he left it to get away from the silence.

All the empty rooms throughout the house made him feel claustrophobic within their nothingness. Only in the servants' quarters was there bustle and chatter and occasional laughter.

He had walked far, very far, and was as yet unaware of it, his mind in constant thought. Only when he looked up and saw the diadem of trees, so familiar from long ago, did he realise that he had unconsciously been walking towards Annesley Hall.

He paused by the old familiar tree where he used to stand waiting for her, gazing towards the old oratory walls where they used to talk and flirt together. What an innocent he had been then.

His eyes moved over the house, this back part of it, seeing it as he had never seen it before. It was huge and long and wide and built solely of rich red bricks, solid and lasting. Four floors high, with a high arch leading through to the stables.

Why had he ever thought she would sacrifice this for Newstead? This house was young and fresh and modern, but Newstead was an *old* place, with *old* paintings of kings and queens on some of the bedroom walls, a place of antiquity.

Then as he looked longer, he changed his mind. All the identical red bricks of the Annesley building were too flat, without any variance; whereas Newstead was of yellow stone with beautiful carvings on the outside walls, delicate images carved in stone by an artist, perhaps many artists. A place of antiquity, yes; but also a place of beauty and charm.

He looked at the land around him. And here ... the land around Annesley was all grass and fields and barren hills, whereas Newstead was surrounded by woods and waterfalls and beautiful lakes.

He turned and began to stroll back in the direction of Newstead, remembering how he had often said to Joe Murray, when heading off to London — "*I only go out into society to get me a fresh appetite for being alone.*"

So maybe it was the same with one's home? Suddenly Newstead did not seem such an empty place to live after all. The long walk had driven the ghosts from his mind and helped him to see the sun again, feel its mellow warmth.

He inhaled some deep breaths of fresh air into his lungs and then he saw her ... she was walking towards him in the distance, coming through one of the fields. Her head was bent and she had not yet seen him ... a lonely figure with a shawl wrapped around her ... so unlike his flirtatious Mary in her pretty bonnets. Today she was hatless and under the sun's light he could see the bright sheen of her light brown hair, uncoiled and hanging loose around her. His heart gave a lurch. He had never seen her with her hair uncoiled before.

"Mary?"

The sight of him seemed to give her a shock, but then her faint smile showed a hint of pleasure. "What are you doing here?"

"Walking."

"It's a long walk from Newstead to here, Byron."

"And one I did many times in the past when I was younger."

She stood in silence gazing around her, her face pale,

yet to him she was still a vision of feminine loveliness, a dazzling light after the darkness.

"And there," she said suddenly, pointing to a large patch of grass under the shade of a tree, "that is where we used to have our picnics and you would tell me made-up stories, do you remember?"

"It's not good for me to remember."

"No," she said wanly, "nor I."

After a silence, he said quietly, "Mary ... what is wrong? Are you unhappy?"

She bent her head and shook it, hiding her face. "Why should you think I am unhappy? Like you, I have been out taking a walk in the morning air. There's usually not another soul about."

"Something *is* wrong. I can see it."

When she lifted her face, her dark brown eyes were heavy with tears. "We all have to pay for our mistakes, Byron. Are you still paying for yours?"

Perplexed, he asked, "What mistake did I make?"

"Loving *me* ... the poem you sent to me ... after you came to dinner at Annesley two years ago ... it was full of love."

"All my poems are full of love, because all my love poems are about you."

She wiped a tear from her face and shook her head. "I don't believe you. All that time you were abroad, I'm sure any poems you wrote were *not* about me."

"*All* were about you. Even my Greek poems are about you in sentiment. I base all my females on Mary Ann Chaworth, the one girl I love, the girl who spurned me."

"Stop!" She had gone very white. "Byron, I am *married*. It's not fair to my husband for you to say these things. It's not fair to *me*. You and I ... we were friends and neighbours. You were just a *boy*, but Jack was grown up..."

"And are you happy with your grown-up?"

"Yes, yes, *yes*. I have always been happily married. So why should you question it?"

"Because you are walking around the countryside looking as pale and as fraught as the unhappiest girl I ever saw. If there is any way I can help you, Mary, then pray *let* me!"

She stared at him with her glistening dark eyes, slowly shaking her head, and then she walked past him and away from him without uttering another word ... until she stopped, looked back at him, and asked, "Is it true? Were you so very *hurt* when I married Jack?"

He shrugged. "Not so *very* as you may have been told."

"So you were *not* hurt?"

"No, thankfully, because when I went to the apothecary seeking some of Socrates' hemlock, he told me that particular poison don't kill people nowadays."

Her smile stretched into a slight laugh. "Still jesting as always, Byron."

He looked at her with his direct gaze. "What else can I do when it comes to you, Mary? It's either laugh or cry."

Her smile faded, she lowered her eyes, yet did not move, so he walked towards her, touched her arm, until she looked up at him with eyes full of confusion.

He spoke to her softly. "He's ten years older than you, your grown-up. Is that why you thought he would make you happy? More so than a passionate boy would?"

"Byron ... please ... "

"I'm told he's now the Master of the Hunt, a magistrate, and the future Sheriff of Nottingham ... and you were the girl who always did so love Robin Hood of our own Sherwood."

She shrugged slightly. "I was innocent then. A girl who believed in romantic heroes and fairy tales."

His eyes were now searching hers. "And is he romantic, your grown-up?"

Indignation flickered in her eyes. ""You forget yourself," she whispered.

"But not *you,* Mary, I never forget you. All I want to know is if he has made you happy, or is it now all a pretence on your part?"

"There is no *pretence,*" she countered angrily. "Byron, you must understand, when we were younger our love was *innocent,* but now I am Mrs Chaworth-Musters, a wife and mother and one of the most respected ladies in the county."

"Mrs Chaworth-Musters, wife and mother and one of the most respected ladies in the county ... " he repeated. "But where is my *Mary,* the happy girl you *used* to be?"

Mary gazed around her, as if she too was wondering where that girl had gone. "We were so innocent then," she said wistfully.

"But not any more. Neither of us are so innocent now as then."

She looked at him, and his beautiful searching blue eyes held her gaze like a magnet, disturbing her, thrilling her, making her want to die because he had caught her unawares and now, seeing him again, only made her feel her misery more acutely.

"Your Master of the Hunt ..." he said very softly, "does he make you happy when he makes love to you at night?"

The question was such a shock; it left her speechless.

"Does he arouse you to pleasure and make your bed a sweet place to lay? Does his fingers touch those places where a girl loves to be touched?"

His words had brought a high colour to her face and he gently touched it. "Love touches everything."

"And yet," she said in a low strange voice, "you must hate me very much now, to speak to me in this insolent way."

Undeterred, his fingers moved through the long

flowing tresses of her hair. "Whenever I think of you, which is often, I always say to myself, 'I love that girl'."

She gave a small cry of anguish and pushed him away. "Byron, stop it, say no more. Why torment me and yourself in this way? It's pointless, foolish, and I have a marriage and a reputation to uphold."

"*Mary!*"

Both turned to see Ann Radford standing a few yards away, staring at them with a face of fury.

"Oh, it's that she-cat cousin of yours," said Byron quietly. "I can see *she* hasn't changed."

"She must have seen us from the garden terrace," Mary murmured.

Byron agreed. "You can see halfway to Newstead from the terrace."

"She must have seen you touch my hair ..." Mary quickly stepped back from him, her eyes full of pain.

"Goodbye, Byron, and please ... don't come walking near Annesley again, for both our sakes. Please stay away."

He stood watching her as she quickly walked away, almost running, and after a glare at him Ann Radford put a hand on her shoulder and hurriedly escorted her back to the house.

He stood for a long time gazing at the empty space where Mary's running figure had vanished so quickly, feeling once again the awful burden of his years of unrequited love. Nothing had changed it. No other female had banished it. A chill came over him, caused by the wind that had suddenly blown up from a soft breeze and was now shaking the trees.

It reminded him of the past, of how Annesley had always seemed more prone to winds than Newstead ... but then Newstead Abbey was nestled down in a valley, and Annesley Hall sat on top of a hill, surrounded by a vista of barren hills.

His gaze was thoughtful as he looked around at the landscape that had once entranced him, but now no more, because all his boyish dreams had vanished like vapour into thin air, vanished as quickly as the girl he still loved.

Hills of Annesley, bleak and barren

Where my thoughtless childhood strayed

How the Northern Tempests, warring

Howl above thy tufted shade.

Now no more, the hours beguiling,

Former favourite haunts I see;

Now no more my Mary smiling

Which made it all a Heaven to me.

He walked on, realising she was right. She was married and it was time to stop looking back at what might have happened, or what might *never* have happened.

Yet, as he walked, he found himself softly saying the final line of each verse of his poem, 'Maid of Athens' ... *"Zoë mou sas agapo..."*

My life, I love you.

Chapter Forty-Nine

~ ~ ~

Approaching Newstead Abbey and admiring anew the palatial magnificence of it's ancient architecture – he saw that venerable old living antiquity, Joe Murray, come rushing towards him, his strong mastiff face drawn with concern.

"You've been gone for so long on your walk, more than *five* hours, I was getting worried about you!"

"Will you give me a helping hand, Joe? My leg is feeling the strain."

"I will, my lord. You just put your hand on my shoulder, and I'll help you to lighten the weight on your foot."

Joe leaned into him and Byron put his arm around Joe's shoulders, exaggerating his limp as they slowly walked on together.

The old man's head was bent slightly, his eyes carefully making sure his lordship's right foot didn't trip, whilst beside him Byron was smiling.

His leg felt no more strain than it usually did. His request for help was just an excuse to give Joe a hug without appearing to do so. There was more than one kind of love in this world, and for old Joe he felt a very deep and pure love, as one might feel for a long-caring father ... or in Joe's case, a long-caring *grand*father.

"So," Joe asked, "what are your intentions now, my lord? To stay living here at Newstead?"

Byron had been thinking about that very question for days, hence the long walks.

"That *was* my decision, Joe, to stay here on my estate for a while and maybe one day write a poetic masterpiece, but now ... well, now, I don't think that would be wise."

"Why not?"

"I met Mary Chaworth today."

"Oh, did you? ... I wish you hadn't."

Joe frowned as they walked together, remembering that time in the past when his lordship and Mary Chaworth spent so much time together, a time when either a frown or a smile from that girl could *rule* him, and change his mind or his mood in a flash.

And now, it seemed, she had done it again, changed his mind about living at Newstead.

"So where will you live?" Joe asked. "You'll not be going back abroad, I hope?"

"No, no ... most of my friends now live in London, so I may as well live in London too." He looked at Joe. "You can come with me, if you wish."

"Me? Live in London?" Joe stared at him as if thinking he must be mad.

"And who will look after our Newstead if I go? Who will look after Nanny Smith and the rest of the staff? Who will make sure all the silver is polished? Who will make sure all the bed linen is changed every week whether they've been slept in or not? Who will be here to look after you when you come home to Newstead on visits? Who will—"

"You, you, and only *you*," Byron cut him short. "I'll take Fletcher instead."

"You will have to take Sally as well. It wouldn't be fair to separate them again."

"She can come along as my housekeeper if she wants."

They had reached the compound where Bruin had once lived, but empty now, because he too had died while Byron was away.

"I'm so glad I had Bruin's portrait painted before I went abroad," Byron said reflectively.

"I don't like it though," Joe said, "the way you have your paintings positioned on the landing upstairs, with a picture of *me* stuck between a picture of a dog and bear – and then to top it all, a painting of Woolly the wolf-dog above me. Thank God you didn't have Sidney the rabbit painted before he disappeared."

"I wish I had though," Byron smiled. "I was so fond of Sidney. He and I had many long talks together. I think he collapsed and died from the weight of all my secrets. He found them too shocking."

As they entered the house Joe suddenly remembered what he had been itching all morning to tell his lordship.

"Oh, by the way, I now know who the traitor in our camp is. The one who kept reporting to your mother. I have not dismissed him, not until I tell you who it is."

Byron closed his eyes and shook his head. "I don 't want to know. If he kept my mother happy with his tittle-tattle then I'm grateful to him. What does it matter now anyway."

"So you don't want him dismissed?" Joe asked.

"No, that would be an act of disrespect to my mother's memory."

"Good, because I think it would be wrong to dismiss him. He's been a good and loyal worker at Newstead for many a long year now, and I *do* believe him when he says she forced him to do it or lose his employment."

Byron had no wish to be reminded of that side of his mother's nature. There comes a time when some things are best forgotten, and spoken of no more.

~ ~ ~

It was after four o'clock in the morning, and he was still sitting at the desk in his bedroom writing, when the candle flickered out and left him in darkness.

His hand automatically moved to the desk drawer to

take out another candle, when the bright view from the window caught his gaze ... the moon was full and the sky was alight with heavenly stars.

The sight and beauty of the night instantly changed his mood and brought his mind alive to the wonders of this earth and this beautiful planet on which he lived.

He stood and moved over to the window to gaze up at the vast crystalline sky ... *Stars, the poetry of Heaven*.

And, just like that sky up there, he realised his own future was wide and open before him with other possibilities now. He knew his feelings for Mary Chaworth would never be completely vanquished, and would always haunt him; but in future he would keep his passion under strict containment and move on with his life.

He was still only twenty-three and his fate was not to be a failure, of that he was determined. In some way he would prove his worth in this life.

The false dawn was beginning to tint the sky with prophetic rays of tomorrow and in a few days he was leaving Nottingham to start a new life in London, and now he was very tired, so to bed, to bed, *to bed*.

As he moved towards the curtains of his four-poster bed he saw the ghost of the Black Friar in his robes whisping into the room, his hands folded inside his sleeves, his cowl over his bent head, and as always he brought a feeling of peace to the room, naturally so, because when alive he had been a quiet and religious man, devoted in life to the love of God.

And although Byron knew the old rule of not speaking to the Friar as he silently passed through, he could not stop himself from smiling and whispering to himself as well as to the vanishing ghost of the Friar – "Good morrow."

~ ~ ~

A STRANGE WORLD

The Second book in the Lord Byron Series

At twenty-seven, Lady Caroline Lamb reads the story of a young aristocrat's strange journey through unknown and barbaric parts of Europe in *Childe Harold's Pilgrimage*, and declares her opinion that the author would certainly be *"mad, bad, and dangerous to know."*

A few weeks later she actually meets him, and becomes obsessed to the point of erotomania.

From the wilds of Albania to a life of luxury as one of the *beau monde* in Regency London, George Gordon Lord Byron is astounded at the burst of fame that engulfs him on the publication of Childe Harold.

"I awoke one morning and found myself famous."

Meticulously researched, and adapted into novel form, *A Strange World* is a vivid and truthful portrait of the most iconic young man of his time, and Britain's first superstar.

Thank You

Thank you for taking the time to read '*A Strange Beginning*' the first book in The Lord Byron Series. **Please be nice and leave a review.**

*

I occasionally send out newsletters with details of new releases, or discount offers, or any other news I may have, although not so regularly to be intrusive, so if you wish to sign up to for my newsletters – go to my Website and click on the "Subscribe" Tab.

*

If you would like to follow me on **BookBub** go to:-
www.bookbub.com/profile/gretta-curran-browne
and click on the "*Follow*" button.

Many thanks,

Gretta

www.grettacurranbrowne.com

Also by Gretta Curran Browne

LORD BYRON SERIES

A STRANGE BEGINNING

A STRANGE WORLD

MAD, BAD, AND DELIGHTFUL TO KNOW

A RUNAWAY STAR

A MAN OF NO COUNTRY

ANOTHER KIND OF LIGHT

NO MOON AT MIDNIGHT

***

LIBERTY TRILOGY

TREAD SOFTLY ON MY DREAMS

FIRE ON THE HILL

A WORLD APART

***

MACQUARIE SERIES

BY EASTERN WINDOWS

THE FAR HORIZON

JARVISFIELD

THE WAYWARD SON

***

ALL BECAUSE OF HER
A Novel
(Originally published as GHOSTS IN SUNLIGHT)

RELATIVE STRANGERS
(Tie-in Novel to TV series)

ORDINARY DECENT CRIMINAL
(Novel of Film starring Oscar-winner, Kevin Spacey)

9 781912 598168